What Happened in Granite Creek

A Novel

by Robyn Bradley

I

Koty

Chapter 1

Koty, you could talk the balls off a brass monkey. When Wayne first said these words to me, they were wrapped in a chuckle and a whole lot of warmth, pillow talk after making love back when I'd barely graduated into womanhood. I giggled and went right on talking, even though I didn't have a clue what a brass monkey was. Today, after almost twelve years of marriage, he still uses that phrase to describe me, usually to one of his cronies: "Man, that woman could talk the balls off a brass monkey," but it's delivered with a combination of loathing and derision. Thing is, his assessment is no longer accurate: I stopped talking to him a long time ago. He just hasn't noticed.

The only thing Wayne does notice these days—or thinks he notices, anyway—is patriotism, or people's lack of it. The more the television says that most Americans favor our getting out of Iraq, the more yellow ribbons I'll find tied around the trees in our front yard. I've stopped explaining my side: that we entered this war based on lies, that too many of our men and women are dying with no end in sight, that it's another Vietnam. I was surprised the time he let me get out all these thoughts in one breath while waiting for the inevitable brass monkey crack. Instead, he stared at me in a way that made me wonder if I'd somehow broken through to the old Wayne, the decent young man I'd fallen in love with when I was sixteen. The expression on his face was something I hadn't seen before. Then, he spat two words—"fucking idiot"—and I realized what the look was: hatred.

So Wayne and I don't talk about this war, or his right-wing leanings, or anything at all, really. For a long time, I'd been able to take solace in the fact that even in Granite Creek, our live-free-or-die patriotic New Hampshire town, more and more people were defecting to my side. Problem is, now the tide's turning in Wayne's favor, and all because of this soldier from Iraq— Jamie Briggs, a hometown favorite who no one gave a rat's ass about, I'm sure, until he lost both arms and both legs to an IED in Fallujah. Suddenly, patriotism has been given a second life in the form of parades and rallies and "Support Our Troops" bumper stickers. Even though the government provides money for injured soldiers' housing renovations, Wayne and his buddies decided to donate their services and help fix up Jamie's mother's house with things like widened doorframes, a wheelchair ramp, and something called a "roll in shower." This way, Jamie could use the government's funds on his future home (in theory). Wayne finished his portion of the install today and tells me all this over dinner.

"I guess the guy's been kind of down since he returned home. Depressed even," Wayne says.

"Oh, that's too bad," I say, half-listening as I scoop more mashed potatoes onto Rosie's and Iris's dishes and catch a glass of milk before Daisy knocks it over with the elbow she scraped up this afternoon.

"His mother is worried about him. Doesn't want him to be by himself during the day while she's at school. Some folks have volunteered to help out and show their patriotism by sitting with him for an hour here, hour there. Talk to him. Keep him company."

"That's nice," I murmur, while breaking up a footsie fight underneath the table. "That's enough," I say, mostly to Iris, my middle child and instigator of trouble. The girls giggle.

Wayne clears his throat, wanting my attention. "You'll be on the one to three o'clock shift."

"*What?*"

"I volunteered you for the one to three o'clock shift. His mother teaches at the high school. She's done at two-thirty, can be home by three."

We stare at each other, and the kids hush up. The only thing his stony face reveals is a slight twitch under his left eye, and that's because I know to look for it. The worse the twitch, the angrier he is.

"Wayne, I—"

The twitch, thankfully, disappears. He holds up his hand, no doubt anticipating my objections, perhaps even hoping for them. "This isn't negotiable, Koty."

"But what am I supposed to do for two hours with—"

"You'll talk to him. You'll listen to him. You'll show this soldier the respect he deserves."

I shake my head, my mind still trying to wrap itself around this. Wayne's been obsessed with all things military ever since his older brother, a decorated soldier from the first Gulf War, was murdered over a decade ago, jumped outside of a gay bar. Including me in his obsession, however, has not been part of his usual MO. "What if he doesn't want me there? What if we have nothing to talk about?"

For a moment, his eyes flicker, as if he hadn't quite thought about that, as if this boy's real needs might be something other than what Wayne has said they are. Then he laughs, deep and scornful. "I've heard you on the telephone, yapping with your sister for hours. I've had to listen to you yammer on for the last thirteen years. Koty, you can talk the balls off a brass monkey."

"But what if he needs to—"

Wayne pushes his chair back, stands, and throws his napkin on the table. "Why do you always have to make things so difficult? I've let it slide, your lack of patriotism and support for your country, for our troops. No more. You're going. End of discussion." As he stomps out of the kitchen, he calls over his shoulder, "He'll be expecting you tomorrow."

\#

I arrive with a Bundt cake that I made early this morning, before getting the girls ready for school. Jamie Briggs's house is on the other side of the woods that abut my own, on a quiet stretch called Still River Road, though you could argue most roads in Granite Creek are quiet. Ours used to be a bustling town full of stonemasons who turned New Hampshire's famous granite into everything imaginable—stone walls, steps, monuments, culverts. Like so many art forms, however, masonry had fallen victim to mass distribution and cheaper final products. Wayne's great-grandfather and grandfather built many of the legendary stone culverts throughout New England, including in Granite Creek, like the one down from the Briggs's house here on Still River Road. The name's misleading, however, since the "river" isn't anything more than a dried up creek that fills with water only after it's rained good and hard for three days straight. The culvert on the Briggs's street is like the one on mine: nothing more than a high-ceilinged stone tunnel beneath the overpass some twenty feet above. The cavernous passageway is the perfect place for local teens to hang out, drink, and do God knows what else.

Because my girls love to roam these woods as much as I do, I always warn them to steer clear of the culverts, unless I'm with them. No need for them to slice their feet on broken beer bottles or worse—my having to explain that the weird balloon-thingy on the ground is a used condom. What I don't tell anyone, though, is that sometimes I'll wander through the tunnels by myself. Their rich scents—moss, earth, mist—are magnificent, other-worldly, even.

I mount the steps to the bucolic two-story structure with a farmer's porch. On this porch stands an old woman who seems vaguely familiar, dressed in her Sunday best: white pillbox hat, lavender A-line dress with belt and matching white-trimmed jacket, stockings, and sensible beige pumps. I didn't realize we were supposed to get dressed up, and now I feel self-conscious in my cut-offs, flip-flops, and blue T-shirt, no doubt stained from today's cooking. I'm suddenly aware of my naked skin and the zit forming on my forehead. At least I showered, although I've resorted to piling my unruly hair high on my head, since the summer heat is still with us, even though it's mid-September.

"Hi," I say, as cheerful as possible. "I'm Koty Fowler. The one-to-three shift."

"Thank the Lord you're here." The caked-on rouge emphasizes the deep crevices in her skin, and her bright magenta lips remind me of a clown. The scent of mothballs fills the air, probably emanating from the old woman's hat.

"Is something wrong?" I ask.

She purses her lips, leans into me, and stage whispers, "He swore at me."

I swallow a laugh. "He what?"

"He took the Lord's name in vain. Now, I understand he's been through a lot, but I will not put up with being spoken to like that."

"Well—"

"And," she interrupts, "he did the same thing to the gentleman who was here before me. He said even filthier things to him."

Wonderful. "I'm sorry to hear that Mrs.—"

"Chester. Dorothy Abrams Chester."

"Well, Mrs. Chester. Maybe he's still adjusting to all this."

"Well, my dear, he's going to be adjusting without me." With that, she marches down the steps and to her car. She gets in, puts on her seatbelt, and backs out of the driveway. I watch until she disappears down the road, knowing it's just me, this house, and whatever waits inside.

If everyone is giving up their posts, Wayne can't possibly expect me to keep mine. Knocking on the door, I wait a minute before remembering the kid is alone, in a wheelchair. I don't even know where in the house he is. *Shit.* I push the door. "Hello?" I call. Nothing. I stand in the middle of a living room furnished in colors that remind me of a wheat field in August. Not a pillow out of place, not a visible sign of dirt or dust anywhere. The scent of vanilla fills the air, and photos decorate the mantel over the fireplace. I spot one of him, Jamie, expressionless in his uniform. What was he again? A Marine? Soldier?

Sighing, I walk down a hallway, sneaking peeks into each room I pass: dining room, study, bathroom—all so glistening clean and perfect that I wonder for a moment if anyone actually lives here or if this is, perhaps, a dream. At the end of the hall is a partially open door. I knock softly, push it, and suck in my breath at the vision before me. A guy who is more metal than man sits in a wheelchair by the window that looks out onto the backyard and the woods. His white tank top reveals where his limbs end and his prosthetics begin: above the elbow on his right arm, below the elbow on his left. His "legs" remind me of the bionic man and are thicker than I expected them to be with a pair of white Nikes stuck on the ends. Wayne mentioned that Jamie had gotten quite adept at using his artificial limbs while he rehabbed at Walter Reed, especially his legs since Jamie is considered a "below knee amputee" and using prosthetics is, according to Wayne, a little easier when your knees are still intact. Nothing seems easy about what I'm looking at right now, however. As I enter his room, Jamie doesn't glance in my direction or act as if he even knows I'm here.

"Hi," I whisper, and then clearing my throat, I say it louder. "Hi."

He turns his head slowly, as if it pains him to do so. He appears older than I thought he would. For some reason, I was expecting a boy, even though I know he's twenty-six, only four years younger than me. His hair and eyes are the color of the cherry wood cabinets my sister had installed in her new kitchen. His hair's cropped short, but his chin has a couple days' worth of stubble. A deep scar runs from the corner of his right cheekbone to his earlobe. If I could color the aura around him, it would be blood red, black, gangrene.

"I'm Koty." I pause. "I made you a Bundt cake." Pause. "Would you like a piece now?" As I say the words, I pray he doesn't say "yes," because it occurs to me I might have to feed it to him.

He says nothing and turns back to his window.

"Right. I'll put it here." I place the platter on a bureau covered in framed black-and-white photos, including one of a man dressed in army fatigues and a helmet. The backdrop is jungle-like, and even though the man appears relaxed, smoking a cigarette, his eyes reveal a darkness that makes me shudder. Wayne told me Jamie's father served in Vietnam. He died over a decade ago of lung cancer, leaving Jamie and his mother alone in this big house.

"Koty," Jamie murmurs. "What the hell kinda name is that?"

"It's short for Dakota."

"Dakota?"

"Yep. Means 'friend.'" This is true, although in my case, the name means the place where I was born: Minot, North Dakota, where my dad was stationed in the Air Force. Unlike Jamie's father, he never went to war, thank God. He was a computer geek. Not that it mattered since I ended up losing him to a stroke when I was a kid. "You can call me Dakota, if you want. I like it better anyway."

He faces me again. "I ain't calling you nothing since you ain't coming back. I don't need no goddamn charity babysitter."

"Right," I say, thinking this is my cue to leave, but something keeps my feet planted to the floor.

"Well?" he yelps.

"Well, what?" I fall into a nearby rocking chair.

"Go."

"I was told to stay."

"Fuck whoever told you to stay."

"Yeah, well. Easy for you to say."

"What the fuck is that supposed to mean?"

"My husband wants me here."

He tilts his head. "What'd you say your last name was?"

"I didn't. It's Fowler."

He seems surprised, and I wonder what he's thinking. "You're Hank Fowler's wife?"

"No. Wayne Fowler. Hank's brother."

He blinks. "Well, I don't give a shit who you are or who sent you. I don't need no goddamn—"

"—charity babysitter," I interrupt. "I heard you the first time."

"Good." He turns back to his window.

Wayne was wrong about my ability to make conversation. I'm speechless. I have no idea what to say to a quadruple amputee. I spy the digital clock on the nightstand, and my eyes wander to it every three minutes, which feels like every three hours. We don't say anything, don't cough, don't sneeze, don't clear our throats. He stares out his window, and I try not to stare at him. Instead, I focus on the items in his room, like his queen-sized bed that's covered in needlepoint pillows and the endless shelves of CDs on his wall, mostly country music, my favorite.

"You like country?" I finally say and wait. No response. "I do, too. It's one of my favorites. My kids think I'm weird, though." I shrug, trying to ignore how odd it feels to be having a conversation this way. "I don't care. Reminds me of my parents and my childhood, you know? They loved country. The good stuff: Mickey Gilley. Willie Nelson. Johnny Cash."

Jamie cocks his head, his nostrils flaring and every inch of him alert, and I wonder if he's going to speak. A door slams and a voice calls out,

"Jamie, I'm home," and before long a woman appears in the doorway. I stand.

"Hi." I smile and extend my hand, but she's watching Jamie, her eyes filled with the kind of hurt and worry that only we mothers can understand. I remember her from high school, the stories about the crazy home economics teacher who went on and on about family values. I never had her, but Kat—my sister—did, and I remember her stories as well my friends' tales of woe that they shared around the lunch table about Mrs. Briggs. "I'm Koty Fowler," I say.

She gazes at me, and I sense recognition in her pale blue eyes. Her lips form a smile, but her weathered face stays sad. "Yes, I remember you from school," she says while shaking my hand. *Of course*, I think. *Can't forget the teenager who got knocked up*. With that thought, a memory dislodges from my gray matter: there had been a small group of teachers who hadn't wanted me allowed back in the high school when I became pregnant "out of wedlock." Had she been one of them?

"I'm Barbara Briggs," she continues as she walks over to her son, puts her arms around him, and kisses his head. My heart aches at the sight, my own mother's death from cancer not even a year ago still all-consuming. "How are you today, handsome?" When he doesn't respond, she sighs and returns to me.

Desperate to fill the air with words, I notice my Bundt cake on the bureau. "Here." I thrust it at her chest. "I made this for you."

She takes it from me and inspects it, and I wonder if it's passed muster. "Thank you," she says. "How thoughtful." She heads for the door, and I follow but stop in the doorway.

"Bye, Jamie," I say.

Nothing.

"Thank you again," Mrs. Briggs says when we arrive at the front door. I nod, and it's only when I get back in my car that I realize I've been holding my breath.

#

At dinner, Wayne asks me how it went.

"He says he doesn't want me to come back."

"It'll take him some time to get used to the idea of having help. Needing help."

"But—" I stop when I see the nasty in Wayne's eyes. He's moody and drunk again, upset that the cops aren't following up on the latest "lead" he and Hank have discovered about their brother's murder.

"Tomorrow," he says in his don't-argue-with-me tone, "will be better. And the day after that."

#

Tomorrow isn't better, however. Neither is the day after that. True to her word, Mrs. Chester doesn't return. The town is slowly running out of patient souls since Jamie's foul mouth effectively chases everyone away.

"Get outta my goddamn house," he greets me whenever I enter.

"Thank you. And how are you?" I retort before taking up my position in the rocking chair, where I watch him stare out his window.

#

By the seventh day, I figure I've done my penance. What I need to do is get Jamie to say something so filthy, so offensive, that even Wayne won't make me go back.

"So," I begin one hour into my two-hour visit. He startles at the sound of my voice, but he doesn't turn around. "How's the walking going?"

"Fuck you."

"That good, huh?" I don't feel proud of this, of my smart-ass answer, of being mean to a kid with no arms and no legs, but I'm desperate. Losing two hours of housework has me behind on my chores. These hours when the kids are in school are precious. I can't get anything done with them underfoot. I've spent every afternoon for the last week and a half in this godforsaken house. Enough is enough.

He faces me. "You're lucky I'm in this chair. Otherwise I'd come over there and stick this metal arm in your fucking eye." He holds out his fake arm in what I gather is an attempt to be menacing, and I laugh. I fucking laugh at a quadruple amputee.

"Look," I sigh. "I'm sorry. You don't want me here. And, frankly, I don't want to be here either."

"So go. It's not like I'm stopping you."

"My husband," I whisper and, for a moment, I sense understanding in his eyes.

"Your husband is the biggest hypocrite of them all. He's hell-bent on this war, and whenever someone tries to recruit him to go over, he sounds like an old lady, making every medical excuse in the book why he can't. If I weren't in this chair, if my legs and arms worked, I'd kick his sorry ass instead of letting him act all mightier than thou with his so-called charity and patriotism and desire to keep the memory of his faggot brother alive."

I sit, stunned. That about sums it up, stated more powerfully than even the conversations I have in my head. Wayne's brother's alleged homosexuality has—and always will be—an off-limit topic in my household, even though I'm convinced that's what got him killed. He was jumped outside a gay bar, his head bashed in, his assailant—or assailants—never found. In a strange way, it's a relief to hear someone call it as they see it, despite his ugly language.

"You should tell him to go over," he continues. "Maybe he'd listen to you."

The truth is a big part of me wants Wayne to go over to Iraq and never come back, at least the Wayne who emerged after his brother's death. But I can't say that. "Well," I say quickly, "if I believed there was a point to this war, I might." Instantly, I wish I could hit rewind and eat my words.

He lowers his eyes and shakes his head. "You're honest, at least. I'll give you that."

"Jamie, I—"

"Jesus, don't ruin it by trying to take it back."

"Hey, even though I don't believe in this war, I do believe in you and your fellow troops. I support *you*."

He snorts.

"It's the truth," I whisper.

"Koty, do us both a favor."

"What?"

"Tell your husband you're done here."

#

"You're going back," Wayne says, after I announce that I've had enough.

"But—"

"You can 'but' all you want, Koty. You're going back. It's the right thing to do. You have to support our troops."

"If you're so set on supporting our troops, you sit with him."

Wayne pauses, his fork in mid-air over his meatloaf. "I work all day putting food on this goddamn table." His voice is a low rumble, like far-off thunder. "What the fuck do you do?"

I stare at my plate. I think of the mountains of shit-stained drawers I launder, the floors I scrub, the meals I prepare, the kids I conceive and birth and bathe and dress and watch over and love and read to and worry about, the clothes I iron and sew, the paycheck I stretch to feed five mouths, the smiles I plaster on my face for the sake of my kids, the husband I mourn—the good man I married and loved, instead of this person he's morphed into. Part of me wants to scream, "You stupid ignorant asshole! Look at yourself! What the fuck happened to you?" and gather up my kids and take off. I tried that once before, though—years ago when it was just Rosie and Iris—and the girls begged me to bring them back home. How could I say no? They love their father, and I keep praying the man I fell for thirteen years ago—the man who would fully appreciate their love, and mine—will return someday.

"The kids are in school," he continues. "You'll go. You'll sit. Even if you don't speak one single word, you'll show your support for this soldier, to this country, for this war that they're fighting to protect people like you who don't know the difference between a goddamn terrorist and a mailman."

#

The next morning, after Wayne's already left for work, Daisy wakes up with the sniffles, something I'd normally send her to school with, but I keep her home. By eleven o'clock, she's feeling fine, and I decide to have some fun with my little girl and bake some cookies, knowing that I can easily coax her to play sick when Wayne gets home. She's an actress, my little one, forever playing dress-up and creating stories to go along with her latest outfits. We don't call her Daisy Diva for nothing.

The phone rings at twelve forty-five. The kitchen's covered in flour and sugar, and pink and blue frosting fingerprints dot the counter, cabinets, refrigerator door, and my white T-shirt.

"Hello," I sigh.

"You leaving soon?" It's Wayne, and I can hear the buzz in his voice. Never a good sign when he's drinking during the day, something he can easily get away with since he works in the family plumbing business with his brother Hank.

"Daisy's home from school. She's sick."

"Where is she?"

"Bed," I lie while staring onto the backyard where Daisy's playing, right at the woods' perimeter. The only thing I love about this old house is its location. I sometimes pretend the forest out back leads to another life, a fairytale place far away.

"Is that why I'm watching her run through the yard half naked?"

I whip around and race through the kitchen to the living room. Wayne's pickup—the words "Fowler & Sons Plumbing" emblazoned in black lettering on the side—sits in the driveway. I can't see him in the cab.

"She was sick this morning," I whisper, my eyes darting around our front yard. "She's better now."

"Bring her with you. Might do the boy some good."

"She's still sniffling. I don't think bringing germs into his house is what Jamie needs."

"Bring her to your sister's then," he says, his voice pointed, threatening. In all of Wayne's ugliness, I can't remember his voice ever quite sounding like this.

"But, I—"

"Goddammit, Koty, don't fucking argue with me."

His voice is too close now, right behind me. As I turn, his fist connects with my upper lip. The swelling is immediate. I taste blood.

For an instant, horror registers in the old Wayne's eyes, horror at what he's done and what he's become, but then he blinks and that man is lost. He walks out without saying a word, the scent of alcohol following him. I don't move until I hear the squeal of his tires, and then, nothing.

#

When I arrive, Jamie's house is in darkness. The smell of rain is in the air, and all I can think about is the wash on the line back home, Daisy crying as I dumped her at my sister's, the look on my sister's face—*Again, Koty? How long are you going to put up with this?*—the mess my kitchen is, the mess I am. I climb the steps, open the front door, and jog to his room as if getting there faster means I'll be able to leave sooner. His bedroom door's almost completely closed, and, without thinking, I burst through.

His wheelchair faces the bed, and he's staring at the deep blue comforter. I spy tears trickling down his face. And his erection. He's somehow managed to roll down the top of his shorts, his dick standing at attention, waiting for a command from a hand, a tongue, a woman. Only then does the enormity of the situation—his situation—descend upon me. Here's a twenty-six-year-old man who can't do the one thing he should be doing at twenty-six, what he was made to be doing at twenty-six: fucking everything in sight, not a care in the world. Even during those times when a guy can't find a woman, he can take care of it himself. Except Jamie can't. Up until now, I hadn't thought beyond his four artificial limbs, hadn't thought about what was between his legs and his neck—a penis and a heart, both alive, both burning, both in need of attention.

I shiver in the doorway. I know I should turn around, walk out, pretend this never happened. His dick bends now, wilting under my stare.

I walk forward.

A *Playboy* lies on the floor, perhaps smuggled in by one of his well-meaning friends who stopped by to visit. I move his wheelchair back, kneel before him, take him in my hands, and stroke. His breath catches and his trance ends. All the anger and rage I saw in his face on that first day has been replaced by despair. His eyes rest on my bruised and swollen lip, but I don't let him question it. I stroke him harder now, and his eyelids flutter. A groan emerges from deep within his throat. I want to say "it's okay," but I can't manage the words, don't know if they're right, don't know if this is right, and before anything escapes from my mouth, his head dips, and he presses his lips to mine, tentatively, shyly, at first, and then with an urgency that surprises me, exhilarates me, despite the pain from my bruised lip. His stubble tickles my face. I haven't been kissed like this in so long, a lifetime ago.

It happens fast. The rain pelts the windowsill; the white curtains billow.

When it's over, I hold him as we both breathe heavy, our sweaty foreheads touching. As I wonder who will back out of this position first— *Should it be me? Should it be him?*—he does the unexpected: he kisses me again. He kisses my eyes, the tip of my nose, and my swollen upper lip, lingering on it, licking it, as if his touch alone can heal me. There was a time long ago before three kids, before Wayne's brother's death, before Wayne turned into the asshole he is today that I'd been kissed like this. At least, I think I did. I'm not so sure anymore. The only thing I'm sure of is this moment with me on my knees, holding a soft penis in my hands, kissing a man made of metal, a man who is not my husband, a man who I want to kiss more, a man who I want to kiss me.

My fingers meld to his skin, and my knees stiffen. Without a word, I detach myself, stand, and walk into the bathroom, where I wash my hands and wipe them on the fresh white towel that I use to sponge him clean. I pull up his shorts, and I hold up the *Playboy.* He juts his chin in the direction of a trunk I hadn't even noticed by his closet, its top open. Inside sits a multicolored afghan, a catcher's mitt and ball, some books, some framed pictures that I don't bother to look at. I grope underneath everything until my hand touches glossy paper and what I suspect to be more magazines. I tuck the *Playboy* inside, wondering how he got it out in the first place.

The buzz of his wheelchair fills the air. He's taken up his perch by the window. I sit in my usual rocking chair, clasp and unclasp my hands, wondering if I'd dreamt what happened.

The front door slams.

"Jamie, I'm home," his mother sings. I sense her standing in the doorway. I turn and smile, and as I do, I feel the pain and pull from my fat lip. How am I supposed to explain this?

Mrs. Briggs doesn't pay me any attention. Instead, she studies her son, her eyes filling with tears. After a moment, she composes herself and faces me. "Hi, Koty," she says. "Looks like rain's headed our way."

"Yes, ma'am." I think of my laundry again. "Well. I should get going."

She nods.

I nod.

I stand.

"We'll see you tomorrow, I guess," she says, and I wonder if this is her subtle way of offering me an out.

I wait until I know her eyes have focused on mine, on my fat lip. We hold each other's gaze for a moment, until she politely averts hers, and I can almost hear the reasoning going on in her mind: *My plate's full; I don't have time to deal with this girl's problems on top of everything else; I have my son to look after.*

"Sure," I finally say, but I'm not looking at her. I'm staring at the back of Jamie's head. Only then do I realize I'm fingering my swollen lip. I wait, hoping to see a flicker of something, anything, from him. *Nothing.* "See you tomorrow."

#

I race down the front steps and realize my breathing sounds hollow, like I'm fighting for air, like I've run a marathon instead of the few feet of driveway to where my gas-guzzling mom-mobile sits. What happened in there? What was I thinking? I grip the steering wheel, lean into the headrest, and close my eyes. "It was nothing," I whisper. "I was helping him, comforting him. That's all. It will never happen again."

Rationalization is an interesting thing. It's where the soul intersects with the brain. Because I could tell myself over and over that I'm a size six, or that Wayne's a good husband, or that I'm happy, but unless my soul believes it to be true, there's no way in hell my brain will accept it. Which is why when I whisper the words, "It will never happen again," a little voice inside my head whispers back, "You're full of shit."

Chapter 2

"Koty, what are you doing in there?" Mom pounds on the door. "We're gonna be late."

I hunker down in my covers and cradle the phone, willing it to ring. Chad Dacey talked to me in English today and asked for help—*my help*—on his Jane Austen paper. I gave him my number. What if he calls?

"I'm not going," I announce, even though between my down comforter, the music blaring from my CD player, and the closed door, I know she won't hear me.

She barges in, shaking her head. "How can you hear yourself *think* when you play it that loud? Seriously, Koty. Let's spare the neighbors."

She totally doesn't appreciate the sheer awesomeness of Alan Jackson. I peek over the covers and watch as she fumbles with the buttons on the player. She gives up and turns to me, exasperated. "Two minutes," she says without even asking me why I'm in bed with the phone on my pillow. "Up, out, and in the car." She marches to the door and continues talking. "Don't make me ask you again." Which makes me want to scream at the top of my lungs "I don't remember you ever asking me in the first place, Mom!"

But I don't. Instead, I hop out of bed, go to my mirror, and push away thoughts of Chad, for now, as another image clamors for my attention: the cute guy I saw visiting his grandfather at the nursing home last night. We made eye contact when I passed him in the hall and he nodded at me, I think, a faint smile on his lips. I asked one of my favorite nurses who he was. "His name's Wayne," she'd said. "Visiting his grandpa."

I smile at the memory, at the possibilities. I pinch my cheeks and apply cherry lip gloss, even though I hate the way it tastes. It makes my lips look pinker and plumper than the peppermint. I smudge the eyeliner beneath my lower lid, struggling to find the right balance between sexy and skanky, and sigh at my nasty curly hair, forever an auburn halo around my head. Mom won't let me get it straightened and refuses to talk about it, always saying, "No. End of discussion!" before we even start.

The car horn beeps.

Sighing, I examine my reflection one more time, shrug into my winter coat, and walk down the hall, singing off-key the lyrics to "Gone Country," oblivious to the life-changing events that are about to happen next.

#

My mother is either the biggest optimist or the most deluded person on the planet. I'm not sure which. See, my father has been living in what's called a persistent vegetative state for six years, after he had a massive stroke and his brain was deprived of oxygen. This oxygen deprivation was long enough to rob us of him, or at least of what made him my dad, but not long enough for his body and brain to completely shut down and die. The doctors said he'd never recover, but my mother refuses to listen, determined he'll wake up one day and we'll all pick up where we left off. In many ways, that's what the last six years have felt like, as if everything's suspended in time, at least at my house. I mean, who keeps a partially decorated Christmas tree up for six years because that was the last thing Dad was doing when he had his stroke? (I've often wondered what would have happened if it had been a real tree instead of an artificial one.) Who packs away a person's winter clothes every spring and brings them back out every fall, and has done this for the last five changes of season? Who renews subscriptions to *Time* and *Sports Illustrated*, even though no one else in the house reads them? My mom, that's who.

#

"Can I drive?" I mouth as I approach the car, my mother already belted into the driver's side and my older sister, Kat, belted in next to her in the passenger seat. I'm taking my driver's license exam in exactly twenty-three days, and I need all the practice I can get.

Mom rolls down the window. "What?"

"Can I drive?"

"No. Get in. We're already late." She says it so matter-of-factly, as if she can picture someone impatiently pacing the floor, checking his watch every five minutes. I know enough not to argue, but I make sure to slam the car door as loud as possible.

"Shit, Koty. Close doors much?" Kat says.

I ignore her. "Can I drive home?" I ask Mom.

"We'll see," Mom says, which I know is parent-speak for, "Probably not." I sink down into the seat, stare out the window, and wonder how many times we've traveled this route. I attempt to calculate it in my head, but give up quickly. Kat's the one who's good with numbers, not me. She got a perfect score on the math portion of the SATs, which got her early admission—and most likely a humongous scholarship—to the University of New Hampshire, where she'll be starting in the fall. I'd ask her to do the calculation, but we don't particularly like each other, mainly because she's a carbon copy of my mother, while I'm, apparently, the evil, bratty, unfeeling child who hates visiting her sick father. My greatest fault has always been my intense desire to act my real age instead of pretending to be some eyeball-bleeding virgin martyr who's good at algebra.

"It's not fair." The words escape my lips before I can stop them. I shouldn't talk back, especially when Mom is in one of her moods, which she no doubt is tonight.

"Excuse me?" Mom says. "What's not fair?"

"Never mind."

She taps her fingers on the steering wheel. "You know, young lady, I'm getting sick and tired of your attitude."

"What attitude?" I say, but even I cringe at the whine in my voice.

"Um, *that* attitude." She brakes hard as the traffic light ahead goes from yellow to red. "I'm sorry you think that whenever you don't get your way, life isn't fair. But you know what, Koty? Life *isn't* fair. Is it fair that your father lays sick in a nursing home and that his youngest daughter needs to be practically lassoed into visiting him?" She hits the gas when the light turns green, and our heads smack the headrests. "I think not."

"Whatever," I mutter while sinking even deeper into the seat and trying my best to get out of range of the rear view mirror. She simply lowers it so she can make eye contact with my reflection.

"Koty," she says. "Watch it."

"What the hell did I do now?"

"Watch your mouth."

"What? Kat said something a lot worse five minutes ago."

"This isn't about Kat. It's about you."

"Right. And my attitude." I roll my eyes. "Whatever."

Mom pulls into the Holy Saints Healthcare Center parking lot. She finds a space, parks, and turns to face me. "Maybe you should stay in the car and adjust your attitude before going in."

I cross my arms. "Fine."

Kat smirks as she gets out while Mom locks the car and doesn't look back.

"Fine," I whisper, tears stinging my eyes. I don't like being alone when it's getting dark, even in a locked car in the parking lot of some stupid nursing home. I sit for all of sixty seconds, tops, and decide my attitude has adjusted long enough. I get out and realize I've forgotten my mittens. It may be March—almost spring—but in New Hampshire, that doesn't mean squat. As I jump up and down, trying to circulate blood through my cold limbs, I spot someone at the main entrance, smoking. *It's him*, I think. *The guy from last night. Wayne.* I take a deep breath, exhale, and somehow my legs propel me forward. I attempt a saunter, even though I'm not sure what a saunter is or if it will help in this situation. As I get closer, I feel his eyes on me. He nods as I approach.

"Hey," he says.

I stop. "Hey." I don't know what to do next: linger, go inside, what? He answers my question for me by extending his hand. I take it in mine, and it's dry and rough.

"I think we passed each other in the hall last night," he says. "I'm Wayne."

"I'm Koty."

"Koty," he repeats. "That's different."

"Short for Dakota. Means 'friend.'"

He nods again. "Cool."

He takes a drag on his butt, and I hope he doesn't offer me one. I've smoked only once, with my friend Bethany behind her shed two summers ago. I thought I was going to cough up not only my lungs, by also my spleen, appendix, and whatever organs are in the general vicinity of a person's chest. (I'm not good at anatomy, either.)

"Your dad's here, right?" he asks.

I nod. *Had he been asking around?*

He puffs and exhales. "My gramps is here. Knee replacement. He's getting rehab."

"Nice of you to visit."

He shrugs. "Nurses said your dad was stationed at Pease."

So he had *been asking around.* "Yeah."

"What was his rank?"

"Staff sergeant."

He nods. "My brother served in the Gulf War. Marines."

"Cool."

"That sucks about Pease. They never should have closed it."

This, of course, is something I've heard a lot over the years. I still think the official closure announcement of the Air Force base, which happened, like, weeks before Dad got sick, is what triggered his stroke, but I've never told anyone that. "Yeah."

"When did they end up kicking your family off base?"

I shake my head. "We never lived on base. My mom didn't like it."

"So where do you live?"

"Here. Granite Creek."

"Go to the high school?"

"Uh huh."

"What year?"

"Sophomore."

"Like it?"

"It's okay."

"You ever say more than one or two words at a time?"

I feel my cheeks grow warm. "If I got something to say."

He throws his cigarette to the ground and steps on it with the toe of his Doc Martens. "So how come you didn't go in with the people you came with?"

"I dunno." I dig my hands into my pockets.

"You come here every night," he says, and it's not a question. "That's what one of the nurses said."

"Yeah."

"For how long?"

"You mean how long do we stay, or how long have we been coming?"

"Both."

"We usually stay until visiting hours are over at nine."

"And how long have you been coming?"

For some reason, I sense he already knows the answer. "A long time."

"That must be hard."

"Don't have much choice."

He lights up another cigarette but still doesn't offer me one. He gestures toward Mom's car. "Is that what that was about tonight? The fact you don't have a choice?"

I think about my squabble with Mom, about all our squabbles, quarrels, arguments. It's true: we never argue about Daddy. We argue about everything but him, even though he is, no doubt, the reason behind our fights.

"Maybe," I say. "Can we talk about something else?"

"Sure. What would you like to talk about Ms. Dakota?"

"I don't know. Where are *you* from?"

"I'm from here, too. Born and raised."

"Oh. And you're …" I struggle, searching for words.

He inhales and blows perfect circles in the air. When he's finished, he looks at me. "And I'm …" he mimics. "What do you want to know? My age? I'm nineteen, almost twenty. Am I in college? No. But I graduated high school, top of my class, lest you think I'm an idiot."

"Oh. So, what do you do?"

"I had been working with my gramps as an apprentice of sorts. He's a stonemason. He fucked up his knee, though, and had to have surgery. So for now, I'm doing this." He thrusts his left shoulder toward me while pointing to something on the chest of his windbreaker, a patch in the shape of a soft-serve ice cream cone. Words cover the cone part.

"'The Yogurt Shack,'" I read aloud. "Where's that?"

"Other side of town. You know the strip mall with Pizza Palace? In there. I'm the manager."

I think about the yogurt that Mom eats for breakfast, how she stirs the fruity goop that's on the bottom of the container. I never liked the stuff. "Is it any good?" I ask. "The yogurt?"

"You like ice cream?"

"Sure."

He smiles. It's a great smile. "Tastes just like ice cream."

"Cool."

"How 'bout you?" he says. "Got a job?"

"Not yet. This summer, I hope. Depending on, you know, stuff." I gesture toward the sliding glass doors, as if that's explanation enough.

"Right." He hoists himself onto the railing. "So."

"So," I repeat.

"Can I ask you something?"

My heart-wings flap like a million butterflies. *Is he going to ask me out?* "Sure."

"Is your dad ever gonna get better?"

I suck in my breath. No one's ever asked me that. In fact, that question—as far I know—has been asked only once by anyone, period: me, six years ago, to Dad's doctor when Dad was still in ICU. I'd been by myself in his room, keeping watch, while Mom took Kat to the cafeteria to fetch us some dinner. I liked the doctor who was on rounds because he always talked to me like I was a person, instead of a kid. His answer was honest and simple as he crouched before me and shook his head.

"No," I answer. Wayne doesn't say anything, *but his eyes do*, I think. They say, "*I'm sorry, that sucks and despite the fact you're standing out here talking to me, I can tell how much you love him, how you struggle between your duty here and being an ordinary sixteen-year-old kid while your mom and sister are suspended in time, hoping for the impossible.*" Or maybe I'm hoping that's what his eyes are saying, because I so desperately need someone to say it.

"Listen," he says. "When you're ready for a job, come by the Shack. I'll hook you up with however many hours you can handle."

"Really?"

"Yeah."

"Thanks."

"No problem." He puffs, exhales, shakes his head. "It sucks, you know."

"What does?" I ask, confused.

"The fact your father is in here, has been in here, all this time. And doesn't deserve it, no doubt."

"No one deserves it," I say, and that's when his eyes say something else: "*No, not true. Some people do.*" I'm about to question him, when the sliding doors open and Kat bursts through. Her face is flushed, tears streaming down her cheeks.

"Koty," she says. "It's Dad. You better come quick."

Chapter 3

September 2008

"Hope you brought a book."

"Excuse me?" I stand on the Briggs's porch and shiver, even though the sun smothers me in furry-like heat. Zeke takes a deep drag off his butt, and thick smoke hangs in the air. He's an old-timer, former cop, with alligator skin—in both texture and color.

"He's in bed."

"Who is?" I ask.

"The kid. Said he was tired. Asked me to get him into bed. Had me help him take off his, you know, his fake legs and arms, and then had me strip him down to his boxers. Don't blame him. Feels more like July than September."

"Oh."

"Anyhow, I think he fell asleep. Will make life a little easier for you. He actually wasn't that bad today. Only told me to go screw myself once, rather than the five times he normally does." Zeke laughs and coughs at the same time. "How's Wayne and the girls?"

"Fine."

"Good, good. Well, don't let me keep you. Just gonna finish this and head on home."

"Right."

I push open the door, hold my breath, and pray that Zeke is right, that Jamie is sleeping, but deep down I know I don't want him to be.

"Mommy's got purple eyelids," Daisy had said when I dropped her off at Kat's this afternoon. Her sniffles had blossomed into a full-blown cold overnight, but it still wasn't reason enough for me to stay away from taking care of my "charge," as Wayne has come to call Jamie. I think Wayne was expecting more of a fight, but all I did was finger my swollen lip and keep quiet.

Kat eyed my purple eye shadow, the eyeliner under my lids, my hair piled neatly—for once—on my head. "Yeah," she murmured, confusion spreading across her face. "You trying out for a Ms. New Hampshire pageant or something?"

"She's gonna sit with Jamie," Daisy answered, pushing through the screen door and into the chaos of my sister's living room.

"Ah," Kat said. "I get it. Give the guy some eye candy. You're definitely better looking—even without makeup—than that old battleaxe of a mother of his."

Kat was a straight-A student in high school, except for one class: Mrs. Briggs's Early Childhood Development, which in any other school district would have been one of those easy classes, like woodshop and gym. Not so at Granite Creek High.

"What's a battleaxe?" Daisy called out from inside Kat's living room, her hearing excellent, albeit selective since she always fails to hear me when I say, "Time to pick up all the clothes off your floor." She'd put a Hollywood starlet's closet to shame.

"Nothing," I yelled back. "Just a little joke between your Aunt Kat and me."

Kat laughed. "Watch yourself, Koty. That woman can melt brains with her eyeballs."

#

"You going to come in or stand there all afternoon?" Jamie asks.

I swallow, awake from my trance, and marvel at the fact I have no recollection of walking down the hall, opening Jamie's bedroom door, or leaning against the doorjamb. I focus on him now, and the heat rises from my belly, to my chest, to my neck, to my face. It's the first time I've seen him without his prosthetics, just a torso, head, and appendages that end abruptly. I gawk, mesmerized almost, but when he opens his eyes, I turn away.

After what happened yesterday, I'd felt sick the whole afternoon and night. Does touching another man's penis, stroking it until he comes, constitute cheating? Kissing like we did, with that urgency, something I haven't felt in ages—that must be cheating, right? Or does cheating have more to do with desire? Is the act itself just that—an act—but is wanting it, thinking about it, desiring it with every cellulite-inch of your body, is that what transcends the act to infidelity?

"Didn't think you'd come back," Jamie says.

"Yeah. Well." I pause, not knowing what else to say or even where to look. I study the knots in the floorboards.

"It's why I got that old geezer to put me into bed."

"Right."

He doesn't say anything else, and when I glance up, his eyes are closed. He rests on top of the white sheets, the blue bedspread turned back to the foot of the bed, and I wonder if I should cover him, even though sweat drips down my neck. For some insane reason my mind drifts. What did he look like when he was found? Were his limbs blown off completely or were they still attached?

"You don't have to stay," he says. "Anyone comes asking, and I'll tell 'em you were here."

"Like that would work."

He opens his eyes. "Then what are you going to do? Stand there all day?"

I blush. "Right." I settle onto my usual perch—the rocking chair—and the floorboard squeaks beneath my weight.

"You know, I won't bite, Dakota." It's the first time he's called me by my full name.

"I know."

"Do you?"

"Sure."

"Yesterday—" he begins.

"—was a mistake," I finish. "Can we forget it?"

"We can," he says, and that's it.

We sit this way for ten, fifteen, twenty minutes. He closes his eyes again, and I inventory my surroundings for the gazillionth time, wondering if this was his childhood room. It's very adult now—no posters of ball players or hot women or fast cars or whatever you'd expect a boy to cover his walls with. It's simple, neat, clean, too perfect, almost, like the rest of the house, and I decide that his boyhood bedroom must be upstairs. The only thing with personality? The shelves of CDs lining the wall. I stand, walk to them, and run my hands along their spines, noticing they're in alphabetical order. Only then do I realize I'm trembling, and images from yesterday—his erection, his lips, his eyes—pop into my head. *How could I have let that happen? How can we possibly go on now?*

"So you said you liked country," he says.

I remain facing the CDs. "Yup. I like real country. None of that country-pop stuff."

He chuckles. "No Taylor Swift, then."

"My kids like her. I don't dislike her, but she's more pop than country, that's for sure." I swivel on my heels, but the minute my eyes make contact with his, I look down. "You know what I mean?" I turn to the shelves again and pull out a CD: *Ring of Fire: The Best of Johnny Cash.* "Now this," I say, holding it over my head so he can see it, "is good shit."

"Agreed."

I pop the CD into the player, turn up the volume, and read the list of track titles. "I think 'Ring of Fire' is probably my favorite Johnny Cash song."

"Recorded in '63," he says. "His biggest hit. Charted for seven weeks."

I can't help but look at him now. "You know your country music," I say, impressed.

He shrugs. "It's a cool song."

"Yeah. It is." Tongue-tied, I stare at him.

"So," he begins.

"So," I say.

"So ... what if I don't want to forget it?" he says.

My brain twists. "Huh?"

"What happened yesterday. What if I don't want to forget it or pretend it never happened? What if I want ... more?"

How is it possible for your heart to sink and rise at the same time, like that feeling your stomach gets on a rollercoaster when you realize you're going over the top and it's the best feeling in the whole world, even though you know there's a good chance the contraption you're in could derail at any moment?

"Jamie, we can't. I mean, my God. How can we?"

Anger—or maybe hurt?—registers in his eyes. He shakes his head and starts coughing while trying to sit up. I go to him, positioning myself part way on the bed, figuring I can help, but then I watch as he brings himself to a sitting position on his own. *Without legs or arms. Wow.*

"You okay?" I whisper, trying to ignore his scent—a combination of soap, baby powder, sweat—trying to forget the salty taste of his lips, his hot breath, the feel of him in my hands.

"As if you care."

"C'mon. I do care."

"Bullshit. Listen, I don't need your pity," he mumbles. "Or charity hand-jobs."

"Jamie—"

He turns his head, attempting to look at me, but I move and shrink into the pillows until I'm out of his line of sight. I don't want to make eye contact. I don't want to see his mouth, or the scar on his cheek, or the day-old stubble on his chin.

I don't want to want.

Instead, I focus on his T-shirt sleeve and the stub of an arm poking out. I wonder if he has any tattoos. Or had any.

"It was more than that, wasn't it?" he whispers.

"What?" I ask, confused.

"What happened yesterday. It was more than you feeling sorry for me, wasn't it? Maybe not at first. But when we kissed …"

He doesn't finish, but it doesn't matter, because I could easily complete his thought. Because when we kissed, something happened. Because when we kissed, it seemed like the two of us were whole again: no broken body parts, no broken marriage, no broken self.

My eyes fill until tears jump out. "It *was*," I whisper. "But—"

"But what?"

"Jesus, Jamie. I'm married."

He doesn't respond, but, again, I know what he's thinking. I'm married in name only. That what I have with Wayne Fowler isn't a marriage anymore.

"Besides," I continue, trying to sound stronger, "You're—"

"I'm what? Huh? What are you trying to say, Koty? I'm a fucking cripple, is that it?"

"No!"

"That all I'll ever be to anyone is a goddamn burden?"

"That's not what I was going to say."

"No? Then what?"

"You're young. You deserve someone who can be yours completely."

He snorts, and even I cringe as the platitude echoes in my head.

"Listen," he says. "Will you quit hiding and put some pillows behind my back?"

"Yeah, sure."

I get off the bed, and Jamie wiggles his butt backwards, toward the headboard. I place two large pillows behind him.

"That better?" I say.

He nods, closes his eyes, and I'm about to sit in the rocking chair again when I notice his right arm—well, what's left of it—move. Almost as if it's gesturing to something.

"You okay?" I ask.

"There's enough room here for you to sit."

I consider the strip of white sheet where he wants me to sit, where our legs would touch, what's left of his anyway. Well, why not? It's not like he's going to attack me. It's not like anything will happen. I'm supposed to comfort him, right? Isn't that the whole point of these visits?

I sit by his side and stare at my lap until I feel him watching me. I look up. His eyes are open and there's such sadness in them that I want to turn away, but I don't. I can't.

"Does it hurt?" he asks.

"What?"

"Your lip."

I shrug. "I should be more careful when horsing around with the girls."

"Your girls didn't do that to you."

I draw air into my chest, the excuses ready to pour out like they always do, but something stops me. Maybe it's the sadness in his eyes or the fact there's probably nothing you could lie to this man about that he couldn't see through. What he lost in body parts, he's made up for in intuition, I bet, in the knowledge that evil exists everywhere, whether it's the local plumber's family on the other side of the woods or the quiet dirt road in the Iraqi desert.

"I'm sorry," he says, "if I made your lip hurt more."

"You didn't." I pause and will myself not to say what falls out of my mouth next. "In fact, I think you made it feel better." Before reason has a chance to win, I lean in and kiss him. I'm about to pull back when he speaks.

"Wait. Don't stop."

As our lips meet again, I fumble for the top of his boxers. He shakes his head, his lips moving side to side against mine. "No," he whispers, and his hot breath tickles my cheek. "Just this."

And so we do just that.

Chapter 4

"Mom?" I twirl the green strings of the Yogurt Shack apron around my fingers and clutch the khaki polyester pants and melon-pink polo shirt. Mom sits in Dad's old recliner, and two laundry baskets sit at her feet piled high with clean sheets, towels, and face cloths. I vaguely remember having left her in this position a couple of hours ago. Kat straddles one of the stools at the kitchen counter, a book, calculator, and pad of graph paper in front of her.

"Mom?" I say again, louder.

Her eyes search for me, even though I'm standing right in front of her.

"See?" I hold out the apron. "I got a job. At the Yogurt Shack. Forty hours a week. Well, once school's over."

"Yogurt?" Kat wrinkles her nose. "Blech."

"It's frozen yogurt. Tastes like ice cream."

"Yeah, sure it does. Where is it?"

"Same strip mall as Pizza Palace."

Kat taps her pencil against the counter. "How do you expect to get there?"

"What do you mean?"

"How. Do you. Expect. To get. There." Kat speaks in her slow "you're an idiot" voice, but loud enough, apparently, to bring my mother back from wherever she's been.

"Gee. Maybe. A car," I say as slowly, but louder.

"Koty, please." Mom massages her fingers into the skin above her eyebrows. "Not so loud. I have a headache."

"Kat started it."

"Kat started it," Kat mimics and laughs. Sometimes I hate her.

"I don't care who started what," Mom says. "Please stop." She points to my apron. "What's that?"

I swallow. "My uniform. For my new job."

"Job?"

"Yeah. Didn't you hear me before? At the Yogurt Shack."

"Oh."

"I was asking her," Kat says, "how she expects to get there. You know, now that you're back to working full-time and all."

"We have two cars," I say quickly. "Two perfectly good cars. It's not like I don't have a license."

Mom clears her throat. "One."

"What?"

"We have one car."

This, of course, isn't true. We have two. We have Mom's. And we have Dad's old Cutlass, which has been sitting dormant in the garage for the last six and a half years.

"What about Dad's car?" I say.

The air leaves the room. Kat becomes absorbed with her book. Mom stares at me.

"Well?" I cross my arms, expectant.

"You're not driving that car," she says simply.

"I didn't ask to drive it. You could drive it, and Kat and I can share your car."

"No one is driving that car."

"Which car?" I press, even though I understand which car we're talking about. "You mean your husband's car? Your *dead* husband's car?"

She trembles and her face reddens. Kat jumps off the stool and goes to her, touches her shoulder. Mom clutches Kat's waist and sobs.

"Why couldn't you let it go?" Kat whispers as her eyes meet mine.

"You mean the same way you two have let Dad go?" And I turn and walk out.

Chapter 5

Jamie and I continue for the rest of the week and onto the next with our afternoon delight: him already in bed by the time I arrive, and me sitting by his side. We kiss. We talk a little, about light stuff mostly, like country music or our favorite movies (his: *Full Metal Jacket*; mine: *Forrest Gump* and *Walk the Line*), pet driving peeves (his: people who don't use their turn signals, like his mother; mine: people who tailgate, like Wayne), and best Christmas present as a kid (his: Roger Clemens's extended rookie card, which his father paid a pretty penny for; mine: tickets to see Garth Brooks, along with a meet-and-greet backstage).

Sometimes we talk about important stuff, like how much we both miss our fathers, how much it sucked to lose them as kids, how my childhood seemed to stop at ten, that I never got to open the Barbie Dreamhouse Mom and Dad bought that Christmas because we didn't have a Christmas—and Christmases were always so hard after that. I'll even talk a little about my girls, what it is about them that makes me proud (Rosie: her compassion; Iris: her determination; Daisy: her imagination) and what makes me worry (Rosie: her vulnerability; Iris: her schoolyard fights; Daisy: her diva attitude at age six, Lord help me). But mostly, we make out. I've taken to keeping a bottle of moisturizer in the van and rubbing down my raw chin and lips before I get home. I don't try to touch him below the belt, and he doesn't ask, even though his arousal is obvious. There are moments when I want to, when I want nothing more than to feel his hands on my body, but then I remember that he has no hands, that this is just a dream, and that to go any further would be disastrous. Somehow, kissing doesn't feel like "real" cheating, even though I realize that I'm once again rationalizing the situation. Still, it amazes me how I don't feel guilty, not since that time, anyway, when I jerked him off.

In the beginning, we're good about making sure we stop long before his mother comes home, but soon even that falls to shit, and we take chances, her footsteps right outside the door, and me jumping off the bed, flinging the bedspread on him to cover said arousal, and then feigning fascination with the pictures on the bureau.

"My husband," Mrs. Briggs had said one day as she picked up the frame and handed it to me. "Is everything all right in here? I thought I heard something fall."

"That was me," I said. "I'm the biggest klutz around. Always tripping over my own two feet."

"Least you have 'em," Jamie laughed, and Mrs. Briggs gaped, her blue eyes wide. "What? It's true, Ma, isn't it? What I'd give to trip over my own two feet again."

As she walked me out that day, she asked, "He's talking to you?"

"Yes."

"I see." She sounded surprised, and not pleasantly so, like she couldn't understand why her boy was opening up to this white-trash baby-making housewife. "He's still not talking to anyone else. That was the first thing he's said in my presence in months."

I shrugged. "Maybe I'm easy to talk to."

She nodded and smiled, and I watched her mentally rally. "Well, it doesn't matter how or to whom. Fact is, he's talking. My prayers have been answered." Then she paused. "At least, one of them."

#

It's Friday now, and as I linger in his doorway while saying good-bye, the hardest part of my day, the what-ifs enter my brain. I wonder how I'll get through the next two days, if guilt will set in, if his feelings will change, if my feelings will change, if on Monday we'll be back to square one with him hostile and me just being me.

My mind takes a mental photograph of everything: the afternoon shadows that fill the room, a faded floorboard, the blue of his bedspread, the expression on his face that grows darker and more pensive with each step I take toward the door. Does it say, "Don't leave"? Or are his thoughts already onto something else? Perhaps a memory so sad, so awful that it's impossible to share. The one thing we haven't talked about: his reality, the war, what happened over there. I like to think I'm as much of an escape for him as he is for me. Part of me wonders if I'm simply avoiding difficult conversations.

"Well," I say. "See you Monday. Have a good weekend."

He doesn't respond, and I realize for him, right now, I'm already gone.

I hurry down the hall and out the door and fumble with my keys, even though I haven't locked my van, when a voice calls out, stopping me.

"Koty?"

I turn and watch as Mrs. Briggs closes the front door, wraps her yellow sweater tight around her chest, and descends the porch steps. She wears sensible black flats that accentuate her thick ankles. "Cankles" is what I heard Wayne teaching the girls the other night as they watched Hillary Clinton on the news stumping for Barack Obama.

"Do you have a minute?" she asks, breathless, when she catches up with me.

"Um, sure," I say, hesitant, fearful. Had she heard something? *Seen* something?

"Since Jamie's been talking to you," she begins and then stops. "Since the two of you seem to have developed some sort of—"

"Bond?" I offer.

Her eyes flicker, and I sense she's not thrilled with my word choice. But she says, "I was wondering if you could try to push him a little."

"Push him?"

"Yes."

"I'm not sure I understand."

Her eyes fill with tears, and she sniffles and hugs herself tighter. I don't know what to do: touch her, look away, go away. She seems so proud, so distinguished. Wouldn't witnessing her breakdown violate her more than it would help? Her family-values lectures were legendary back in Granite Creek High School, tinged with fire and brimstone. How can I possibly comfort her?

"He was so different, you know. At Walter Reed," she says.

"Different?"

She nods. "Positive. Determined. His injuries were so extensive, his prognosis so bleak. But he exceeded everyone's expectations. Any time someone told him he couldn't do something, he proved them wrong in short order. Some of them—the doctors and therapists—warned me that it would likely catch up with him, at some point. The reality of his situation, the stress. Depression, even. I didn't believe them. When he was discharged for good this past summer, I thought everything would be okay, mainly because he was coming home, with me. How could he not be okay when he has his mother to take care of him?"

She pauses, and I'm not sure if she wants an answer. I've known Jamie Briggs for barely three weeks, yet, in some ways, I suppose I know him more intimately than anyone else, even his mother.

"His transition was jarring," she begins and her eyes are faraway, lost in memories. "After the parade, after your husband and the others revamped the bathroom, the shower, installed the ramp in front. After everyone was gone, and it was him and me left staring at each other, I lost him. The change was so dramatic. I called the doctors, and they prescribed medication. You know, anti-depressants. He refused them when he was in the hospital, and the truth is, he didn't need them. Not then. But he's refusing them now, and he does need them. He needs something. I'm at a loss as to what. I thought maybe having company during the day when I was teaching—I thought that might lift his spirits, but he seems to hate me for having orchestrated it. Hates all the people, all the help." She stops and her eyes refocus on me. "Except for one. You."

"If it's any consolation, he hated me at first, too."

"So what changed that?"

Dear God. "I don't know. It just changed, I guess." My cheeks heat up. I hate blushing, hate the fact that it's so completely out of my control and reveals so much.

"I see," she says.

"What do you want me to do?" I ask quickly.

"Everything he learned, everything he accomplished over the last thirty months, he's going to lose it, or go backwards anyway, if he doesn't embrace life and accept where he is."

"You want me to help him embrace life?"

"I want you to help him try. Convince him to take his meds for the depression. To consider counseling. To walk—he can, you know. He needs assistance getting the prosthetics on, but once they are, he can be very independent. If I could afford to retire now, I would, but I had to put a second mortgage on the house to help with travel expenses and pay the bills when I took the leave of absence in the beginning to be with him. People don't know," she says, shaking her head. "They don't know all the sacrifices. Not just the ones he's made, which are obvious, but the ones I've made. Trust me when I say this: I'd do it all over again. But to see him shutting down like this." She stops, and the tears fall. "It breaks my heart. So I'm asking you, from one mother to another: help my son. Do whatever you need to do, but help him."

Her final words, though shrouded in tears, are pointed and filled with deeper meaning. Or maybe I'm reading too much into it.

"Mrs. Briggs, I'd love to help, but I think you give me too much credit."

"Do I?"

"Yeah. I think so."

"All I'm asking, dear, is that you try," she says, and I wince. I hate when people call me "dear," especially when it's delivered in a tone that you use with a five-year-old. "Please," she says, more sincerely, tears streaming down her cheeks. "Woman to woman, mother to mother. Try. And if not for me, then for him. For Jamie."

I hate guilt trips as well, even though they work and I'm not above using them on my own kids.

"Okay," I finally say. "Okay."

#

The truth, of course, is that Mrs. Briggs's request affects the fantasy world I've created, the sanctuary in coming here and making out with Jamie, chatting with someone who seems to care and appreciate what I have to say, escaping from the world of wife and mother, if only for two hours five days a week.

I haven't felt this way since high school, since the old Wayne, since life was so very different. And that's if I ever felt this way before, which I'm not even sure of anymore. Besides, I already have an inkling of how this will go, which is why my belly hurts as I mount the stairs on Monday, let myself in, and wander down the hall to his room. I knock and push the door open.

"Hey," he says, and his face brightens. He's in bed, his prosthetics off as usual, awaiting me, awaiting the "us" we have for one hundred twenty minutes. My feet remain planted on the threshold.

"It's nice out today," I say. "What do you say we get you dressed and in your chair and we'll go for a walk?" I grimace and catch myself. I should have asked Mrs. Briggs about his legs and arms, about getting a lesson in putting them on. "Well, a stroll. You know what I mean. Let's get out."

I turn to his closet, which might be the most organized closet I've ever seen. "Here, I'll pick out something for you to wear." I pilfer through his shirts and slacks, which have been pressed and hung according to color. I sigh, afraid to look at him, because he's being too quiet. "Well," I say, giving in and facing him. "How 'bout you tell me what you want to wear?"

He stares at me, and I can't tell if he's bewildered or amused. "What are you talking about?" he says.

I point to the window as if that's explanation enough. "It's nice out. Thought we could go outside, get some fresh air. It'd be good for you."

Then I see it. His face transforms into something I recognize: anger.

"Oh, would it, now? According to who?"

Whom, I want to correct him, but I don't. English was the only subject in which I excelled in school, despite the fact "motherfucker" is the longest word in my vocabulary these days. "It just would. Wouldn't it? I mean, when's the last time you've been out?"

"What, are you my mother?"

"No, but she wants you to get out, too."

"Wait. You and Ma have been talking? Behind my back?"

"No. Well, not exactly." I sigh. "On Friday, she stopped me on the way out and asked me if I'd encourage you to, you know, do stuff."

"And I suppose you said 'Okeedokee—no problem'?"

"What was I supposed to say?"

"That it's not your job to get me to do anything."

"I tried that. She wouldn't listen."

"Well, maybe you should have tried harder," he huffs.

"Sounds like good advice," I say, calm. "Maybe you should follow it."

"Don't fucking start with me, Koty."

I cringe, wounded. "Don't act like my husband."

"What did you say?"

"You heard me.'"

"I'm not your husband," he says. "I don't hit you."

"No, that would require you to stand. And use your arms."

"Fuck you."

"That all you can say? C'mon, Jamie. Your mother's request isn't that weird. You were in the hospital for, what, almost three years? From what I hear, you were doing everything, exceeding all expectations. But now you spend all your time in your bed or in that damn chair looking out the window. Do you want to lose everything you learned and worked so hard for?"

"Since when did you become a medical expert?"

"The same time as you. Never."

"Get out. I don't need this shit."

"What are you so scared of?"

"I said get out."

"Tell me, Jamie."

"Get the fuck out of my house!"

I walk forward and cross my arms. "No."

"Bitch," he mutters.

"You can call me every name in the book, but I'm not leaving. Not until you talk to me." I sit down on the side of his bed, which, on the one hand, I realize is cruel since there's nothing he can do to get away. On the other hand, I have no choice. I can't leave him. Not like this.

He screws up his face and reminds me of Iris when she gets into one of her snits: petulant, pouting, impossible to reach. What the hell was I thinking? That we'd go on making out—and that's it—forever? Despite the fact Jamie probably thinks I'm just some girl, he means much more to me than he realizes. He's awakened something inside. Seems to me I owe it to him to try to break through whatever it is that's holding him back, in case I do mean more, in case he does listen. Or maybe I want to matter again to someone other than my own blood.

I reach for the side of his face, and he recoils at my touch, but I don't stop. He has nowhere else to go. He can shrink into the pillows and headboard and pray that he disappears, but he can't escape me. Not now. Not yet.

He closes his eyes and gives in. I stroke the side of his face. His jaw clenches, twitches.

"You have no fucking idea what it's like," he whispers as he opens his eyes. "What this is like."

"You're right. I don't."

"You can't make it better, Koty. My mother can't make it better."

"Weren't you making it better yourself? I mean before, when you were in the hospital?"

"I was a hero at that hospital, and I'm not talking about a military hero. I was a fucking rock star. 'There he is—the quad amputee. Look at what he's done. What he's accomplished. Such an inspiration.' And I was. To all the other amputees."

"Don't you think you're an inspiration here, to all of us?"

"You don't get it, do you? Here, I'm a freak. I'm a carnival attraction. I'm a person who people pity. Or can't look at. Or who shake their heads at because I was sent to Iraq for a war based on lies." He pauses. "Sound familiar?"

"That's not true."

"Please. Don't."

"Okay. Let's say I give you all that. Why go off on me when all I suggest is that we go outside? Why go berserk knowing your mom—who from what I understand was pretty much by your side for the last three years—wants you to try to, you know, live."

"Putting on those damn legs and arms and showing off my moves to everyone and being the local inspiration and war hero—that's not living. That's performing."

"What's living then?"

"What you and I have been doing for the last three weeks." I reach for his face again, but he turns his head away. "Don't."

We sit in silence, and after a while, I begin to think I should go. Then, he speaks.

"There was this physical therapist I had. Eddy. Eddy never celebrated my big accomplishments, like walking in eight months. He was happy for me, but he was never part of the cake-cutting celebrations. Eddy was excited about the small things, the seemingly trivial little exercises I'd master with him when no one else was watching. I asked him one day why he was like that. He said I needed to learn to live more in the moment. To enjoy the little successes along the way. To find joy in those everyday things because there was going to be more of them than the big things. So when you ask me what I think this is, that's it: a little success that I take great joy in."

I glance around the room and wave my hand across his bedspread. "I don't understand. How is this a little success?"

"Who would think that I—you know, the crippled kid living with his mother—would have a beautiful woman all to myself for two hours a day to kiss and talk to and even laugh with?"

He thinks I'm beautiful? "I don't know, Jamie. Seems like this should qualify as a big accomplishment. You know, when you describe it like that."

I smile, hoping it's contagious, and reach for his face again. This time he lets me.

"No," he whispers as I stroke his cheek. "A big accomplishment would mean I'd have you longer than two hours a day."

His words and the meaning behind them make my belly flip-flop.

"Why do you stay with him anyway?" he asks, and I wish I could explain the old Wayne in a way that would make him understand. But people's memories tend to be short on the good, long on the bad, and considering Wayne's been this way for as long as my oldest has been alive— well, I'm lucky if anyone remembers the old Wayne, least of all me.

"I've got three kids."

"You heard of something called abuse? Verbal, physical. It's all the same."

"He doesn't mean it," I say so easily. Too easily.

"No? You think someone who kicks a dog doesn't mean to kick the dog?"

"Am I supposed to be a dog?"

"Might as well be, the way he treats you. And the way you obey."

"He wasn't always like this."

"No? How was he like?"

"He was sweet. Tender."

"Yeah, right. Sounds like the Fowler family this town knows so well."

"Honest. He was. He was an entirely different person when I met him. But that was before his brother died. Before he started drinking. Before he started spending more time with his family. Besides, he's not like his father. Not completely. And he's not like Hank. I can count on one hand how many times he's hit me. He's always sorry afterwards. Always." I stop, cringe, and carry on. "I know that's probably what most women in these circumstances say, but in this case, it's true."

"Those are excuses."

"They're excuses now, but they're also reasons, or at least they were, back then, for why he changed. How fast he changed."

"I hear his brother was a homo who got his head bashed in."

I've always hated the words "homo" and "faggot." Maybe I hate labels. "He wasn't out," I say.

"Right. He couldn't be."

"Why? Why in this day and age can't people love who they want to love?"

He shakes his head, unwilling or unable to answer, and we're quiet for a while.

"I suppose you're anti-gay, too," I say. "Being a military person and all." I'm surprised at the pissiness in my voice.

"I got nothing against gay people," he says. "But they have to know, the things being the way they are, that the military isn't a welcoming place for that lifestyle. Whether it's right or wrong or should or shouldn't be isn't the issue. The reality is that the military doesn't support it, there are a lot of homophobic people in its ranks, and you're putting everyone at risk by entering the military if you know you're gay. I'm not saying what happened to Wayne's brother was right. It wasn't."

"It wasn't the military that killed him."

Jamie shoots me a look, and for the first time I realize the rumors may hold some truth. There had been speculation that Carl had encountered some fellow soldiers the night he was killed, military men who did not appreciate Carl's extracurricular nighttime activities, even though he swung a wrench by day and had served in Desert Storm.

"If it wasn't the military, it probably would have ended up being someone else," I say. "Even himself. God knows his family never would have accepted it."

"And I thought you said Wayne was sweet. Tender."

"He was. He also loved his brother more than anything. Carl protected him from their father, watched out for him, was the father he never had, the mother he never had. Wayne was the peacemaker trying to keep everyone happy. Everyone has a breaking point. Carl's death was the crack for Wayne. Alcohol warped and widened it. He'd always been so scared of drinking, seeing what it had done to his mother, choosing specifically not to go down that road. He was right, you know. To be as scared as he was of it. Because it took only one bottle. *One* bottle, Jamie, on the heel of his brother's murder, and he was gone. It was like the man I'd fallen for had up and left."

The weight of Jamie's eyes are heavy on my own.

"You still love him," he says simply.

"I love the man I met thirteen years ago. That man shows up from time to time over the years. I guess I keep hoping he'll eventually come back home for good."

"And if he doesn't?"

I shrug. "Like I said. I've got three kids."

"Exactly," he says, his one-word reply pointed and meaning so much more.

"I don't want to talk about it, okay? It is what it is."

"Is that the approach you want me to take?"

"With what?"

"With everything. Accepting my sorry state like you've accepted yours?"

"No. Of course not."

"Then I have an idea."

"What?"

"You want me to stand, to walk? Okay. You do the same. I want you to stand up to him."

"What do you mean?"

"You heard me."

"Easier said than done."

"Exactly."

"Fine." I lean back and cross my arms.

"Let's shake on it," he says and then his face breaks out into a grin. "Oh, right. Well, then. A kiss will have to do."

Chapter 6

M&M fights. Whipped cream showers. Strawberry sauce. Sticky floors. Waffle cone batter. Hot fudge. Peanut butter cups. Mixed nuts. Sanitizer. Wet mops. Cherries jubilee. Dark forest sundaes. Dirty dishes. Broken AC. Sweat. Crushed butterfingers. Soda fountains. Brewed coffee, special blend.

The sights, the sounds, the flavors of my sixteenth summer on the planet.

Mom and Kat both said the novelty of my first job would wear off in a week, or after the first paycheck, or at the precise moment when I wanted to do something else, like go to the beach but realized I couldn't because I was committed to a schedule, to forty hours. But it's mid-July now, and after two months, I still love my job and everything that goes with it: my co-workers, the regular customers, even my boss.

Okay, especially my boss.

See, Wayne Fowler's like no one I've ever met before, not that I know or hang out with many (okay, any) twenty-year-old guys. Being around him these last few weeks has made up for the last six years of hell and family drama, like maybe I had to go through all that crap with my dad's stroke and coma and death to experience this, whatever this is, because the truth is I'm not even sure. I mean, it's not like anything's happened between Wayne and me. I'm not even sure he notices me. You know, in *that* way.

I flirt like crazy, I'll admit it (okay, the best I know how, which isn't saying much). Melissa and Tucker and Jodi and our assistant manager Locust (his real name is Lucas, but he swarms all over us girls, so we call him Locust) say Wayne likes me, but I don't know. I mean, wouldn't something meaningful—a wink, a conversation, *something*—have happened by now? He is my boss and all, but so what? It's 1995, not 1955, and he's not that much older than me. I keep hoping and dreaming and thinking maybe he does and if he'd kiss me, then—

"Hey, space cadet," Locust says, awakening me from my daydream. I look around the back room of the Yogurt Shack as if it's the first time I've been here. He gestures to the smoking waffle iron that sits on a sleek silver counter in front of me. "I don't think burnt waffle cones will sell all that well."

"Shit!" I throw open the top, cough, and wave my hand over the blackened pancake like a mad woman.

Locust laughs. "That's what happens when you do too many whip-its, Koty."

"First one I've burnt all day," I say, ignoring his comment because I still don't know what a whip-it is, but I'm too proud to ask. I scrape off the charred remnants with a putty knife.

Locust sidles up next to me. "Let me show you how it's done, kid."

"Yeah, okay, master cone-maker." I roll my eyes in case he misses the sarcasm in my voice. "I'm going to bring these out front first."

I carry the tray of waffle cones into the front of the store and place it on the counter next to the coffee machines. Melissa stands in front of the topping bar and waits for a customer to decide on what candy concoction he wants on his sundae.

"What're you guys doing back there?" she says. "The place smells like burnt toast."

"Waffle cone mishap," I say.

Melissa shrugs, apparently bored by my answer, and heaves an extra heavy sigh, her subtle way of telling the customer to hurry up. I'm about to leave her to her heaving when something catches my eye through the plate glass windows that look out onto the parking lot. It's Wayne helping a frail hunched-back old man into a car, and I wonder if he's remembering his grandpa. He died from an infection a few weeks after my dad, and I know he misses him like I miss my father (okay, I don't know for sure, but I sense it). It helps to have someone around who understands what it's like to lose the person you love most in the world, even though, as I've told him, I lost my dad six years ago. His death in March was simply a formality.

"See? Your Romeo doesn't discriminate. Teenagers, old people, you name it," Melissa says as we watch Wayne wave to the man and then continue with his cleanup, a black garbage bag bulging behind him with trash from the parking lot.

"Whatever," I say and pray my response sounds non-committal and cool. Girls like Melissa have a new boyfriend every other week. Then there's me, boyfriendless since the third grade when Robbie Dobbs and I "dated" for a day and we shared his strawberry Quik during lunch. I retreat to the backroom and my waffle cone duty: pour batter, close lid, and imagine nine million different ways to get Wayne to open up about his grandpa so that he can see what a good listener I am.

"Jesus, Koty," Locust says, and he's next to me again, throwing open the lid and waving his hand over the smoking pancake. "We need to find you a task that doesn't involve fire."

The back door handle jiggles once, twice, and in walks Wayne, whistling, with three dented cans of Dr. Pepper.

Locust smirks. "Check it out, Chief. Koty's burning down the place."

"No doubt because you're distracting her," Wayne says.

"She don't get distracted by *me*, Chief."

"Doesn't," I correct. "And you're right. I don't."

Wayne fiddles with the radio mounted above his desk, changing the channel from Locust's Top 40 station to—oh my God—*country*. I think I'm in love.

"What the hell is that?" Locust says while wrinkling his nose.

"Country," I say. "You know, good music?"

Wayne smiles. "You like country?"

"Uh-huh."

"Knew I hired you for a reason," he chuckles.

"Riiight," Locust says. "I think I'll leave you two alone with your death-by-banjo music. I'm gonna help Melissa out front."

"You do that," Wayne says as he shuffles through a sheaf of purchase orders. "But remember to actually help. Not gawk."

"Don't worry." Locust winks at me. "I'm a good multi-tasker." He stalks off, a pipe cleaner in Yogurt-Shack-issued polyester pants that sag down his butt.

"Remind me," I say. "Why do you keep him around?"

Wayne shrugs. "He doesn't mind opening. I'm not a morning person."

"Me either," I say.

"Really? You always seem like you're in a good mood, no matter the time of day. At least, you have been on those rare occasions when I've had to open and you've been scheduled."

"Maybe I like being here." *Oh, God, did I just say that?* My cheeks warm and I concentrate on stirring the batter and scooping it onto the waffle iron. I close the lid. I feel his eyes on me.

"Are things at home still tough?" he says, and I glance up in time to see him shaking his head. "Sorry. It's none of my business."

"It's okay. I mean, it's no secret. The dark cloud hovering over my house usually tips people off." I see his eyes become distant, fixed on something past me, past all of this. "Now I'm sorry," I say quickly. "I didn't mean to make you uncomfortable."

"You didn't." He walks over, pulls on some plastic gloves, lifts the lid to the waffle iron that I've forgotten about (again), saves the well-cooked pancake, wraps it on a cone-shaped piece of plastic, and deposits it inside a cone-shaped paper sleeve. He's standing so close that I can smell his wintergreen gum, his go-to remedy that's helping him stop smoking. "So how come that dark cloud doesn't hang over you?"

"I dunno." I shrug. "I don't want to be sad forever. It's not what my dad would have wanted. He wanted to see us happy, for me and Kat to dream big." I stop, a memory popping into my head. "You know, the summer before he got sick, we spent a week on the Cape. One day, we got on Route 6 and drove all the way to the tip of the Cape in P-Town. Dad told me that you could drive that road clear across the country. Kat didn't believe him, but I did, and I said that I'd do it someday. Rent a jeep and drive." I stop and stir the batter. "I haven't thought about that in a long time."

"So what do you dream about now?"

"Oh, nothing too exciting." My face heats up again, and I study my Reeboks, stained in various yogurt flavors: cantaloupe, strawberry cheesecake, cappuccino. *You*, I want to scream. *I dream about you.* "What do you dream about?" I sputter, and he smiles while my stomach flip flops.

"I asked you first."

"So? I asked you second. "

"You," he says. "I dream about you."

"Me?"

"Yeah. And Melissa and Jodi and Tucker and Lucas," he says, ticking off the names of his employees. "I have way too many work-related dreams."

"Oh. Right."

"You ever dream about this place?"

"Sure."

"Am *I* ever in your dreams?"

"Maybe," I say, trying my damndest to sound coy, but cool.

He smiles, opens up the waffle machine, and pours a scoopful of batter.

"Yeah?" he asks, and I wonder if I hear hope in his voice.

"Sure." I lick my lips, feeling my confidence mount. "And Jodi and Tucker and Melissa and Locust."

He laughs. "Good answer."

"I thought so," I say, and I laugh, too.

#

Later in the backroom of the Shack, the radio blasts "Gangsta's Paradise" by Coolio, the Top 40 station winning over country, thanks to the fact Jodi and Melissa have returned, even though they'd gotten off at three o'clock and it's now closer to eleven. Locust had promised them some cheap strawberry wine and pot in exchange for God knows what. They huddle with him and one of his pimple-faced friends on the other side of the room, passing the bottle back and forth and giggling, while Wayne and I perch on the silver counter, him with his legs touching the floor and me with mine swinging away. I desperately want to hold on tight to what I'm experiencing in this moment: the hot summer air, the freedom, the possibilities with Wayne sitting next to me. I smell him and the remnants of his musky cologne mixed with sweat and wet mop and wintergreen. Sounds disgusting, but it's an aphrodisiac, making me dizzy.

There is something here, between us. I'm not imagining it. I don't think so, anyway. Am I? I mean, we haven't gone out on a date or done anything more than hang out back, sometimes alone, sometimes like tonight, with others, after we close the store. But we talk. We talk in those ways that I've longed to talk to someone, the way I used to with Kat and Mom before they became too sad to listen; before I transformed into that kid in school with weird family baggage, in my case a sick father who lived in a nursing home; before I forgot that I'm still a kid and dreams are what it's all about. Wayne listens, more than he talks, actually, but this seems okay, like he's thankful to have someone who trusts him enough to talk to him and confide in him.

The soulful voice of Darius Rucker from Hootie & the Blowfish comes on the radio singing "Let Her Cry" about a woman with a drinking problem who cries all the time (at least, that's how I interpret the song; yeah, I've lost the country battle at home with Kat, who prefers this stuff). Wayne's eyes, which had been squinty and laughing not five minutes before when we hosed the backroom with whipped cream, suddenly become wet and serious.

"What's wrong?" I ask.

He shakes his head.

"Well, something's the matter. You got serious all of a sudden." I look around the room at the squashed peanut butter cups on the brown-tile floor. "Don't worry. We'll make Locust clean it up," and I laugh, hoping it will be contagious, but he simply stares—at what, I don't know.

"Hey," I say, waving my hand in front of his face. "'Fess up. Something's going on."

"It's this song."

I stop and listen. "Yeah," I say. "So? You got something against Hootie & the Blowfish? I mean, they're no Garth Brooks, but—"

"It's not that," he sighs. "Whenever I hear this song, I think about things. My family and stuff. You know?"

I nod, but I don't know, not with any certainty anyway. Here's the little I do know about Wayne and his family, from Wayne himself: he's the youngest of three. He's close to his brother Carl, the middle kid and the one who served in the Gulf War, but he's not close with Hank, the eldest of the Fowler boys. The family business is plumbing. Wayne hates plumbing. What he loves: working with stone, like his grandpa had done for over sixty years, a legendary stonemason in Granite Creek.

This is what I know about Wayne and his family, from what I've heard around town: his mother drinks too much. His father has a temper, beats his wife and sometimes the kids, at least he did when they were growing up. His father also refused to learn the masonry trade, disappointing Wayne's grandpa to no end, and instead went into—of all things—plumbing. Hank and Carl followed their father into the "new" family business, until Carl enlisted in the Marines.

And this is what I've figured out on my own: Hank and Mr. Fowler don't understand Wayne's decision to go into some earth-crunchy business like frozen yogurt so that he can save up money. Hank and Mr. Fowler also don't know that Wayne's got a side business restoring old stone walls and that it's his dream to be a stonemason, just like his grandfather.

"My biggest fear," Wayne whispers, "is ending up like them."

"You won't," I say, and I believe it.

Later, after we finish cleaning up the shop, we spill out the door and into the warm night, the peepers peeping full blast.

"We're going to the beach," Locust announces while his entourage of drunken underage girls follow the bottle he waves toward his red Camaro. "C'mon."

"Should you be driving?" Wayne asks.

Locust winks. "Not a problem, Chief. Stuff's for them. Loosen 'em up. C'mon. You and Koty can follow us."

Wayne glances at me. I shrug as if to say "your call," but I'll admit the image of the two of us cuddled by a fire on the beach sounds tempting.

"Go if you want," he says.

"I don't want to," I say when I realize he's backing away toward his truck. "But I could use a ride home. It being almost midnight and all."

I'd won the car battle with my mother after all, with Kat and I sharing Mom's car and Mom driving Dad's Cutlass, until I "graciously" (Mom's word) decided to let Kat have the car during her last month at home before college. As long as Kat dropped me off to work, I promised I'd be able to hitch a ride home with one of the other girls, when my hope and desire was that Wayne would become my personal chauffeur and being alone in his truck would prompt, well, something. This is night number one of my Grand Plan, and I'm thrilled to see how well it's working as Wayne nods his agreement in bringing me home. I wave good-bye to Locust and his wenches and climb into Wayne's pickup.

"Thanks." I carefully belt myself in, every inch of my body ready to spark. "I live on Stony Brook, which is off Main."

"You sure you don't want to go with them?" he says as he starts the engine. "Where's your car, anyway?"

"My sister has it. And are you kidding? The last thing I want to do is watch those girls do things with Locust and his friend, and all for some cheap wine. *Please.*"

He smiles but becomes silent, and I wonder if he's still thinking about that song and his family. I study his profile. It's what my mother would call a strong profile, even though she had trouble articulating exactly what she meant when, as an eight-year-old, I'd ask her what a weak one looked like.

"Besides," I say, feeling a bit reckless, as I rest my hand on his arm. "I'd rather be here with you."

He doesn't respond, doesn't even acknowledge my flirtation, and I yank my hand back as if I've touched fire. With each passing yard, I feel a little more humiliated and burrow deeper into the seat, desperately hoping it will swallow me up. How the hell will I face him tomorrow and the next day? My God, Locust and Jodi and Melissa and all of them are going to have a field day when they find out what happened, because they will—they'll find out. They'll see how uncomfortable we are with each other and they'll hound me and him until one of us breaks and spills the fact I made a pass at him and was promptly rejected.

"What number?" he asks.

I exhale, unaware that I'd been holding my breath. A few seconds more, and I might have passed out. That would have taken care of everything.

"Sixty-four. Two doors down on the right."

He pulls to the curb, and I fumble for the handle, tears stinging my eyes.

"Koty, wait." He reaches for my arm and tugs it until I turn and face him.

"Listen," I start to babble. "It's cool. You're not interested, and that's, like, totally fine. I feel like the biggest loser right now, but I'll get over it, and I'm sure we'll be laughing about it, you know, in, like, thirty years or something."

"You think I'm not interested?"

I shrug my answer, because I know if I attempt to say anything else, I'll cry. He smacks the steering wheel and shakes his head.

"I'm interested," he says. "I've been interested since I saw you at that damn nursing home. It's just that …" He stops, and the whole world pauses. "Fuck it," he whispers as he reaches for my face and kisses me.

Chapter 7

October 2008

Thirty lurks behind the occasional white hair I pluck from my scalp, thicker and coarser than my auburn curls from hell. I ignore the saying that for every white hair you pull out, seven more will grow in its place, but I'm starting to think the old wives' tale is correct. Examining my head becomes a regular part of an otherwise haphazard beauty routine.

Thirty lurks in the rolls of fat around my waist, a testament to having carried three human beings, birthing two the natural way, and having one pulled from my insides. The fatty deposits grow larger and at a much faster rate, despite the fact I'm not eating more. Sometimes, all I want to do is yell, "Fuck you, metabolism!"

Thirty lurks in the way men gawk at me, or don't anymore, their eyes roaming over Rosie's budding chest, and I want to scream, "You fucking pedophile, she's eleven. *Eleven.*" At eleven (okay, almost twelve), she stands nearly as tall as I do, and her face carries the concerned expression of an old woman who's witnessed things nobody should see happen between a husband and wife.

Thirty lurks in the restlessness that I feel, in my mother's words, haunting me, "What you want in ten years will be entirely different from what you want now," reminding me how much I miss her and how right those words are in one sense: I do want something different. But also how wrong they are: I'm not sure what that different thing is.

Thirty lurks in the routine that's become my life of making breakfasts and lunches, doing laundry, vacuuming floors, putting away dishes, planning dinners, mending shirts, monitoring homework, breaking up fights, praising the good behavior (Rosie, Daisy), admonishing the bad (Iris, nine times out of ten), succumbing to my wifely duties of having sex, which happens less and less, with Wayne falling asleep in his chair, drunk, and me so goddamn tired at night that I probably wouldn't notice if he tried anything at two a.m. anyway, when I imagine he comes stumbling to bed.

Thirty lurks in the suggestions Jamie's made about the possibility of the two of us, in old dreams I have coming back to life, in the what-ifs that echo in my head.

I try to remember what I thought thirty looked like when I was a kid. I realize, however, that I never dreamed that high. The number thirty seems so out of reach when you're ten or sixteen or even when you're twenty.

So how can I long for a different thirty, for a thirty that could have been, when I never had an image of thirty to begin with?

How can I feel so mixed up about a number—a number that's not even that old, white hairs aside, a number and decade that Kat assures me I'll learn to embrace, if not at first, then eventually?

"Mom? Mom!"

Iris's insistent voice brings me back to the present. The running faucet overflows the pitcher in the sink. I turn it off. Iris stands before me, determination in her eyes. Rosie and Daisy sit at the kitchen table, Rosie doing homework, and Daisy staring, rapt, at the little black and white TV on the counter. "What?" I say.

"I've been trying to get your attention for, like, forever." Iris screws up her face and crosses her arms. She may be only ten, but she won't be denied, strong-willed little girl that she is.

"Sorry." I dry off the pitcher and put it in the fridge. Iris is right behind me, arms still crossed.

"So can I?" she asks.

The timer on the stove dings. I open the oven door, poke my potatoes with a fork, and decide they need another five minutes. "Can you what?"

She rolls her eyes and blinks through bangs in desperate need of trimming. "You weren't listening!" She unfolds her arms, grabs a yellow sheet off the counter, and waves it in my face. I take it. It's for something called AIM: Academics, Integrity, Marksmanship. *Marksmanship? My kid wants to shoot guns now?* There are different age levels, including eleven and under called "pre-sub," whatever that means.

"Mommy," Daisy pipes up, pointing to the television. "Look! They found another body."

"What?" I turn to the TV. *Another* body? How is it my six-year-old is aware of *any* bodies?

"They said it was buried off the highway, just like the others." She points again to pictures—mug shots, most likely—of several women's faces. "That one looks like you."

For the love of God. "Okay, enough. Rosie, change the channel, will you?" Four—now, apparently, five—bodies of prostitutes had been found near highways in New Hampshire and Maine, the story of the summer in our quiet town.

"But it's the *news*," Rosie says. "You always have the news on when you're making dinner."

"I know. Just change it, okay?"

Rosie shrugs and obeys, changing to re-runs of *That '70s Show*, which she knows I don't like her watching. Still, it's better than too-close-to-home murder mysteries. Iris pulls on my shirt again and points to the flyer clenched between my fingers. "So, can I do it?"

I hand it back to her, wash my hands, and start rinsing the spinach. "No."

"What? Why not? It's for kids."

I glance up as she points to something on the paper, but all I see is her filthy fingernails. When's the last time I battled her into taking a bath? "I'm sorry, but a ten-year-old doesn't need to know how to fire a gun. End of discussion."

"But Dad does."

"And Dad's a grown up."

"But it's *for* kids."

"Iris," I sigh as I arch my stiff back, another symptom of older age. "You already made that point. I don't care."

"But that's not fair."

Wayne walks in, freshly showered, leaving wet footprints on the old hardwood floor. He tweaks Daisy's cheek and opens the fridge. "What's not fair?"

"Mom won't let me do this," Iris says as she holds up the flyer. He takes a Dr. Pepper—he's in one of his dry-drunk periods and hasn't touched a drop since the day he gave me a fat lip—closes the door, and stoops to read it. When it comes to rearing the kids, Wayne's always stayed in the background. I'm good cop, bad cop, all wrapped into one, not that the bad cop is needed often, at least not with the other two. Kids are smart and intuitive. They know what they can get away with, and it became clear from an early age to all three of them that Wayne wasn't one of those people you pushed past his limit. He's never hit them, but he's never needed to either, not even with Iris, since I've always run interference with her bad behavior, something I've always attributed to middle-child syndrome and nothing more. At least in the early years. But now, I'm not so sure.

"Where'd you get this?" Wayne asks.

"At the library."

"And you want to do it?" he presses.

"Yeah."

He rubs his chin. "Why?"

"Because you do," she replies. "We could go hunting together someday." I never said the girl wasn't smart.

"But, Iris," I say. "I don't understand. You love animals. Why would you want to kill one?"

She fingers the sterling silver dolphin charm on her necklace and squints at me through her bangs, all serious. "I've given that some thought," she says, and I smile in spite of myself at how grownup she's trying to sound. "I don't want to hurt animals. But hunting helps with overpopulation, like deer."

I shake my head because she's obviously been listening to Wayne and Hank carrying on about the pros of hunting.

Wayne must sniff my annoyance because he speaks up, trying to deflect. "Shooting a gun—that's a big responsibility, Buttercup. You know you're not supposed to touch Daddy's guns, right?"

"Yes, sir. I know."

"Well," he says, eyeing me. "Learning the proper way to handle a firearm is the first step in safety."

"Wayne," I interrupt, and his eyes meet mine. "No." We hold each other's gaze, but I'm determined and perhaps bolstered a bit by Jamie's encouragement. I won't back down from this one, and I know he knows it. Deep down, where the old Wayne lurks, I know he knows I'm right, too.

Finally, he lowers his eyes to Iris and tousles her hair. "Your mom and I will need to talk some more about this one, Buttercup."

"Which means 'no,'" she says, while stomping off. Daisy slides off the kitchen stool and follows her, while Rosie remains glued to the TV. Wayne and I stare at each other again.

"Thank you," I say.

"For what?"

"For not disagreeing with me just for the sake of disagreeing."

He taps the top of his can and lifts the tab. "That what you think I do?"

Yes. "Sometimes."

He holds the can to his lips, gulps, and sighs. "Yeah. I guess you would think that."

#

I expect a fight with Iris when I put her to bed, but she gets on her PJs, brushes her teeth, and is under the covers before I have to ask twice. She's giving me the cold shoulder, but I can handle that: I'm grateful for the silence.

It's Rosie's question that I'm not expecting when I go in to kiss her goodnight. She sits propped against her pink and purple pillows while reading *Harry Potter*. She's read all seven books twice, at least, and has started on number one again. I sit on the edge of her bed and put her bookmark, one that Daisy made for her out of pipe cleaners and feathers and buttons, inside the page. "Lights out, kiddo." I kiss her forehead and push a wayward strand of curly hair out of her eyes. I wish she and Daisy hadn't inherited my curls. They're cute and all, but a bitch to take care of. Only Iris lucked out with straight hair, the same brown-black as Wayne's.

"Mom?"

"Hmm?"

"Why do you think Dad always disagrees with you for the sake of disagreeing?"

"What?"

She blushes like I do. "You said that. This afternoon when Iris was asking about shooting lessons."

"I don't believe I said 'always,'" I say carefully.

"Then why do you think he *sometimes* disagrees with you for the sake of disagreeing?"

"I don't know why I said that. I think I was having a bad moment."

She studies my face, and I study the pieces of Wayne and me in hers: his brown eyes, my lips, his square jaw. "Are you going to get a divorce?" she asks.

"What? No. Of course not." I tuck a curl behind her ear. "See, sometimes husbands and wives, moms and dads disagree. It can be frustrating when it happens, but that doesn't mean when we disagree I'm always right and he's always wrong. It doesn't mean we're going to get divorced, either. It just means we disagree sometimes, that's all. Okay?"

She smiles what I hope is a relieved smile. "Okay."

"Now, bed."

She scoots down into her covers. I stand and bend to kiss her head. "I love you," I say.

"Love you, too." She rolls over and closes her eyes.

I head for the door and glance back once before flicking off the switch, and practically walk into Wayne, who's been listening outside her room.

"Jesus," I hiss.

"Nice save," he whispers.

I pad down the hall to our bedroom. "Don't know why she got that in her head."

He follows me. "Well, we don't," he says as he peels of his sweatshirt and jeans.

I sit before two baskets of laundry that somehow multiplied and begin folding. "Don't what?"

"Agree. On anything." He plops onto the bed.

I shrug and say nothing.

"I want to teach Iris," he says.

"You want to teach Iris what?"

"How to shoot."

I snap a towel. "I thought we already discussed this."

"No. We said we *would* discuss it. That's what we're doing now."

"She's ten."

"And she wants to learn."

"She's a child."

"Yeah. A stubborn, strong-willed kid who's made it clear to us she wants to learn. She might not touch my guns now, Koty, but she will someday. I'd rather her know the right way, know what she's dealing with, than to go experimenting on her own and shoot her goddamn leg off. Or worse."

"Or," I say while snapping the towel in the air, "you could get rid of your guns from the house. Don't know why we have 'em here anyway."

"It's called protection. It's called sport."

"It's called unnecessary, as far as I'm concerned."

He rolls over onto his back, hands laced behind his head. "Once again, we disagree."

"Well, yeah. Listen, I'm willing to be perfectly agreeable to reasonable things. Teaching a ten-year-old how to shoot a gun is not reasonable."

"I'm not asking you for your permission."

"So what are you doing then? Disagreeing to disagree?" I reach for another towel. "Just like I said."

"Right," he says. "My goal in life is to disagree with everything you do."

"Certainly seems that way."

He rolls onto his stomach and watches me. "Listen. Give me this one thing. I don't ask for much, not when it comes to them. There's a lot I disagree with when it comes to the way you're raising them—"

"Like what?" I say, surprised at how much his criticism hurts.

"Jesus, will you let me get a word in edgewise? I might disagree, but I let you direct, because I realize a united front is more important than having two parents pitted against one another, like the way I was raised."

I roll my eyes and keep folding. Referencing his parents is not the way to win me over.

"Anyhow," he continues. "I want this time with Iris. She's interested in something I'm interested in."

"Oh, c'mon. You bought that? She was manipulating you."

He stops, shakes his head, and rolls onto his back. Two years ago—heck, two months ago—I would have been jumping up and down at this attempt at conversation, at an actual discussion on his part. So why am I pissing all over his parade?

"For the record," I say, unsure what's right or wrong anymore, "I still don't approve of teaching a child how to fire a gun. But if you do this—if we agree to it—and if I see any change in her behavior, any more aggression at school, or change in grades, then we stop. You stop. That needs to be the deal you make with her. Perfect behavior."

"That's asking a lot of a kid who's never shown any sign of perfect behavior in her life."

He has a point. "Well, no worse, then. And better in some areas. Less lip to me. More consideration for her sisters. No fights in school."

"Okay," he says.

"Okay," I say.

"Did we just agree on something?"

"Looks that way."

He lets out a whistle. "Only took thirteen years."

Chapter 8

What color is happiness? Yellow, like the sunflowers he leaves under my windshield. Raspberry-swirl, like the sunrises when I'm sneaking back into my house in the morning. Cocoa, like the deliciousness of his eyes. Charcoal, like his favorite T-shirt.

Think the rainbow spectrum.

On steroids.

I am in love.

I've told no one this, not even Wayne, but he must know. How could he not see my skin goose bump every time his arm brushes against mine? The way my cheeks heat up and, no doubt, turn pink when I catch him watching me? How my voice smiles every time I hear his on the other line? How breathless I become after we kiss and lick and grope and—

"You sure you're ready for this?" Wayne asks, interrupting my naughty thoughts.

"Of course." I reach out and rest my hand on his knee. He stiffens and grips the steering wheel tighter. "What's up? Why are you so nervous?"

"You'll understand. After you meet them. Listen, I can't promise anything, okay? My old man—he's sometimes offensive. And if my mother has been, you know …"

I squeeze his knee. "Don't worry. I know." I don't, of course. But how bad can his family be, especially since I've been living with a family in mourning for almost seven years?

Wayne takes a right down Little Creek Road. Woods line both sides, ablaze in gold, orange, red. We travel forever, it seems, and the road twists and turns, rises and dips, the houses becoming farther and farther apart. We cross a short bridge, and instead of guardrails, a stout stone wall lines either side. Wayne stops, and I peer out the window, trying to see over the wall's ledge.

"My great-grandfather built this culvert over a hundred years ago," he says. "My gramps was a teenager and helped him. It's all built from granite. Not like the concrete or steel they use today."

"Is this the creek the town is named after?" I'd never thought about the origins of my town's name until now.

"Nah. That one is on the other side of town. This creek here is mostly dried up. Can fill pretty fast with water when it storms, though."

I nod, trying to think of a smart question to ask about culverts, even though I'm not sure what one is.

"What?" he asks, as if he can read my mind.

"I don't think I know what a culvert is," I say, and my cheeks grow warm.

He smiles. "Just a fancy name for a mechanism that channels water, usually under something like a railway or road, like this one. They come in all shapes and sizes, but the one beneath us is round and large in diameter— you can stand up straight in it and then some. There's another one on the other side of the woods." He pauses, his eyes faraway. "I used to play in them when I was a kid. I loved the smell, you know? Dank and mossy." He glances at me. "Probably sounds weird to you."

"Actually, it sounds cool."

He laughs. "Well, I know what we'll do on our next date: take a romantic walk through the culverts."

I punch him playfully in the arm, and we start moving again, traveling for another two or three minutes.

"Well," he says, pulling into a dirt driveway and parking behind a van that reads "Fowler & Sons Plumbing." "We're here."

The house, which is set off the road, is an older-looking two-story farmhouse with a wrap-around porch in desperate need of a coat of white paint. I clap my hands and reach for the door handle, but Wayne grips my arm, stopping me.

"Twenty minutes," he says. "Tops. We're not staying more than twenty minutes."

I shake him off. "Right. Twenty minutes. We're having an early dinner and then catching a movie. Got it."

We step out and walk up the driveway, where angry voices greet us. An older man—Wayne's father, I'm guessing—stands on the porch with his arms crossed, observing two men standing in front of the van. They're going at it, the taller one in the other's face.

"Shit," Wayne says under his breath. I reach for his hand and hold it tight.

"Get your goddamn sissy ass out of my sight, you hear?" the tall one screams. As we approach, Wayne's father makes eye contact with me, and his mouth forms words I can't hear. The other two men glance in our direction.

"Hey," Wayne says, mounting the porch steps with me in tow. Then, to his dad: "Didn't Mom tell you we'd be stopping by?"

"She mentioned something," his father says.

"Right. Well, this is Koty." Wayne turns and gives me a weak smile. "Koty, this is my father, Norval. Everyone calls him Norv." He points to the guys in the driveway. "These are my brothers, Hank and Carl."

I offer my hand to his father. He considers it for a beat before accepting it. His grip is strong, hard. "Nice to meet you, Mr. Fowler."

He nods, says nothing, and releases me. I smile at Hank, the tall one, who looks like his father—meaty-necked, red-nosed, black eyes—and then at Carl, who looks like an older, tired version of Wayne.

"Nice to meet you, Koty," Carl says. "You'll have to excuse us here. Just a classic Fowler family feud, that's all."

Wayne ignores the comment. "Mom inside?" he asks, but doesn't wait for a response, making his way to the screened door, dragging me by the arm.

"Yeah," Carl replies. "Good luck with that."

Wayne holds the door open for me, and I enter. The house feels swallowed by shadows. We walk down a dark hallway lined with wicker baskets overflowing with magazines, shoes, and unidentifiable crap. Wayne had warned me that his mother had a "thing" for baskets. The hallway leads to the kitchen, where a woman smoking a cigarette sits at a small table by a window overlooking the backyard and woods. She's thin and yellow-skinned with hair that looks like a dandelion gone to seed. Her left hand is wrapped around a bright pink mug, but I suspect she's not drinking coffee or tea. Wayne warned me about this as well.

"Mom," Wayne says. She turns in slow motion as if it pains her to do so.

"They finally stop arguing?" she asks. Her voice is hoarse and filled with grit.

Wayne shrugs. "I don't know. Maybe." He pauses. "Mom, I want you to meet Koty."

"All they ever do is bicker and bitch," she says and then sips from the mug and puffs on the butt. "The whole lot of 'em."

"I know, Mom. I know. Listen, can we talk about something else? I want you to meet Koty."

She fixes her muddy brown eyes on me, and I smile. "Hi, Mrs. Fowler. It's nice to meet you." I allow my eyes to do a quick intake of the kitchen, which is like any kitchen, if you ignore the smoky film clinging to the cabinets and walls. And, of course, all the baskets, dozens of them, some even hanging from the ceiling. "You have a lovely home."

She laughs. "You like it? You can have it."

"Mom," Wayne says, closing his eyes. "Please."

She waves away his words as if they're flies—annoyances and nothing more—and turns back to her window.

Wayne doesn't hesitate. He takes my hand and leads me back the way we came. When we step onto the porch, his father and Hank are gone, but Carl sits on a weather-beaten rocking chair and stares straight ahead.

"Told you," Carl says.

I glance at Wayne whose cheeks have turned a color of pink I've never seen before. His lip forms a tight straight line.

"Koty, can you give me a moment?" he asks. I nod and watch as he disappears into the house. I shift awkwardly from one foot to the next.

"So you two work together, right?" Carl says, still staring straight ahead.

"Yeah."

He nods. "That's cool."

"You work with your father and brother, right?"

"Yep. It's a barrel of monkey laughs, let me tell you."

Loud, angry voices erupt from the house. Wayne. His mother. I can't make out what they're saying.

Carl shifts in the chair and gazes up at me. His eyes are the same color as Wayne's and filled with kindness. "Don't worry," he says. "Wayne'll be okay. But do me a favor, Koty."

"What's that?"

"Don't let him end up back here. No matter what."

I nod, not knowing how to respond to that, as Wayne explodes through the screen door, jumps down the porch steps, and runs to his truck. I race to catch up, and when I do, he's already behind the wheel. I climb into the cab. He turns the key in the ignition and begins backing up before I have a chance to close the door.

We drive in silence for five, ten, fifteen minutes, and the whole time I wonder whether I should say something or let him be the first. I note his clenched jaw, his hands gripping the steering wheel, but I also note how the tension lessens with each mile, the farther away we get from his house, until finally his body, his face, his whole aura relaxes.

"So," he says as he pulls onto a main drag, "where do you want to eat?"

Chapter 9

"You're quiet today," Jamie murmurs. He sits in his chair, prosthetics attached. No more waiting for me in his bed. This makes our heavy make-out sessions a little more awkward, for me anyway, but we manage, or I do anyway. "Koty?"

"Sorry. Tired, I guess." I yawn for effect.

He nods, accepting my answer even though I'm sure he doesn't believe it.

"Do you have nightmares?" I ask suddenly, and I'm not sure where the question is coming from. "You know, of when it happened." I wait for a transformation in his face: anger, sadness, something. Nothing happens. He simply nods. "A lot?" His jaw twitches, and he nods again. "I'm sorry," I say because I am, and because I don't know what else to say.

We sit in silence—how normal this stance has become when we're not locked together at the lips—and my mind imagines those nightmares, even though it has no context, no clue, no possible comprehension of their true contents.

"Sometimes," Jamie begins slowly, his eyes far away, "certain noises, certain smells become a trigger, and everything comes flooding back. But louder. Harder. There are days, even now, when all I want to do is rub my eyes because I can't get the sand out, the dirt, the grit. Thing is—"

"There's no sand to begin with," I finish for him.

"And no fingertips to rub my eyes." He holds up his left arm, the one that has a hand-shaped prosthetic on the end. "No matter how good I get with this, something like that—getting dirt out of my own eye—I'll never be able to do again." He shakes his head. "During rehab, they were all like 'Focus on what you can do. Not what you can't do.' That was easy enough to swallow because you're in a room filled with people in similar sorry states as yourself. But here," he shakes his head, unable to finish.

"Why'd you join?"

"The Army?" He shrugs. "My dad. 9/11."

I gesture to the pictures on the bureau. "Your dad fought in Vietnam?"

He nods. "He was there when Saigon fell."

I want to ask an intelligent question so I search the cobwebbed sections of my brain that house information learned during my high school American history class. But all I can come up with in response is, "Wow."

"Ma always said the man who left and the man who came back were two different people. But she didn't care. She was hell-bent on getting pregnant. It was the one thing left in him that he could give her. Did you know she'd had six miscarriages by the time she was your age?" He sits, lost in memory. "Anyway. He died when I was sixteen. I was pretty messed up after. My grades went down the shitter, which devastated my mother, with her being a teacher and all. I think she'd hoped I'd go on to college, meet a nice girl, take part in a normal, quiet, non-military profession, have two point five kids and a dog. The whole package, you know?"

"Yeah, I know. I never had her as a teacher, but I heard about her strong 'traditional' family beliefs."

"One thing about her: she may be old-fashioned, but she's up front about it. All of it. Family values and all. You know where she stands."

"True."

"Anyhow, after graduation, I took some classes at the junior college in the fall and spring, but my heart wasn't in it. Flunked out. Worked odd jobs during the summer. That was 2001. Then 9/11 happened. Became obvious after that what I needed to do. What I had to do."

"Do you regret it?"

"No, of course not. I don't regret fighting for my country."

"Because it's a noble cause?"

"I think noble is giving your life for your country, for a brother, for a friend, for a child. I defended our country. It was an honor and a privilege to do so."

"Is that you talking, or the military?"

"What the fuck sort of question is that?" he says, his eyes on fire.

"Jamie, I—"

"What, you think I can't think for myself, have my own thoughts and opinions? Is that it?"

"No, but, let's face it. The military is known for brainwashing its recruits. You join, you drink the Kool-Aid, and that's—"

"That's what?"

"And that's it. At least that's what they make you think, right? Their way or the highway. That this so-called 'war' in Iraq is about terrorism, when it's got more to do with oil and greed and politics and God knows what else. You don't need to put up a front for me. If you regret it, I won't hold it against you. I would if I were you."

"You'd what?"

"Regret it! I mean, look at you."

"Right. Look at me. The fucking cripple. The fucking cripple you feel sorry for and give charity hand jobs to."

One charity hand job, I feeling like saying. *One.* "That's not what I meant, and you know it."

"All I know is that I was fighting for something real, something that mattered, and in the span of two minutes, the one person who I thought actually understood that just destroyed the last fucking thread these fucking plastic hands have been holding onto."

"I'm not saying you didn't believe in the cause or that you weren't fighting for something worthy. I'm only saying how can you not wonder what if? What if you hadn't joined the military? What if?"

"Do you ever wonder what if?"

"You mean about you? Yeah, actually, I do."

"No," he says. "Not about me. About you. Do you ever wonder how your life would have been different if you hadn't gotten pregnant, if you'd seen the scumbag your husband was before you married him? Do you wonder what your life would be like today if you weren't the mother of three kids and the wife of an alcoholic who is from the worst family this town has ever seen? Don't you ever wonder what if?"

"No," I hear myself say, even though deep down, I know it's a lie.

"Why not?"

"Because that sort of second guessing is way too painful."

"Exactly," he says.

"Hey, I'm sorry."

"Forget it."

"I mean it. I'm sorry."

"Fine," he says, but the tone of his voice suggests otherwise.

"Jamie, the last thing I want to do is hurt you. It's obvious I have. I'm sorry for that."

"I said forget it. But do me a favor?"

"What?"

"Next time you think—and I know you will—'what would my life be like without Wayne?'—know that it's still an option. You could have a life without him."

"Oh, sure."

"And with me instead."

Earth stops. Hell freezes. Pigs fly. I'm sure I heard him wrong. "What?"

"You heard me."

"You're not serious?"

"Why wouldn't I be? You know, our differences aside about this war and despite the fact you can go from sweet to bitchy in less than thirty seconds, I've never talked this way to a woman before—"

"Talking is one thing," I interrupt.

"I've never felt this way either. There. Happy?"

I'm stunned. "I'm married."

"I know that."

"I have three kids."

"Know that, too."

"I'm going to be thirty in a few weeks."

"And your point is?"

"Jamie—"

"No, wait. Don't say anything. I'm not asking you to say anything. I'm asking you to think about it. To visualize it."

"Visualize it? You're kidding, right?"

"No, I'm not. Picture it."

"And then what?"

"I don't know. You'll need to tell me."

"Jamie, I can't."

"You deserve a good life."

"My life isn't bad now, not always, anyway. Besides, you're confusing Wayne with the rest of his family, and he's not like them. Not completely." I think back to the reasonable conversation we had the other night, to how he can be when he stops drinking, when he focuses on other things—like his kids—rather than Carl's murder. "In fact, the other night, Wayne and I had a good conversation. A parenting conversation."

"What about?"

"Guns, of all things."

"Guns?"

"Yeah. Iris—my middle child, the ten-year-old—wants to learn to shoot. Some organization called, I don't know, AIM, or something like that. I told her no. But Wayne disagreed, of course."

"So what did you decide?"

"I gave in. Wayne made a halfway decent argument. We actually discussed something for the first time in a long time. I told him if I see any change in her behavior, that's it, though."

Concern spreads over Jamie's face. "You got firearms in the house?"

"Yep."

"How many?"

"I don't know. Wayne hunts, so he has a bunch of rifles or whatever for that locked up in a gun cabinet."

"Anything else?"

"He keeps a gun in our bedroom."

"Loaded?"

"Yeah. I think so."

"Locked up?"

"No," I say, and memories of an argument about it come storming back. "Don't tell me to convince him to lock it up, because I'm not going to win that battle."

"What kind of gun?"

"Um. I'm not sure."

"You know how to use it?"

I shake my head. "I don't want to know."

"You should know. For safety. If they're in your house, you should know the proper way to use them. Especially with kids around."

"Now you sound like Wayne."

"Well," he says slowly. "If we're both saying it, maybe there's some truth to it." He pauses. "Learning how to defend yourself and your kids against him is important."

"Wayne may be a lot of things, but he's not violent in that way."

"Oh, yeah? What way is that? The way he busted your lip a few weeks ago?"

"He's not Hank or his father."

"The genes are there. The DNA."

"With that reasoning, what does that say about my girls? They have his genes. Are they prone to violence then?"

"Maybe, yeah."

"No," I say, but I doubt myself, an image of Iris, in second grade, rolling around on the playground with a boy twice her size. She'd won the fight, bloodied the boy's nose and sent him doubled over in pain with a swift kick to the groin. Middle-child syndrome, I'd tried convincing myself. I push the memory aside and sit up straight. "No. Definitely not."

He studies my face. "Okay, then. Do it because if there are guns in the house, Wayne shouldn't be the only one who knows how to use them properly. Do it because you live on a secluded street that backs into secluded woods. Do it for me."

"Have I ever mentioned I hate guilt trips?" He says nothing, and I sigh. "Okay. Fine. I'll learn."

"I can teach you," he offers.

"You?" I can't mask the incredulity on my face or in my voice.

"Yeah, me," he says, and I can't tell if he's annoyed at my skepticism or not. "If you can follow directions, then I can teach you."

"Okay," I say, positive it will never happen, but not about to burst his bubble.

"And don't forget you owe me an answer about what I asked you to visualize."

"Jamie—"

He holds up his arm. "Shh. Not now. After you've thought about it."

I nod even though I'm positive that won't ever happen either.

Chapter 10

April 1996

We sit on the edge of Wayne's bed, staring at the third pregnancy stick he's made me pee on. Like the other two, this one shows a red plus sign. Wayne and I had gone all the way for the first time on New Year's Eve. It was a natural next step for me, given the last six months of our relationship. But a few weeks ago, our condom broke. Then, I missed my period.

"Well," Wayne whispers. "I guess that's that."

I lift his stiff arm, cuddle against his warm chest, and listen to his heartbeat. "It's going to be okay. I mean, it's not ideal, but it would have happened. Eventually, right?" When he doesn't respond, I pull back and peer into his eyes. "Wayne?"

"Yeah," he says. "Right."

#

I try convincing myself that Wayne is simply worried about what people will think, since his family lives on permanent rumor control. Last thing the Fowlers need is their youngest knocking up a girl who's barely of age and who is his employee to boot.

I expect more support from Mom. After all, she and Dad married young. You don't have to be a math major to know she was already pregnant with Kat when she and Dad got hitched. They'd always seemed happy to me, from what I can remember, at least. I mean, what else could explain her utter devastation and despair during the years Dad languished in a nursing home? She loved him. She missed him. He was her world.

"You don't have to keep it," Mom says quietly, evenly, after I tell her.

"What are you talking about?"

"I'm talking about reality, Koty. Oh sure, you think it's all romantic now, but a baby changes everything. You have no idea how much."

"But you and Daddy—"

"Times were different then. Yes, abortion was legal, but it was still the biggest of taboos."

"It's not now?"

"No. Yes. Listen—you're only seventeen. You have your whole life ahead of you."

"That life includes Wayne and this baby." I cross my arms. "Mom, I love him."

She frowns and shakes her head.

"What?" I bark.

"What you want now is going to be entirely different from what you want ten years from now. Trust me."

"How do you know what I want? When's the last time you ever asked me anyway?"

"Don't raise your voice at me."

"Why not? It's the only way I've gotten your attention these last seven years."

"Do not turn this around and put it on me. You got yourself pregnant. I had nothing to do with it."

"You won't have to have anything to do with it now. God forbid."

"Koty, you have no idea what you're talking about."

"No, Mom. You have no idea. I will marry Wayne. I will have this baby. I will graduate school. I will have a life."

"I, of all people, want you to finish high school. I will move mountains to make sure you get your diploma, but do you have any idea how hard it's going to be?" She waits a beat but begins again when she sees me drawing air into my chest to protest. "Don't answer that. It's a rhetorical question. Of course you have no idea. How could you? From the soaps you watch? From the movies you've seen? You're going to be getting up two to three times a night. You can kiss a normal night's sleep good-bye for the first two years, and that's only if you get a good baby, which Kat was, and you weren't, colicky little thing that you were. Do you know how tired you're going to be? Exhausted doesn't do the feeling justice because it's about ten steps past exhaustion, right before the insanity exit. So if you think you have a hard time concentrating now on your trigonometry and world history, wait until you have a newborn and you're trying to hit the books."

"Gee, Mom. Thanks for the vote of confidence."

"Reality has nothing to do with confidence. You can be the most confident sleep-deprived woman on the block, but it won't change the fact that you'll be sleep deprived."

#

I'm the only one who looks at my situation with any bit of romanticism. Kids at school snicker and whisper behind cupped hands, and every corner I turn, I bump into pity. Pity in my teachers' eyes, pity in Kat's eyes, pity from people on the street or in the mall once it's obvious that I'm not thick around the middle, but pregnant. Wayne grows quiet and pensive, but I push it aside, attributing it to the things I'm reading, how it's common with fathers-to-be as they start thinking about things like taking care of a family. Still, the last time I felt this lonely was during those early years after Dad's stroke. Right after it happened, we had all the help we'd ever need with hams and pasta salads showing up on our doorstep, teachers excusing absences and offering extensions on assignments, kids from school sending Kat and me homemade cards, and Dad's colleagues on base taking up donations for our family. Once it became obvious to everyone (other than my mother and Kat) that Dad wasn't going to wake up and get better, however, things changed.

Patience comes in limited supplies, I think. People certainly don't want to waste what little they have on a lost cause. The food stopped coming in. Same with the phone calls and homemade cards. Kids at school were awkward around me. What do you say to the girl whose father is almost dead? Death and resurrection have clear instructions: condolences for one and congratulations on the other. As for persistent vegetative states? Hallmark doesn't have any cards for that. The one word I'd use to describe those years is this: hushed. I don't want that to be the word describing my pregnancy. I mean, my God. Every change in my body, every tumble and somersault from the little being growing inside me leaves me in awe. Sure, I studied biology and anatomy, but here I am experiencing it firsthand. I want to laugh and giggle and smile and share and scream from the rooftops about the life inside me, the hope, the possibilities. But everywhere I turn—Wayne, Mom, Kat—I find myself biting my tongue, swallowing my joy, hushing myself, and the baby inside.

Chapter 11

October 2008

The sun pokes through the blinds. Somewhere, a fire burns, its scent wafting through the barely open window. Trees rustle the last of their leaves. The bed is empty, and I know it's late. Late for me, at least. I roll over and glance at the clock: 7:02.

The reality of today dawns on me.

It's my thirtieth birthday. It's also my twelve-year wedding anniversary. Giggles and "Shh's" erupt on the other side of my partially closed bedroom door, which opens, tentatively at first. My girls greet me in various stages of dress for school. Iris carries a tray (no doubt because she insisted), Daisy claps her hands and sings "Happy Birthday" off-key, and Rosie monitors them, hovering like a mother hen. I sit up in bed, smile as wide as I can, and spy Wayne lurking in the doorway.

Iris places the tray on my lap, the breakfast plates decked out in scrambled eggs, pancakes, and bacon. To the left sits a little white vase with a daisy, purple iris, and red rose.

"Look what Daddy bought," Daisy says, pointing out the flowers as if I could miss them. "One for each of us." She beams fifty thousand watts of light, and the only thing I want to eat up is her.

I lock eyes with Wayne. His are hard, almost empty. I say almost, because in this moment I detect something else, though I can't say what, and I wonder what he sees when he looks at mine. Regret? Resentment?

Disappointment? Longing? A part of me wants to welcome him in this moment, but another part of me—that place inside that knows this is the calm before the November storm that has occurred every year since Carl's death—wants to fast forward to another life.

"Thank you," I say simply.

"Happy birthday," he says. "It's the big one."

I adjust my position as Rosie and Daisy climb into bed and snuggle next to me. "That it is. Oh, and happy anniversary, by the way."

He nods, says nothing, and disappears, leaving me alone to celebrate with our daughters while my insides contract in pain.

Chapter 12

"Look." I lift my shirt and point to my bare belly, thirty-three weeks and counting. "A foot."

"Mm," Wayne says.

"You didn't even look." I grab the papers from his hands, directions for the crib he's trying to put together. Despite her abortion suggestion, Mom has warmed up to the idea of a grandchild and saw to it that I had a proper baby shower. The crib was her present to us.

"Hey," he says, as I throw the directions across the floor. "You're the one who's been nagging me to put this damn thing together."

"It can wait." I take his hand, always dry and rough from the sanitizer solution he uses at work, and place it on the baby's appendage. "See? Feel it?"

He goes still and closes his eyes. Then he shakes his head.

"What's the matter?" I ask, alarmed.

"How are we supposed to do this?" he whispers.

I'm in that stage where anything and everything makes me cry, including weather reports on CNN. "Together," I choke as the tears spill. His eyelids flutter open, but he doesn't reach for me, or hold me, or try to comfort me. Without a word, he removes his hand from my belly and continues assembling the crib.

#

I can't get comfortable in bed anymore, my belly overwhelming my body. I try on my side, my back, and onto my side again.

"Koty, please," Wayne murmurs, his back to me.

"Sorry."

The phone rings. I hoist myself onto my arm so I can see over Wayne's shoulder to the digital clock on the nightstand: 5:04. Early yet, and still dark. I need sleep. I have a physics test in three hours. The phone rings again.

"Wayne?" I shake him. "You gonna get that?"

He groans, picks up the receiver, and holds it to his ear. "Yeah?" he mumbles. He sits up fast, alert, and flicks on the light. "What? When?"

What is it? I mouth to him, but he ignores me.

"I'm on my way." He hangs up, his feet hit the floor, and he rummages through the dirty clothes on a nearby chair.

"What's going on?" I ask.

"That was Hank." He pulls on jeans and a wrinkled T-shirt. "Something's happened to Carl."

"Oh my God. What?"

He runs his hands through his hair, not that it does any good, with tufts sticking up in a million different directions, and puts his wallet in his back pocket. "I'm not sure. Hank told me to get to the hospital."

I push the covers aside. "I'm going with you."

"No."

"What? Don't be silly. Of course I am."

He comes over to my side of the bed and crouches in front of me. He rubs his hands under my nightgown and along my prickly legs. Shaving has become too difficult. "Listen to me, Koty. I need you to stay here. Hank sounded pretty unhinged, so I can only imagine what my parents are like."

"Don't you want me there?" I say, hurt. We've been married for only a few weeks, a quick trip to City Hall on my eighteenth birthday, and I'm already feeling the difference between dating and marriage. Wayne's been quieter, more distant.

He releases my legs. "Don't start."

"Don't start what?"

"This isn't about you or what I want. What I *need* is for you stay here, then go to school. Don't you have a big test today?"

Tears pool behind my eyelids. I nod.

"The baby," Wayne says, and his voice softens. "I need you to think of our baby. You don't need the added stress."

"But how will I know what's going on?"

"I'll pick you up after school."

"What if you need me before then?"

"I'll be with my family."

"I thought I was your family, too."

He clenches his jaw and stands. "I don't have time for this. I gotta go." He grabs his keys off the bureau and disappears before I can protest further. I hear him unlinking the chain on the front door and slamming it shut.

I roll out of bed and pull up the shades, but it's too dark to see him. I hear him, though, as he slams the truck door, revs the engine, and takes off down the street. I stand there forever it seems.

The baby hiccups.

A siren sounds in the distance.

I stub my toe on the way back to bed.

I lean against the pillows, rub my belly, and do my best to ignore the feeling that my life has somehow changed in the space between a phone call and a man getting dressed.

Chapter 13

When I arrive at Jamie's on my birthday, he's already outside. He grips a walking stick in his prosthetic hand.

"You okay?" I say. "What's going on?"

"Everything's fine. Got a surprise for you."

I shake my head, confused. "How'd you get out?"

"You said you wanted me doing more, right?"

"Yeah, but—"

"Old-man Zeke helped me out. Listen, you want to see your surprise or not? C'mon." He starts to walk, slowly, tentatively, and I realize I've never seen him walk more than a few paces, mostly from his bed to his wheelchair or vice versa. He stops and glances back, but I say nothing and simply follow him around the side of the house and out back, where a card table is set up. On the table rests a gun, a square box, a rectangular piece of metal, two sets of goggles, and four small wedges of foam. I have no idea what kind of gun it is, but it's similar to the one Wayne keeps in our bedroom drawer. About fifty feet away, where the woods meet the lawn, some of the trees are outfitted with targets: black circles against yellow.

"Happy birthday," he says, almost shyly, and I can tell by the curious expression on his face—is it hope? Excitement?—that this is a big deal to him. I tread carefully.

"I don't know what to say. Did you set this up by yourself?"

"Nah. Zeke helped me. My mother, too."

"Your mother?"

"She can handle herself around a gun. She hates hunting, but she respects the sport and knows how to use a firearm. Bow and arrow, too, believe it or not." He watches my face and then smiles. "C'mon. I know it's overwhelming, but it will do you good to know how to use one of these. And it would do me good to know I can still show someone how."

I take a deep breath. "Okay. Where do we begin?"

"Safety first. You put on one set of safety goggles. Then you put the other set on me."

I slip the goggles over my head and adjust them around my eyes, and then I do the same for him. "Are we using real, you know—"

"Ammunition? Yes. You'll treat it with more respect if it's real. So no messing around. Understood?"

I nod and for the briefest of moments can picture him as he might have been four years ago, dressed in fatigues and whole. A leader.

"Okay," he says. "That right there is a nine-millimeter semi-automatic handgun. It's a good one to learn on."

"Is it loaded?"

"No. I want you to pick it up by the grip with your right hand. Barrel facing away from you and me." I obey. "Good," he continues. "We're going to go over the external parts. Along the back of the gun, that thing sticking up? That's the hammer." I touch it and nod. "Now run your hand along the top. That's the slide. See the part of the slide that's different? It's shiny? That's the ejection port. Now look at the left side. See that piece that looks like it could move back and forth? Put your left thumb on it and slide it."

I do and the top part of the gun slides back.

"Good. That's the slide catch. It locks the slide to the rear. To close the slide, simply push down on that lever." I go ahead and push. "Great," he says. "Go ahead and do that again. Open the slide." He pauses and waits. "This is what we'd do if we wanted to make sure the gun was empty. You can never be too safe. Keep the barrel pointed away from you and me, but look inside the ejection port. See anything?"

"No."

"Always do a visual check and a physical check. Put your finger inside and sweep it around. Do you feel anything?"

I do, and feel nothing but the metal of the cylinder. "Nope."

"Good. It's empty. Okay. Now release the slide catch."

I pause, remembering what I've learned, release the lever, and the slide closes.

"Good. Put it on the table for now and pick up the magazine clip." He gestures to a rectangular piece of metal. I pick it up. It's cold. "Feel the flat side. Always remember, flat side to flat side."

"Flat side to flat side," I repeat.

"See that box right there? Those are the bullets. Go ahead and open it. Pick one up." I hesitate, and he says gently, "They can't hurt you the way they are now, Koty." I nod and follow his directive. "Feel it," he instructs. "Notice there's a pointy side and a flat side."

"Flat side to flat side."

He nods. "Exactly. You'd insert each round, one by one, into the magazine, flat side to flat side."

I glance at him. "You want me to do that right now?"

"No, not yet. First, I'm going to show you how to insert the magazine. You can put those down. Pick up the gun again in your right hand. Good. Push the slide back and visually check and physically check to make sure it's empty." I follow his directions and the rhythm of his voice. "Wrap your right hand around the grip. Right. That part of the gun that's against the heel of your hand is called the backstrap."

"The backstrap," I repeat.

"Now pick up the magazine in your left hand. You want the flat side of the magazine to go against the flat side of the backstrap."

"Flat against flat."

"Right. So go ahead and slide the flat side of the magazine into the magazine well so it's against the flat side of the backstrap." He watches as I follow his directions. "Perfect. Now if you had ammo in there, you'd release the slide mechanism, and it would chamber the first round and be ready to fire. Remember where the hammer is?"

I pause and then point to the back of the gun at a little hammer-like piece of metal.

He nods. "When it's down like that, in the rear, it's ready to fire. But let's say you don't want it to be ready to fire. This particular nine millimeter model has a de-cocking capability. See along the top left toward the back?" He watches me. "Right there," he says. "Go ahead and press down that lever." I do and there's a click and the hammer rises to the top. "See? It sends the hammer home. Even if there were a live round in the chamber, if you pulled on the trigger, it wouldn't fire."

"So it's a safety feature," I say.

"Exactly. Okay, I'm going to have you release the magazine clip. When you have your hand wrapped around the grip, you should feel something right about where your middle finger is."

I search with my fingers until I detect what feels like a button. "Okay. Got it."

"When you press on it, it's going to release the magazine clip, so have your left hand underneath so you can catch it. Go ahead and press on it."

I do, and the magazine clip falls into my hand.

"Perfect," he says.

"You're a good teacher."

He smiles. "Ready to load live ammunition?"

No, I think. *I'll never be ready for that.* But I'm not doing this for me anymore. I'm doing it for him. "Okay."

"Put down the gun, and pick up the magazine. Have the flat side against your palm. Good. Now we're going to insert the rounds. Remember what I told you?"

"Flat side to flat side."

"Right. You'll insert each one so that the flat side of the round is up against the flat side of the magazine. Push down on each one and then load the other. If you want to remove a round, see that red insert? Keep pressing on that, and each one will pop out. So go ahead and load the rounds."

"How many should I put in?"

"It holds fifteen rounds, but how 'bout you put in four. Don't want to overdo it on your first day."

He watches as I do each round, one by one.

"Okay," I say. "That's four rounds."

"Good. Put the magazine down, and pick up the gun, and check to be sure it's not loaded."

I place the magazine on the table and reach for the gun. "But we know it's not."

"You can't be too careful. Remember how to check?"

I nod, and release the slide mechanism. The slider moves to the rear. "Okay, I visually check," I say peering inside the ejection port and to the empty magazine well below. "And I physically check." I wiggle my finger inside. "It's empty."

"Good. Now what?"

Flat against flat. "I insert the magazine with the flat side against the ..." I search for the correct word.

"The backstrap," he prompts.

"Right. The backstrap." I insert the magazine clip.

"Give it a good tap on the bottom so that it's seated right. Perfect. Now hold the gun out in front of you, aiming the barrel away from us. I'm going to have you release the slide, and that's going to chamber a round, okay?"

I exhale. "Okay."

"Go ahead and release the slide."

I do. "So this is a loaded gun that I'm holding?"

"Yes."

If you'd asked me fifteen minutes ago how I'd feel in this moment, I don't think exhilarated would have been the word I'd have used, but that's exactly how I feel.

"Relax, Koty," he says, his voice low and soothing. "You're doing great. Do you remember the safety feature?"

I hold the gun out in front of me, feel the metal against my hands, and only then realize sweat is trickling down the side of my face. "The hammer," I say, surprising myself at how easy I'm picking this up.

"Right. You need to de-cock the hammer. Remember how?"

I nod and put my finger on a lever and glance at him to make sure I've selected correctly, even though I know I have. He nods, and I press down. The hammer moves up.

"Good."

"It's safe now?"

"As safe as any loaded gun can ever be."

"So when am I going to shoot?"

He laughs. "Eager now, aren't we?"

"Well, you got me this far."

"This is true." He gestures to the table and the foam thingies. "Put the earplugs in your pocket for now and let's have you walk away from the table. We're going to have you stand right in the middle of the lawn, aiming for the targets on those trees."

I gather up the earplugs, walk to a spot, and wait for Jamie to come next to me.

"There are several different stances I can teach you, but for now, stand with your feet about shoulder width apart and have your right leg, since you're right-handed, a couple inches behind the left. Bend the knees. This is the Weaver stance."

I stand, separate my legs, put the right foot a few inches behind the left, and bend.

"Good," he says. "Raise your right arm, hand wrapped around the grip, but bend your arm at the elbow. You don't want to hold it out straight because your arm will get tired pretty fast. Now your left hand is going to provide stability. The palm of your left hand will essentially be touching the bottom of the magazine clip, and you're going to have your hands so that thumb meets thumb."

"Like this?"

He studies my hands and frowns. "Not exactly." I adjust, but he shakes his head. "This is where it would be so much easier if I could show you."

"But look at everything you've shown me so far. Let me try again." I reposition, thinking less about his directions and more about what feels natural, and wrap my hands around the butt of the gun. My thumbs meet.

"You got it," he says. "Now, there are two parts of the gun that we haven't talked about yet. See those two protrusions from the top as you look over the top of the gun? The one nearest you is called the rear sight and the one farthest away is the front sight. Line up your target in between them, but keep your eyes on the sights, not the target."

I take a deep breath. "Okay."

"Now, when you squeeze the trigger, the gun's going to recoil. It will feel like the gun is jumping in your hand. Don't let it alarm you—that's what's supposed to happen. Stay calm and focused and hold onto the gun. Got it?"

"Got it."

"With your left hand, take out the earplugs and put 'em in your ears and then mine."

I nod and carefully dig into my pocket and pull out two earplugs. I insert one into my left ear and fumble with the right. Then I do Jamie's, his eyes studying my face the whole time. "You're going to do great," he says, two ticks louder than his normal speaking voice. "Now get back in position."

I obey and glance at him for approval. He nods.

"You need to cock the hammer," he yells, and I do. "Good. Okay, whenever you're ready."

My first instinct is to close my eyes and squeeze the trigger, but, instead, I breathe and swallow, and as I do, the world stops. Suddenly, it's just me, the target ahead, the gun in my hand, the possibilities. I keep my eyes on the sights, take another deep breath, and squeeze the trigger.

My arms jump, as Jamie warned, but I don't let go. My eyes close, though, at the end, and I'm instantly angry with myself.

"Not bad," Jamie says, his voice muffled because of the earplugs. He leans into me and says in my ear, "You got three more rounds. Don't take your eyes off the sights."

I do it again and again and one final time, the last one being perfect, or as close to perfect as I can imagine, my eyes open, the center of the target almost hit, the power coming from me and my hands. Part of me wonders if I should be concerned at this transformation, but a bigger part of me wants to scream, "Fuck it! You're thirty! Live!"

I turn and face Jamie, whose smile is wider than any smile I've ever seen on him or anyone else. I don't see a damaged man standing before me with metal arms and legs, wounded in body and soul. I see a man with a broad, manly chest. Sexy brown eyes. Lips that know how to tease every sensation out of my own. I can't remember ever feeling so goddamn horny in my life. I walk up to him, gun by my side, open my mouth and kiss him, long, hard, and deep. My left hand reaches for his crotch, and I feel him get hard beneath my touch. He pulls back, breathless.

"Hold up, cowgirl. You still have a gun in your hand. Safety first."

We walk back to the table, and he watches as I remove the magazine and do my visual and physical inspection. I remove my earplugs, tossing them on the table, and then his, my hands lingering on the side of his face, my lips to his. I feel buzzed, drunk almost. I massage his hard on, and we kiss again, but he pulls back abruptly, his eyes darting from side to side, his nostrils flaring.

"What's wrong?" I say, glancing around the yard.

"I heard something." He pauses, eyes alert, jaw twitching. "We should go back inside."

I have to remind myself that Jamie's senses are on overdrive, something that the IED couldn't destroy. He hears things long before the sounds bounce off my eardrums. Still, I can't help but wonder if he's imagining it, since I don't hear anything, his backyard and house protected from people thanks to his desolate street, the nearest neighbor a good quarter mile away. "Okay," I say, trying to hide my disappointment because I can already feel the magic of the moment evaporating. Like any drug you try for the first time, the high so unexpected and so pure, I wonder if it will be possible to ever get it back.

#

It takes time, walking with Jamie from the backyard, to the side yard, up the wheelchair ramp, and into the house to the study where he has me put the gun, the magazine clip, and the ammo in a safe. We start down the hall toward his room. I can tell I'm running late and peek at my cell and see several missed calls from the kids' school. *Shit. What'd Iris do now?* I'm about to stop in the hallway and tell Jamie I should get going, but as if he can read my mind, he speaks.

"C'mon. I got another birthday present for you in my room."

"You mean a shooting lesson wasn't enough?" I follow him down the hall. He nudges the door open and there sits a vase overflowing with red roses.

"Happy Birthday," he whispers in my ear. "Managed to get all thirty in one vase."

"They're beautiful." I finger their delicate petals, satin against my skin, and breathe in their scent. Then, it hits me: what this looks like. *Shit.* "Jamie, what's your mother going to think?"

"Don't worry. She was in on this. I told her it was your birthday—a big one—and said we should do something nice for you."

I bite my lip, unconvinced, and an image falls loose from my memory: the little white vase with this morning's breakfast, the simple rose, daisy, and iris inside. What am I doing? I need to get out of here. I need fresh air.

He moves toward the bed and motions for me to join him, but I hesitate.

"I should get going." I glance at my watch. "I'm already running late, and the girls will want to spend time with me today."

"Oh, right," he says. "What are the big birthday plans for tonight?"

"It's actually my anniversary, too."

"Anniversary?"

"Mine and Wayne's. You know, wedding anniversary?"

His face darkens. "No, I didn't know."

"He and the girls want to take me out to dinner," I say quickly. "That's what we usually do. Together. Family time."

"Right. Well, don't let me stop you." He gestures to the roses. "Don't forget to take them with you."

"Oh, I can't."

"You can't what? They're yours."

"I know, but I shouldn't."

"Why not?"

Because they remind me too much of you. Because they're likely to invite questions I don't want to answer. Because I need to keep these worlds separate. Instead, I simply say, "Because."

"That's not much of reason."

"Jamie, they're beautiful. Everything about this afternoon was beautiful, special."

"But?"

"But how's it going to look if I bring home thirty red roses from you?"

"*And* my mother," he adds. "This was from both of us. Even the little card sticking out the middle of the flowers says so."

"Well," I say, fingering the card, which I'd overlooked: *Wishing you a happy birthday! Thanks for all of your help. The Briggs.* "Wayne might not see it that way."

"Are you going to pussyfoot around him for the rest of your life?"

"Jamie, we need to be careful."

"I'm not scared of Wayne."

"Well, you should be. Because if he knew what was going on—"

"What *is* going on, Koty? Have you thought about that?" He turns away suddenly, head tilted. "My mother's home."

I strain to hear what he hears, but all that greets me is silence. "Right. Well, I need to go." I wait for a minute, hoping he'll face me. When he doesn't, I walk to the door.

"Happy birthday, Dakota," he whispers, but I pretend I don't hear him and keep on walking.

Chapter 14

December 1996

It's two weeks before Christmas, and I'm due any time, but instead of joy and anticipation, the words that shroud our life are sadness, anger, and despair.

I bottle up everything. The birth of a child should trump death, even a tragic one, but this is only a hunch on my part, or perhaps it's hope.

I lean back in the seat and rub my belly like a crystal ball, wishing I could glimpse the future. When will the old Wayne return? Will our baby's birth be enough to lure him back? I glance at his profile and want to reach out and wipe away the sadness from his face. But I don't. On more than one occasion these last few God-awful weeks, I've watched him shrink away from my touch. I can't stand to see it, not today.

My last checkup. Well, maybe not last, but I have a feeling it will be my last, that the next time I see Dr. Kobb, it'll be during labor. I've been reading about instincts, about how women know their bodies and babies, and I wonder if this is true.

I'm nervous. I'll admit it. How much will it hurt? How long will it be? Will the baby be okay? Will I be able to breastfeed right away? Will I love it enough? Will Wayne?

Wayne.

He drives, silent, eyes on the road, not speeding, not exactly anyway, but with more urgency. The person in front of us stops short. He hits the brakes.

"Hey, asshole," he shouts as we pass the car, a Volvo with a forty-something goateed man driving. "Put your dick on and learn to drive!"

I'm about to respond when Wayne gets right on top of another car and turns on his hazards.

"What are you doing?" I ask.

"This dude's a danger to everyone around him. I'm warning people."

"What? That's crazy."

"You want to get in an accident? Because I don't. I'm trying to protect you and our unborn child." His voice is gruff, uneven, without any trace of tenderness. He sounds like his father. "By the way," he continues, "I've been meaning to tell you. I'm leaving the Yogurt Shack."

"What? Now? But how can you do that when I'm about to—"

"Let me finish, will you? I'm going to work with my father and Hank."

I'm sure I've heard wrong, that this is a joke, that he'll burst out laughing and exclaim, "Koty, I'm not that crazy!" But he doesn't. "You don't like the plumbing business," I say.

"Guess I'll have to learn, won't I?"

"What about masonry and all your dreams?"

"Koty, in case you've forgotten, my brother was murdered, the same brother who helped run Fowler & Sons Plumbing. They need the help. It would be pretty silly to change the name to Fowler & *Son* Plumbing, now wouldn't it?"

I shake my head. "This isn't you talking. This is Hank. Or your father."

He laughs, long and deep, the sound emanating from a place so dark, so unfamiliar, that I shudder.

"As they predicted," he says. "They said you'd think they were forcing me, that I'm making this decision under duress."

"You are."

"No. You're wrong. I'm making this decision for me."

"What about us? Our baby?"

We've arrived at the medical building, and Wayne pulls into a parking space, puts the car in park, and leans his face into mine. He's going to kiss me, I think. He's going to apologize and tell me everything's going to be okay. Then I see the anger in his eyes. It matches the meanness in his voice. "Don't ever question what I do to take care of this family. Got it?"

I nod, unable to speak.

Chapter 15

For normal families, November means high school football games. Raking leaves. Early wish lists for Santa. Happy moments around a Thanksgiving table.

Not for us. November is the month I walk on eggshells waiting for the inevitable break. It always comes, ever since that phone call about Carl's death twelve years ago. I've gotten used to the ebbs and flows of Wayne's drinking. Kat says I'm an enabler. Kat, however, has a college degree and a way of being independent. She has step-kids, boys no less, not flesh and blood that depend on her like three daughters depend on their mom.

I've gotten good at this, adept even, at creating our lives around Wayne's "schedule." November is always a bad month, so I work extra hard at managing the kids, making sure dinner is never late, keeping the house as spotless as possible, doing everything within my power to make it so he can't find an excuse to go off on me or, God forbid, the girls, even though something inevitably triggers him. Maybe this year, I reason, will be the year where I figure out the right formula. Maybe this will be the year when the trigger no longer fires.

A woman can dream, can't she?

#

The beer cans are stacked in a pyramid, and the dinner dishes await me in the sink. I've gotten Daisy bathed and playing happily in her room, no easy feat on a Sunday night, but Iris and Rosie sit at the kitchen counter, with Rosie trying to show Iris how to do fractions. "Trying" being the operative word, since both girls keep casting sidelong glances at their Uncle Hank as he spouts on and on about some sort of nonsense. Everything Hanks says is nonsense, warped and fueled by a life of non-stop booze since he was thirteen, and it's moments like these when I'm grateful I married Wayne, not Hank, even during our hellish Novembers.

Hank doesn't visit much, mostly because I sense he knows I can't stand him, nor him me, but his wife is taking one of their boys to look at colleges this weekend, or at least that's what Wayne had said this afternoon when he announced we'd need to set another plate at dinner for Hank. "College?" I'd said. "I didn't realize there was a clown school in driving distance." I'd immediately regretted my words, since if there was one thing Wayne was whether sober or drunk, it was loyal to his family. But he grinned. Which goes to show how stupid our nephew is and that his mother lives in la-la land if she thinks any school will accept him.

Hank and Wayne spend dinner making plans for the annual hunting trip they take in Carl's memory and discussing the latest conspiracy theories one or the other has hatched in connection with Carl's murder. I tune it out and notice that even the girls are extra quiet, chewing their meatloaf and sipping their milk and looking to be excused as fast as possible, except, of course, for Iris whose ears perked up at the details regarding the hunting trip. No doubt, she was the one who insisted on dragging Rosie out to the kitchen to go over fractions.

Hank cracks open another beer and leans back in his chair. "The whole country is—how did Ma used to say it?"

"Going to hell in a handbasket," Wayne says, and Hank nods.

"Exactly." Hank takes a long swig, a thoughtful expression on his normally vacant face. "You voting?"

"Yup."

"Goddamn liberals are out to make McCain look like he singlehandedly caused this financial meltdown. Of course, I don't think putting some unknown broad on the ticket was the right move. Don't get me wrong—she's pretty as hell, but all that means is I'd rather fuck her than vote for her."

Wayne stifles a laugh but catches my eye. "The girls," he says to Hank and gestures toward Rosie and Iris.

Hank rolls his eyes at the warning. "On the radio this morning, I heard them saying that Obama is leading in the polls. Can you believe it? Like we need one of them leading this country."

Wayne shakes his head, but says nothing. I'd learned long ago to avoid talking politics with Wayne, who leans more and more to the right with each passing year.

"One of what?" Iris asks.

"Girls," I say because I need to nip this one in the bud, and fast. "You'd probably be more productive if you did your homework in Rosie's room. Let the grownups talk their boring talk out here."

"Nah, wait," Hank says. "This is important. A civics lesson. You see, Iris, don't let them liberals you got teaching you in the school tell you those people like Obama are like us."

"What people?" she asks.

"He means African Americans," Rosie says.

Hank chuckles and slaps his knee. "You hear that? African Americans. That's bullshit. You can change the label, but that don't change the fact a nigger is still a nigger."

"Girls!" I say loud enough to startle all of us. "Rosie's room. Now."

Rosie gathers up their books and papers, and Iris glances from Hank to me. She draws air into her chest, a question hanging on her lips, but I purse mine in my best "don't you dare speak now" look and point to the hallway. "Out."

I watch as they disappear down the hall. "Listen," I say to Hank. "Keep your politics to yourself."

"Excuse me?"

"You heard me."

"Hey, I'm calling it like I see it. Or are you missing the fact a nigger is running for the White House?"

"I don't want you using that language in this house or around my girls. Understand?"

I cross my arms and we both look at Wayne, as if we're expecting him to referee this debate, but all he does is stare at the table.

Hank shakes his head in disgust. "Figures." Hank pushes his chair back and stands. "Pussy-whipped, as usual. I'll see you tomorrow, Wayne. That is if you're allowed to come out and play." He walks out, muttering under his breath about my goddamn ignorance.

I wait a beat and then turn to my dishes. All remains quiet for a good five minutes, and I feel my body relax, even though I hadn't been aware of the tension in my muscles to begin with. Wayne isn't completely unreasonable. Having his daughters hear their uncle call a presidential candidate the n-word isn't right, and I know he knows that, regardless of what he thinks of Obama politically. I wasn't out of line; I simply asked Hank to stop using that language. He's the one that walked out in a huff and who tried to turn it around into some gesture about Wayne always taking my side, which everyone in this family knows is not true. Perhaps Wayne will sulk, go to bed, sleep it off, and have forgotten about it by morning. That happens sometimes. No doubt, I'll hear about it again, later this month, most likely when something does send him over the edge, but for now?

I sense something behind me and turn around. Wayne stands in front of me, his face so close to mine, I can smell the beer on his breath.

"You get some sort of perverse pleasure embarrassing me?" he says. His voice is quiet. Too quiet, like the calm and stillness I imagine right before a tornado tears through a farmhouse in the middle of the night.

"Embarrassing *you*? Are you okay with him using language like that around our daughters? Because I'm not."

"That was Hank being Hank. You know that. The girls are old enough and smart enough to know that."

"The girls should not be hearing any man referred to as a nigger. I don't care if it comes from Hank or a black rapper. It's wrong."

He chuckles, still low, still too quiet. "Oh, that's right. I forgot. Koty Fowler knows all that's right and wrong, is that it? If you say it's so, then it must be."

I push past him and gather the empties on the table.

"Well?" he asks.

"I'm sorry. Was there a question in there?"

He waits a moment, stunned perhaps at my smart-ass reply, and grabs my arm, twisting it until I face him. "What did you say?"

"Wayne. You're hurting me. Let me go."

He twists harder, and a door down the hall creaks open.

"The girls," I begin, pause, and catch my breath, "don't let them see you like this."

"Don't let them see me like what?" he says, but he releases me, casting my arm to my side as if he'd touched a leper. Daisy plods into the kitchen.

"I want ice cream." She peers up at me, expectant. When I don't respond, her eyes move to Wayne. "What?"

I rub my arm and grit my teeth. "Is that how you ask?"

She rolls her eyes. "May I have some ice cream, *please*?"

"Better," I say and head toward the freezer.

"That's right, Buttercup." Wayne claps his hands. "You listen to your mother on all things related to propriety. She knows, let me tell you. But

whatever you do, remember this: don't vote a nigger into the White House."
He stalks off, and I hear him open the front door and slam it shut. A part of
me prays he doesn't get behind the wheel and opts for a long sobering walk
instead. Another part of me wishes for something more sinister.

"Why'd Daddy say that word?"

I pull a pint of Brigham's chocolate—her favorite—out of the freezer
and place it on the counter. "Daddy's upset. He didn't mean to use that
word." I wonder if an almost-seven-year-old can glean how lame my excuse
sounds. She frowns the way she does when she's thinking hard or trying to
remember her multiplication tables, her nemesis.

"Why did he say it then? That's a bad word, right?"

"It *is* a bad word. You should never call anyone that word. Not ever." I
pluck the ice cream scoop out of the dish strainer, pull a bowl from the
cabinet, and try to scoop. The ice cream is too hard and my arm hurts. I place
the pint in the microwave and set it for five seconds. "Daddy was repeating
something Uncle Hank had said after dinner. He was trying to make a point
with me." The microwave dings, and I pull out the ice cream, which is soupy
along the perimeter. I scoop two large balls into the bowl while Daisy climbs
up onto one of the stools. For an extra treat, I grab a Kit Kat from the leftover
Halloween candy, crush it up, sprinkle it over the ice cream, and hand Daisy
a spoon. "Whaddya say?"

She grins wide, revealing her missing front teeth. "Thank you."

I return to the dishes in the sink and stare out the window into the
darkness, the clinking of Daisy's spoon to bowl our only accompaniment.

"Mommy?" she says after a while.

"Hmm?"

"What does *pro-pry* ..." She wrinkles her nose, trying to remember the
word.

"Propriety?" I prompt.

"Yeah. Propriety. What does that mean?"

"It means proper behavior and good manners, basically." *And it means everything your father isn't when he's drinking.*

"Oh."

The subject needs to be changed. Now. "So speaking of all things proper, we have someone's seventh birthday party to finish planning. Let's see. What's on the list?"

She grins wide again. "Moonwalk."

"Check."

"Pizza."

"Check."

"Piñata."

"Got it."

"Ice cream cake."

"Is there any other kind?" I remove her empty bowl and rinse it. "Sounds like we're in good shape. Have we heard from everyone you invited?"

"Twenty-one yes's and three no's." Daisy, the most social of my kids, wanted to invite her whole class, boys and girls. God help us. "And you said Rosie and Iris could each have a friend, too."

"Yep," I say. Rosie had already asked her friend Ashley. Iris hadn't asked anyone, in typical Iris fashion. I keep hoping she will. Everyone needs a friend.

"Aunt Veronica, Uncle Hank, and Aunt Kat and Uncle Dennis will be coming too, right?"

For a moment, I'm stricken by how sad it makes me to hear that string of names without my mother's tacked on at the end. Well, not her name per se. The girls called her Grandma, of course. It's the reference to her that I miss. Wayne's father has kept to himself in Florida for the last five years since Phyllis died, so our girls don't know him and didn't know her, but they knew and loved my mom. I can't believe it's almost been a year.

"Yes to Aunt Veronica and Uncle Hank," I say. "But remember Aunt Kat and Uncle Dennis are going to visit your step-cousin Bobby at college since it's parents' weekend."

"Oh, right." Daisy nods. "Well, maybe you should invite a friend."

"Me?"

"Yeah, since Daddy has Uncle Hank and Aunt Veronica and Rosie will have a friend and maybe Iris, too. You should have a friend. Maybe what's-his-name. The guy you visit every day."

Jamie. My God, she means Jamie. "I don't think that would be a good idea."

"Why not?"

"Well, for starters, he doesn't really know anyone."

"He knows you."

"I mean no one besides me." The front door opens and shuts. Wayne's back.

"So?" Daisy says. "He can make new friends. Like with Daddy."

"Who can I make friends with?" Wayne tousles Daisy's hair and ignores me.

"The guy Mom visits. When he comes to my birthday party."

"If," I say. "*If* he comes. Like I said. Probably not a good idea."

"Why not?" Wayne leans against the counter, crosses his arms, and fixes his eyes on me. "Sounds like a nice gesture."

Ah, yes. So this is how it will go: Wayne acting like a two-year-old and disagreeing with everything I say.

I ignore him and help Daisy down from the stool. "I'll ask him tomorrow, but now it's time to brush your teeth and get ready for bed."

#

The next night at dinner, Daisy asks me if I invited Jamie.

"I did," I lie. "He wanted me to tell you thanks for the invite, but he won't be able to."

Daisy pouts. "Why not?"

"He said he wouldn't feel comfortable." *Fuck. Why didn't I simply say he had other plans?*

"How come?" Daisy asks.

"Because of, you know, everything."

"I thought you said he was walking again," Wayne says. "Even taking walks outside."

"Yes. He is. But birthday parties with thirty kids running around? Let's face it. That's not for everyone." I take a quick sip of milk and notice Iris pushing her food around her plate. "How'd your math test go today, Iris?"

She glances at me, but Wayne speaks before she answers. "You didn't ask him, did you?"

"What?" I say, trying hard not to choke.

"You didn't ask him to come to the party, did you?"

"Didn't I say that I did?"

Wayne stuffs a piece of steak into his mouth. "So if I called him and asked him right now, he'd know what I was talking about. Right?"

I wipe my mouth and feel the girls' eyes on me.

"Mommy?" Daisy asks.

"Okay. I didn't ask. He's been through a lot. He's not a fan of crowds or loud noises or having people stare at him. I didn't want to put him in the awkward situation of feeling he had to go because I was asking."

"But it's a party," Daisy says, and her eyes shimmer with tears.

Wayne takes a long drink of beer. "Seems to me you should let the guy make his own decision. Considering people have been making decisions for him since the time he enlisted, he might like to be able to accept or decline an invitation on his own."

"Fine. I'll ask him tomorrow."

Wayne glances at the clock. "Why not ask him now?"

"You want me to go over there now?"

"You heard of a thing called a telephone?"

I start a "but," and then realize it's useless. Wayne outing me in front of the girls is one more slap in the face for speaking up to Hank last night and "embarrassing" Wayne. I push my chair back, stand, and bring my dinner plate to the counter, even though half my meal remains. I reach for the phone before realizing I don't even know Jamie's number.

"I don't know his number. Listen, I'll ask him tomorrow."

"That's why they invented four-one-one," Wayne says.

I call information, get the number, and dial the Briggs's house. I get his mother on the phone, identify myself, and ask for Jamie. I hear the surprise in her voice, but she doesn't question me. I wait for a long moment and turn my back to the kitchen table because I can't stand all the eyes on me.

"Koty?" Jamie says. "Everything all right?"

"Hi, Jamie. Yes, everything's fine. Listen, I'm calling because my daughter Daisy would like to invite you to her birthday party. It's a week from Saturday. At our house."

"Birthday party?"

"Yes." *Please say no, please say no, please say no.*

"Whose idea was this? Yours?"

I don't answer.

"Was it Wayne's?" he asks.

"Yes."

"Is he there right now?"

"Yes."

"Do you want me to come?"

Oh, God, why are you asking me this? "Daisy would like it if you came. She said she wants me to have a friend at the party, too, since Rosie and Iris each get to have a friend." I twirl the cord around my finger.

"Okay," he says, but I hear uncertainty in his voice.

"Great," I say. "I can give you more details when I see you tomorrow."

"Right. Bye."

"Bye." I return the phone to its cradle. "He said yes," I say without turning around. Daisy claps.

"Yay!" she says.

I plaster a smile on my face and return to the table, gathering dishes, including Iris's untouched meal, in no mood to question her further about math tests or anything else. Maybe she's getting sick. Just what I need.

When I get to Wayne's dish, he places his hand on mine. "Now, was that so hard?"

#

"So what was that all about?" Jamie asks the next day. We're walking in his backyard, toward the woods, and with every step he takes, it seems he becomes more free. We don't touch or kiss outside—we keep that for behind closed doors—and it's hard in moments, especially those when I'm filled with pride as I watch him, so desperate to give him a hug.

It's a beautiful fall afternoon: crisp air, blue sky, and tension and excitement (depending on which side you're rooting for), thanks to the presidential election.

"It's what I told you last night. You're invited to Daisy's birthday party, a week from Saturday. She thinks I should have a friend there."

"Smart girl, considering you don't have any in that family you married into."

"You can back out, you know." For a second, I think he might be hurt, but the moment passes.

"Do you want me to come?" he asks.

"I want you to do whatever makes you feel comfortable."

He shakes his right "arm" at me. "Comfortable is something I gave up about three years ago."

"You know what I mean."

"Yeah, I know what you mean. You're thinking it's easier to keep your worlds separate. This one and that one."

"Well, yeah. Don't you agree?"

He shrugs. "For now maybe. Someday though—"

"It's not someday yet."

"When it is, though, you'll need to make a decision."

"About what?"

"About this. About us."

Hearing him say the word "us" as a unit, suggesting something more than simply a volunteer effort on my part is both terrifying and exciting. *And impossible*, I remind myself. We begin walking again.

"I'll go," he says.

"You don't have to."

"I know. But I'd like to meet your kids."

"Jamie, Wayne will be there. We need to be careful. This isn't a date."

He rolls his eyes. "Of course, crazy lady. I know." A hawk squawks overhead, and we watch as it soars in the sky. "So," he says. "I've been thinking."

Oh God. "Yeah?"

"Yeah. About what I want to do with my life."

"And?"

"Did you know I used to be a camp counselor? Back when I was a teenager?"

"Nope."

"I used to go to overnight camp during the summer. Hated it the first week I was there. I was ten, I think. I ended up loving it. I loved the independence. I loved all the activities: archery, canoeing, swimming. I loved it so much that I became a counselor. For two summers, anyway. It's the only thing that kept me sane after my father died." The hawk we've been watching flies lower and in one sudden movement swoops to the earth below and out of our line of sight. Jamie turns to me and continues. "What I loved best about being a camp counselor—shit, this sounds like the start of some dumb essay for school. Anyway, what I liked best was teaching the little kids how to do stuff. It reminded me of the times I spent with my dad before he got real sick."

"I bet you were good at it."

"I don't know. I like to think that I was." He shrugs. "It's something I thought about a lot. I figured when I got back from Iraq, I'd volunteer at Drill Sergeant School. I was already an NCO, and I knew volunteering would show that I was committed to becoming a drill sergeant. I thought that would be a good way to use my skills. Make a career I could be proud of. That my dad would be proud of. But then, well, this happened." He extends his prosthetic arms out wide. "Forget the Army. How could I teach, at any level, like this?" He pauses and nods. "You changed all that."

"Me?"

"Yep. When I taught you how to use a gun, and you did—you were able to do it—I realized that maybe I could still teach. Even like this."

"So you want to be a teacher?"

"Not a teacher like my mom. I want to teach people like me. People who think they can't do stuff—fun stuff—because of their physical disabilities."

"Veterans?"

"Yeah, but not only veterans. Everybody. Especially kids."

"Sounds great," I say, because it does.

"Yeah. On paper, anyway. The actual 'doing' part—that's the stumbling block."

"You'll figure it out."

"Maybe we could figure it out together."

I close my eyes because I can't stand seeing his face and the fact he still finds hope in mine. "Jamie, I—"

"Think about it, okay? I'm not even talking about you and me as, well, you know. I'm talking strictly from a business standpoint. From a friend standpoint. From two people who are hoping to get a little more meaning from life, despite the lemons they've been given."

"You calling my girls lemons?"

"No, but I bet getting pregnant at seventeen wasn't part of your dreams when you were a little kid."

"I don't regret them, you know. Not for one minute."

"Never said you did."

"Wayne was different, too. Back in the beginning."

"So you say."

"He's not as bad as you make him out to be. He's not a monster."

"Koty, a man doesn't have to be Satan incarnate to make him the wrong man for you."

"What are you saying? I have twelve years invested in this marriage, in this family. You don't just walk away."

He reaches for me, not so much in a romantic way, but an earnest one, and I imagine it's moments like this that make him frustrated since I'm sure he wants nothing more than to touch my hand and feel skin against skin.

"What about if you have something to walk *to*?" he whispers.

"Jamie, my God. This is insanity. You are not asking me what I think you're asking me, right? We've known each other, what? Two months and change?"

"So what? When you know something in your heart, in your gut, you know it. I've based my life on gut feeling, Koty. I know how I feel. I've known it for a while. Call me crazy, but I think you know it, too."

"I have a life. I made my bed."

"Bullshit. You made a mistake. You've paid for it and then some."

"You think I can walk away? It doesn't work like that. Besides, it's not just me. I'm a package deal. I come with three kids."

"I'm well aware of what you come with. I'm okay with that."

I rub the sides of my arms with my hands, trying to keep warm, even though this particular day is a mild one. I kick at the leaves with my sneaker and shake my head. "We're not having this conversation now."

"If not now, when? When he finally goes off the deep end for good and does the unthinkable?"

"That's already happened once. He learned from that."

"What did he do?"

I bend and pick up a rock and throw it as far as I can into the woods. "He shook Iris. When she was a baby. Well, two years old or thereabouts."

"He shook her?"

"Yeah. He'd been drinking. He was angry because he had new evidence about his brother's murder, and he felt he was getting the runaround from the police, and he was frustrated. And Iris was being Iris."

"Wait. You said she was two."

"Yes, but you have to understand that Iris has had a strong personality from day one. She's a lot like Wayne, actually. It's why she loves him so much. She's his favorite, too."

"As long as he hasn't been drinking and she doesn't irritate him, right?" He shakes his head. "So what happened after he shook her?"

"I left."

"You left? You mean, for a few hours?"

"No. I walked out. I took Rosie and Iris. I was six months pregnant. I got in the car and I drove and drove. It was a Sunday night. August. Heat wave. Then, it started to rain. Monsoon, actually. We stayed in Hampton Beach for a few days."

"Then what?"

"I came back."

"Why?"

I shrug. "Because my girls asked me to. Jamie, as imperfect as it is, we're a family. I know what it's like to grow up without a father. So do you. As imperfect as Wayne might be as a husband, and even as a father, he loves his kids. And they love him."

He doesn't respond, and I glance at my watch. His mother will be due home any time. I start walking toward the house, and Jamie follows. We cross the yard to the side of the house and then to the driveway. We stop in front of my car. I pull my keys out of my pocket.

"You got everything?" he asks.

"Yep. Left my purse in the car."

"So am I still invited?"

"Are you still invited?" I ask, confused.

"To Daisy's party."

"Sure. You're more than welcome." I open the door, climb inside, turn the key, and open the window. "Well. See you tomorrow."

"Question," he says.

"Yeah?"

"I thought you said November is usually his bad month. Anniversary of his brother's death and all."

"It is."

"But he shook your daughter in August."

I sigh. "Jamie—"

He holds up his arm, the one that actually looks like an arm and a hand. "All I want to know Koty is this: when's his good month?" He nods, steps back, and makes room for his mother as she pulls into the driveway while I reverse direction, thankful that I don't have to answer him.

Chapter 16

December 1996

I find him in the basement of our apartment building. I've been struggling with the laundry basket, my large belly in the way, and I've resorted to carrying it on my head, like the images of women from far-flung third world nations you see in *National Geographic*. He sits on top of the dryer, a bottle of something in his hands. He doesn't offer any help, no acknowledgement of my predicament. I don't think he sees me, period. My body numbs.

"Wayne? What are you doing?"

His eyes try to focus, but those sexy eyes I'd fallen for, the ones that used to gaze at me not even a year ago with interest and love, are empty, blank.

"What does it look like I'm doing? I'm having a drink."

"But—"

"But what?" he spits.

"You don't drink."

"Well, I do now."

I reach for him, place my hand on his arm, but he recoils at my touch.

#

Two days later, I go into labor. It's not like the books, the magazines, what they tell you in Lamaze classes.

"She's perfect," I say, and I can't stop the tears. I cradle the little being to my chest, wondering the whole time how I possibly lived for seventeen years without having experienced happiness like this before.

"Well," Wayne says. He stands in the doorway to the bathroom, holding the hospital-issued pink water pitcher. He places it on my bedside tray. "This is filled."

I smile what I imagine to be the widest smile in the world. He doesn't smile back, simply presses his lips together and nods.

"I'm gonna get going, okay?" He shrugs into his jacket. I have a new parka for him, wrapped under our little Christmas tree at home.

"No, wait," I say, confused, hurt. "Aren't you staying? The nurse said they'll put out a cot."

"I—" He hesitates. "I'm tired. You're tired."

"Well, yeah. I hear we should probably get used to that."

"Right. I know." He pauses. "I need some time, Koty."

"Time for what?"

"Time. That's all. I'm sorry. I know that's not what you want to hear." His voice goes quiet, and he stares at his feet.

Rosie stirs in my arms, her eyes fluttering open, searching. My tears come again, and Wayne's by my side. He rubs my back, kisses my head, says something into my hair, but I can't make out the words. Then, he's gone.

It's not like the books. Or the magazines. Or what they tell you in Lamaze classes.

Chapter 17

The scene is surreal: my husband chats with the man I spend my afternoons kissing and confiding in, while the man, no doubt, loathes every minute in my husband's presence.

Standing next to Jamie, Wayne looks old, or at least older than a thirty-three-year-old man: his hair has grayed and thinned on his crown, and his eyes, which I swear were once the size of quarters, seem smaller, tired, and without any spark. Because there was a spark once, right? It was one of the things that drew me to Wayne in the first place.

Wasn't it?

"Mom." Rosie tugs on my sleeve. Her friend Ashley, wide-eyed because she's an only child and not used to such backyard hubbub, lurks behind her. "The pizza's here." She points to Wayne who is now paying the delivery guy and juggling a tower of boxes. I wave him over to the picnic table where we're standing and give a prayer of thanks for the fiftieth time today that we've lucked out with such nice weather for mid November. Warm enough that we can all be outside comfortably, but cool enough that Jamie can be covered in slacks, shirt, and windbreaker—you wouldn't know by looking at him that he was missing four limbs. Kids can be cruel, and I'm grateful the only spectacle is the Moonwalk.

"Go tell Daisy and her friends that the pizza's here." I glance toward the inflated monstrosity, which Hank is supervising. The castle-shaped contraption, in all its yellow, red, and royal blue glory, appears even more out of place against the backdrop of the woods with its browns and grays. I spot Daisy's curls through the netting on the sides of the castle and watch as kids slide down an inflated exit ramp.

"Where's Iris?" I ask.

"I dunno," Rosie says. "Inside, I think."

"Well, go get her, too."

I help Wayne rip the covers from the pizza boxes as kids descend upon us from every direction. "Pizza," someone yells.

Daisy squirms her way under my arm as I pass out paper cups and plates. Sweat drips down her flushed face, and the pink dress she insisted on wearing is stained with something purple and sticky. I start a bottle of hand sanitizer around the table.

"I want pepperoni," one voice calls out.

"I want plain."

"I want sausage."

"There's plenty," I say. "Let's everyone start with one slice, and if you want more, you can have it. Don't forget there's ice cream cake, too."

"And the piñata," Daisy says and her friends erupt in cheers and tomato sauce smiles.

Wayne ushers Jamie and Hank to the adult picnic table, and for the first time that I can remember, I wish Hank's wife had shown up, even though she's notorious for cancelling out on Saturday events due to hangovers. I watch as Wayne helps Jamie slide onto the bench. Jamie clenches his teeth, and I wonder if his discomfort is physical, emotional, or both.

As I'm pouring Kool-Aid and passing around cups, Rosie appears by my side again. "Mom, Iris says she wants to stay inside."

"Why? Is she sick?"

"No. She says she's not hungry. Where are we supposed to sit?"

We have three picnic tables. Two have been pushed together for all the kids. The adults have the third one, borrowed from Hank.

"Would you two mind sitting with the grownups?"

Rosie nods, takes Ashley's hand in her own, and leads her to the other table. They slip in between Wayne and Jamie. Satisfied that all the kids are fed and watered, I approach the grown-up table with the pitcher of Kool-Aid, even though Hank and Wayne are drinking Mike's Hard Lemonade. I glance at Jamie who has a slice of pepperoni in front of him, half eaten, and I realize that in all the time I've known him, I've never seen him eat. We've always been occupied with conversation or—

"You going to stand there all day or sit down?" Hank asks and the rest of them look up at me. I plunk the pitcher of Kool-Aid in front of them.

"I'm going to see what's up with Iris." Then, to Wayne and Rosie: "Keep an eye on all of them, okay?"

#

I find her fetal-like on the bed. She faces the wall, and my stomach sinks, because maybe she is sick. I sit on the edge of the bed and place my hand on her shoulder. She cringes at my touch.

"Iris, sweetie. Don't you feel well?"

Nothing.

"Iris?"

"What?"

"Look at me."

"Why?"

"Because I asked you to."

She sighs and turns to me, and I see Wayne. They have the same wide-set eyes that are so brown-black you can't easily distinguish the pupil from the iris. Right now, they're full of anger, not the usual mischief.

I stroke her hair, which unlike the other girls' hair or mine is silky and straight. "What's wrong? C'mon. You'll feel better in the fresh air. We lucked out with the weather today. Everyone's outside eating pizza."

"I'm not hungry."

I hold my hand to her forehead long enough to determine she doesn't have a temp before she shakes me off. Now it's my turn to sigh.

"It's your sister's birthday. There are thirty-plus people in our backyard having fun, and you're up here sulking about God knows what."

"I'm not sulking."

"No? Then what are you doing? Because you're not sick as far as I can tell. I don't have time to play twenty questions. I don't care if you're hungry or not, but you're not going to be rude and antisocial on your sister's birthday. You can sit with Rosie and Ashley at our table."

"I'm not sitting at your table."

"There's no room at the kids' table."

"Whatever. You don't get it."

"I don't get what? Why don't you want to sit at my table?"

"I'm not sitting with him."

"With who? Uncle Hank?" My mind leaps to a million different conclusions, each one a little more sickening than the first.

"No, your friend." She says the word "friend" with equal amounts of disgust and derision before turning her back to me and curling up even tighter.

"Jamie?" I ask. She doesn't respond, but I think I see her nod into the pillow. "Why don't you want to meet Jamie?" Maybe Hank is to blame. I can remember at least one occasion when he was complaining about the "retards" the local Stop & Shop uses as baggers. Iris had been there. Wayne was wrong. They're kids, and they are influenced by what we adults say and do. Except I've always gone out of my way to show my girls that you treat people—all people—with respect. Rosie and Daisy do. So why can't Iris?

The schoolyard fights, her skipping school, her mouthing back more than usual, all this plays in my mind in one endless loop. I've had enough. "You get up right now, young lady. You will show this man the respect he deserves. He lost his limbs protecting this country for people like you and me." I ignore the fact that Wayne used almost the exact same words on me nearly two months ago.

"No."

"Excuse me?" With one swift movement, I wrench her up and deposit her in a heap on the floor. She gapes, her mouth hanging open. I'd never laid a hand on any of them before. "Up. Now. And so help me you better behave yourself, Iris. I've had enough of your attitude."

Horror sweeps over her face, and I spot Wayne again in the flush of her cheeks, the rage in her eyes, the furrow of her brow. I can't stand it anymore. I walk to the door and pause only long enough to say, "If you're not down in two minutes, young lady ..." I don't finish the rest, knowing she'll do a better job than me at filling in the blanks.

#

Iris steps onto the deck and surveys the backyard. She spots me waiting for her by the table. She stuffs her hands in her pockets and walks at a snail's pace. As she approaches, she scowls at me as if to say, "Satisfied?"

"Jamie, I'd like you to meet Iris. Iris, this is Jamie Briggs."

I'd like to say her face softens once she sees him up close and personal, but if anything, it grows darker and her eyes narrow.

"Hi," he says. "Nice to meet you.

She doesn't respond, and I nudge her shoulder. "Yeah," she says, her voice flat, "Nice to meet you, too." Then she walks to the other side of the table and sits next to Wayne. My anger intensifies. I glance at Jamie who, thankfully, doesn't seem to notice or be bothered by her snub, no doubt because he's probably as uncomfortable with the situation as I am.

"What's up, Buttercup?" Wayne asks. "Where've you been?"

"Inside," she says.

Wayne places a paper plate in front of her and lifts the lid to the nearest pizza box. "You hungry? Better eat up before your Uncle Hank scarfs it all."

"Hey," Hank says, his mouth full. Iris shakes her head.

"You feeling okay, kiddo?" Wayne asks. She shrugs her answer, and his eyes search for mine, but I focus on the kids' tables and decide it's time to get on with the rest of the party, convinced that if I do, this day will somehow end sooner.

"Okay," I say, to Daisy and her friends. "Who's ready for the piñata?" The kids jump from the table while yelling, "I am! I am!" and I know twenty-six sets of parents will be cursing me later because of the sugar high these kids are a few bat swings away from experiencing. I lead the charge to the rainbow-colored donkey-like vessel that swings from the lowest branch of a tired old maple tree in our side yard.

"Don't you think we should let them digest a little?" Wayne whispers as he comes up behind me.

"This will help them burn off some energy. Then they can bounce some more in the Moonwalk. Then, ice cream cake." I point to my watch, which reads 1:15. "We only have them until three, and we still have to do this, cake, and presents."

Wayne shrugs, waves over Hank, and the two take charge of blindfolding the kids, handing off the bats, and lining them up with the piñata. I glance at the table where Jamie sits alone watching me. Rosie is leading Ashley and Iris around the kids' table, where they're collecting dirty plates and cups and dumping them into an extra large black trash bag.

I take a deep breath and walk to Jamie.

"Hey," I say. "How you doing?"

He nods. "Okay. How are you doing?"

"I won't have any trouble sleeping tonight, that's for sure. You need anything? Something to drink? A little more to eat?"

"I'm good, thanks." He flicks his chin toward the kids. "They're cute. Especially yours."

"Yeah, well. Thanks. Iris's attitude isn't, and I apologize for that."

"What do you mean?"

"Nothing. Just Iris being Iris. Speaking of which, I better oversee the cleanup."

As I head to the kids' table, Iris glowers at me, and I have an overwhelming desire to stick my tongue out at her. I don't because I'm the adult, the responsible one. Instead, I ignore her attitude and help clear the table, our work punctuated by the smack of the bat against the piñata and shouts of "Almost!" and "So close" and "Yes!" After what feels like forever, the thing finally breaks, and the kids swarm over the bounty and fill paper bags with their loot. Rosie and Ashley corral them back to the table, where I've had the ice cream cake sitting out so it could soften. I light candles. We sing happy birthday. I slice pieces of cake and pass them around the table.

"That everyone?" I ask, grateful for the moment of quiet as the kids stuff their faces.

"What about them?" Rosie points to the other table, where Hank, Wayne, and Jamie sit. I slice three more squares of cake and plop them onto plates.

"I'll help," Iris says, and she takes two plates and two plastic spoons and heads over to the table.

Good, I think. *Maybe guilt is getting the best of her. It usually does.* Rosie and Ashley help themselves to some cake, and I'm debating whether to indulge when a loud "whoop" sounds from Wayne's table. We all look up in time to see an entire square of ice cream cake squashed and dripping down the front of Jamie's jacket. Iris stands nearby.

"I'm sorry. I tripped," she says when she sees me marching toward her. Jamie clenches his teeth while Wayne wipes down the front of his jacket.

"Accidents happen," Wayne says.

"Accidents," I repeat. "Right."

"Hello," a voice calls out, and I turn around. It's Mrs. Briggs, waving and making her way from the side yard to where we all are. She smiles and then sees Wayne bent over Jamie. She rushes over. "Is something wrong?"

"No, no," Wayne says. "Iris here had a little accident delivering the cake to your son. Nothing a washing machine can't fix."

"Here, let me do that," she says while taking the paper towels and sponging down Jamie's front. Jamie stares ahead, his eyes far away, and I know every moment is killing him, his helplessness on display in front of two men he hates, dozens of kids, and me.

It's my turn to glower at Iris, who stands up straight, triumphant, and holds my unwavering gaze.

"Let's go," Jamie says.

"Oh, but I'm early." Mrs. Briggs balls up the dripping towels. "I thought it would be nice to watch the kids a little bit." Then, to me: "It's easy to forget how cute they can be, since once they enter high school, that's all gone."

"Yeah," I say. "The cuteness can leave a lot sooner than that even."

"Daisy still has to open her presents," Rosie says.

"I'm tired," Jamie says. "Let's go, Ma."

"You sure?" She sounds disappointed but doesn't protest further. "Okay, then." She helps him stand. Jamie nods at Wayne and Hank and gives a brief smile to Rosie and Ashley. He glances at me, and his eyes reveal such hurt, such misery, that I have to turn away.

"Thank Daisy for inviting me," he says, and I nod without looking at him.

"Girls," I say to Rosie, Ashley, and Iris. "Go clear off the table and start bringing Daisy's presents over. Wayne, the camera." I bark my orders and ignore Jamie's shuffling steps as his mother helps him navigate the uneven terrain that is my backyard.

I go through the motions, logging who gave what presents to Daisy so she can write thank you notes and oohing and ahhing in all the right places as she opens packages filled with Bratz dolls, hair accessories, books, and games. Rosie, Ashley, and Iris sit by her, handing her the gifts, throwing away the wrapping paper, and dutifully handing any cards to me. Iris's demeanor has improved greatly since Jamie's departure. She giggles and smiles and even claps her hands, and I can't help but wonder how guilty I should feel for disliking my own child as much as I do right now.

#

"We need to talk to Iris," I say to Wayne as I crawl, exhausted, into bed that night. He leans on his pillows and reads *Field & Stream*, the only thing I've ever seen him read religiously and which he now hands off to Iris when he's done, a recent development that followed her interest in firing guns.

"'Bout what?"

"About what happened today."

"What happened?"

"You know, with the ice cream she dumped on Jamie."

"That was an accident."

"No. It wasn't."

"What makes you say that?"

"Um, her behavior right before it happened. She was holed up in her room because she didn't want to be around someone like Jamie. Someone with disabilities."

"She said that?"

"Not in so many words, but she didn't deny it either," I say.

"Why would she be mean to someone with disabilities?"

I roll my eyes. "Oh, gee, I don't know. Because your brother is prejudiced and spouts pejoratives at anyone who's not like him."

Wayne smacks the magazine against the blanket. "Don't fucking start."

"Don't fucking start what? Maybe you don't care that what you're exposing our daughter to is affecting her worldview, but I do care."

"Why does it always come back on me, huh? What I do and what Hank says, huh? Hank was sitting with us at the table, for Christ's sake. He's never said anything against the kid."

"Maybe not about Jamie specifically, but he says enough. Like using the n-word the other night or when he calls the baggers at Stop n' Shop retards. I mean, where else would she get this attitude from?"

"School. Her friends. TV. You know, the last few times I've dropped by the house in the afternoon when you're off visiting with that kid and running late, I've found them all parked in front of the TV watching idiotic shit."

"While I'm 'visiting'? You mean doing the visiting you said was non-negotiable a couple months ago?"

"Yeah, two hours. Not the three-plus hours it's been turning into on some days."

"So now it's my fault our daughter is getting into fist fights and wanting to learn how to shoot guns and is prejudiced against people with physical disabilities."

He rubs his face. "One of the reasons I work as hard as I do is so that you can be home with them and raise them right."

"Raise them right according to whose standards? The Fowler Family way of raising kids?"

Wayne throws off the covers, and the magazine falls to floor. "If I didn't know better, I'd say you were trying to piss me off."

"Well, it's not hard to do." I cross my arms. He stands in his boxers and stares at me as if I'd sprouted donkey ears.

"Maybe she's getting her attitude from you," he says as he walks out and slams the door.

"Or maybe," I say as the quiet settles around me, "I'm getting it from her."

Chapter 18

May 1998

If there's one thing I've learned from my last pregnancy, it's this: don't underestimate the power of hormones. They'll sucker-punch you every chance they get, even when you feel you're already being bitch-slapped by the universe. I've warned everyone about them: Wayne, Kat, my mother, and even Rosie, who's not even one and a half and who simply giggles whenever I say in high-pitched baby talk, "Mommy is losing her fucking mind." (Thankfully, her tongue has trouble wrapping itself around the letter "F." On more than one occasion, I swear I've heard her say "nucking." My vocabulary has gone down the toilet during the last two years of marriage and motherhood.)

Somehow, Kat—who's dating Dennis, a divorced father of two boys (in the old days, this would have been considered scandalous, but my getting knocked up at seventeen has cleared the road for her to date a guy fifteen years her senior)—and my mother understand the hormone effect. Wayne? Not so much. Which explains why he's not getting my hints—eye twitches, eyebrow raising, and excessive yawning—as his parents sit on the couch opposite me in our toy-strewn apartment living room. While I should be thrilled that Norv and Phyllis Fowler have taken a sudden interest in Rosie and me, their timing, as usual, isn't great, considering I have only three weeks to go before I pop, the temperature this week is unusually hot and sticky for May, and I have an eighteen-month-old who's decided she no longer wants to sleep through the night or take an afternoon nap.

"Well," I begin, carefully, slowly, because I can't stand their presence anymore, but I know I need to hide my true feelings. "It was so nice of the two of you to stop by, but I should probably put Rosie down soon." I smile as sweetly as I can and hope they get the hint and say their good-byes.

Norv gestures to Wayne. "You haven't told her, have you?"

"Told me what?"

Phyllis clucks, shakes her head, digs through her purse, and pulls out a pack of Marlboros.

"Oh, no. Please," I say while rubbing my stomach. "No smoking inside."

She scowls and clucks two more times. I want to hit her.

"Mom," Wayne says hurriedly, no doubt sensing my desire to karate chop his mother since he practically lifts her off the couch and pushes her toward the sliding glass door. "How 'bout the balcony, okay?" She humphs once, opens the screen to the balcony, and steps onto it, muttering something the whole time that sounds a lot like "ungrateful bitch." Wayne closes the slider to shield me from her smoke, or perhaps her rants.

"Told me what?" I ask again.

"My parents," Wayne begins. "They're moving to Florida. End of the year."

"Yep," Norv nods. "Right after the holidays."

"Oh," I say, confused. While a Florida-bound set of grandparents might be considered a loss to any other family, Wayne's parents have always kept me and Rosie at arm's length. Not that I've particularly minded, considering the more I discover about Wayne's family—the fights, the drinking, the everything—the more I dislike them.

"And the house—" Norv continues.

"—is ours," Wayne interrupts. "They're giving us their house."

"They're *what*?"

"The house, Koty. My parents are giving us their house."

"Why?"

"Why?" Norv laughs. "Why not? Hank's all set with his place. But you two!" He pauses and waggles an arthritic finger around the living room. "This place is barely big enough for one person, let alone a family of four." Then, as an aside to Wayne: "Told you she wouldn't like it."

"Dad," Wayne says. Then, to me: "It's a generous gift. A house, free and clear. Big backyard. Plenty of space."

He's right. It is. So why do I feel like I want to throw up and take Rosie and run and never look back?

#

"So," I say as I roll my whale-of-a-body onto the bed that night. "Are we taking it?" Nothing more had been said after the Fowler's announcement this afternoon. Wayne's mother finished her cigarette, came back inside, and walked past all of us to the door without so much as a "so long" or "goodbye." About thirty seconds after her exit, Norv had patted Rosie on the head, nodded at me, slapped Wayne on the back, and followed her out. Wayne and I had done our best to avoid one another for the rest of the day.

"We'd be fools not to." He walks to the window and opens it. I can almost hear the air escape, leaving behind the tension between us.

"It's just that—" I begin but stop, unable to find the words.

"It's just what, Koty? This doesn't have to be hard, you know."

"I know."

"Do you?"

"Yes."

"Then why are we even discussing it? You're the one who's been talking about a house. Not me."

"I know, but—"

"But what? It's not the house you dreamt of, not the exact one you wanted? Well, guess what? That's not the way it works."

"I thought it would be, you know, different."

"Yeah, well. Welcome to my world."

"What's that supposed to mean?"

"Nothing. Forget it." He falls into bed next to me and kicks aside the sheet and blanket.

"Hey," I say. "C'mon. Don't be like that. Don't go to bed angry."

What I want: for him to hold my hand, to lay his head on my belly, to talk to our unborn child, to talk to me the way we talked when we first dated.

What he does instead: flicks off the lamp on his bedside table and turns on his side with his back to me, without uttering another word.

What I'm left with: his brother Carl's words echoing in my head: "But do me a favor, Koty. Don't let him end up back here. No matter what."

Chapter 19

November 2008

When I pull into Jamie's driveway the Monday after Daisy's party, I know something is up because his mother's car is there. She greets me at the door, wrapping herself as she always does in her yellow sweater.

"Jamie okay?" I ask.

"He hasn't been himself. Since Saturday, actually." She pauses. "Did something happen at the party?"

I shake my head. "Just the accident with the ice cream cake."

"Well, he's not talking. Hasn't eaten. I called in sick today, but I need to run to the grocery store. I figure if anyone can get through to him, you can." She takes a deep breath. "Do you mind staying?"

"It's what I came to do."

She steps aside, lets me in, and then shrugs into a coat hanging on a hook by the door. "I won't be long," she says.

"Take your time." I watch as she leaves and then turn to face God knows what. "Knock, knock," I say as I reach his door and push it open. He sits by the window in his wheelchair, his prosthetics off. "Jamie?"

He doesn't respond, doesn't face me, doesn't acknowledge my existence at all. I drop my purse to the floor and sit in the all-too-familiar rocking chair while images of our first couple of weeks together zip through my mind. This couldn't all be because of Iris and the cake, could it? Something else must have happened. Right? We sit in silence for five, ten, fifteen minutes until I can't take it anymore.

"So," I say. "Daisy wanted me to make a special delivery. She made you a thank you card." I open a wide side sleeve in my purse and pull out the construction paper creation. I wave it in the air, trying to get his attention, but he doesn't stir. "Jamie, please. Talk to me. I'm sorry about what happened. I think you probably know it was no accident that Iris dumped that ice cream on you. I'm not sure why. She's confused, I guess, about people who are different. Maybe you're right. Maybe being around an environment where she's subjected to the nonsense that Hank and Wayne spout about people, maybe that's skewed the way she looks at people with disabilities." Even as I say the words, something doesn't fit. Wayne, after all, is the person who introduced me to Jamie. Wayne celebrated Jamie's return to Granite Creek and played an integral role in his rehab at home. Wouldn't Iris have taken this in and not those other conversations? And then there's Iris herself, my little girl who walks to the beat of her own drummer, who'd probably be happiest being homeschooled on a farm with animals as her only companions. She may be difficult, but she's not without compassion.

"Doesn't matter," Jamie says. "Your daughter did me a favor."

"What do you mean?"

"She showed me that no matter how hard I try to convince myself otherwise, things will never be the same. That the things I wanted three years ago, I can't have."

"I'm not following."

He turns his head, and I suck in my breath, because that's how visible the hurt is on his face. "I'm always going to need help. I'll always be a burden to someone. My mother. Care providers. The system. You name it."

"We all need help."

"Oh, really? You need help wiping your ass?" He shakes his head. "Even when it's something I could probably manage on my own—like wiping up ice cream off my shirt—people automatically assume I can't take care of it. That actually might be worse. Not the fact that I do need help with some things, but the fact people will always think I need help with everything. That I'm perpetually broken, unfixable."

"Jamie—"

"No. Don't. There's nothing to say. Don't make it worse or belittle me more by trying to convince me otherwise."

"What about the other day and what we were talking about? About you wanting to teach people with disabilities and show them that they can still do things? What about the fact you successfully showed me how to fire a gun? What about all that?" I pause and swallow. "What about us?"

He stares out the window again, and I wonder what he sees. When I look out my kitchen window at home, I see respite and solace and peace in these woods. Since September, I've imagined the direct path to this very house and this man who has reignited feelings in me, feelings I took for dead, feelings I figured I no longer had a claim to since I'd made my bed, and my bed was with Wayne. What does Jamie see? I bet he suspects evil lurking behind every shrub and that the brown and gray tree trunks remind him of sandstorm-filled skies in a land I'll never know beyond images in magazines and news reports.

"There is no us," he says. "There's only the dream of it."

I jump out of my chair and kneel before him. "You don't mean that. I know you don't mean that." I rub the side of his T-shirt clad torso and then allow my hands to drift. After that first time in September when I jerked him off, we'd never done anything more than kiss. In a way, that's helped me temper my guilt. *It's kissing*, I'd tell myself, *not full-blown sex*. For Jamie, I think it was out of respect for me that it had never gone any further. He'd been raised a gentleman with values that you respect and protect your women. Or perhaps he was wooing me. Or maybe he wanted to wait for the day when I could be all his. I ignore these thoughts and stroke him through his pants, feeling him grow hard beneath my touch. He groans.

"Stop," he whispers. "Please. Stop."

I hesitate for a moment, allowing my hands to linger, but then I comply and move my hands up his sides, to his shoulder, to his neck, and to his face, his eyes registering something I've never seen before. Is it possible to be in so much pain that you're beyond tears? Jamie sees through me, past me, to a world where things are different, for both of us.

"What can I do?" I whisper.

He waits a beat before responding. "Leave."

"Jamie, we've talked about this before, and it's not as easy as—"

"No. Not him. Me."

"What?"

"You've done enough. There's no point. It's too hard, for me."

"But we're friends. We've become friends. Friends don't just stop being friends."

"I know, but I can't do this anymore."

"What am I supposed to tell Wayne?"

"Tell him I'm cured." He laughs wryly. "Seriously, Koty. He saw me on Saturday. Ice cream accident aside, he probably thinks I'm assimilating nicely into my surroundings as a bionic man. I'm sure he didn't envision you doing this forever." He pauses. "I mean, did you?"

"I don't know what I thought. I've been trying not to think."

"I know. I know."

"Why do I feel like we're breaking up?"

He nods. "In a way, I guess we are."

"I don't know if I can do this."

"There's nothing to do, Koty. We're going back to the way things were."

"I don't know if I can do that."

"Well, that's within your control, whether I'm around or not. It always has been. Don't go telling me it's not."

"It's not so simple."

"I never said it was simple, but it is doable."

I lean back on the heels of my sneakers. "What about you? What are you going to do?"

He rotates his head as if to say "you're looking at it" and shrugs.

"That's not an answer," I whisper.

"Well, I don't have an answer."

"I could give you the same line that you just gave me," I say.

"What's that?"

"That what you want to do is within your control. Teaching. Putting together some sort of organization or place for people like you."

"You should go," he says.

"Can't. Told your mom I'd stay until she got back."

He turns to the window. "She's back."

I strain to listen, and, sure enough, his senses once again detect things before I do. I stand and arch my back, my legs stiff. Mrs. Briggs appears in the doorway, holding a package of bread.

"Hi," she says, her face expectant and hopeful. "They were putting out fresh bread, and it smelled so good I couldn't resist. How 'bout I toast some up for all of us? A nice snack on this raw November day."

I'm about to speak, but Jamie beats me to it.

"No thanks, Ma. Koty is about to leave. We've decided we don't need her to babysit me anymore."

"Oh, honey," she says. "I don't think that's the best idea."

"Ma, I'll still have the other services. A couple hours of complete independence is what I want. I'm not asking."

She fingers the crinkles in the paper bag, and while I can tell she's worried at the thought of her son being alone, I sense something else. Exhilaration, perhaps, that her son has spoken up and made a demand and that he's showing signs of life. A spark.

She smiles. "I suppose we won't know until we try it. Thank you for all of your help, Koty."

I nod, and she excuses herself, her footsteps echoing down the hall.

I cross my arms. "Don't for a second think that I believe the line of crap you just gave to your mother."

"You can believe whatever you want."

"I'm not saying good-bye."

"And I'm not going to argue. You asked me a little while ago what you could do? Do this."

I've lived with stubborn long enough to recognize its stench. Even though the chasm inside my heart—the one that grows wider with each loss beginning with my dad, my mom, Iris (because it doesn't take a rocket scientist to see I'm losing hold of my middle child), and the Wayne I fell in love with a lifetime ago—even though I feel the tug and pull and wrenching of muscle and artery and vessel, I pick up my purse and walk out the door because there's nothing left to do.

Chapter 20

This house will remain in a permanent state of undoneness until the day we die, despite Wayne's assurance when we accepted his parents' generous "gift" that we'd refurbish and renovate and make it our own. It could be ours, I suppose, if Wayne ever finished what he started. But he and Hank are always busy fighting, working, fighting, drinking, working, and searching for Carl's killer. I'd support this last mission more if every time Wayne worked on it, it didn't pull him further and further away from his family, from his responsibilities, from the Wayne he was before he found and latched onto this anger and hatred toward everything and everyone. Part of me wants to scream, "Don't you see us? Me and your daughters, alive and in the flesh, here in front of you?" Any time I dare say such a thing, he looks at me with such—I don't know, blankness—that I shut up.

#

The baby kicks and turns inside of me, and I adjust my position on the couch. Sweat trickles down my neck even though a ceiling fan (which I convinced Wayne to install at the beginning of the summer) whirs overheard. The calendar ticks too slowly toward my due date of November 23, but despite my pregnancy fatigue, I still keep praying this one will arrive late. November has notoriously been a hard month for Wayne and me, and this child—any child—deserves to enter a world filled with love and calm rather than one filled with anger, torment, and booze, which is how the past four Novembers have been.

Exhausted, I stretch out on the couch, feeling more and more like a beached whale, while Rosie sits in her bathing suit on the floor and attempts to read *The Berenstain Bears' New Baby* book. Iris stands next to her in nothing more than a sagging diaper that I suspect needs changing. It's Sunday night, and probably every other family in our town is recovering from a day of togetherness—mommy, daddy, kids—by watching a movie together or sitting out on the porch in the summer heat. Not us. As always, it's only the girls and me.

Today, I've taken two walks through the woods, hunted for toads, removed one tick, made ice cream sundaes (I'm still wearing the remnants of one), watched as an overtired two-year-old tortured her older, but meeker, sister by standing in the middle of the sprinkler and not allowing said older sister her chance to run through. I've applied and reapplied sun block to various body parts no fewer than three hundred twelve times (and always missing random quarter-sized areas on certain appendages). I've grilled vegetables and hamburgers in ninety-six-degree heat and still have three loads of laundry to do—that is if I ever expect my children to wear something other than diapers and wet bathing suits.

This miserable heat wave is supposed to break tonight, with a cold front and rain due in, but the ladybug thermometer that the girls and I go out on the front porch to read two or three times a day remains stuck at a sticky eighty-eight degrees. I wonder if my feet will ever be the size of something other than eggplants or if my craving for cheese curls will ever diminish. My head pounds and I try to ignore the image of our dinner plates still piled high in the sink while Wayne sits at the kitchen table, where he has been all day, surrounded by papers stained by coffee cups and lemonade splatters and pencil smudges, the cordless phone within easy reach as he waits for a call back from the police department. "I think I found something," he'd announced proudly last night and told me he had placed a call earlier that afternoon to the detectives working Carl's case.

This should be welcome news to me, and it would be, I suppose, if we didn't have this conversation every six months or so when Wayne or Hank think they've discovered something new. Kat refers to them as Starsky and Hutch, and I always warn her when she brings Mom over to visit not to call Wayne this to his face. They haven't been by to visit in three weeks. Kat's used Mom's chemo treatments and this heat as an excuse, but I know they can sense when Wayne's due for a downward spiral.

No doubt, the cops feel the same way as I do about Wayne's latest evidence, a new "eyewitness" account by a notorious town drunk if there ever was one, since it's already past seven o'clock and he hasn't received a call back. I wish I could be supportive and consoling, but I've lived through too many of these episodes of high hope followed by destructiveness. Wayne, I've decided, is an intermittent drunk, a label I invented, as opposed to Hank who is a full-time functioning alcoholic, which I think is a real term, since Hank drinks every day and somehow functions, albeit with foul breath, bloodshot eyes, and a perpetually dark mood. Wayne's drunkenness is chronic, yes, but it becomes destructive only when something triggers him. He's not like Hank, who always has a flask within reach, and he's not like his father was, drunk and abusive. Wayne goes through periods of not drinking even, and whenever he loses it on those three or four occasions a year that he does, he's sorry afterwards. So very, very sorry. Sorry to me. Sorry to the girls. And for the briefest of moments, the old Wayne is back. When Kat asks me why I stay, why I put up with it, that's why. Because the old Wayne is still in there. I keep hoping beyond hope that the next time he emerges, I'll convince him to stay for good.

"You let him hit you," she'd said once, and I told her she had it wrong, that I don't "let" Wayne do anything, that it sometimes happens, and that he's always sorry. "What if he ever hits one of the girls?" Kat asked.

"Simple," I'd replied. "I'll leave."

#

I strain now to make out the words to Wayne's one-sided conversation with whoever is on the other end of the phone, but his voice is low and hushed until the final moment when he yells: "Do your goddamn job and look into it!" Crashes and bangs ensue in what I imagine is a scene of overturned chairs and a refrigerator door empty of its magnets and finger-painted masterpieces. This reaction, I know, is a red flag and an indicator that the coffee-drinking Wayne I left alone an hour ago is now downing something harder.

"Mommy, what's Daddy doing?" Rosie asks.

"Daddy's frustrated," I say.

"What's frustrated mean?"

"You know how you feel when you tell Iris to stop touching Monkey, but she does it anyway?" Monkey is Rosie's favorite stuffed animal. "Kinda like that."

Wayne stumbles into the living room, running his right hand through his hair, his left hand wrapped around the neck of a beer bottle. He paces back and forth, something that drives me insane, but I know enough not to say anything when he's like this.

"They're idiots," he says.

I hesitate, unsure if I should question him, but maybe he needs to get it off his chest. "What happened?"

Red rises up his neck and cheeks. His nostrils flare as if he can't get enough air. He hasn't shaved in three days, and gray scruff covers his chin. Under different conditions, I might consider it sexy.

"They don't want to fucking listen," he says. "I call with evidence—new evidence—and they don't even want to give me the time of day. I should go kick their fucking ass."

"Wayne!" I nod in the kids' direction. Rosie and Iris gawk at their father, their eyes wide, while he rolls his.

"Do you want to hear or not?" he sighs. "You're the one who asked me what happened."

"I do, but maybe we should talk about it later. Unless you can—"

"Unless I can what, Koty?"

"Unless you can keep it G-rated. They're kids."

"Yeah, well. They'll need to grow up someday and learn how the real world works. How it screws you up the ass and straight to hell. Isn't that right, Rosie?" he says in a loud baby-sounding voice. He bends at his knees and gets right in her face. "Someday you'll learn how fucked up this world and everyone in it is. Might as well do it now. Right, kiddo?"

"Wayne!" I shout as Rosie's lip quivers—she can barely stand it when I raise my voice at her—and her eyes fill with tears. She discards her book, climbs onto the couch, and attempts to wedge herself into the crook of my arm, which is difficult with my hippo belly, and even more uncomfortable given the heat. I rub her back as she burrows her face into my shoulder, and my eyes seek out his. He's focused on Iris now, who has walked up to him, fascinated instead of scared. She begins to laugh.

"What are you laughing at?" he says.

"Wayne," I say. "She's two. She doesn't understand."

He rubs his face and shakes his head, and I'm thinking he realizes the insanity that he's become.

"You want to know what some people said to Hank the other day?" he says, chuckling in that you're-not-going-to-believe-it sort of way. "They said, 'Why you so hot on finding out what happened to your faggot brother? Seems to me whoever done it, did us a favor. One less faggot in the world.'"

He emphasizes the word "faggot" and it hangs in the air. For a moment, I think he might start to cry until a little voice pipes up.

"Faggot," Iris repeats and laughs. Okay, so it actually sounds more like "fug it," but we know our little mimic well enough to know what she's trying to say. "Fug-it, fug-it, fug-it!" she continues, her chubby little legs moving up and down and her right hand clenched around Monkey. Of course.

For a moment, the earth stops, the ceiling fan ceases to spin, Rosie's sobs dissolve into nothingness, and it's just Wayne and Iris standing in the middle of some horror film with me watching and knowing what's about to happen next, and unable to stop it.

He tosses his bottle into the fireplace, grabs Iris by the shoulders, lifting her off the ground, and shakes her hard. I move fast, despite my belly, my eggplant-sized feet, and my sheer exhaustion, adrenaline pulsing through every cell of my body. I shove Rosie to the side, charge Wayne, slap my hands over his, and find a sound so guttural and primal from deep within my womb that when the words "Stop it! Stop it! Stop it!" fill the air, we both pause and look around, trying to identify where the horrified, tortured scream is coming from. He gapes and loosens his grip enough for me to know that if I put my hands around Iris's waist and pull her toward me, he won't hinder my efforts.

Iris whimpers in my arms, probably unsure of whether to be scared or to say, "Again, Daddy!" as if Wayne's some human carnival ride. Shock registers in his eyes, as I'm sure anger, horror, and disgust do in mine.

"Get out," I say, my voice low and even.

"Koty—"

"Get. Out."

"Wait. I'm sorry, I—"

"Get out now!" I scream, and Iris jumps in my arms. Rosie sobs into a couch cushion. Wayne's lip trembles, tears in his eyes. He nods, walks toward the door, and stops.

"I'll be back later. We'll all cool off. Talk about what happened."

He exits the room before I can respond, "The hell we will," and I hug Iris while I listen to the screen door squeak open and close and the sound of Wayne's truck as he backs down the dirt driveway toward the road.

"Where Daddy go?" Iris asks. Her face is pink, and I examine her eyes, particularly the whites and the pupils—isn't that what happens to shaken babies, something rips in their eyes?—but they appear fine. I touch her neck and let my fingers wander down to her bare shoulder, and I'm sure I can detect Wayne's fingerprints and the yellow and blue-gray colors of bruises. *Shit, shit, shit.* I can't believe he finally did the one thing I was ninety-nine point nine percent sure he'd never do.

If I know him—and God knows what happened tonight should make me question that—he's gone off to one of two places: Hank's house with his mousey wife and snot-nosed kids or the bar. Either way, he'll be drinking. There won't be any talking or reasoning tonight. What he did to Iris is a preview of what's to come later: him and me arguing. The great dry-out that'll begin tomorrow and likely lead up to November, the birth-month of our third child when the same scenario will repeat, the soundtrack to our marriage one endless skip of sadness.

This logic spills out of my head with ease, and I'm surprised at how calm I am. That is until Rosie starts tugging on my shirt. I reach down to cover her hand with my own and realize I'm trembling.

"Mommy?" she says, her face tear-stained. "Daddy scared me."

"I know, sweetheart. I know."

And I do: I know what I need to do next. I sit on the couch, both kids somehow on my lap, and dial Kat. The answering machine keeps picking up. Odd for a Sunday night at almost eight o'clock. Dennis travels a lot, and she has his kids every other weekend, but I can't remember if this is an on weekend or off. And, of course, she has Mom. Chewing my lower lip, I decide to try Mom's number. They put a line for her in the house, even though she doesn't get many calls. "She can still feel somewhat independent," Kat had explained to me. But that line goes unanswered as well. Something's wrong.

"Shit," I mutter under my breath.

"Mommy!" Rosie says. "That's a bad word."

"I know. I'm sorry. Rosie, you need to let me up. I need to get Aunt Kat's cell phone number off the fridge." Rosie obeys and I haul myself and Iris off the couch and waddle into the kitchen, which, as I'd imagined, looks as if a bomb went off. An overturned chair, papers, and magnets litter the floor.

Rosie comes up behind me. "What happened, Mommy?"

"Help me find a dark pink sticky note." I bend and pluck a yellow one from the floor. "It'll look like this, but it will be dark pink. Almost red. Can you help Mommy do that?"

She nods and falls to her knees and roots through the papers while I scan from above.

"Found it!" She holds up the sticky note and a smile spreads across her face. I snatch it from her grasp and spy Kat's handwriting. *Yes.* I dump Iris to the floor to play with Rosie in the paper piles, reach for the receiver on the wall, and dial. Kat's one of the few people I know besides Wayne and Hank who has a cell phone. "I need it for Dennis's kids. It's good to have for emergencies," she'd told me. "You should consider getting one."

"Koty?" she says after one ring and I wonder how she knows it's me. I don't ask.

"Yeah, Kat. It's me. Where are you?"

"I was going to call. It's Mom. We're at the hospital."

"What? Why? What happened?"

"It's okay, it's okay. She was feeling dizzy. Then she was having chest pains."

"Oh my God. A heart attack?"

"No. That's what I thought, but they don't think so. They think it's something to do with the medication she's on. They're going to keep her overnight for observation. I'm going to stay with her. The AC is out at our house, and Dennis is away until Tuesday." She sighs and with it, I hear the utter fatigue in her voice. Mom's been living with her for almost three years now, and the last six months have been hell thanks to Mom's relapse. "Everything okay?" she asks.

"Yeah," I say. "I tried you at the house and got worried when I couldn't get you or Mom, that's all."

"You're lucky you got me now. No reception inside the hospital. I decided to get some fresh air while the nurses get her settled."

"Right."

"You sure you're okay? You sound weird."

"Yeah. Everything's fine."

"Where are the girls?"

"Right here. Say hi to your Aunt Kat, Rosie." I hold the phone away from my ear while Rosie yells, "Hi, Aunty Kat," and Iris babbles something unintelligible. "See? We're cleaning up and getting ready for bed."

"Okay. Well, I should get back up and do the same."

I swallow a sniffle. "Tell Mom I love her, okay?"

"You can tell her yourself tomorrow, Koty. She's going to be fine. At least for now."

"Tell her. Please."

"I will."

"And Kat?" I pause and twirl the cord around my index finger. "Thanks."

"For what?"

"For taking care of Mom all this time. I wish I could do more—"

"Forget about it. You got your hands full and then some. I'll talk to you tomorrow."

"Right. Bye."

"Bye."

We hang up.

I stand in the middle of chaos, and Iris begins to fuss. She holds her chubby little hand to her head, like she does when she falls and hits it against something: the corner of the coffee table, the edge of her crib, a wooden block she holds in her own hand.

Crouching down, I scrutinize her face. "What?" I say. "What's wrong?"

She points to her head and cries and whimpers, "Hurt," a child's way of saying she has a headache from the shaking her father inflicted not even fifteen minutes ago, and I've got the angry in me all over again. We're not safe here, not tonight, not tomorrow, maybe not ever.

"Let's go," I hear myself say.

"Where?" Rosie asks.

I don't answer her. Instead, I scoop Iris up and walk down the hall to the bedroom they share. Rosie follows. My brain commands and my body responds: change Iris's diaper, put her in her pajamas, fill a diaper bag with as much as it will carry, direct Rosie to her closet, help her strip off her suit, hand her shorts and a T-shirt, pull a sweatshirt off a hanger in case the forecast is right, fill another small bag with underwear and socks and toothbrushes. In my own bedroom, I repeat the process and find the stash of money I keep in my jewelry box, not much, a few one hundred dollar bills, my mad money for birthdays and Christmas and now this.

We pile into the old Cutlass, the car my mother refused to let me drive after my father died, and we get on Interstate 95 because it's the easiest thing for me to do, and we drive and drive and drive.

"Where are we going, Mommy?" Rosie asks after a while and between yawns. Iris sleeps, head hanging to the right like it always does, but I find that I keep glancing in the rearview mirror anyways to make sure she's still breathing. What if something is wrong? What if he caused brain damage and it's one of those insidious things that take time to fully manifest, an aneurism or hemorrhage? Maybe I should bring her to the hospital to get her checked out. But what do I say? My husband was shaking the snot out of her until I stopped him? What kind of mother lets her husband do that?

"Mommy?" she asks again.

"An adventure," I say, and I wonder how many mothers use this phrase when they don't know where they're going or worse—they do, like the doctor or dentist's office, but would rather not say since it will invite more questions, more anxiety, more tears.

I drive.

I can't go to Kat's either, and not because she isn't there: it's because Kat doesn't need my shit on top of what she's dealing with already with Mom. Besides, it's the first place Wayne would go.

Wayne. What will he think when he comes home tonight? I've never left before. I've never even threatened it. Leaving is what other women do, women who are in situations that'll never get better. Will he be so drunk that he'll pass out on the couch and not even notice we're gone until he wakes up Monday morning? Will he search for us? Call the cops? Is leaving and taking the kids even legal? What should I do? Turn around? Continue on and never look back, even though I know that's not realistic? I'm twenty-three years old, for God's sake. Two kids. Pregnant with my third. Barely graduated high school. A dead father. An almost dead mother. A sister who has her own life, who can't be expected to take care of me and my kids.

I drive and glance in the mirror. Rosie sleeps now as well. I ignore the urge to yawn and instead roll down the window and feel the air on my face. A light mist hits the windshield, the rain we've been so desperate for here at last, and I wonder for the briefest of moments if this is a sign from God, the universe, maybe even my father. But a sign to do what?

I rub my face. When did this become my life? But I know the answer. I can pinpoint the moment when everything changed: the morning we got the phone call about Carl. I mean, things hadn't been easy before that and Wayne was stressed and quiet and all, but that's what did it, right? He wasn't destined to turn into his father or to end up like Hank. Right?

Or am I kidding myself? Have I been kidding myself the whole time? Was the moment everything changed the night when Wayne said "Fuck it" and kissed me for the first time back when I was a kid working at the Yogurt Shack? Was that it?

I go through tolls and realize I'm heading out of New Hampshire and into Massachusetts. Where the fuck am I going? The rain picks up and I turn the wipers on full blast, only to realize that it doesn't help and the blades need changing. I glance at the gas gauge and the arrow is approaching the neon orange danger zone of empty. *Shit.*

I don't even know where I am exactly, just that I'm on this interstate. I wonder where it ends, if I could follow it until it's no more and start over fresh, wherever that is. Where would that be? Florida? Georgia? Or does this interstate eventually head west toward Arizona or California?

I need gas. I need a plan. I yawn. I need a place to get some sleep. I won't put my kids in danger again.

I get off the next exit, and only realize as I'm on the ramp that I don't even know where it's leading to except that there is a gas and lodging sign as I approach the end of the ramp. I follow the arrows and drive. It's a Sunday night. In August. Near the seacoast. I pray to God I can get a room. We gas up. We drive. I spot a Days Inn. A vacancy sign. I coax Rosie out of her car seat and carry Iris without waking her. Get us checked in by a grandmotherly woman who takes pity on me and helps me with our bags. I lay Iris on my bed, and tuck Rosie into hers and stroke her hair until she falls asleep.

I tremble and sit on the floor in between the two beds, my back against the nightstand. Then, I cry.

#

Sunlight pours through the window and for a moment, I have no idea where I am. I turn my head and pain shoots up my stiff neck. It all comes back to me. We're in a hotel. My bladder is about to burst (how I got through the night without peeing amazes me). I fell asleep leaning against Rosie's bed. *Rosie.* I wrench my neck, despite the pain, and watch her steady breathing. I feel eyes on me, and I move again while massaging my stiff muscles. Iris is on her side, staring at me.

"Morning, sunshine," I whisper.

She blinks, but doesn't respond. I crawl to her, sit on my haunches, and stroke the side of her face. "You okay, sweetie?"

At first, nothing. Then, I see it: one solitary tear clinging to her lower eyelash.

"Iris," I say. "Can you hear me? Does something hurt? Tell Mommy." I cup her chin. "Say something. Please."

She wiggles herself free from my grasp and buries her head in her pillow. I sigh, but I have to pee. I haul myself to my feet, limp to the bathroom, avoid the mirror, do my business, wash my hands, and come back out.

"Mommy," a sleepy voice says. "Where are we?"

I glance over at Rosie, who's sitting up in bed. Curls frame her face and the sunshine hits them just right, giving a halo effect.

"On an adventure," I say with as much cheer as I can muster. I bounce on her bed and tickle her, hoping that Rosie's giggles will be enough to snap Iris out of her funk. I glance over at her bed, and Iris is sitting up now as well, frowning, but watching us at least.

"You know what time it is?" I ask Rosie.

"What time?" Rosie says.

"Time for a pillow fight!"

Rosie whoops as I snatch the pillow out from under her and bop her on the head. She scurries to the other side of the bed, grabs the pillow, and hits me back. The whole time she's laughing. As expected, this is too much for Iris.

"Me, too!" Iris says and before I can help her down from the bed, she slides herself off and toddles to us.

"You, too? Okay!" I lift her up and hit her gently with a pillow, and her giggles fill the air along with Rosie's.

If only all problems could be solved so easily.

#

We spend the next two days on an "adventure vacation" as Rosie and even Iris describe it when other vacationers ask. I buy us swimsuits and towels, and we go to Hampton Beach. I dig deep inside my well of energy and walk with Iris up and down the beach as Rosie splashes in the ocean. We make friends with other families with kids, and when someone asks where my husband is, I simply explain he has his own business and had to work. Rosie absorbs this lie and repeats it whenever asked, and I think even she starts believing. Perhaps I do, too.

Even though I'm beyond exhausted and have no idea how to get from one hour to the next or how long I'll be able to keep up this charade, I don't call home or Kat or the hospital and instead pretend that if we return (when we return), it will be to a different life. My fantasy, though, doesn't completely take over reality. I find my back stiffening any time I spot a police cruiser or see a cop on the sidewalk. On the second day, I even wonder if the manager at the hotel is looking at me funny, as if he knows something or has seen a picture of me. I refuse to turn on the television or tune into the news in case, somehow, we're the top story, the family who disappeared.

We're running low on cash by the third morning, and at breakfast while I'm counting bills and change, Rosie clinks her fork against her glass of milk.

"Enough," I say, and she stops for a moment before starting again. "What did I just say? You're going to break it. Please stop."

She ignores me, glares at her glass, and continues clinking. Sighing, I remove it from her reach. She frowns and clinks her fork against the plate with her half-eaten pancakes.

"Rosie. Stop. Now."

She clinks louder. I place my hand on hers, and anger fills her eyes. "When are we going home?" she says.

"I don't know."

"I want to go home. I miss Daddy."

"Daddy! Miss Daddy," Iris repeats. I ignore her.

"Mommy and Daddy need to work some stuff out."

Rosie tilts her head. "So we'll go home. So you and Daddy can work stuff out. Right?"

How do you explain to a four-and-a-half-year-old that it doesn't work like that, not with grownups, even if you wish it did? You can't.

#

We drive mostly in silence under a hazy sky. The girls snooze on and off in the backseat. I play the radio and am relieved that we don't hear any breaking news bulletins about a pregnant woman and her two missing kids.

As I turn onto our street, the kids stir in the back, drinking in the surroundings and recognizing where we are. A police car sits in the driveway behind Wayne's pickup truck. My stomach turns, and I think I might be sick.

"Yay! We're home." Rosie claps her hands and unlatches her car seat while I take Iris out of hers. Wayne and two cops stand on the porch, while Rosie races up and into Wayne's outstretched arms.

I eye the cops, waiting for ten million questions, even handcuffs. I recognize one, Officer Panzieri. He was in Kat's class at Granite Creek High. The two of them descend the steps, and the first one nods, tips his cap, and says "Ma'am." I nod back. As Panzieri passes me, he pauses. Iris watches him, her eyes wide and fixed on the dime-sized mole he has on his cheek. He pats her bare shoulder, his fingers lingering on the barely-discernible yellow-green bruises on her upper arm. "You had your husband worried. Your sister and mother, too."

"Yes, sir," I say. I can't remember the last time I ever called anyone "sir," but it seems appropriate.

His eyes move from Iris to me. "Everything all right, ma'am? Anything we should know about or that we can help you with?"

"Everything is fine."

He studies my face. "Okay, then. You folks have a nice afternoon." He tips his cap, walks to his car where the other cop waits in the driver's seat, and gets in. Iris waves as Wayne and Rosie join us, and we watch the car back down the driveway and disappear down the road.

"Daddy," Iris says, and she opens her arms to him. He doesn't pull her from my grasp. Instead, he holds out his arms as if to say to me, *It's your call. I'm not taking her from you.* I inch closer until Iris can wrap her arms around his neck, at which point Wayne pulls her close and hugs her, his eyes closed tight. When he opens them, I can tell he's been crying, the white parts bloodshot, the lids puffy. I try to remember the last time I saw Wayne cry. If I've ever seen him cry. He must have cried at Carl's funeral, but I have no memory of this: all I remember is his anger, his fist through a wall, his drinking.

"We went on an adventure," Rosie says as she leans into him, the top of her head barely grazing the bottom of his belt.

Iris nods. "Beach!"

"Well, that sounds like fun," he says. "I wish I could have gone with you."

"We wished you were there, too, Daddy," Rosie says. "That's why we came home."

"Is it now?" he says, and his eyes stay on me, expectant.

Rosie tugs on his T-shirt. "It's hot. Can we run through the sprinkler?"

"Sure," he says. "Why don't you get on your bathing suit, and I'll meet you out back, okay?"

"Yay!" Rosie spins and runs into the house. I reach for Iris.

"I need to change her first," I say and follow Rosie.

"Koty," he says, and I stop, turn around, and wait. "I'm sorry." When I don't say anything, he continues. "You had me worried. Your sister and your mother, too. Speaking of which, you need to call them."

"Is my mother—"

"She's fine. She's out of the hospital. But worried."

I nod and climb the steps. He's right behind me.

"Koty."

"Yeah?" I sigh. He waits until my eyes focus on his.

"I am sorry. That wasn't me the other night. You know that."

"No, Wayne. That is you. That's you when you're drinking."

"I haven't touched a drop since then." He shakes his head and rubs his face, and I can smell his stink. "You had us worried. Where'd you go?"

"We just drove."

"Where?"

"Hampton Beach. We drove until we stopped, and that's where we stopped. And then we came home."

"That's it?"

"Yeah," I say as I pull open the screen door. "That's it."

Chapter 21

November 2008

It's the first holiday season without my mother, and my sadness, which I thought I had under control, feels as fresh and raw as it did the days and weeks after she died. Everything makes me cry: the laundry that multiplies in the basement when I'm not looking; Wayne's suitcase, a fixture on our bedroom floor for the month that I watch go from empty to filled to partially empty after his hunting trip until *I* decide to finally put everything away; the report on the solar system that I help Rosie with every night for two weeks straight; the line at the local turkey farm when I wait my turn to fetch my pre-cooked frozen bird (the first time I cooked a turkey back in my early twenties was also my last, thanks to our oven turning off mid-roast). The excuse for my tears—the fact I miss my mother—is the only saving grace I have since everyone, even Wayne, accepts this explanation without question. I do miss her, of course, but I know it's not the only reason I feel so incredibly sad: I miss Jamie as well.

I haven't seen him since the day he asked me to leave, and the only one surprised that I stopped going was Iris, at least that's how it seemed when I'd announced that Jamie and his mother felt he didn't need as many services since he was getting by on his own and that I wouldn't be spending as much time there.

"So, like, how often will you be going?" Iris had asked.

I spooned beets onto Daisy's dish, and she wrinkled her nose. "I don't know. Not in the near future, anyway."

"Really? You'll be staying home?" Iris's voice held such an odd combination of surprise and something else—hope?—that I paused mid spooning and considered her. Maybe Wayne was right. Maybe the kids needed me home, or, at least, they needed to know I was home doing mom stuff while they were in school. Security blanket of sorts. God knows the time I spent with Jamie ate into my household chores, so after-school time was less about spending special moments with my kids and more about trying to cram everything into fewer hours. "Yeah," I said. "Really."

"Timing's probably good," Wayne added, "since Hank and I have the hunting trip. Plus the holidays."

Daisy clapped her hands. "Yay! Christmas."

"And Thanksgiving," Rosie said. "And my birthday."

Iris scowled. "That's not a holiday."

"Well, now, Buttercup," Wayne said. "Your mom and I would disagree with that. We think all your birthdays are like holidays."

Iris glanced at me. "So you're not going ever again, right?"

"Where? To Jamie's? I didn't say never. Just not for a while." But even as I said it, I wondered if it would be forever.

#

"You expecting other people I don't know about?" Kat says while surveying my mountain of potato peels and shucking off her coat.

"People can bring home leftovers."

She comes up next to me with her hands on her hips. "By 'people,' you mean me and Dennis?"

"And Hank and his family."

"Oh, God. You didn't mention they were coming."

"Didn't I?" I say, even though I hadn't. On purpose.

She washes her hands in the sink, dries them on my pumpkin-colored hand towel, and reaches for the plate of brownies and chocolate chip cookies she'd brought in with her. "Um, no. I would have remembered that."

I hand her a knife and turnips. "Oh, sorry. My bad. Peel?"

"I'd be careful handing me a sharp instrument right now." She pops a brownie into her mouth, accepts the knife, and starts hacking at one of the vegetables. "What time will we be graced with their presence?"

"Whenever the football game's over."

"That where Wayne and the girls are?"

"Yep."

"I told Dennis to get here around one thirty and dinner would be at two."

"Good. Did the kids make it to Linda's okay?" I ask, referring to Dennis's ex.

"You mean the Barracuda?" she says. "Yes."

We're quiet, having covered the list of our immediate relatives, and then the familiar pang of sadness hits me. Normally, Mom would be here with us, chopping and cooking and bantering back and forth.

"Dammit," I say while wiping my eyes with the back of my hand.

"You cut yourself?" Kat says, while I shake my head and throw down the knife. "You okay?"

"It's Mom," I say. "I can't help but think of her on days like today."

Kat nods. "Yeah. Me, too."

I excuse myself and escape into the bathroom, cleaner than it has been in months, thanks to Operation Clean House, which I launched a week ago when Wayne left on his trip. Keeping insanely busy, or at least busier than my regular life of caring for three active girls, a house, and a husband, has been the only way I've gotten through these last two weeks.

Leaning over the sink, I splash water on my face but am careful not to make a mess, sopping up any excess with a washcloth I toss into the hamper.

I turn the wand for the blinds until they're fully open and stare out onto the backyard and the woods, trying to see if I can make out his house. Crazy, of course, since Jamie's backyard has got to be a good quarter mile away from mine. In one moment, it's a comfort, thinking he's on the other side. In the next, I'm sniffling and dabbing my eyes. Is he thinking about me? Does he miss me? Is this how I'll be living the rest of my life, longing for those I've lost, of the future I could have had if I had taken a chance?

Someone knocks softly on the door. "Koty?" Kat says. You all right?"

No, I think. *I'm not all right.* Instead, I examine my reflection, wipe my nose one last time, open the door, and follow Kat back to the kitchen.

#

We've managed to squeeze everyone—all eleven of us—at the main dining room table, its extra leaves in place. It's tight quarters: Hank and Veronica and their two kids, Henry and Michael, on one side, Wayne and me at the heads of the table, and Dennis, Kat, and the girls squeezed on the other side. Kat leads us in grace (if I left it up to the Fowler side, there'd be no mention of thanks and God), and everyone digs in, plates filled and then refilled. Hank's boys are tall and lanky but can pack it away. Veronica, always meek and quiet, barely fills her plate, but her scotch glass is always full. Hank and Wayne drink beer out of grand Pilsner beer glasses that Wayne only uses on special occasions. Kat and Dennis drink white, and a full wine glass sits in front of my dinner plate, even though I'll probably pour most of it down the sink. I don't have the stomach for alcohol. The conversation is filled with local high school football scores, college searches for Henry, and talk of business—Wayne and Hank's Bad Plumbing Adventures (as I've come to call their company), Dennis's ski and snowboard sales, and Kat's accounting business. Veronica handles the books for Hank. Then there's me: housewife extraordinaire. Thirty years old and going downhill fast. The thought's enough to cause me to lift the wine glass to my lips and take a sip and then another. Wayne raises an eyebrow because he knows how much I hate booze, but he doesn't say anything.

"Well, I don't care what this so-called bank bailout and stimulus package are supposed to do for the economy. Everything's gonna go down the toilet now that we have this nig—" Hank pauses and casts me a derisive smile. "This Negro coming in."

Dennis clears his throat, and Kat concentrates on folding her napkin.

"What?" he continues. "You disagree?"

"Next Thanksgiving," Dennis says.

Hank looks around the table, confused. "Huh?"

"I think we should postpone this discussion until then."

"Why's that?"

"Because I find it challenging to debate the success of a man's tenure in office when he isn't even *in* office yet."

I hide a smile as I take another sip of wine. Go Dennis!

Hank shakes his head. "There's a liberal mindset if I ever heard one." Henry and Michael snicker. Veronica wraps her hand around her tumbler. Kat sighs. My girls sit quiet, waiting for the volley back. And Wayne? Wayne sits there, Hank on one side, Dennis on the other. The voice of reason versus the devil. Problem is, the devil's a blood relation. We all know where Wayne's loyalty lies.

Dennis smiles. "We liberals don't have a monopoly on logic. At least not yet."

I glance at Hank and can see him mentally dismantling the sentence in his head in an effort to understand its meaning. "Yeah, right."

I don't know if it's the wine or the absurdity of it all, but I laugh. Out loud.

"Something funny?" Hank says.

"Sorry," I say. "I was thinking of something else."

"This conversation boring you?"

I lock eyes with his. "Maybe we should leave politics for another time. It's a holiday."

"Hear, hear," Kat says and stands. "Koty, I'll help you start clearing dishes."

Hank rolls his eyes and turns to Wayne, who simply stares at his plate.

"Hey, Michael," Dennis says to Hank's youngest. "I hear you got a good arm. Want to throw some spirals in the front yard?"

Michael's eyes light up and he pushes his chair back, but he must remember where he is, who he is, and what he's doing, because he stops short and looks at his parents. "Can I?"

Hank stares at Dennis now, who holds his gaze. "Yeah. Sure."

Disaster averted, at least for now, the girls get up and wander into the living room. Henry stands, pulls out his phone, and follows them. Veronica gulps her drink and begins clearing her side of the table, while Hanks sits and stews.

"Hey," Wayne says, hitting him on the arm. "I got some cigars. Let's go out back." Hank doesn't respond, but he stands and heads for the kitchen where another beer and the back door await. Veronica and Kat carry out the first round of dinner plates, leaving Wayne and me alone, staring at each other. He doesn't appear angry this time. In fact, his eyes are heavy with fatigue and something else I can't quite name, and I wonder if his thoughts resemble my own: if he feels we're both trapped in something impossible to get out of, if he questions where the last twelve years of his life have gone, if he thinks about another woman the way I think about Jamie.

A pot crashes in the sink.

"Stop it, Iris," Daisy yells from the living room.

A cat meows underfoot.

"Wayne, you coming or not?" Hank calls out from the kitchen.

Wayne blinks, and the window to his soul closes. "We'll be out back," he says.

#

I stand at the sink hours later, Julie Andrews belting out "These Are a Few of My Favorite Things" from the TV in the living room as the girls watch *The Sound of Music*. The water runs from the faucet over my cracked and dry hands, which have seen more dishwashing today than they have in the last three months combined.

Kat and Dennis left a little while ago, armed with Tupperware filled with stuffing and turkey, turnips and mashed potatoes, and other remnants of our Thanksgiving meal. Hank, mellowed by bottomless glasses of beer and cigars, stayed well past eight o'clock, although Veronica shuttled the kids home earlier and then returned to pick Hank up. No major fights, no broken dishes, no feelings wounded beyond repair. So why do I stand here wanting to scream, convinced my chest will explode if I don't? How can I possibly live the rest of my life like this?

My eyes, which had been staring into the backyard's darkness, refocus on my reflection in the glass. I turn off the faucet. Dry my hands. Prepare a plate of sweets: brownies, chocolate chip cookies, marble cheesecake, lemon squares, pumpkin-filled whoopee pies. The day had been mild for late November, but the temperature has since dropped. I grab the hoodie hanging over one of the chairs and pull it over my stained UNH T-shirt, a Christmas present from Kat eons ago. I take a deep breath, pick up the plate, and march into the living room. Wayne leans back on the recliner, his eyes at half-mast, the girls on the floor in front of him, too close to the TV screen as far as I'm concerned, but I don't say anything. A Toys "R" Us commercial plays, and the kids watch, rapt.

I hold up the plate. "I'm bringing this to the Briggs."

Wayne opens his eyes, and the girls look up. "Who?" he says.

"You know, Jamie Briggs and his mother?"

"Now?"

"Yeah. We have so much. I thought I'd be neighborly."

"It's nine-thirty."

"I know, but I've been in the kitchen all day. I need fresh air. I need to get out."

He shakes his head. "Suit yourself."

The movie continues, and Rosie and Daisy return to their stupor. Iris watches me. "You said you weren't going over there again," she says.

"No. I said I wasn't going there every day. I didn't say never again." I walk out, but feel her eyes on my back. Still, I don't turn around. I don't even think of turning around.

#

Barbara Briggs's car isn't in the driveway when I pull in, but there are lights on in the house. I get out, climb the steps, and ring the doorbell. Nothing. I knock. I take a deep breath and try the doorknob, knowing it'll open since no one locks their doors around here. Music fills the air with the unmistakable grit of Johnny Cash's voice in "Folsom Prison Blues." I take a deep breath and follow the music down the hall to Jamie's room, his door wide open. He sits with his back to the door at a desk I haven't seen before. A computer sits on top, and the monitor glows, casting a funky blue light in an otherwise dark room.

"Hi," I say, but the music's too loud, the second round of applause from the song overwhelming the room. "Hi," I say again, louder. He whips his head fast. How could I have forgotten in two short weeks his sensitivity to sudden sounds and surprises? His face goes from startled to confused when he sees it's me.

I walk to the CD player and turn down the volume. "Great song," I say, while glancing at the monitor. Only then does it occur to me I might be embarrassed by what I see. I mean, what if it's porn? Instead, I see the home page for the Small Business Association of New England. *What is he doing?*

"What are you doing here?" he says.

"I had to see you."

"Koty—"

"I'm sorry. I know you asked me not to, and I did. For two weeks. But I couldn't take it anymore. I mean, we're friends, right? More, maybe, but friends first, and today, on all days, when we're supposed to give thanks for what we have—" I stop because I'm rambling and not making any sense. "Anyhow. I'm thankful for you. That's all." I hold out the plate. "I came to give this to you and your mom." I swallow and wait for him to say something, anything, but when he doesn't, I fill in the empty space. "Where's your mom anyway?"

"I left her at her sister's. My Aunt Shirley. Had one of my cousins take me home. She was having fun. I was tired and wanted to leave. Wanted to be by myself."

"Right." I place the plate next to the keyboard. "Well, like I said, I wanted to stop by and say hello. And now I'll say good-bye." I head for the door.

"Koty, wait."

I hesitate before turning around, and in that time, he stands and starts toward me. When I finally face him, I feel silly and hang my head. It's obvious this is such a bigger loss to me than it will ever be to him, a man who has lost more in his twenty-six years than most men do in a lifetime.

"Hey," he says. "Look at me." I obey. "One of the hardest things I've ever done was telling you to go away." He pauses and exhales. "I don't know if I have it in me to watch you walk away again."

Warning bells go off in my head, in my ears, in my heart. I ignore them. I reach for his face, kiss him, and don't stop.

Chapter 22

November 2001

I feel a combination of drunk and fatigue like I never experienced with the first two. The nurses are encouraging me to get up and walk because they're concerned about blood clots, a complication, apparently, of C-sections, but all I want is to hold my baby and sleep. Mom and Kat have taken Rosie and Iris home, and I want to worry about that arrangement, too, with Kat having to juggle her job, two step kids, and Mom's chemo while Dennis travels, this being his busy time of year. But I'm too tired to worry about Kat or Mom or my kids or Wayne.

Wayne.

He's in the Maine woods, hunting with Hank and mostly out of cell phone range, their annual trip to mark Carl's death. Killing innocent animals doesn't seem like the best way to avenge a murder, but he never asked me what I thought of the idea when he announced his plans—what, four years ago now—to mark that first anniversary. (Did he ever ask what I thought about anything? I can't remember.) We'd fought, since I didn't want to be alone with a baby just shy of one, and he'd told me to get a grip, that he was going, and that I should get over it. It was the first time he laid a hand on me, a slap across the face. He apologized profusely for weeks afterwards, and for an eye blink, I had the old Wayne back. Perhaps he would have stayed, too, if not for that damn hunting trip with Hank. Instead, he came back ugly and unrecognizable.

#

Wayne knows I've given birth, that's what Kat said, since he called the house last night to check in from the town store up in Maine. When he hadn't gotten anyone at our house, he tried Kat. He said he'd start back in the morning since Daisy had already made her arrival, if you can call it an "arrival" when you're yanked from a womb.

I wonder how he felt when Kat told him it was another girl, another mistake as far as he's concerned. But there will be no more "mistakes." I've made sure of that. I'll tell him (when, I'm not sure) I had my tubes tied for medical reasons, that Dr. Kobb recommended it, that I signed the consent form, that it made sense, that three is enough, even if it means no sons.

Part of me fears his wrath. A bigger part fears his apathy.

I've named her Daisy Louise. Mom teared up when I told her this, my baby's middle name a tribute to her first, and I wonder if Wayne will care. He's never suggested names or fought me whenever I announced the final choice. His only request, and this came right after Rosie was born: if we ever had a boy, that we name him Carl. The best I could come up with was "Carol" as Iris's middle name.

#

"Do you want to hold her?" I ask when he finally shows up.

He shakes his head, says nothing. He looks like hell, dressed in stained jeans and a plaid flannel shirt with holes.

"You don't want to hold your newborn daughter," I press, a combination of hurt and chutzpah. He presses his lips tight, shakes his ahead again. "I don't understand you," I murmur while lowering my eyes to Daisy's face so I can't see his reaction.

"I never asked you to," he says.

"Never asked me to what?"

"Understand."

"It's not something you ask your wife to do. It's not something wives ask their husbands to do, either. It's just something that's done. You try to understand each other. That's what a marriage is all about." The power in my voice after having spent ten hours in labor, in the presence of this beautiful untainted little being, surprises me, and, no doubt, Wayne. I know he won't yell and holler in the hospital, but I half expect him to get in my face, childbirth and newborn be damned, and talk to me with a voice that reminds me of the rumble strip on a highway: jarring and ominous. But he doesn't. Instead, he's quiet. I'm quiet. Little Daisy Louise is quiet, her cupid doll lips sucking air.

Finally, he speaks: "If it's any consolation, Koty, I don't understand myself either." And then, he's gone, the shadow of old Wayne following him down the hall.

Chapter 23

December 2008

Shadows fill the room, and I think about my first time here, back in September, when summer's heat lingered and sunshine poured through the window for the duration of my visit. Now, everything grows darker and colder so fast. I shiver.

"Hey." His voice is soft and warm like a blanket. His breath tickles my ear. "You warm enough?"

I nod, even though my back is to him, spooned against the part of him that's still complete and whole. Making love to this man has been nothing like I have ever experienced before. I expected it to be awkward, at least a little, that first time we had sex on Thanksgiving night. But it wasn't. Jamie is in tune with his body and what it can do—probably more so than anyone I know. His shoulders are beautiful, broad, strong; his abdomen hard and solid, as are the muscles in his legs. He has scars—many—but they only add to his allure. Every inch of him is alive, as if he's making up for the parts he no longer has, and it amazes me how someone who is considered "broken" to the outside world can fill me up so fully, so completely.

"Was there an answer in that movement?" he asks, as he rubs what's left of the upper part of his left arm against the upper part of mine.

"Yes. Warm enough."

"Then what is it?"

"What's what?"

"Something's on your mind."

I sigh, and with the exhale, tears trickle down my face, and for some godforsaken reason, I'm transported back in time to those first hours and days after Dad had his stroke, when his life hung in the balance, and we didn't know what was going to happen next. At least, I didn't, not at the time. It was the not knowing that was so goddamn hard. The same feeling permeates every inch of my body, every corner of my soul. Because this— whatever this is—can't go on forever, or indefinitely. An end point, a breaking point, perhaps both need to happen. On one side or the other.

He nudges me, but I pretend to be asleep, at least until the tears stop and dry. I rouse and disentangle myself from him and the sheets. He watches as I put on my bra, underwear, jeans, and sweater.

"You going to tell me what's up?" he asks.

"What's up," I say, "is the time. I need to go."

He rolls his eyes. "Like that's stopped you from staying. Come here."

I obey and walk to the edge of the bed.

He gestures to the space next to him. "I won't bite, Dakota."

I sit down as he struggles to sit up. I wait as he gets himself situated, amazed at the amount of body strength it must take him to do it, and help adjust the sheet over his lower body. I remember the joy when my girls first learned to sit up and roll over on their own. Such a basic but important building block to everything else they'd ever do. Something I'd taken for granted until I met Jamie.

"I do need to get going," I whisper.

"Okay. But before you go, tell me what you're thinking. Because I know it's something."

I shrug. "I don't know. I'm thinking a million different thoughts."

He nudges me with his right "leg" and smiles. "Anything good?" he asks in a suggestive tone.

Now it's my turn to roll my eyes. "Not those type of thoughts."

"Then what?"

"I don't know."

"Well, if you don't, who does?"

"That," I say, "is an excellent question." Instinctively, I reach for him. This is where I'd be squeezing his hand, or he would mine. But there's nothing to hold onto. Instead, I return my hands to my lap.

"I love you," he says. "You know that, right?"

My insides spasm and ripple as those three words echo in my head. The thing is, I do know, but I can't say it back. Not yet. Maybe not ever. Even if I do feel it.

He leans against the headboard. This time, I reach for his face, hold it in my hands, my nose grazing his. "I know." I kiss him.

"Then leave him," he whispers.

"Jamie, please—"

"Promise me you'll think about it. I know it won't be easy. I know. But nothing about either of our lives has been easy. We can do this." He pauses, and I know when he says "this" he means so much more than us. It means his dream of building something here, in town. Of doing something with his life. Of seeing me do something with mine.

"I don't know. Jamie—"

"Dakota," he says, "just promise me, okay?"

#

I'm at the front door, officially late now, with my hand on the knob when a voice behind me speaks.

"So was that lip service?"

I whip around. Mrs. Briggs stands, arms wrapped around herself in the same old yellow sweater.

"No pun intended," she adds wryly, eyeing me the way you do cat vomit, dog shit, a used condom in the Walmart parking lot.

"I didn't hear you come in," I say.

"Of course you didn't."

"Listen. I can explain."

"No. You can't, but let *me* explain one thing."

"What's that?"

"I'll be damned if I let you break another piece of him."

We stare at each other, her with narrowed eyes and me with ones that I'm sure are screaming, "I can't fucking believe this."

"It's not my intention, nor has it ever been, to hurt your son."

"Do you love him?"

"Excuse me? I don't think that's any of your business."

"Because if you don't," she says, ignoring me, "then I suggest you stop coming here. End it now, before he gets in any deeper."

Too late, I think. "I can't," I begin, but that's as far as I'm able to go. I can't what? Wait to leave my husband, my children? I can't wait to take my children and run away with Jamie? I can't wait to tell Jamie how I feel, *if* I feel?

"I see," she says. She stands up straighter, if that's even possible, and points to the door. "I believe you were leaving."

"Right," I say and I do.

Chapter 24

The mail stack grows until the end of the month when I force my ass in front of the computer and simultaneously go through everything and pay bills online. The computer has an unfortunate location, however—the living room—where any number of distractions await, like watching *Hannah Montana* with Rosie, playing endless games of Operation with Iris, or dressing up dolls with Daisy, all of which I'd rather do for the rest of my life without a break rather than deal with our Visa bill.

Tonight, though, it's late. The kids are in bed, finally, and I sit at the computer, exhausted and a little pissed off since Wayne is out playing darts with Hank and whoever else frequents the bar on Tuesday night. I wiggle the mouse and the computer monitor comes to life, revealing a website on vasectomies, of all things. Rosie's supposed to be in an advanced science class, but somehow I don't think this has anything to do with her homework, so it must be Wayne's doing, and my first thought is, why does he think he needs a vasectomy? My second thought is this: I'm going to have to tell him I had my tubes tied when Daisy was born, something I'd never gotten around to doing, even though I'm not entirely sure why.

#

I browse the facts on the website and learn that nearly one out of six men over the age of thirty-five have a vasectomy. (Wayne will be thirty in May.) A million vasectomies are performed in the US every year. It's non-invasive and can be done on an outpatient basis with a local anesthetic. The descriptions and visuals of the procedure suck me in so much that I'm startled when I hear the front door open. Wayne walks into the living room, followed by the scent of stale cigarettes and beer.

"Hey," he says and then he notices what's on the screen. "Oh. Glad you found that and not one of the kids."

"Yeah. I was wondering what was up."

He takes off his jacket and throws it on the couch. "At my physical last week. Talked about it with Doc. I was researching the risks online. Figured I'd check it out before bringing it up with you." He pauses. "Truth is, I don't know. Part of me thinks it's a good idea, but another part of me wants a son."

Shit. "You don't need to get a vasectomy."

"Well, maybe we should think about it some more. I mean, the three kids are a handful. There's no guarantee it would be a boy anyway, if you got pregnant again, that is. I know you're on the pill and all, but that's not always foolproof, as we both know."

"I'm not on the pill. And you *really* don't need to get one."

He knits his brow, confused. "What? Why not?"

"You just don't."

"Wait. Do you think I'm cheating or something?" He rubs his hand over his face. "You're not on the pill? Shit, Koty. What're you thinking?"

I take a deep breath. "I got my tubes tied after Daisy," I say, and his face turns pink. "I'm sorry. I should have told you."

"Damn right you should've. Like before you had it done." He shakes his head. "I don't get a say in any of this?"

"We can barely afford the ones we have."

"Oh, so it's my fault, is that it? I can't provide for a bigger family?" He points his finger at me. "Don't you turn this around and put it on me. You lied. You've been lying."

"You weren't there when Daisy was born. You were on your hunting trip, and the doctor asked me if I wanted it done, since he was already inside. It made sense for me to do it, given everything."

"By everything, you mean money?"

I nod. *Among other things.*

"Okay. I could probably accept that explanation—had you told me three and a half years ago when it happened. "

"I said I'm sorry."

"You're sorry?"

"What else do you want me to say?" I study his face, trying to discern if he's more angry than sad or the other way around.

"Any other secrets you're keeping from me?"

"It wasn't a secret."

"That doesn't answer the question."

"No. No other secrets."

He picks up his jacket and puts it on.

"Wayne. What're you doing? I said I was sorry." He doesn't respond and walks out of the room toward the front door. I follow. "Wayne. C'mon. Let's talk about it."

He opens the door. "Little late to be talking about *it*, don't you think?" He marches onto the porch and bounds down the steps two at a time, and all I want to do is scream after him, "You want to know why? *That's* why." But, of course, I don't.

Chapter 25

December 2008

I drive and drive and drive, circling neighborhoods that aren't my own, searching for what, I don't know. All I can picture is Jamie's haunted face as I left him, his mother's accusatory demeanor, the confusion in my eyes as I stare at my reflection in the rearview mirror.

When I finally decide I can't put off my children, my husband, my responsibilities anymore, I follow the lonely street that leads to our lonely house. Wayne's pickup sits in the driveway. I glance at the clock. Four o'clock already. *Fuck.*

I take a deep breath, mount the steps, open the door, and plug my cell into its charger on the junk table by the door. The house is unusually quiet, no TV, no whining, no fighting. But then I hear the clink and clank from the pipes when the shower's on. I glance in the living room and spot Daisy's backpack in front of the Christmas tree that we had erected over the weekend. Pine needles cover the floor. I walk to the kitchen, and the smell of the roast I had the good sense to put in the crockpot this morning fills the air along with the pine, scents I normally take comfort in, but today, in this moment, in this light as darkness falls around me, I don't. The mail lays scattered across the table along with Rosie's books and one of Daisy's pink mittens. No signs of Iris.

I deposit my keychain on a hook on the wall and check the house phone for messages. Nothing. My kids are here or out there somewhere, and even though I would usually give my left foot for silence like this, for a moment that's all mine, I want noise. I need noise. I don't want to be alone.

I wander down the hall, enter our bedroom, throw my purse on the floor, stare at myself in the mirror, and notice my sweater is on inside out. I pull it over my head, turn it right side to, and put it back on, ignoring Jamie's scent clinging to my skin.

Wayne waltzes in behind me, a white towel wrapped around his waist. Alcohol emanates from his pores. Well, at least we both stink.

"Hey," he says to my reflection.

"Where are the girls?"

"Rosie and Daisy are out selling Rosie's candy bars. Iris is at someone's house." He drops the towel to the floor—which is where it will likely stay until I pick it up—and pulls on his boxers.

"Whose house?" I fiddle with the jewelry on top of the bureau.

"Um." He pauses. "Kenny something or other. Landau? Does that sound right?"

"We picking her up?"

"Nah." He pulls a gray T-shirt over his head. "The mother's dropping her off at five."

"Oh." I watch him in the mirror, and his eyes connect with mine. He comes up behind me and squeezes my ass, a non-verbal gesture that says, *Hey, it's been awhile. We have the house to ourselves. How 'bout a quickie?*

"I'm taking a shower," I say, desperate to the get the scent of sex off my body. The whole room smells like a bar, and I hope I have better luck washing my stink off than Wayne had washing off his.

"Now?" he says, and for a moment, I think he might sound hurt. It has been awhile, neither one of us initiating any sort of physical contact.

I paw through the clean clothes in the basket on the floor and pluck a pair of underwear, sweats, and T-shirt. "Yeah."

"You sick?" he whines, and I want to slug him. As if that has ever stopped me from performing my "duties" in the past.

"Period," I mutter, knowing that'll shut him up and should keep his hands off me. Wayne's never liked having sex when I've been on the rag.

I scurry past him, down the hall, and into the bathroom, turn on the shower, and tear my clothes off. As the mirror steams, I watch my image evaporate. *What the fuck am I doing? What the fuck am I doing?* I step in the shower and turn the water so hot that it stings my skin.

Mrs. Briggs's words echo in my head. *I'll be damned if I let you break another piece of him.* Jamie's words echo, too. *Promise me you'll think about it. I know it won't be easy. I know. But nothing about either of our lives has been easy. We can do this.*

How can a man so jaded in all the ways of the world, a man who's seen unspeakable horrors, a man who's lost everything, who's sat on the brink of death, only to be yanked back without his leg and arms, see possibility in the impossible?

I think I know why. Jamie has never been in love before. The first time, no matter how unreasonable, impossible, or whatever, there's hope. I remember sitting on the edge of my childhood bed, a child myself, cuddled under Wayne's arm while reading the pregnancy stick and thinking, *We'll make it work. We'll make it work, because we have no choice.*

I thought we would, too, that we could. I thought it for a very long time. Shit, there's a part of me, even now, that still thinks it. Even though it's bullshit. Even though whatever love Wayne and me had is gone. Isn't it?

I turn the water off and stand naked until I begin to shake. I towel off, put on my fresh clothes, toss the ones I'd been wearing in the hamper, and open the door to the chaos that is my life.

Voices emanate from the kitchen. Adult voices. Authority voices. Angry voices.

I walk in.

Wayne stands stiff and tall with his hand on Iris's shoulder. A woman stands across from them—who is she? She seems familiar—dressed in working mom attire: cheap suit, flats, long winter coat. Behind her stands a boy, about Iris's age, maybe older. Again, familiar but not. I allow my eyes a quick scan of the counter, where I spot four beer cans, empty, no doubt.

"What's going on?" I say.

"This here is Mrs.—" Wayne begins.

"Landau," she interrupts. "Liz Landau." She doesn't hold out her hand, and I don't offer mine.

"What can we do for you, Mrs. Landau?"

"Right. Well, I was telling your husband about the disturbing scene I encountered when I got home from work today. Involving your daughter."

I look at Iris, but she keeps her head hanging low.

"What happened?"

"Our family cat," the woman sniffled. "Your daughter was torturing it."

At the word "torturing," Iris lifts her head. Her eyes are angry and filled with tears, but they're not remorseful.

"There's got to be some mistake," I hear Wayne say, even though I'm not so sure. The events of the last few months race through my head: her obsession with guns, her schoolyard fights, her ditching school, and now this. But another image enters my head, too: Iris, sleeping curled up with Cream Puff. It's Daisy's cat, but the animal has always gravitated toward Iris. Iris was the one who cried when we found a wounded vulture in the woods. Iris is the one who thinks a trip to the zoo is the best way to spend a birthday. Iris is the one who loves zebras and has stuffed animals and posters of every animal imaginable covering the walls of her room.

"I'm afraid not. I saw it with my own two eyes. She was holding its ear."

"Well, maybe she was looking for a tick or something," I say. "Kids are curious, you know."

"No," she says, shaking her head. "You're not hearing me. She was *holding* its ear in her hand. The one she'd cut off."

"What?" I gasp, and Iris and I lock eyes. There's hate in them, and if I didn't know better, I'd think the hate was directed at me. Wayne squeezes her shoulder hard enough that she winces, but she doesn't shrug him off.

"Look at her hands." Liz Landau points to Iris's hands, which hang innocently at her side. "You'll see the blood. I didn't clean her up. Just put her in the car and carted her here while my husband took the cat to the vet."

I cross my arms and stare down my middle child. "What the fuck were you thinking?"

"Koty," Wayne whispers, and I can't help but laugh at the absurdity of it all. Iris chopping ears off animals she used to love, me cursing in front of total strangers, and Wayne the voice of reason.

"You're all a piece of work," Liz Landau says as she crosses her arms. The little boy who'd been hanging back peeks from behind his mother, a triumphant look on an otherwise sallow and scrawny face. "I should report this to the cops. Hurting animals is a crime, you know. And a predictor."

"A predictor?" I ask, my bitch barometer rising.

"Of future degenerative behavior."

"Lady," I say, "you watch too much *Law & Order*."

"And you need to watch what your kids are up to."

"Enough!" Wayne's voice rumbles and shakes the house. His eyes tell me to shut-the-fuck-up, and I do. He turns his attention to the woman and her boy.

"That won't be necessary, Liz. My wife and I will deal with it. I promise you that. Iris will pay the vet bill." He walks toward her and places his hand on her arm. "Okay, ma'am? Let us deal with this. Let us take care of our daughter." Even drunk, he can be charming.

She looks up into his face, a face I'm told time and time again by other moms, by old ladies I meet in the market, is handsome. I don't see that anymore, but a vision of what he used to be, of the handsome man I fell for, I do remember.

She sniffles, dabs her eyes with a tissue I hadn't noticed before, and nods. He ushers her down the hall, and I hear the front door open, muffled words, and the door close.

Iris and I stand in the kitchen. She crosses her arms and scowls.

"Do not," I begin, my body shaking, "look at me like that."

"Like what?"

"Like that."

"Whatever," she says.

"Don't you 'whatever' me, little girl. What has gotten into you? What were you thinking? Do you even think anymore?" She doesn't respond, so I grab her by the shoulders and shake her. "Well?"

"I'm thinking I wish you were dead!" she yells as Wayne returns to the kitchen. Her words hit me with such force I practically fall backwards.

"Iris—" Wayne begins.

"I didn't do it," she says, and then she points a finger at me. "You didn't even ask if I'd done it. You just assumed I did."

"A woman and her son stood in the middle of my kitchen telling me they caught you cutting off the damn cat's ear. I mean, c'mon, Iris. If you were innocent, I think you would have professed it then."

Her face goes stony. I glance at Wayne. He's studying Iris.

"What happened, Buttercup?" he says.

I laugh. "I don't fucking believe this."

"Let's give her a chance," he says, "to tell us what happened."

"Right. Because if she says it to you, it has to be true." Even I'm surprised at how strident my voice sounds, but I don't care anymore.

Iris stares at the floor and trembles in her Sketchers. "What do *you* know about truth?" she says, but her voice is so faint, I'm not even sure I heard her correctly.

"Excuse me?" I say. "Care to repeat that?"

She raises her eyes, and beyond the black of her pupils is a monsoon of tears. "I know," she says. "I. *Know.*"

"You know what?" I sigh, but as the words leave my lips, I stop short. *Wait, what does she know?* My mind rewinds through all the images from the last three months. Jamie and I have been careful; we only kissed in his room, only made love in his room. Except, there it is: my mind pauses on a memory. Me shooting the gun in his backyard. Me kissing him. Me touching him. Him hearing something, or someone. *Oh, God.*

Iris trembles. "I saw you. And him. That guy you're supposedly 'sitting' with every day."

"Iris—" I interrupt.

"I saw you kissing him. And hugging him. And touching his—"

"Enough!" I look from her to Wayne, who stands dumbly in between us. The red starts at his neck and quickly spreads across his cheeks, his nose, until I expect to see sparks fly out of his hair follicles. His eyes narrow and cloud over. Iris shuts up, and I realize I'm holding my breath. *Oh God, oh God, oh God.*

The front door slams, and Daisy's incessant chatter enters the kitchen before she does, with Rosie right behind her.

"I helped Rosie sell seventeen candy bars," Daisy announces. The candy sales are part of a school fundraising effort for what I can't remember. Her cheeks are as pink as her sole mitten, which she pulls off her hand and throws on the kitchen table. She spots the wayward one on top of the mail stack. "Oh, there it is!"

Rosie rolls her eyes as she opens the fridge and helps herself to some Kool-Aid. "Yeah, right. Help. Or something like it."

Daisy crawls onto her chair, plucks a banana from the fruit bowl, and begins to peel. "I'm hungry," she says in between mouthfuls. "When's dinner?" When I don't respond, her eyes move to Wayne, to Iris, and back to me. "Mommy?"

"You girls are going to stay at your Aunt Kat's tonight," Wayne says, his voice low, but even.

Rosie swallows and places her glass on the table. "But it's a school night."

"Go pack up your things," he continues, ignoring her. "Homework. Pajamas. Clothes for tomorrow. We'll be waiting for you. In the van."

"But—" Rosie says.

"Goddammit, what did I say? Get your stuff and get in the van."

Rosie's mouth hangs open, but to her credit, she doesn't let another word escape. Instead, she takes Daisy by the hand and shepherds her down the hall toward their rooms. Iris follows them, refusing to make eye contact with either one of us.

"I'll stay here," I whisper. "The roast should be ready." I turn to the counter next to the stove where the crockpot sits, but he catches my arm and twists it harder than he ever has before.

"The hell you will." He releases me, leaving angry red fingerprints on my wrist, and goes to the fridge, takes out a can of beer, opens it, and chugs. "Call your sister. Now."

I punch Kat's number into the phone and ask if she can take the girls tonight.

"But it's a school night," she says.

"I know. Please."

She pauses, no doubt waiting for more of an explanation than that, and I expect her to press me for details. Maybe she senses the tension, or maybe her subconscious does. Whatever the reason, she doesn't question me further about it, just asks if they've eaten yet.

"No," I hear myself say. "And Daisy's hungry."

"Well, I've got nothing in the house. I hope pizza's okay, this last minute."

"Pizza's great."

We say good-bye, and I hang up the phone and face Wayne, who's leaning against the counter, watching me with an expression that's not quite hate, not quite despair. He finishes his beer and tosses the can on the counter, in the general direction of the other empties from this afternoon.

"You shouldn't be driving," I say, and I think I'm going to be sick.

He grabs the keys from the hook on the wall and flings them at my face. I catch them, but not before the silver *K* on my keychain catches me below my right eye.

"Then you will."

I close my eyes. "I can explain," I hear myself say, but when I open them, he's already gone from the kitchen. The front door slams.

Daisy bounces into the kitchen, already dressed in her pajamas, and holds her pillow, Elmo, and a backpack that's bulging with so much crap that Rosie struggles to zipper it. Rosie's backpack sits at her feet along with a small suitcase on wheels. Iris stands behind them, empty handed.

"Where's your stuff, Iris?" I say.

She keeps her eyes down and points to the suitcase.

"Are we having dinner at Aunt Kat's?" Rosie asks.

"Yes. Pizza."

"Yaaaay!" Daisy spins and tosses Elmo into the air. Rosie laughs and snatches it from her grasp.

"Hey, gimmee," she says, and Rosie obliges.

Such an innocent scene, packing up my three girls for an overnight stay with their favorite aunt, while my husband and I can have a night alone.

If only.

If only.

Chapter 26

October 2006

Wayne and I, we've done everything backwards. We got pregnant, then we got married with no honeymoon period to speak of since we went straight to a place called Difficult Times and stayed there for almost a decade. But maybe, just maybe, we've gotten to a good place, a place that I always knew was possible with the old Wayne, who, happily, has been making more and longer appearances. This is my hope, anyway, as I wave bye to the kids as they stand in Kat's door and see Wayne and me off to celebrate my twenty-eighth birthday and our ten-year wedding anniversary.

We ride in silence, my hand on his knee, and it feels comfortable. Comforting, even. The good started coming round this past summer, a fun summer, the girls the perfect ages for beach days and trips to Storyland. Kat and Dennis had given us an early anniversary present, a new gas grill, and we—yes, together, me and Wayne—cooked out every night, even when it rained: grilled veggies, steaks, burgers, fish, and chicken I marinated ahead of time for twenty-four hours. He still drank, but not nearly as much as he had, only socially, for the most part. We made love. We had hot sex. We fucked, sweaty, hard, until we both collapsed on the bed, sweat trickling down my back in the summer heat.

The fall had gotten off to a good start as well with all the girls in school full time, giving me some much-needed breathing room, with a chance to take an English literature class at the local community college. I'll admit, though, that Wayne's been a little quieter this past month and drinking more, too, but he works hard, long days and deserves to relax, right? Besides, the fall has that effect on some people, right? Maybe he's got that disease. What's it called? SAD: Seasonal Affective Disorder. Maybe he's tired. He's allowed. We're both allowed.

"Hey," I say. "Whatchya thinking?"

He keeps his eyes on the road and shakes his head. "Nothing."

"Aw c'mon. You must be thinking something."

He casts me a sidelong glance, and his eyes narrow, filled with annoyance. "What did I say?"

I remove my hand and place it on my lap. "Sorry."

We pull into the parking lot of our favorite Italian restaurant, which is packed for a Tuesday night.

"You remember to make reservations?" he says.

"I thought you had," I say. Dinner on my actual birthday and our anniversary had been his idea after all, but I don't say this.

He gets out of the car and walks toward the entrance without even waiting for me. I run and catch up. We squeeze our way past people to the hostess.

"How long's the wait?" he asks a high school-aged girl with glossy blonde hair that she flips from side to side with her left hand.

"How many?"

"Two."

"Thirty-five minutes."

He shrugs at me as if to say, *Well?* and I know how I need to respond.

"That's okay," I say. "We can go somewhere else."

We make our way back to the truck and climb inside.

"Where to?" he says.

"I don't know." *How can I salvage this?* "Maybe we should get takeout. Go home. Watch a movie." I reach for the side of his face. He's growing his winter fur, as Iris says, and I rub my thumb down the length of his jaw. "Take advantage of an empty house." He reaches for my hand and pulls it away. "What's wrong?" I ask.

He doesn't say anything for a long time. Instead, he grips the steering wheel with both hands, his knuckles turning white. "Every major anniversary we have—one year, five year, ten—is a reminder."

"Of what?"

"That it's a major anniversary for Carl, too."

This, of course, I know. I didn't realize, however, the profound effect it had on my husband, how the death of one could trump his living and breathing wife, his living and breathing marriage.

"It was your idea," I say.

He turns to me. "What was?"

"Going out tonight. If it hurts so much, why'd you suggest it?"

Headlights hit his face, illuminating the pain in his eyes, and then disappear, leaving us in darkness. "It seemed like a good idea at the time. It seemed like this year, maybe, I had a handle on it." He turns the key in the ignition, puts the car in drive, and navigates his way onto the main road. Wayne's never been one to articulate his feelings, and even this small admission is probably more than he can bear. I say nothing in response, because there's nothing to say. I know he doesn't want me to say anything, so I pray that my bearing witness to his pain will be enough for him to move past it, once and for all.

Chapter 27

A car horn beeps. A seven-year-old giggles, "C'mon," and races down the hall, out the door, and into the backseat of a van. A twelve-year-old big sister buckles her in, and then herself. The middle girl—ten, going on God knows what—sulks, trying desperately to hide her tears, no doubt aware of the misery she's unleashed with her revelation.

I sit in the driver's seat, staring at the rearview mirror, and watch the scene play out behind me.

"Drive," Wayne says, and I do. I switch my brain to autopilot and navigate streets and turns on instinct, on memory. I pull up in front of my sister's one-level house, the house she and her husband moved into so Kat could better care for our dying mother, who became the child she could never bear.

I accompany the girls up the walkway. Kat greets us at the door, her smile wide, her confusion over the last-minute plans forgotten in light of Daisy's perky voice and endless chatter. I try to catch her eye, to signal to her my desperation, my fear, but she doesn't see it. Or she doesn't want to. Or she's so used to it that she doesn't even notice anymore.

As I walk back to the car, Wayne's changed positions, is in control of the wheel, and I think about my options: turn around and go into Kat's house (and do what? Scare and confuse my kids even more? Put them in potential danger?). Run (to where? Jamie's? Wayne would check there. He'd kill him. Or me. Or both of us.). Or take what I have coming to me?

My stomach churns acid.

I get in the passenger's side, and Wayne's halfway down the street, it seems, before I can close the door or buckle myself in.

"Now let's get one thing straight," he says. "This ends."

I'm not sure what "this" refers to. Me and him. Me and Jamie. Me, period. I nod anyway.

Somehow, we get home in one piece. *Home.* I wonder if I'll ever feel this way in this house again, if I'm about to be kicked out, or if Wayne will choose to leave.

Wayne slams his hand against the steering wheel.

"I'm sorry," I whisper, but I know it's not enough.

He turns to me, his face contorted in anger, in misery, in sadness. In it, I see him: the man—no, the boy—I met in front of a nursing home a lifetime ago when everything was different.

"Time for dinner," he whispers.

I follow him into the house, watch as he slams plates and forks and knives on the table. "Well?" he says.

I lift the cover off the crockpot, and the steam hits me in the face. I stick a fork in the carrots and potatoes. Done. Like me. Like this marriage. I assemble the roast on a plate. Spoon the carrots and potatoes into bowls. Wayne goes through one beer and then another by the time I have everything on the table. He opens two more cans and holds one out to me. I shake my head and wrinkle my nose. The odor nauseates me.

"No," he says. "Tonight, my wife and I are going to enjoy ourselves. Have us a couple of drinks so we can talk. And get relaxed. For later." His voice lingers on the word "later." He holds out the can. "Take it."

I do, hoping that will be enough. He watches me expectantly.

"Well," he says. "Drink."

"Wayne. Please."

He bangs his fist against the refrigerator door sending magnets and drawings and report cards to the floor. "Drink, goddammit!" he screams.

"Okay, okay." Only when I hold the can to my lips, do I realize how much I'm shaking. I gulp once, twice, grimace as I force the liquid down my throat. I gag.

"Better, honey?" He drains his can, throws it into the sink, opens the fridge, and gets another two cans. "Sit," he says, motioning to my chair. I do. "A toast," he continues, holding up his can, watching me expectantly. I close my eyes and lift mine. "To us." He hits my can with his, hard. Beer jumps out of the top. "Can't have a toast, unless you drink."

"Please," I plead.

"You have a choice. Drink yourself. Or I'll pour it down your throat."

I open my eyes and stare at his, filled with loathing. I drink.

"Keep going."

I drink.

"You can do it."

I drink.

"Thatta girl." He places another can before me. "Now, eat."

He digs in as if he hasn't seen food in a month. The room spins. He plops some meat and carrots onto my plate and points to the beer can.

Wooziness washes over me. I shake my head, but he picks it up and holds it in front of my face. I take the smallest sip I can manage, gag, and wretch. Satisfied I'm in hell, he turns back to his food.

"So," he says, his mouth full. "Were you ever going to come clean? Or were you waiting for all our daughters to catch you in the act?"

I burp bile and beer. "I'm sorry."

"I'm sorry, I'm sorry," he mimics. "That doesn't answer my question."

"What?"

"Were you ever going to tell me?"

My stomach turns. "I don't know."

"What *do* you know?"

I shake my head.

"Do you love him?" he whispers. "Do you know that?"

"Wayne—"

He slams his hand on the table. My fork falls to the floor. "Answer me! Do you love him?"

"I don't know!" Tears spill down my cheeks.

"Oh, for chrissakes, save it," he spits, pieces of meat and carrot flying from his mouth. "Just fucking save it."

"I never planned for it to happen. It just happened."

He spreads his right hand over his heart. "Oh, yeah? Well that's a goddamn relief now, isn't it? You didn't plan to fuck the cripple. You did it by accident. I realize I'm not the brightest bulb on the tree, honey—you've made that clear over the years—but how does that happen, huh? Fucking by accident?"

"It wasn't—"

"Oh, sorry. That's right. I'm sure it wasn't fucking. Such a vulgar term. I'm sure you and the kid—yeah, how old is he anyway? Does he shave yet? Yeah, I'm sure it was 'making love.'" He takes a swig of beer and wipes his mouth on the back of his arm.

"I can't talk to you when you're like this."

He eyes me while he takes an extra long gulp and crushes the can with his bare hand, hands that at one time, I used to marvel at, trace their contours with my index finder. "When I'm like what?"

"This."

"Yeah, and what exactly is 'this'?"

"A drunken asshole. I mean, my God, Wayne. What the fuck happened to you?" Amusement plays on his face. He grins. I push my chair back and stand. "I've had enough," I say. I turn to walk away, to where I don't know, but he grabs my arm, digs his nails into my skin, and twists until it almost breaks.

"Oh, honey," he says, his voice low and even. "We're just getting started."

Chapter 28

"We got the last Wii in the store," Kat says, holding up a box to Mom who sits propped up on pillows in bed. Mom is bundled from head to toe, always cold, a bright pink cap covering her peach-fuzzy head, her hair starting to return since she's stopped all chemo. Her eye sockets are sunken, her face gaunt. Kat keeps telling me I have to prepare myself, that this is it, and that everyone knows it: the doctors, Kat, even Mom herself. The goal right now is to have her see one more Christmas. I've never liked goals that seem impossible to reach, and seeing my mother this sick, this helpless, this small—it brings up too many bad memories of the days when Dad was sick and of years lost as a result, and I find myself crying more now than I ever have, as if I'm making up for all the tears I didn't shed then when I was so desperately trying to be a kid.

Kat paws through the five enormous shopping bags at her feet: Best Buy, Toys "R" Us, Barnes & Noble, Macy's. She plucks a colorful box with a clear plastic window. Inside is realistic parrot-like bird perched on a branch. The bottom of the box reads "Squawkers McCaw," one of the hot items from Hasbro's "Fur Real Friends" line.

"This is for Iris," Kat says. "Since I'm sure Koty and Wayne don't need a real one in the house, even though Iris says it wouldn't be a problem."

"Yeah. No problem for the cat." I shake my head. "Iris and her animals. We'd have a farm if it were up to her. But if she keeps up with these antics in school, she won't be getting anything." It's only November, and I've been called to the school no fewer than six times for various reasons: Iris shoving some girls who were making fun of her for wanting to play with the boys at recess, Iris giving lip to her science teacher because she thinks he's "dumb" and doesn't know what he's talking about, Iris being Iris.

"Don't be a Grinch," Kat says, and I inwardly cringe and think uncharitable thoughts. What the hell does Kat know about parenthood anyway? She's an every-other-weekend stepparent to two boys who are teenagers and mostly on their own. But before I can let these thoughts consume me, Kat moves on to another bag and produces a jewelry box with a sterling silver claddagh ring. "For Rosie," she says, while placing it on top of Mom's blanket.

Mom coughs, nods, and attempts a smile. "Lovely," she wheezes. "And Daisy?"

"Ah, yes, DD," Kat says. I've never glommed onto the Daisy Diva nickname or its acronym, probably because I'm afraid it might be too accurate. "It took some convincing, but Koty's okay with my giving her a sewing machine, plus lessons, by me, of course."

I shrug. "She seems young, that's all."

"She's creative," Kat says. "Besides, she asked for it. What other seven-year-old do you know who watches *Project Runway* every week?"

"It'll be good for her," Mom says. "And for you. Gives Kat some time with her, and you some time alone."

"Um," I say. "That takes care of one of them. I'll still have the other three, you know."

Kat arches her left brow. "Three? Did you have another kid when I wasn't looking?"

"I was referring to Wayne. He might as well be the fourth child."

Kat chuckles and Mom smiles, but they move on to another bag without questioning me further. I guess this is what it's come to—my life is predictable: troubled middle child, diva youngest child, oldest child getting into jewelry and makeup, and husband who acts like a spoiled brat more days than not. It's become expected and the norm, so much so that any complaints on my part are met with polite chuckles, smiles, nods, and then, nothing.

The bags finally emptied, Kat surveys the bounty from our five a.m. day-after-Thanksgiving shopping venture. "A good start," she says. "I better go hide some of this stuff before Dennis gets home." She gathers up some of the boxes and whisks them out of the room, leaving Mom and me staring at each other, something I can't stand because it's as if death himself is giving me the hairy eyeball. Kat's been the one "dealing" with our mother's illness, her second relapse, her hospice care. I can't. Everyone has a breaking point, and this might be it for me. I feel the cracks forming already, widening with each breath she gasps, each moment we have left. I've been avoiding being alone with her, and I know she knows it.

I jump to my feet. "I should get going."

My mother sputters, attempts to sit up straighter, and holds out her trembling hand. "Wait," she says, while patting the side of the bed, gesturing for me to sit. I do, in spite of myself. "I've been wanting to talk to you."

"Okay."

"When your father had his stroke, I fell apart. For six long years, I was broken. Kat, too, because I let her, because I welcomed the company." She pauses and takes two deep breaths. "I'm sorry. I'm sorry for doing that to you, for doing that to your childhood."

"Mom, you don't need to apologize—"

"Let me finish. I do need to apologize. I need to say it, and I need you to hear it, because I need you to keep this in mind when you lose me. Don't fall apart. Don't lose yourself in mourning. You have too much to live for. Your girls. Your marriage. And *you*, Koty. You have yourself, too."

She holds out her hand again, and this time I take it in my own, all the while nodding my head furiously, trying not to cry. "Mom, please."

She smiles a thin smile. "No amount of 'pleases' will change what's coming. I'm okay with it. It's time. I'm tired. But I need you to promise me something." She stops, closes her eyes, and leans back in the pillows. "Promise me that you'll *live,* that you won't fall apart."

"How can you ask me that? You're my mother."

"Precisely," she says. "I can ask that because I'm your mother. And because you, too, are a mother. A wonderful mother to those three girls. I'm sorry for that, too, you know."

"For what?"

"For ever suggesting you didn't need to keep Rosie. You proved me wrong when your father died and showed me that it is possible to go on and be happy. And you proved me wrong when you got pregnant. You, my love, are a wonderful, wonderful mother."

Before I can speak or sob or run away, Kat returns and gathers up more of the goods. "I think I need an extra room for all this loot."

"You'll have one soon enough," Mom says with a laugh.

"Ha, ha," Kat says so easily, as if she's completely at peace with my mother's upcoming demise.

I stand again, determined to get out the door this time.

"Leaving?" Kat asks.

"Yep."

"Grab some of those bags, will you? Bring 'em to my room before you go." She picks up three boxes, bright and cheery in their reds and greens and golds, and balances them carefully as she makes her way out the door. I collect bags from Macy's and Sports Authority, the whole time sensing my mother's eyes on me. I walk quickly to the door and am almost through when she speaks.

"Dakota," she says. I turn and face her. "Remember what I said. Promise me."

I nod, and with that one gesture, I do.

Chapter 29

December 2008

He snores now, passed out.

For what felt like hours, I'd been outside my body, watching him do his thing despite a voice pleading, "No, stop! Please, no." Another voice, his, had responded back: "You are my wife. I am your husband. This is what wives and husbands do." But now I'm back inside this body, my body, which aches and hurts all over, from the inside out.

I'm naked.

I'm cold.

I'm dirty.

I want to wash myself off. I fall out of the bed, wretch, dry heave, pick myself up, and claw my way to the bureau, surprised that my legs work.

I'm dirty.

I open the top drawer, his boxers and my underwear and nighties, side by side. My hands shaking, I rummage through the material, grab a piece of fabric, and pull a nightgown over my head, desperate to cover myself. Only then do I realize what I've selected, one of the slutty pieces of "lingerie" he bought me over the years. I slam the drawer shut in disgust, not even bothering to change. Wayne doesn't stir, the deepest sleeper I've ever met, even more so when he's passed out drunk, but something inside the drawer rattles.

Of course.

I open it again and grope beneath our undergarments until my fingers graze the cold metal. My fingers curl around its finger-grooved grip, my will stronger than it's ever been, my desire fueled by hate for him and love for my children, for Jamie, for myself, a combination more dangerous than any weapon of mass destruction. Shaking and sobbing, I climb back onto the bed, sit on my knees, hold it to my sleeping husband's head, remembering what Jamie taught from that one lesson, and beg myself to do it. But I stop. Gulp air. "Nooooo," I wail through gritted teeth, and the sound that emanates from deep within me doesn't even sound human. I re-aim the gun at my own temple, take a deep breath, close my eyes, see my children, and sob all that much harder because I can't, I won't leave my kids with him, can't do this anymore, can't get away from him, not fully, not forever, not as long as he's alive. I move the gun back to Wayne's head.

Tears and snot seep onto my tongue, and all I taste is salt. I put my finger on the trigger, knowing my girls will be better off with my sister after I kill Wayne and myself, without a mother in jail, and Jamie's words throb in my ears—*Noble is giving your life for your country, for a brother, for a friend, for a child.* "For you," I whisper.

"No!" a voice screams, and something tackles me. Me and it fall to the floor and roll and roll until we're out the door and into the hallway. *Bang.* My cheek's on fire, bursting with pain. Warmth oozes down the side of my face, my neck, and colors the front of my nightgown red. Something's wounded, but it's not me, it can't be me, because I hear crying coming from somewhere else. I struggle to sit up and identify the source. It sits, a lump against the wall. It's holding the gun.

"Iris," I say, but no sound comes out of my mouth. I try again. "Iris."

Her glassy eyes search for mine, while I touch my cheek and pull back a bloody hand.

"It's okay. It's okay. Come here, baby," I whisper as I try to make sense of it all, of what just happened, of what was about to happen, of where we are. The hallway. Outside my bedroom. *Wayne.* I crawl toward the door and glance in. He remains passed out, oblivious. A random memory releases in this absurd moment, him joking once, long ago, that when he's out, he's out. That he could sleep through the apocalypse.

"Iris, come here," I say again, and this time my voice sounds more like my own. "Give me the gun. Iris, please."

She doesn't move. Her eyes are wide, her face is pale, but her hand is clutched too tight around the gun. "Iris," I begin again, reaching out my arms. "Give me the gun. Before your father wakes up." I attempt to crawl but stop when I see her move, lifting the piece, pointing it at me.

"No," she says.

"Iris!"

"I won't let you hurt him."

"Iris. Listen to me."

"Whore," she says, but her voice breaks because she's crying.

The word hits me with such force, more force than a bullet ever could.

"Whore!"

I shrink back, further and further, until I'm against the wall.

"Whore!"

Blood drips from my face. My stomach lurches into my throat. I inch along the wall, down the hallway.

"Whore!"

I pick myself up, frantic and desperate to get away from her, chased out by one hate-filled word, a word spoken by my own child, my own little girl. I stumble down the hall and trip over the pile of shoes by the door, including my own. I pull on my sneakers and haul myself up, hands gripping the junk table covered in permission slips, wayward homework assignments, and my phone. My head pounds, the blood drips, and the pain inside is beyond anything I've ever experienced. I pull the cell from its charger, don't think, and run.

II

March 2014

Chapter 30

Iris

My first gay memory, almost nine years ago: I'm seven years old and playing in one of those plastic wading pools with Isabella, who is the prettiest, prissiest girl I've ever been friends with. I must be at her house, because I have no memories of my sisters, no memory of anyone but the two of us.

I watch Isabella giggle and splash about in her neon pink bikini, and that's when desire overwhelms every inch of my second-grader body. I need to know if her *down there* looks like my *down there*. I sidle up next to her, giggling as well. Water clings to her inch-long blonde eyelashes. Her skin is berry brown, her hair almost white. I reach out and stroke her soft cheek. She smiles, still giggling. My hand slides down her cheek to her neck, and then across the shimmery pink material of her bikini top, until it stops below her belly button. The fabric from her bikini bottom grazes my skin. She's not giggling anymore, and I peer into her curious face. I slide my fingers until they're between her skin and the bikini's fabric. She goose pimples. I pull, hesitating at first, and then with more determination.

I peek.

Her *down there* is just like mine: creamy white with a fine slit. I let go. "You can look at mine," I whisper and my legs shake. I feel her fingers tug at my bathing suit briefs suctioned to my body. I feel the air *woosh* around me down there. I feel her eyes on it, on me, and my heart beats like a thousand hummingbird wings. I want her to look down there forever. I want to feel what I feel down there forever, all juicy and wet.

Of course, at the time, I had no way of verbalizing any of this, but I remember as if it were yesterday, even now at the age of fifteen. Isabella was curious, sure. For me, however, it went beyond curiosity. It always has. It's what ruined everything, too.

#

I know something's up the minute Dad calls for a family meeting. The fact we never have family meetings is the first clue. His pale face is the other.

We sit around the kitchen table, and even though Dad insists we eat as a family as much as possible, it feels different being together like this, awkward even. Daisy snaps her banana-scented gum, her fingers with their wild neon green nail polish (she says it's going to be *the* color for spring) texting a mile a minute over the latest iPhone she got for Christmas. Rosie's eyes are wide, her pupils dilated, and I wonder if she knows what this meeting is about.

Dad clears his throat, once, twice. He sips his cranberry juice. He drops his chin to his chest. "I don't know how to tell you this, so I'm just going to say it." He pauses. "They've found your mother's body."

From the corner of my eye, I see Daisy's hands stop in mid air. Rosie gasps. I sit still and wait, watching him. He lifts his head, and his gaze meets mine.

"Where?" I whisper.

"Maine."

"Maine?" Rosie says. "Why was she in Maine?"

"Where in Maine?" I ask.

"In a wooded area off the Maine Turnpike. Land being excavated. A construction crew found human remains." His voice is matter of fact, almost like my chemistry teacher when he's explaining the details of our next experiment.

"Was she," I start and stop. "Was she murdered?" For the last five years and three months, we've heard countless theories about Mom's disappearance: running off, suicide, something more sinister.

"*Iris,*" Rosie hisses, and she gestures toward Daisy as if to say, "Not here."

I ignore her. "So?" I say again to Dad.

"The FBI believes so, yes."

"FBI?" Rosie says.

"Do they know how she died?" I ask.

Dad closes his eyes. "Iris—"

"Tell us, Dad. You have to tell us."

He nods, opens them, and focuses on me. "Her injuries, or so I've been told, were consistent with a fall from a significant height." He stops, his eyes never leaving mine. It's as if we're the only ones in the room, my sisters invisible.

"Wait. She *fell*?" Rosie says.

"That's what I've been told," Dad says, though he doesn't sound as if he believes it either.

"But it was murder, right?" I say. "Like, she was pushed or something? Or did she jump?"

"They're still investigating," he says. "They don't know the who or the what or the why yet."

"So then they don't know for sure if it was murder or if she jumped," I say.

"She didn't bury herself, Iris," Rosie says, clearly irritated that I'm suggesting suicide. Daisy leaps out of her chair and runs to the bathroom.

Rosie follows her. I stay put, staring at Dad. His eyes, filled with so much pain and fear, stay fixed on mine. I've grown accustomed to this. It's how he always regards me. With Rosie and Daisy, he looks at them the way a father should: with pride in moments, with annoyance in others. But with me, it's always been this, or at least it has since that night when everything changed. When Mom disappeared along with my memories of a twelve-hour period.

#

I find Rosie and Daisy in Daisy's bed. Her room is typical for a twelve-year-old kid, I guess, in that it's covered in clothes: the bed, the floor, the butterfly chair. The thing that makes Daisy different is that she makes all her own clothes. She has every season of *Project Runway* on BluRay, and she subscribes to *Vogue* (Dad refuses to let her get the adult version of *Cosmo*, but I know she subscribes to something online). Aunt Kat used to say Daisy was born a diva, which is how she got her nickname DD: Daisy Diva. She's been getting mad lately when we call her this because, she says, "the childhood moniker doesn't serve someone entering her thirteenth year." Yeah, her words. She can sound extremely grownup, like the genius she's been labeled by the schools. That is, when she's not trying to hide it by talking "valley girl" with all her "like, like, likes."

Daisy doesn't appear like a diva right now, however, with her puffy red eyes and trails of black mascara. Of the three of us, she's the one who cries as easily as she laughs, and sometimes her tears and giggles happen during the same conversation. She leans her head against Rosie, who's always had a maternal streak and slipped into the mother role once Mom was gone, and maybe even before, now that I think about it. If Rosie were an animal, she'd be a mama elephant, of this I have no doubt, always herding us away from trouble, taking care of us, loving us. Daisy would be a peacock, I think, proud to show off her beautiful feathered tail. And me? I'm the platypus, I guess, the freak of nature, the lost middle child, the kid people glance at sideways since everyone assumes I know more about my mother's disappearance than I've ever let on.

I sit on the edge of the bed and touch Daisy's foot, her toenails the same neon green as her fingernails. She wears a silver ring on her big toe. She shakes me off and turns her head into Rosie's chest. Rosie looks at me over Daisy's wild curls, the same texture as Mom's used to be. Dad said he won't let her straighten her hair until she's older. "Like when?" Daisy will ask. "Like when you're forty," is always his reply.

Rosie and me, we speak with our eyes. It's as if I can read her mind, which I know irritates her since she's not as adept at reading mine. Right now, her eyes are asking, "Did he saying anything more?" I shake my head.

"I always knew," Daisy says, her voice muffled but still understandable. She sniffles, pulls away from Rosie, and sits up. "I knew she'd never leave us on her own."

"I think we all knew that," Rosie says while fiddling with the strings from her green and gold hoodie, our school colors, the letters "GCH" on the front above her left boob.

"Maybe now you'll remember something, Iris," Daisy says. "You know, like they say on cop shows and psycho dramas on TV. Maybe this will trigger your memory."

The thought had already crossed my mind. In many ways, it's what I fear most. Daisy's right: we all knew, even in those early hours and days, that Mom was gone for good. While the rest of the town questioned whether she had run off, we knew she wouldn't have left us of her own free will, at least not forever. But it was the *how* and *who* that frightened me. Who took her? Who killed her? What did I see? How was I involved? Was Dad involved?

"Do you think," Daisy says while rubbing her eyes, "that they're gonna, like, come after Daddy again? The cops, I mean." She's the only one who still calls Dad "Daddy."

"Only if he had something to do with it." The words escape my mouth before I can stop them.

"Iris!" Rosie shakes her head, her cheeks pink.

Daisy narrows her eyes and scrunches her eyebrows, which are so light you can barely see them. "You remember something," she says to me, a statement, not a question.

"No. But if he was, you know, involved—"

"He wasn't," Rosie says. She leans back in the bed and crosses her arms. "I know Dad's not perfect, but he wouldn't have. He wouldn't have killed her."

Daisy starts peeling off her nail polish, and flecks of neon green drop onto her bright pink comforter. "Was he involved, Iris? Tell us. If you remember something, you need to tell us."

"I said I don't remember anything. God. Don't you two ever listen?"

"Are we gonna have a funeral?" Daisy whispers.

Rosie nods. "Probably."

Daisy's face crumples, and she starts crying again. Rosie envelops her. I sit and stare. I want to cry, too, but I can't.

#

I wander out of Daisy's room, unsure where to be or what to do. I don't want to be alone, but I can't stay with them and their heartbreak. I make my way down the hall and back to the kitchen. Dad remains at the table, his hand still wrapped around his glass of juice. He hasn't had a drink since Mom disappeared, and even though he doesn't talk about it, I know he goes to AA meetings. I sit across from him. His face is weathered and so much older than other dads his age. "Hey, Buttercup," he says weakly. He used to call all of us "Buttercup," but I'm the only one who lets him use the pet name anymore. At seventeen, Rosie is definitely too old for such cuteness, and Daisy's got her other nickname to deal with. As for me? Even though I'm fifteen—almost sixteen and a sophomore in high school, for crying out loud—it's comforting in a way, the one thing that I can hold onto from before Mom left, since it feels like every other part of my life changed after she was gone. I don't have any friends, and making fun of me is an afterthought for most kids at school, since I do my best to be invisible. No one has any idea how much effort goes into that.

"How are your sisters doing?" he asks.

I shrug. "Okay, I guess."

"And you?" He studies my face, searching for something lost a long time ago, something I'm convinced he wants to remain lost, whatever that something is.

I shrug again and say nothing.

"Listen," he begins slowly. "If you start remembering anything, you need to come to me first. Okay?"

I nod.

"I mean it, Iris. Not Rosie, not Daisy, not Aunt Kat. Me. You can tell me anything. You know that, right?"

I'm gay, Dad. I'm gay. Can you handle that? "What do you think I'll remember?"

"I don't know."

I don't believe him. "You still think I know something, don't you?"

"Given what we know now ..." He stops and takes a deep breath. "Given where they found her and how they think she died, I'd say the chance of your knowing anything is probably slim. Which explains why you haven't been able to remember anything. Maybe there's nothing *to* remember."

"But I must have seen her that night or that morning. Heard where she was going, seen who she left with, right?"

"Iris, stop. We've been through this before. We can't assume any of that."

"Why not?"

"It's been so long and you've been thinking about it so hard and from so many different vantage points that I'm not sure I'd even trust anything you remember at this point."

"What do you think happened to her?"

He wraps his hands around his glass of untouched juice. "I don't know."

"Do you want to know?"

He lowers his eyes and grips the glass tighter. "Time for bed," he says, our conversation over, for now.

Cream Puff, our old cat, comes limping into the kitchen, spots me, and rubs up against my legs. I've always been her favorite. I pick her up, cradle her like a baby, and scratch her belly. She purrs happiness. Still carrying her, I stand and wander back the same way I came, thinking about what I do know: I didn't slice the ear off Kenny Landau's cat. It was *his* experiment. *His* idea. *His* hand. Kenny was more devious than I ever was and hardly got caught for his transgressions. The few times he was caught, he lied better than anyone I'd ever seen. But me? I got in trouble. A lot. Especially in those weeks leading up to Mom's disappearance. So it was easy for everyone, including Mom and Dad, to believe that I'd hurt his cat. What everyone forgot is this: I suck at lying. If I refuse to answer, that's one thing, but if you ask me point blank whether I did this or that or if this or that happened, I'll tell you the truth, even if it doesn't paint me in the best light, even if it doesn't paint others in the best light.

Provided, of course, I can remember.

Chapter 31

Daisy

People think I don't remember her. I remind them I was seven when she disappeared, not three or four. I have memories. Lots of 'em. Like the time we went to the Butterfly Place in Massachusetts, just the two of us, since she tried to give us what she called "one-on-one" time, and she knew how much I loved butterflies, the colorful kind like the blue morpho butterfly and the green birdwing, which I'd read about all on my own when I hijacked the computer one afternoon when no one was paying any attention to me. I was four and a half, and, apparently, this was one of many reasons Mom fought to have me start kindergarten early rather than wait a year, since I was a November birthday. Anyhow, I remember standing with her in the middle of the indoor atrium at the Butterfly Place, bombarded by color: electric oranges, bright yellows, reds that could put sunsets to shame. The flapping of wings. The exotic feel of the air. The freedom. My tummy somersaulted, and I spun around, flapping my arms, desperately wanting to fly, too, but it occurred to me that despite all this flapping, the flying was in vain, for me and for the butterflies. I started to cry.

"Sweetheart," Mom asked, alarmed. "What's wrong?"

"They can fly," I'd said. "But they can't go anywhere."

I also remember the fighting, the times Daddy came home, red-faced and loud, which became our measuring stick for how to behave. He never hit us, and I saw him hit my mother only once that I can remember, a slap across the face, after she'd gotten up close into his. He apologized more to us than he did to her, and I remember his face didn't get red or his voice loud for a long time after that, months even. That's how it went in our family.

Being the youngest, I got away with much more crap than my sisters, but I also was an afterthought, the person whose opinions mattered least, despite the fact everyone thought I was smart. I think that's one of the reasons I turned to fashion. I can express myself, my mood, with clothes without ever opening my mouth, and everyone hears. Everyone listens.

So what's it like to have a mother who vanished? To have a father suspected of being involved in her disappearance? To hear rumors of her affair with another man?

I may have been only seven, and I might not have understood everything I heard, but that's the thing: I could hear, and I did listen, that's the bottom line. In fact, I heard more than Rosie or Iris did, I think, mainly because people forgot I was there or they figured I was too absorbed with designing outfits for my Bratz dolls to be paying the grownups any attention. I started hearing the moment Rosie and I got home from school that fateful afternoon. Mom's car was in the driveway. So was Daddy's work van, along with his pickup truck. Iris was sick, or so Aunty had said once she got in touch with Daddy that morning after discovering that Iris wasn't with us when she woke us up for school.

Anyway, I raced in our house, stripping off my coat and scarf and mittens, leaving them in a trail behind me because I knew Rosie would pick them up (okay, so the "diva" moniker might have been fair back then, but it's so *not* fair now, okay?). I ran through the living room, pausing to see if any new gifts had been added under the tree. *Nothing!* I traipsed into the kitchen, expecting to find Mom and remembering something she'd said earlier that week about baking Christmas cookies. Instead, I found Daddy sitting at the kitchen table, his face pasty white like the glue we used in art class. A candle was burning, Mom's favorite from Yankee Candle Company. The room smelled like apple pie and a hint of something else, like the stuff Mom used to clean the bathrooms.

"Daddy!" I said, breathless, as I wrapped my arms around him. I was an "affectionate child," Mom used to say, and loved doling out hugs and kisses to anyone who'd accept them, and I never felt I got enough from Daddy. Having him home in the afternoon was a treat. Did he hug me back? I don't remember, because right after I was through hugging him, I was looking for Mom. I stood in the middle of the kitchen, waiting.

"Where's Mommy?"

Daddy didn't answer, just stared blankly ahead. Rosie had come in by now, having, no doubt, hung up our coats like the good daughter she was.

"Hi, Dad," she said. "Where's Mom?"

He still didn't answer, and I tugged on his flannel shirt. "Daddy?"

He jumped. "Huh?"

"Where's Mom?" Rosie asked again.

He took a deep breath. "I don't know. She's not here."

"But her car's in the driveway," Rosie said.

"I don't know where she is."

"Maybe she went for a walk," I offered, since I knew how much she enjoyed walking through the woods, almost as much as we kids did. "Oh, wait!" I said. "I know. She's probably visiting what's-his-name."

"Jamie," Rosie said.

"Yeah, him." I opened the fridge and foraged through Tupperware containers. Rosie joined me, closed the door, redirected me to the table, and opened the freezer door for my favorite ice cream: Brigham's chocolate.

I sat at the table and swung my legs. "Is Iris still sick?"

Dad cleared his throat. "Yes."

"I'll check in on her," Rosie said.

"No!" Daddy's voice boomed. Now I jumped, and Rosie dropped the ice cream scoop into the sink. It clanked and clunked. Daddy was a lot of things, but he wasn't a screamer. "She's in bed. I don't want you disturbing her. I'll check in on her. Okay?" He directed the question to Rosie who stood stiff as a statue at the sink, her face ghost white. She nodded. He stood.

"You girls do your homework." He began his retreat out of the room, stopped, and turned around. "It's going to be okay. Got it?"

Rosie and I nodded. "Got it, Daddy," I said, as the hairs on the back of my neck stood up.

#

Dinnertime, and Mom still hadn't returned. I sat at the kitchen table working on my third letter to Santa while Rosie stared at her books, the little black and white TV on the counter our only accompaniment. The waning minutes of *Dr. Phil,* I think. Mom's candle still burned, and I could barely detect that other smell, the cleaning stuff. Daddy wandered in, considered us, glanced at the clock, and opened the freezer door. He pulled out a frozen pizza and bag of tater tots (my favorite) and asked Rosie to cook them. He opened a can of chicken noodle soup, poured it in a bowl, and heated it in the microwave.

"Dad?" Rosie asked. "What about Mom?"

He watched the microwave as it counted down the minutes and seconds. "Try her on her cell. Let's hope she has it with her and it's on."

Rosie nodded, pulled her own cell phone out of her jeans pocket, and hit one button. She put it to her ear and waited. She was close enough to me that I could hear the muffled sound of Mom's message. It had gone right to voice mail. Rosie shook her head. "What should we do?" she asked.

"Hey," I pointed to the TV. The weatherman stood in front of his map, and I read some of the words on the bullet point list: ice storm, power outages, freezing temperatures. "Maybe we won't have school tomorrow." I turned my head, trying to gauge Daddy's reaction, since Mom was usually the first to say, "Don't count on it."

He considered the TV, his jaw tight, but he said nothing. Maybe we *weren't* going to have school, and my belly flip-flopped with the possibilities. School, even at that age when it was supposed to still be fun, bored me. This was because I was more "advanced," according to Mom.

"Daddy?" Rosie whispered. She hardly ever said "Daddy" anymore. He turned to her. "I'm worried about Mom."

The microwave dinged, and he ignored Rosie and opened the door. He snatched two potholders hanging from a clip stuck to the fridge and pulled out the steaming bowl of soup. "I'm sure everything's fine," he said.

"When's the last time you saw her? I mean, did you go to work today?"

"Iris is sick. I stayed home."

"Wasn't Mom here?"

He blew on the soup, selected a large spoon from the silverware drawer, and wrapped a dishtowel around the bowl. "No," he said. "I haven't seen your mother since last night when I went to bed."

"But where would she have gone? Her car—"

"Rosie," he said in that voice that usually made us all quiet. "I don't know where she is. If I knew, I'd tell you." He paused, looked at us, and his face softened. "Listen, your mom and I had a fight last night. When I got up this morning, she was already gone. I think she's mad at me, that's all. Went somewhere to cool off. She's probably at your Aunt Kat's now, yapping away."

Rosie's eyes lit up. "I'll call Aunty."

"No," he said.

"Why not?"

He had a funny expression on his face, like he'd just swallowed something yucky. Finally, he spoke. "Sure. Go ahead. I was thinking I didn't want to worry your aunt if your mom's not there, but she probably is. I'm going to take this soup into Iris. If you get ahold of Mom, tell her I can pick her up."

He disappeared down the hall, and Rosie took her phone, pressed another button, and held it to her ear. One ring, two rings.

"Aunty? It's me, Rosie. Is Mom there?" Pause. "No. Dad said they had a fight last night and that when he woke up, she was already gone and had probably gone somewhere to cool off." Pause. "She's okay, I guess. Still sick. Dad's giving her soup right now." Pause. "Okay. Love you, too. Bye."

"What'd she say?" I asked.

"She hasn't heard from her. Not since Mom dropped us off last night. She wants Dad to call her."

The hairs on the back of my neck prickled again. This time when my tummy somersaulted, I felt sick. "Rosie? I don't feel so good."

She held the back of her wrist to my forehead like Mom always did. "You don't feel hot. How 'bout I cook up the tater tots? Those'll make you feel better."

I clung to her arm as she started to move away. "Wait. What if she's not okay?" She turned, and we stared at each other, the answer to that question hovering between us. I think, even in that moment, we knew. We knew something was wrong. It was dark out. No one had seen Mom all day. Her car was in the driveway.

Rosie shook me off and walked out of the kitchen. I followed her down the front hall. She paused at the table by the door.

"What?" I asked.

Rosie pointed to the table and Mom's empty cell phone charger. "Her phone was here when we left for Aunty's last night. I remember seeing it, because I'd left my candy bars on the table and picked 'em up before we left."

"So she has her phone with her. That's good, right?"

Rosie shrugged. "Do you remember the guy's last name?"

"What guy?"

"You know, him. Jamie," Rosie said, irritated.

I shrugged. "No. Why?"

"What is it?" she said, ignoring my question. She snapped her fingers. "Briggs! Jamie Briggs." Rosie pulled out her cell again. "Maybe she's there."

I stood by her as she dialed 411 and was connected with Jamie's house. She identified herself, asked for Mom, and listened. Finally, she spoke. "Okay. Well, thanks anyway."

"What'd he say?" I asked as she ended the call.

"It wasn't him. It was his mother." Rosie paused and even in the dim hallway, I could see tears pooling in her eyes. "She said Mom hadn't been there at all today."

"Maybe we should go look for her." I opened the door without thinking about coats or boots or mittens or anything else. Ice pellets smacked the porch. I shivered and glanced at Rosie who was staring at the bottom of the table. She bent down, examining something on the floor.

"What is it?" I asked, forgetting about the door and the weather.

"I think it's blood," she whispered as I struggled to see what she was looking at.

"Hey!" Daddy's voice called out. We both jumped. "What're you doing? Close the door, for God's sake."

I obeyed and then faced him.

"I called Aunty," Rosie began, "and Jamie Briggs. Dad, no one's seen her." She paused, her lip quivering. "Something's wrong." She pointed to the floor. "Look. I think that's blood."

Before Dad could respond, something moved behind him. It was Iris, dressed in her pajamas, pale-faced and expressionless.

"Iris?" Rosie ran to her, kneeled, and grabbed her by the shoulders. "Did you see Mom this morning? Did she say where she was going?" Iris stared at Rosie, her eyes empty.

"She has a fever," Dad said quietly while wrapping his arm around Iris's shoulders. "She's pretty out of it. Best we let her rest." He directed Iris back down the hallway toward her bedroom. Rosie remained on her knees. I patted her shoulder.

"Rosie?" I said. My legs felt like jelly, and the juices in my belly churned. "I'm scared." She reached for me, and I fell into her arms. She hugged me so tight I could barely breathe.

"Me, too," she said, rocking me back and forth. "Me, too."

#

Rosie made the tater tots and pizza, but none of us ate. Daddy called Uncle Hank after dinner.

"You two stay put, you hear?" Daddy said when he heard Uncle Hank's truck pull up in the driveway. He pulled on his parka, black leather gloves, and gray wool cap. Uncle Hank appeared in the doorway, quiet for once. "It's a mess out there," Daddy continued. "So I don't want you wandering outside. Got it?"

We nodded.

"I have my cell. You hear something, anything, you call me."

We nodded again. Outside, the wind howled. It sounded like someone was sliding marbles down the roof and throwing rocks against the side of the house. The lights winked. Dad squeezed his eyes shut. "Shit," he said. He opened his eyes. "Rosie, you know where the flashlights are, right?"

"Yes."

"And the candles?"

"Yes, but … you know," she said through clenched teeth. I knew what Rosie was referring to: she didn't like lighting matches. Usually it wasn't an issue since Iris was always jumping to do it and Mom said I was too young. I hated being the baby sometimes.

Daddy sighed. "If the lights go out, use the flashlights for now and call me. Okay?"

Rosie nodded.

"C'mon. Let's go," Daddy said to Uncle Hank, and they were gone.

We stood in the middle of the floor staring at the closed door.

"Maybe we should call the police?" I offered. Rosie shook her head. "Why not? Isn't that what you're supposed to do when a kid is missing?"

"Well, duh. Mom's not a kid," Rosie said. "She's a grownup. Besides, Dad might get mad."

Rosie walked into the living room and plopped down on the couch. I sat in front of the nativity scene and rearranged the donkey and sheep, all made of white porcelain. How many days until Christmas? I'd forgotten to rip the sheet off the day calendar in the kitchen. It's something I did every morning. *Except we weren't here this morning*, I reminded myself. *We were at Aunty's.* I wondered if anyone had ripped it off. What day was it anyway? Hm. Thursday. December 11, 2008. I squeezed my eyes shut and attempted the math in my head, but resorted to counting on my fingers. Fourteen days until Christmas. The ticklish feeling I always got when I thought about Christmas erupted in my stomach.

"Fourteen days until Christmas," I called out and clapped my hands and turned to Rosie who remained on the couch, tears trickling down her cheeks. I'd seen Rosie cry before, sure. But this? This was different. She hadn't been scolded (a rare event, but one that forced her to tears) or gotten a bad grade on her science test. She hadn't been pushed too far by Iris. She hadn't fallen climbing up a tree or found out that Brian Preston (her latest crush) liked somebody else. She was just sitting there, crying. All the anxiety and fear I'd been feeling before barreled toward me. Outside, something groaned, cracked, exploded. I jumped next to her and attempted to burrow my body into hers.

"What was that?" I yelped.

She pushed me aside, trembling, and got up. "I'm not sure."

I slid to the floor and scurried to her side, clasping her hand in mine. We walked to the front door. She opened it. The wind howled. Ice and snow fell on the porch. "It was the wind," she said.

She closed the door, locked it, and led me back to the couch. This time, I ignored the tree, the nativity scene, and all thoughts of Santa and Christmas. I sat practically in her lap, shaking. She took her phone, hit a button, and held it up to her ear. I could hear Mommy's recorded message. Again. She threw it in disgust, and it landed on the floor in front of us. I leaned down, picked it up, and traced my finger on the picture she had on the display window. It was one of her and Becky Lipton, her best friend, goofing around and making weird faces. Then I saw the time—9:35—and gasped. It was waaay past my bedtime. She snatched the phone from me.

"Maybe you should go to bed," she said.

"I want to wait for Mommy."

"Mom'll be pissed you're still up."

Rosie didn't usually use banned words like "piss." Iris did, but not Rosie. "I don't care," I said.

"There's nothing to do anyway. You might as well sleep."

"No."

"Daisy," she said, her voice low. "I'm not asking. If you want to get your ears pierced for Christmas, you better mind me now, or I'll tell."

I turned and faced her. She never sounded like this either. "Fine," I said, and as I got up, I made sure to step on her foot.

"Watch it, jerk," she spit as she began texting.

Something crashed overhead. The lights flickered once, twice. I shuddered and then yawned. Despite my best efforts, I was tired. Exhausted, actually.

"Rosie?"

"What?" she said, eyes still glued to her phone.

"What if they can't find her?"

She paused in mid type and looked up. Her eyes were her own again, kind and understanding. "They'll find her, DD. I promise. Now go to bed. I'll check on you in a little while."

Rosie's promise.

It hadn't been a lie. It's just that neither of us knew then that the "finding" wouldn't happen until five years later.

#

I watch as Rosie sets a teacup on my bedside table. I'm the only one in the house who drinks tea, and no one ever makes it right, but I'm grateful for it anyway. I pick up the cup and let its warmth seep into my hands.

"Better?" Rosie asks, which is enough to make the tears start again. She sits on the edge of my bed and averts her gaze.

"You didn't break your promise," I finally say, and she looks at me, confused. "Don't you remember? That night? You promised me they'd find her."

She nods. "Yeah. I remember. I always felt bad about that."

"You were trying to make me feel better. And trying to get me to go to bed, as I recall." I sip the tea. Peppermint. "Which was probably a good thing, since I didn't sleep much for months afterwards."

"Speaking of which."

"Right," I agree. "Bedtime."

She stands, stretches, and adjusts the scrunchy holding up her hair. There are moments, like this one, when all I see is Mom in her. It's more than the physical, which is obvious, since her hair is the same shade of auburn and the same tight curls as Mom had. It's her mannerisms, too, like the way she laughs or the way she puts her chin in her hand and watches you when you're talking. Out of the three of us, she knew Mom the longest, had the most time with her, so I suppose it makes sense that she would have sponged up more of Mom than Iris or me.

She's almost at my door when I say, "Will you stay?" and I'm not sure if I'm asking Rosie, my sister, or Rosie, the girl who reminds me of my mom. "Until I fall asleep?"

She smiles, nods, and settles into the sliding rocking chair across from me, the same chair that our mother nursed and soothed us in when we were babies. It had been in my room last, so it's stayed. We say nothing more. I sip my tea while she rocks, and for the gazillionth time, I pretend it's really Mom.

Chapter 32

Rosie

I envy Daisy's tears.

I mean, I want to cry. In moments like these, I begin to feel that familiar swell in my throat, dampness behind my eyelids, but then, nothing. I cried a lot in those days and months afterwards until it was clear, in my mind anyway, that she was gone, dead most likely, and not coming back. I cried over the mounting suspicion regarding my father, over the revelation about Mom and Jamie. I cried for Iris and Daisy and for our family. Eventually, I stopped (mostly) because someone in the family needed to rally. I'd always been the one to do it, the good daughter who minded her sisters, who hugged her sad mother, who appeased her angry father. So it made sense that I'd be the person to pick up the pieces. Problem was, the pieces were to a puzzle so large and confusing and made up of one hundred shades of red. Even if I were given three lifetimes, I knew I'd never complete it.

#

I watch as Daisy's breaths even out, slumber having won over sadness, for now, anyway. I leave her bedside lamp on and creep out of the room and into my own, right next to hers. I sit at my desk and stare at my books, my laptop, my cell phone. A few hours ago, I was doing a final proofread of my proposal for an independent study next year—my senior year in high school—in early childhood education, due tomorrow. Problem is, I'm not sure I'll be hopping out of bed in the morning for school, considering what's gone down tonight. I could email it, I suppose, although the directions for putting together the proposal made a big deal about submitting print copies. Seems so trivial now, these stupid directions. I mean, how do you go about your normal day-to-day stuff after learning your mother's body's been found? Her *murdered* body?

I shiver, pick up my cell phone, cradle it in my palms, and wonder if I should call him. I should text him, at the very least. I start typing, but I feel eyes on my back. I turn around.

Holding our old cat, Iris stands in the doorway. Actually, looms is more like it. She's fifteen, but almost six feet tall and Kenyan-runner skinny, like the track star she could be, if she chose to formally participate, which she doesn't. Informally, Iris is a running machine, always jogging at odd hours, and running simply for the sake of running, like that guy in *Forrest Gump*, which was one of Mom's favorite movies. Iris can also eat whatever she wants without gaining an ounce of weight. So annoying. When we went shopping for school last summer, she got jeans that were a size zero. *Zero.* Apropos, I suppose, since the girl suffers from major self-esteem issues and thinks of herself as "a nothing." Her words, not mine.

"Can I come in?" she says. I nod and watch as she falls onto my red beanbag chair on the floor. She stretches her legs, and they go on forever.

"DD okay?" she asks.

I shrug. "As good as can be expected, I guess. How you holding up?"

"I'm here," she says. "You?"

"I don't know. It's weird, you know? How can something that is so *not* a surprise still be?"

She nods, and I know she understands what I mean. Still, I don't feel comfort in this.

"Have you called him?" she asks.

Iris knows me too well, another thing that's annoying. I swivel in my chair and rearrange the books on my desk. "Who?" I ask, trying to sound as innocent as possible.

"You know who."

"Don't know what you're talking about."

"Rosie, cut the shit. Look at me."

I swivel again and face her.

"So have you?" She waits for me to say something, and when I don't, she sighs. "Be careful, okay?"

"Careful of what?"

"It's going to bring everything back up, Rosie. The affair. Her disappearance. Stuff with Dad."

"Old news," I say.

"Maybe. But the breaking news—that's what people will latch onto."

"As they should. I mean, my God, Iris. Our mother's body was found. Our mother's *murdered* body."

She shakes her head. "I'm not talking about that. I'm talking about you. And him."

"There's nothing going on with—"

"Stop," she interrupts. "Think about it. You work at the place he created."

"Well, it's not like there are many places to work around here."

"I've seen the two of you together."

"So?" I say, exasperated.

"I see the way you look at him."

I don't doubt this. I've never been good at hiding my feelings, but what she's failed to notice is that he's never returned the look. Unless! Is it possible she's seen something that I haven't? Hope flutters in my head, making me dizzy.

"Promise you'll be careful," Iris says. "Please."

I need to change this subject. Now. "What about you?" I say.

She blinks. Annoying thing number one hundred twelve about Iris: she doesn't realize how pretty she is, how her doe-brown eyes, long lashes, and zit-free skin appear so perfect all the time, unlike my pimple-prone forehead, nose, and chin.

"What about me?" she says.

"This is going to bring up stuff. For you, too, you know."

She dumps the cat to the floor. "You and Daisy already questioned me. So has Dad. I don't remember anything." She stands, and her eyes search my room, lost. On the rare occasions when she's opened up, she's said she doesn't feel she fits in anywhere. By the expression on her face, I sense this is how she's feeling right now. Without another word, she walks to my door, pauses, and turns around. "The truth is, maybe I'm afraid of what I'll remember. Did you ever think of that?"

I have, but she's gone before I can say it.

#

I drive Dad's old pickup around to the side of the building where I know he'll exit. Thursdays are extended hours at the Center, so I'm not surprised at the crowded parking lot. A wheelchair basketball tournament, I think. I spot his handicap van and park next to it.

I twirl my claddagh ring around my finger and blast the heat, which doesn't work all too well these days. I smack the dashboard, as if that will somehow help, and then feel around the back of the cab for a blanket Dad keeps for occasions like this. *Dad.* He hadn't questioned me when I asked for the keys, but I offered an explanation anyway: that I was dropping off my independent study proposal to a friend because it was due tomorrow and I didn't think I'd be up for going to school. He simply nodded as he sat at the kitchen table, staring straight ahead. I'd peeked in on Daisy, who was sound asleep, and as I shrugged into my coat in the hallway, Iris emerged from the shadows. She didn't say anything and neither did I, not that it mattered. She knew where I was going.

#

Talking and laughter erupt from the side doors as people spill out into the night. Some are in wheelchairs, others limp, and some show no outward sign of disability, even though I know that doesn't mean anything.

I sit and wait until the throngs diminish. Finally, I spot two familiar people. The first is Elmer, the old janitor. He holds the door for Jamie. They stand, chatting, until Elmer laughs so loud I can hear it clear across the parking lot behind closed windows. He slaps Jamie on the back, and then they walk in opposite directions, since Elmer usually circles the building at night looking for wayward teens making out in the dark. Not that he cares; he has a sick sense of humor and likes to scare the crap out of them. I've always liked him because of it.

I watch as Jamie approaches his van, trying to catch the moment when he recognizes that it's me in the pickup waiting next to it, and whether in that recognition there's a hint of something else: happiness, lust, joy, anything. Instead, all I sense is confusion. He comes up to my window, and I roll it down (yes, that's how old the pickup is).

"Hey," he says.

"Hey."

"What're you doing here? Were you at the game?"

"No. Just got here. Wanted to talk to you."

"Now? It's kinda late. Can't it wait until tomorrow? Or whenever you're on next?"

I grip the steering wheel tight and take a deep breath. "They found her, Jamie."

"What?" he asks, his face contorted in confusion.

"They found her." This time, I watch as the confusion dissolves into understanding. His eyes widen, his jaw twitches. He might even be trembling, but I could be imagining that.

"Where?" he asks, his voice flat.

"Some woods off the Maine Turnpike."

"Maine?"

I nod.

He lowers his eyes. "How?"

"She fell," I begin, but I don't know how to finish this. "From some place high up. But they don't know where or who or why. Anyway, I didn't hear all the details."

"She *fell*?"

"Yeah, but, you know, not on purpose."

"So she was murdered."

I nod my answer because I can't bring myself to say it out loud in front of him.

"When did you find out?"

"Tonight. At least, that's when Dad told us."

At the mention of my father, his face darkens. "Well. Thanks for letting me know." He pivots, but I reach out and touch his shoulder, the part of him that's real and not plastic or metal. I need to feel him, and I need him to feel me.

"Wait." As he turns to me, the thing I'd been wanting to happen all night happens: I start to cry.

"Rosie," he whispers, but there's urgency in his voice.

"I'm sorry. I just need someone to talk to. Please."

He sighs. "Okay. But not here."

"The diner?" I suggest, and he nods. On the outskirts of town, right before the exit to the interstate, is a late-night diner that serves breakfast all day.

"Right," he says. "I'll meet you there."

I compose myself and watch as he makes his way to the van, hoists himself inside, and waits for me to drive off first, which I do. I glance in the rearview mirror every now and then to make sure he's still there.

I think Iris thinks that I set out to fall in love with Jamie Briggs, but that's not true. It's not how it works, anyway, not that Iris would know. She keeps herself closed off from everyone in school, sitting alone at lunch—if she even goes. Most of the time she's holed up in the library. Iris doesn't have a best friend. She doesn't have any friends, period. I try including her sometimes with me and my friends, but she always declines, and I'll admit that a big part of me is relieved when she does. As for love? I know Iris is gay. I so don't care, and she'd deny it anyway, I'm sure, if it ever came up, and I can't point to one specific thing that makes me know, but I do. Out of the three of us, Iris has shouldered the biggest burden in terms of Mom. I mean, my God. She might have been there when it happened, even though we're not sure what "it" is. Of course, I carry the burden as well. I was the one who let Iris run off that night from Aunt Kat's house. I often wonder what would have happened if I'd gone after her. I might not have been able to save Mom. But maybe I could have saved Iris.

#

We pull into the diner—there are five cars and two eighteen wheelers in the parking lot—and I note the time: 10:23. Dad doesn't make us follow a curfew, mainly because he doesn't need to. Iris never goes out with people, only to run, and I'm the responsible one who always calls and provides firm times for arrivals and departures. Daisy's too young, although she's the one who'll probably need the most reining in, free spirit that she is.

I shiver in the cold night and walk behind Jamie as he lumbers to the door. The folks sitting by the window glance up and watch—he's always a spectacle wherever he goes, especially when his "legs" are in view like they are tonight, thanks to his gym shorts—but their eyes quickly turn to their bacon and home fries and scrambled eggs.

The waitress tells us to sit wherever, and we choose a booth in the corner by the window and slide in. Jamie is so adept in his world and I'm so used to the way he does things that I don't notice the differences—like how he has to navigate around tables or slide into booths—until I catch someone watching him. Here, though, it's comfortable, since the waitress has seen us both before. He orders coffee. I order pancakes and a water. Business taken care of for the moment, we sit in silence. He gazes out the window onto the parking lot, and I study his profile. He's what my best friend Becky would call delicious and super yummy, despite the scar that extends from his left ear and down his jaw line to his chin. Despite the fact he's thirty-one, fourteen years older than me. Despite the fact he and my mother were—

"So," he says while facing me.

"So," I say, and words fail me as they often do when I'm in his presence.

"How you holding up?"

"Okay. I guess."

"And your sisters?"

"Daisy took it hard. Iris is Iris."

The waitress arrives with his coffee and a glass of water for me. He nods. "And him?" He means my father. In all the time I've ever known Jamie, I've never heard him use my father's name.

I shrug. "I don't know."

He lifts the coffee cup to his lips with a prosthetic hand that works almost as well as mine. It's "truly innovative," according to Jamie, and one hundred times better than the hand he used even a few years ago.

"And you?" he says.

I feel myself begin to tear up, but I'm determined not to lose it this time. I turn my attention to the window and watch as two truckers climb into their cabs, but this leads my mind in a dangerous direction: truckers driving along a lonely stretch of highway, the Maine Turnpike, my mother buried in a grave, unmarked and uncared for. The tears come—I can't control them— and he lets me cry.

My tear ducts finally empty, I take a paper napkin out of the silver dispenser sitting on the table and wipe my face, trying hard to ignore the image that flashes in my head of what I must look like. Even the best waterproof mascara couldn't survive the flood from my eyeballs in the last hour.

"That's about how I'd expect you to feel," he says, but not in a jerky way.

Our waitress appears and sets a plate of steaming pancakes and syrup before me. My stomach turns at the sight of food.

"How are you?" I ask, because I know he must feel something as well.

We stare at each other, and I wonder if somewhere, somehow, Mom is watching us. I mean, there's nothing going on. Jamie's my boss, plain and simple, and that's all he's been since I started working at the Center two years ago. Actually, I first started by volunteering in the kids' room three years ago, babysitting children while their parents exercised. I don't think there's any way Jamie would have hired me if I'd come in off the street. I mean, I can understand why. *That* would have been weird. It still is weird, I suppose, but less so as time passes, since I worked myself into the organization in an innocent way, or so it seemed, when I simply asked the woman who ran Kids' Korner if I could volunteer since I had just gotten my babysitting certification and wanted experience. She was grateful for the help and never paid much attention to who I was, my last name, or the history between my parents and the founder of the Center for Abled Americans, Jamie Briggs. I failed to mention these facts to my father as well, instead simply telling him I was volunteering at a daycare center.

Of course, my motives were far from innocent. After Mom disappeared, I became pretty obsessed with Jamie, convincing myself that he knew something, even though, deep down, I knew he didn't. I was able to hide my obsession for a while, but when I turned fourteen, I saw a way to get closer to him by immersing myself in his world. By the time Jamie realized who I was, I'd been running Kids' Korner more efficiently during my ten hours a week of volunteer work than anyone else. He'd heard the good comments from kids and parents alike, so he let me be. When an actual paid position opened up a year later, I was the logical choice. It was the only logical thing about the whole situation, I suppose. Dad was not happy when he figured it all out, and we even fought about it. But he relented pretty fast. He'd gotten kinda Zen after joining AA, with forgiveness and the twelve steps and all that. Still, I do my best to avoid talking about work whenever Dad is around.

"How am I?" Jamie finally says. "I don't know how to answer that, Rosie." He pauses. "So when will they know?"

"When will who know what?"

He leans into the booth and whispers, "When will they know for sure how she died? Like what she might have fallen off *of*?"

"Oh. I don't know."

"Do they have any suspects?"

"No. Well, I don't think so."

"I always knew, you know? That she was gone. Dead."

"Yeah." I nod. "Me, too."

"Weird," he says.

"What?"

He pauses, and his eyes are wet, shimmering. "That it can still hurt." He snorts, sniffles, and the moment passes. He juts his chin toward my untouched plate of pancakes. "You going to eat?"

I shake my head.

"Well," he says. "We should get going then." He waves his arm and gets the waitress's attention. She scowls at my untouched plate, but says nothing, gathers up the dishes in her left hand and deposits the check on the table with her right. Jamie expertly maneuvers his arm and plucks a billfold out of his front chest pocket. It takes him a little longer than it probably would for someone with a "real" hand, but still. He places a twenty-dollar bill on the table. He's known for his generosity with money.

"I got it," he says as he begins to slide out of the booth.

"Wait," I say because I don't want to go just yet. I still need to talk to him; I still need to talk about Mom. "Did you love her?"

"Don't ask me that, Rosie."

"Why not?"

He slides back in. "Because it was a long time ago. Because it doesn't matter now."

"It matters to me."

"Why?"

You would think the person who'd become obsessed with Jamie Briggs would have been Iris. Or even my father. But no, it was me. In those weeks after she'd gone missing, after Iris told me about Mom and Jamie, after the roads were cleared from the ice storm and the power came back on and life in town began to return to normal, I was desperate for a possible connection to her. What if she was alive? What if she was hiding out with him? What if they were going to run away together? Dad was so concerned about Iris and focused on taking care of Daisy because she was so young that I was forgotten—or at least forgotten for stretches of time that allowed me to wander unsupervised through the woods, lurk around Jamie's house, even go through the mail in his mailbox, searching for handwriting I recognized: a note, a letter, a postcard written in code.

He saw me, at least once, because I saw him as he stared out his window onto the backyard. I'd walked all the way up to that window, his breath made the glass fog up, and I wondered what he was going to do. I knew he couldn't come after me. I knew he couldn't lift the window and curse me out. I knew he couldn't do anything, not that it mattered because he had done enough. He'd had a hand in making her go away, I was convinced. So I did what any unreasonable, uncreative pre-teen could do in the situation. I spit. I hocked one up, just as I'd seen Iris do on countless occasions, and I spat as hard and as far as I could. I watched as the sputum dribbled down the glass. He didn't do anything, only stared. Even though the glass was dingy, foggy, coated in spit, I could see his eyes. The sadness. The pain. I recognized it, because his grief mirrored my own.

From then on, Jamie Briggs became my own private pet project. I followed everything about him, scouring the Internet for articles on his deployment, his injury, his recovery and rehab, his eventual return home, his fund-raising for the Center, its opening, its success. He was my connection to her, more so than my sisters or my father, since I was convinced he'd had her last.

"It just matters, okay?" I say.

"That's not an answer."

"Yeah? Well, you answer my fucking question first and maybe I'll answer yours." I'm surprised at my angry words and voice, but I don't apologize.

He regards me, curious. It's not like me to talk back or to curse—to him, to my father, to anyone. He shakes his head. "Out of the three of you, you're the one who looks the most like her. I've always thought that. But it's what you just said. Shit, the *way* you said it, I guess, that reminds me of her."

"Is that a good thing? Or a bad thing?"

"Neither. It just is."

"You still haven't answered my question."

He smiles for the first time all night. "There it is again. Spunk."

I wrinkle my nose. "Spunk?"

"Yeah. It's a good thing, Rosie. Don't let anyone ever tell you otherwise."

I lean back into the booth and cross my arms. He sighs.

"Right, I still haven't answered your question," he says. "Yeah, I loved her. Happy now?"

I'd always wondered what it would feel like to hear him say those words "I love" and how I've wanted so much for him to say them to me. I don't know if Mom loved him back—I can only assume that she did, that she must have, because I can see right before my eyes what there is to love: his stubbornness, the same stubbornness that got him walking again, no doubt, and that kept him going after the rumors ran rampant after Mom was gone; the drive for equality among men and women who've been injured in these wars, how losing a limb (or four) doesn't make you any less abled in mind or spirit unless you allow it; his strength; his beauty. I find so many people like Jamie—amputees—to be attractive. It feels kinda weird at times, like maybe I'm a freak.

"What was she like?" I ask.

"What was who like?"

"My mom. With you."

"Listen, I answered your question, and that's where it's going to end. Do you honestly think I'm going to tell you—"

"No," I interrupt. "I don't mean those sorts of details. I mean what was she *like*? Was she happy? Did she love you back? Was she going to leave my father? Us?"

"Why you asking me all this? I knew her for, what? Three months, if that? You guys knew her best. Not me."

"I want to know. I need to know. Those last three months, we didn't know her best. You did. Then she was gone. I'll never know that person she was in those final moments. Not knowing, I think, is worse than knowing."

He considers me now in a way that's different from before, as if he sees me in a new light, as if, perhaps, he's starting to see me for me and not as some younger version of my mother.

"I think she was happy in moments," he begins. "Confused as all hell in others." He pauses, exhales. "Did she love me?" He looks up at the ceiling, lost in a memory, and shakes his head. "Hell if I know." He pauses, lost again, but then lowers his eyes until they meet mine. "Was she going to leave your father? I think it was too late, since he had already left her, years ago, at least the guy she'd fallen for and married." He waits while I take this in. "Was she going to leave you and your sisters? No way. She loved you girls more than anything in this world—more than me, if she ever did, more than your father, more than her own life. And that's it, Rosie. No more questions."

I nod, and this time when he slides out of the booth, I follow. We walk out into the cold night and to Dad's pickup. I unlock the door, climb inside, and spy the manila folder on the seat next to me, the name "Mrs. Briggs" written in block letters. I've had Mrs. Briggs for classes during my freshman, sophomore, and, now, junior year. I had nothing to do with orchestrating that. I've always wanted to be a teacher and work with kids, and Mrs. Briggs is the department head for Family and Consumer Sciences, which is why I've had her every year of high school: she teaches the classes in my area of interest. She's also agreed to be my independent study advisor next year, and I'm psyched because I bet she'll give me an awesome recommendation for college. I know my whole Jamie Briggs/Mrs. Briggs connection must seem weird to some people, but it all feels normal now. To me, anyway. Like maybe it was meant to be or something.

"Here," I say while handing him the envelope. "This is for your mom. I won't be in school tomorrow, and this is due. She'll know what it is." I pause. "I overheard you telling someone yesterday at work that you were having dinner with her tomorrow," I say shyly, my face heating up. *My God. He's going to think I stalk him.* "I'll email her and let her know I gave it to you." He nods and takes it, and I close the door and roll down the window. "Thanks," I say. "For listening." My eyes start leaking again. *Dammit.*

"No problem," he says, averting his gaze. "See you around."

"Yeah, see you," I whisper, and I watch through my tears as he walks to his van, settles inside, and drives away.

Chapter 33

Jamie

I've never been good with girls and tears. Not with my mother after Dad died. Not with any of the wives or girlfriends who lost their men in battle. Not even with the little kids at the Center. Then it hits me. Did I ever see Koty cry? This is the thought that goes through my mind as I walk away from Rosie who is on the verge of another meltdown. Understandable, but still—it's just not something I'm comfortable with, and I hope she understands it's not her, that it's me.

Inside my own van—a van that was manufactured and designed specifically for me since that's what happens when you make noise and when you force people to listen to you—I press the button that starts the engine, navigate the machine onto to the road, and try—unsuccessfully—not to think.

I'm not a sentimental man, and sensitivity is not one of my strong suits. I'm a man of action rather than words, and the only time I strayed from this philosophy was during those months with Koty.

Koty.

A day hasn't gone by in the last five-plus years that I haven't thought about her. I suppose the fact Rosie has wedged herself into my life—first at the Center and then with all the work she does for my mother in school—

might have something to do with it, but I imagine I'd think about Koty every day, regardless.

So, did she love me? I can still picture her standing in my doorway after I told her that I loved her. The confusion in her eyes. The quiet on her lips when she didn't say it back. If that's where it had ended for Koty and me, then the answer I just gave to Rosie—"Hell if I know"—would be correct. The problem is, that statement isn't entirely accurate, and all because of the only phone call Koty made the night she disappeared. Records showed she called my house at 10:06 p.m. My mother was out at the store, and I couldn't get to the phone in time. (I don't even think I bothered trying. Who would be calling me at that time of night, anyway?) Then there was Koty's cell phone itself, found in our driveway the next day. Had she tried to come to me? What happened to change her mind? Or *had* she changed her mind? Did something more sinister happen instead, like her no-good husband getting to her first?

He denied it, of course, the one and only time I cornered him and was able to throw it in his face.

He'd come to the Center to pick up Rosie. Usually, Rosie walked or hitched a ride with someone else (never me—I made sure of that), but the day he showed up, it was in the middle of a nor'easter, a storm that the weather folks had originally predicted wouldn't be so bad but had turned into Armageddon in February. We were closing the Center early, and I was one of the few people left in the building. I made my rounds, making sure lights were off and office doors were locked. I'd just passed the front door when in walked Wayne. I didn't recognize him at first. He was covered in snow and wore a hunter's cap that partially concealed his face. He had a beard, too. It had also been a little over three years since I'd seen him in person. He stomped his feet on the doormat, shaking off the snow.

"Down the hall," I said. "And to the right."

His head snapped up at the sound of my voice. He stared at me for a long moment and began to walk away, following my directions.

My body tensed, my chest cavity squeezed, and rage filled every inch of my body. It may have been three years, but Koty's face—beautiful and tortured—appeared before my eyes.

"You may think you've gotten away with it," I called out after him. "But you haven't. Karma's a bitch, my friend. Remember that."

He whipped around and was in my face so fast and so close that I could feel his breath as he snorted, his nostrils flaring. "I'm not your friend," he said, his voice low.

"You were no friend to Koty, either."

He glared at me, his cheeks red. "You motherfucking ass—"

"Dad!"

Wayne turned at the sound of her voice, and I peered over his shoulder to Rosie, her eyes wide.

"You ready?" he said. "I'll be in the car." He stormed off, leaving Rosie staring at me.

"You best get going," I'd said and walked away before she could question me.

Okay, so the situation was weird, I'll admit.

When my mother got wind that one of the Fowler girls was volunteering at the Center, she came marching to my house—I'd long since moved out by then—and badgered me.

"Jesus, Mary, and Joseph!" she'd said. "What were you thinking?"

"Ma, I had nothing to do with it. She's a volunteer for Kids' Korner, and a damned good one, from what I hear. I let the folks there handle the volunteers."

"But, Jamie," she said, shaking her head. "Think about what this looks like."

"It looks like we're moving forward," I said. "I think that's what Koty would have wanted." I watched as her face darkened. It always did whenever I mentioned Koty's name. "Ma, I couldn't help her," I continued. "But maybe—just maybe—I can help one of her girls."

Of course, it wasn't even seven months later, in the fall of 2011 when Rosie started high school, that my mother ended up having Rosie in class. At some point, all of us—Ma, me, and, I imagine, even Wayne—simply let it be.

#

My mind races in a million different directions despite my best efforts to concentrate on the road, the occasional passing headlights, the hum of the engine, the warmth of the seat emanating into my ass. (Yeah, this baby came with all the bells and whistles, and why not? My ass is one of the few pieces on me untouched by war.) The radio plays in the background, white noise up until this moment when I hear the unmistakable horns from "Ring of Fire" and Johnny Cash's gritty voice.

Holy shit.

I've gone back and forth on the concept of God a million times, starting when my dad died. So ask me if I believe in Him, in a higher power, in "signs" from above, and it will depend on the day. I do think, however, that we go on after this world. Energy can't be created or destroyed, so the essence of a human being needs to go somewhere. I doubt the place the energy ends up is anything like the heaven or hell we've all been taught. I have no idea what this somewhere looks like. But I like to think that their energy—my father's energy, my comrades', Koty's—can see me now and can feel something resembling pride.

Chapter 34

Wayne

There was a time I loved Koty more than anything in the world. It was short—too short—and I should have gotten out when it changed, when my brother was murdered, which is when I stopped feeling anything, period. By then it was too late. She was already pregnant. A part of me hoped—prayed even—that the baby would make a difference. We humans are damn fools that way.

I didn't feel anything when Rosie was born. Sad to say, I know, and I'm sorry for it, but lying about it doesn't change the fact. I was still numb from Carl's death, still scared shitless about the future, still struggling with my new-found balm—booze—still amazed at my transformation from mild-mannered good guy to major league prick, just like my old man. Yeah, I was aware it was happening. Shrinks usually say that awareness is the first step in some endless staircase to redemption, whatever that is. In my case, in that instance, it was merely an observation—nothing more.

At some point, my asshole self felt normal, and the "old Wayne"—as Koty would occasionally say when she wanted to piss me off—felt like a foreigner. As my old man used to proudly spout, "Fuck foreigners. All of 'em." It was easy to let go. I can't tell you why. Doesn't matter anyway. All that matters is the fact that I could, and that I did.

So it was easy for some people—okay, a lot of people—to think I had something to do with Koty's disappearance, at first.

The news about this "missing mother of three" didn't hit the airwaves right away, thanks to the ice storm, the worst storm this area had seen in a half century, if not longer. We lost power for over a week. Navigating the roads was impossible in those early days, especially out here on our street, which was littered with fallen trees and wires. People's pipes were bursting left and right, but I didn't help Hank with our plumbing business. I couldn't leave the kids because Koty was gone.

I remember certain details so clearly, like the horror on Rosie's and Daisy's faces when I returned home that night without their mother. They knew it wasn't good. I think they knew that from the very beginning.

"What are we going to do, Daddy?" Rosie had asked, and I realized there was nothing left to do but one thing. I picked up the phone, called the police, and told them my wife—the mother of my children—was missing.

The cop I talked to—I don't remember his name—asked me how long she'd been gone. I told him I wasn't exactly sure, that when I got up this morning around 6:30, she was already gone, that she had probably left some time before that. He informed me—as I expected he would—that I couldn't file a missing person's report until after twenty-four hours. Given the severe weather alert, however, he took down my information and details about Koty: the fact she didn't have her car. The fact her purse was still here. The fact her cell phone wasn't. As he was gathering my information and noted our last name, the old Fowler family legacy once again haunting me, he asked me if there had been any problems, if she'd ever left before.

"We'd been arguing," I said. "And yeah, she left once before for a few days."

"How long ago was that?"

That time Koty had left, she'd been pregnant with Daisy. "A while," I say. "Seven years ago."

We spoke some more, but the rest is hazy. All I remember is the cop seemed less concerned once he made the connection: *It's that old Fowler family, famous for domestic disputes. The woman had left once before and returned.*

"If she doesn't show up by tomorrow morning, you can file an official missing person's report, Mr. Fowler. Hopefully she'll show before then. We're in for a big storm."

He was right. It was a storm that would follow me for the next five plus years, along with Detective Vincent T. Panzieri, a guy who had a hard on for me from the first time we met back in August 2001, when he showed up at my house after Koty had taken the kids and walked out. That time, Panzieri was a rookie fresh out of the Academy, ready to make a name for himself and convinced, based on nothing more than the rumors surrounding my family name, that Koty had left because I was abusing her and the kids. Since then, he'd risen through the ranks to detective, and once he caught wind that Koty had gone missing again, he was all over me like a fly on shit.

"It would help if we could search your home," Panzieri had said after I volunteered to come in for questioning. It had been three days since Koty disappeared, and the roads were starting to clear, even though the rest of the outside world was encased in nothing but ice.

"What for?" I said. "I already told you there's nothing to find. I woke up, and she was gone."

"There might be clues you missed."

I laughed, but inside my stomach knotted. "Clues? You make it sound like a crime scene."

"Was it?"

"What did I say? She was gone when I woke up."

"Then you shouldn't mind us coming in."

"You want to come in? Get a search warrant."

"Now what type of message does that send to your kids, Mr. Fowler? That Daddy has something to hide?"

I resisted the temptation to grab him by the oversized hairy mole on his cheek. "No. It tells them that even in tough situations, a little thing called the Constitution still applies. Get a warrant."

He sighed. "Okay, Mr. Fowler. One more time. From the top."

"How many times do I have to explain it? I'd been drinking. We fought. I fell asleep. When I woke up, she was gone."

"But your middle daughter." He paused and shuffled through some pages on his yellow legal pad, a stack of folders next to him. "Iris. She was there."

"Yeah. Apparently, she'd come home sometime the night before, after I'd fallen asleep. She'd been staying with her sisters at her aunt's house."

"And why was that, Mr. Fowler?"

"Why'd she come home or why was she staying with her aunt?"

"Both."

"You married?" I asked.

He nodded.

"Got kids?"

"Two."

"So you know how nice it is to have a night alone with your wife."

"But you said you and your wife fought."

"We did. Like wives and husbands do. Do you ever fight with your wife?"

"Did you hit Koty?" he asked, ignoring my question.

I held his gaze. *Liars blink, don't they?* "No."

"What did you do?"

Deflect, I thought, because I wasn't sure if I could get through the story again. "Why don't you look back at your notes? All the answers are in there."

He put on his glasses and consulted his pad. "You dropped your kids off at your sister-in-law's house at approximately 6:00 on Wednesday, December 10. You and Koty went back home. Had dinner. Drank. Argued. You fell asleep. Meanwhile, Iris left your sister-in-law's house around 9:15, on foot, and headed to your house, according to your eldest, since Iris doesn't remember. Her reason for leaving is unclear because—again—she can't remember. Since she was on foot, let's say she gets to your house between 9:30 and 9:45."

I nodded. "Sounds about right."

"You have no knowledge of this, since you're out cold because you'd been drinking. Somewhere between that time and when you woke up to use the bathroom at—" he shuffled through his papers again. "At 6:30 a.m. or so, you notice the middle daughter is home and your wife isn't. Your wife's van, however, is still in the driveway."

"Yep."

"You're surprised about your daughter, but regarding your wife, you don't think anything of it, at first, since your wife likes to go for walks."

"Right."

"But your daughter is sick. You call your wife's cell phone, which is also gone and, presumably, with her. She doesn't answer. You leave a message. You text her. You even search the woods, since this is where she likes to walk, but you don't find her. You figure she's angry and needs time to 'cool off' as you say. You realize you might need to stay home from work to take care of your daughter, at least until your wife returns."

"You take good notes."

Panzieri turned a page. "You call your business partner, who also happens to be your brother, at approximately 7:15 a.m."

"Sounds right."

"You stay home. By the time your other daughters come home from school, your wife still hasn't returned. A storm is brewing." He paused, and I knew he wanted me to understand the double meaning. "You and your brother go searching for your wife that night. Nothing. You call the police upon your return. They tell you that you can't file a missing person's report until the morning, which you do. Of course, this also happens to occur during the worst ice storm these parts have seen in over half a century. Convenient, wouldn't you say?"

Fuck you, asshole. "No, sir. Considering my wife was missing, I wouldn't call her being missing in the worst ice storm these parts have seen in over a half century to be convenient."

"You won't allow us to search your house. Or talk to your daughter Iris without your being present."

I leaned forward and tapped my index finger on the legal pad. "See note about Constitution and see note about Iris's age. She's ten. Of course I'm not going to let you question her without my being present. That's my right."

"Indeed it is. But what if she knows something and is afraid to say it in your presence?"

"You're barking up the wrong tree. She doesn't remember anything. She was probably tired when she got home and no doubt a little scared. It's quite possible Koty chewed her ass out and put her to bed and Iris doesn't want to remember that as her last interaction with her mother."

Panzieri smiled. "Interesting theory." He selected a folder from the stack and opened it. "As for Iris, she's a little hellion, isn't she? Bullying at school. Walking off school grounds. Torturing a cat."

What the fuck? "Wait a minute. She didn't torture a cat. There's more to that story. Iris loves animals."

"Oh, that's why she wanted to learn to hunt, right?"

"Where'd you hear that?"

"Your oldest mentioned it to one of the other officers."

"You questioning my other kids without my knowledge?"

"Not questioning. Having a conversation. You own a gun, Mr. Fowler?"

"You know I do. Several. They all have licenses."

He nodded. "Shoot any recently?"

"As a matter of fact, yeah. Target practice."

"Don't suppose we can examine those guns?"

"You can. If you get a warrant."

"*When*, Mr. Fowler. Not if."

Fuck, fuck, fuck. Don't look rattled. "Knock yourself out."

"Do you think your wife simply walked out on you and your daughters, Mr. Fowler?"

I hesitated, unsure how to answer. "I don't know. I thought so, at first. She'd done it once before. But—"

"But she came back. I remember. I was there."

"Right. She had the kids that time. I've thought before she might leave me, but I never thought she'd leave our kids."

"And why on earth would she leave *you*?" he asked.

"For any of the same number of reasons your wife might leave you." I stopped myself before adding, "… you motherfucking asshole."

"What did the two of you argue about that night? If you don't mind my asking."

"I mind, but I'll tell you, since maybe it will help with your little investigation here." I paused, knowing my next move was critical and had to be played right. I swallowed my pride and spoke: "She was having an affair."

Panzieri raised an eyebrow. "And you know this how?"

"The how isn't important. The fact is, she was."

"Bet that made you angry."

"Wouldn't it make you angry?"

He nodded, giving me that. "So do you know who this mystery Casanova is?"

"You don't believe me, do you?"

He smiled. "Who is it?"

"The kid who was injured in Iraq." *Say his name. Just say his goddamn name.* "You know, Jamie Briggs."

"Excuse me? The quadriplegic?"

"Not a quadriplegic. Quad amputee. There's a difference." *Like the fact his cock isn't paralyzed.*

"And he'll corroborate this story?"

I stared him square in the eye, mine on fire, no doubt. "Maybe you should ask him and find out."

Panzieri paused, caught speechless for once.

"Seems like you got yourself a new suspect to interrogate," I said. "We done here?"

#

Panzieri never did get that search warrant. The one benefit of having long and deep roots in a town is that even though you're bound to have enemies, you're also bound to have friends in high places.

Panzieri didn't have much of a case without a body anyway. Every detail in my statement—all the phone calls I made that morning, including the ones to Koty's phone and to Hank—were verified. The fact I alerted the school that Iris was sick and that I stayed with her all day—Iris remembers this much—verified my whereabouts. Koty's cell phone was found at the Briggs's house along with corroboration about the affair. Some folks, including Koty's sister, thought I might have "lost it" and killed Koty after I found out, but no one could remember me doing anything suspicious, like sneaking away to dispose of a body in Maine during the very small window of time before the northeast turned into frozen tundra for the better part of two weeks. After that, most people gave me the benefit of the doubt because they saw how concerned I was about my kids, how I organized a search party once the ice began to melt, how my family put up a reward for information, how I stopped drinking and joined AA and even let go of my obsession in finding my brother's killer. Shit, I became a model citizen, the "good Wayne" returning from the depths of hell.

Of course, only I was aware of the details I'd left out during my conversation with Panzieri, like the unforgivable thing I did to Koty that last night. Or the place I found Iris that fateful morning. Or the real reason why I couldn't let Panzieri and his goons in my house with their fancy equipment that can detect blood long after it's been wiped away by bleach.

Even now, I don't trust him, convinced he hasn't revealed everything he knows about Koty's death. I know his telling me it was "a fall" has got to be some sort of trick to get me off balance, but I play along and don't ask any questions because my number one priority has been—and always will be— protecting Iris.

Chapter 35

Iris

I toss and turn in bed. I'm not a good sleeper, never have been. In the morning, my bedspread will be on the floor, my sheets tangled around my legs. I talk in my sleep, according to Rosie and Daisy, who are in nearby rooms. "What did I say?" I'll ask, and most of the time what they repeat makes no sense, simply words threaded together by an invisible, meaningless string. Sometimes I'll call out for her, for Mom. Sometimes I'll simply plead, "It wasn't me. It wasn't me." Rosie and Daisy will shake me awake, hoping that I remember something. I never do.

Even if I did remember, would I trust those memories now, like Dad said? Memories that have had over five years and three months to decay and transform, to be under the influence of so many suggestions? I'll experience snippets of memory: flashes of images, sounds, scents, but they disintegrate when I examine them too closely, and before long it's like the feeling you have when you're trying to remember a dream, but can't.

What I remember: I knew about Mom and Jamie before anyone else. I found out by accident, but I suppose that's how people find out about such things, isn't it?

I remember the day of the week—a Friday, her thirtieth birthday—and how we had made breakfast for her in bed. Friday was art day in school, and it was the only subject I never had to explain myself in. It was *art*, after all, and open to interpretation. No one questioned my making pictures of two girls holding hands, an innocuous image for a ten-year-old and a positive image for a rough-and-tumble, pain-in-the-ass like me, because it suggested calm and all-around girlishness. Because no one questioned my art, I could live in peace with the knowledge of what I actually meant.

Anyhow, we had a sub in art that day, a disappointment for me, since I liked Mrs. Currier, my art teacher, and all the projects she planned for us. The sub said we could paint, color, or sketch, and while a bunch of the boys made a mess of the paints and some of the girls quietly colored images of real girl things, I decided to make my mother a birthday card. I didn't want it to be some dopey card, either. I wanted it to have meaning. I wanted it to matter to her. Even then, even though I couldn't articulate it, I sensed she'd been distant, drifting away from us the same way you can be standing still in the ocean, thinking you're not moving, and then you look up and realize you've drifted far from where you thought you were. I knew, even though Dad had convinced her to let him teach me how to shoot, that she wasn't happy with the decision, that she somehow didn't trust me. I wanted to show her that I was more grownup than she thought. A lot to pull off in one folded eight-and-a-half-inch piece of red construction paper.

When I was done with my card, I decided I wanted to give it to her, right then and there. Who cared that I was still in school, that we still had two hours until dismissal? I was so proud of my creation, and I needed her to be proud, too, to tell me it was wonderful, that I was wonderful. I needed it to be her and me, which never happened in our house since I was stuck smack dab in the middle of Rosie and Daisy. I wanted her all to myself. So I ditched. I'd done it before, three times, actually, and had been caught only once, and that had been the previous year. I was getting good at it and had a plan: I asked to go to the bathroom at the exact moment the boys were unleashing their "let's torture the substitute teacher" plot. I slipped out a side door and began the fifteen-minute walk home, without any thought of consequences. I was never a kid who could be verbally beaten into submission with threats of punishment. (Little did I know, it would be the last time I ever ditched school.)

During the walk home, I pretended the conversation I'd have with Mom. She'd be pissed, but I knew—*I just knew!*—that my card and my reasoning would win her over. She'd make us hot chocolate, and we'd sit at the kitchen table and talk and I'd have her all to myself, at least for a little while before the disaster I called Daisy and my overprotective older sister, Rosie, came barging in.

When I got to the house, the driveway was empty. I tried the front door, but it was locked. I didn't have a key—that was Rosie's responsibility—so I sat on the porch steps, wondering what to do next, when I remembered about Mom's daily "obligation," as she called it, her visit with some soldier from the war.

"Shit," I'd said out loud. I'd left school for nothing and would likely get in trouble, both at school and at home. I pictured Dad during our talk about guns and how he made me promise to stay out of trouble and show that I could be responsible because that was the only way he and Mom would allow me to learn how to handle a gun.

I stood up and debated what to do next: go back to school and feign illness, pretending I'd been locked in the girl's bathroom barfing up lunch? If I had been anyone else, that scenario would have worked, but I was well known to the principal and all the teachers. I somehow needed to salvage this. If I showed up on the soldier's doorstep, my card in hand, she couldn't get mad at me, at least not there in front of him, right? I could be charming, this much I knew. Sick people like kids. Mom would see the positive effect I had on this guy and realize my intentions had been good and wouldn't be able to bring herself to punish me.

I walked around to the back of the house. I remembered Mom saying this soldier lived on the other side of the woods. I didn't know which house, of course, but I'd look for Mom's car. Easy peesey.

I loved the woods behind our house, even though we weren't supposed to play in 'em without parental supervision, there being old culverts filled with crap, like broken bottles and old tires, that we could "break our necks on" as Mom and Aunt Kat used to say. (Not that that ever stopped me before. I mean, c'mon. What kid doesn't love a tunnel, even a short, above ground one with high ceilings?) Still, I was careful as I walked. I loved being outside in Mother Nature, and I stopped from time to time to gaze up at the sunshine poking through the tree tops and twirled with my arms outstretched until I felt dizzy. I skipped. I sang. I trotted. I galloped. I ran. I was free to be myself, uninhibited, no questions asked, and all I could think about was the last time I'd felt this way, the previous May. Memorial Day Weekend. My tenth birthday. We'd gone to Salisbury Beach and splashed for hours in the cold water that turned our skin purple. We fed seagulls French fries at Markey's Lobster Pound and got big dripping ice cream cones at Hodgies, the best ice cream in all of New England, and we were together, all five of us, and happy.

By the time I arrived on the other side of the woods and scrambled up the embankment to the road, the feeling—*that* feeling—had started to evaporate, and little did I know it would be the last time I'd ever feel it. I looked both ways and wondered which direction to start in first. I listened to my gut and turned left, whistling as I walked, trying hard to hold onto the feeling, but quickly becoming aware at how desolate the area was, even more so than my street. I trudged along the quiet houseless road, reckoning it was about two o'clock, maybe later. What if I was going in the wrong direction? What if I got lost? But then I spied a two-story house and spotted Mom's van parked in the driveway.

I walked up the front steps, knocked, and waited. Nothing. I tried the doorbell. Waited. Still nothing. Then I heard what sounded like a firecracker—*pop*—and voices around back. I sucked in my breath and followed the perimeter of the house to the backyard where I found Mom— *my mother*—holding a gun. A guy—Jamie, I guessed—was standing next to her, saying something in her ear while she nodded. He backed up, awkwardly, toward a table—and that's when I noticed his legs weren't real legs. One of his arms looked like a pole. Mom shot the gun—once, twice, three times—aiming at some yellow targets on the trees in the woods. She turned around and walked to him. Then it happened: they kissed. It wasn't like the obligatory kiss she gave Uncle Hank and Aunt Veronica, mostly air and a little bit of cheek. It was on the lips. I'd never seen my parents kiss like that. Where I had seen it: on some of the stupid soaps Rosie watched, like *Days of Our Lives* and *All My Children*, the actors and actresses sucking face. I couldn't believe it. It felt like she kissed him forever. And then, she touched him. *Down there.*

My head spun. I started moving backwards, unaware of my surroundings, almost banging into a garbage can. I ran. I ran down the street as fast as my legs could carry me, and into the woods. I ran and ran and ran, forgetting everything about culverts and animals and rocks. I ran until I thought my lungs would burst and I exploded through the woods into our backyard. Home. I panted, bent over, and realized I was still holding Mom's birthday card. Part of me wanted to rip it into a million little pieces. How could she do that, kiss someone other than Dad? How could she do that to him? To us? What if she went to jail? (What can I say? I was ten. In my world, bad people went to jail or at least were threatened with it.) What if they got divorced? Should I tell someone what I saw? Dad? Rosie?

I sat on the front steps and waited while questions bombarded my skull like a pinball. I hugged my knees to my chest as fear washed over me. I didn't know what I was scared of. I only knew I was scared.

I heard the phone ring inside the house and bet it was my school principal. No doubt she would try Mom's cell phone next. Suddenly, my brilliant idea didn't seem so brilliant. I didn't care about Mom's birthday, or shooting, or anything. I wanted to go inside, into my room, and hide under the covers until the images of what I saw disappeared.

I sat on the steps and waited and waited and waited. I spotted Rosie and Daisy before they saw me, Daisy's mouth moving the whole time as she galloped in order to keep up with Rosie's legs. Rosie wasn't paying attention to her, like she usually does, because her eyes were focused on something in her hands, and that's when I remembered Rosie had gotten a cell phone, an early birthday present that she had convinced Mom and Dad that she needed for the start of school. She was probably calling Mom right now, wondering where the hell I was when I didn't show up at our usual meeting spot by the swings to walk home together. *Shit.*

Daisy spotted me before long, pointing and shouting and acting like the maniac that she was. She came flying up the driveway, arms a twirling.

"Where were you?" Rosie asked, more concerned than angry.

I shrugged. "I wanted to come home."

"Why didn't you wait for us?"

"No," I said, impatient. "I wanted to come home awhile ago. I left during art class."

Rosie's eyes widened, and her cell phone vibrated in her hand. "It's Mom," she said. *Awesome.* "Hello? Yeah, she's right here. Where are you? Okay. I'll tell her. Bye."

"So?" I asked.

"She said not to move."

"Where is she?" Daisy asked.

"I don't know." Rosie deposited her phone into her purse. "She said she was running late."

"But she said she'd be here today. It's her birthday," Daisy said.

"Well, she isn't, idiot," I spat. "Get over it."

Daisy's eyes filled with tears. Rosie put her arm around her.

"Just because you're in trouble doesn't mean you have to be a jerk." Rosie whispered the word "jerk" as if someone was going to swoop down and slap her across the face for using a bad word. "So why'd you leave, anyway?"

"Because I felt like it."

"What's that?" Daisy pointed to my lap and Mom's card.

"Nothing." I folded the card into quarters and shoved it in my back pocket as Mom pulled in the driveway. She jumped out of the van, her face pink and her eyes wide, and I was convinced I was dead meat. But instead of yelling at me, she simply marched past us, unlocked the door, and walked inside. Rosie and Daisy followed, letting the screen door slam behind them. Finally, Mom came back out and sat down next to me.

"The school called," she said. "Mind telling me what's going on?"

What's going on? You were kissing another guy. You were touching another guy. You're going to make Dad sad. Are you going to get a divorce? What will happen to us?

I remained silent.

"Listen, Iris. This isn't what I need today. Frantic calls from your principal and from your sister. You walking out of school for no apparent reason."

You! I wanted to scream. *You're the reason. I walked out for you.* Instead: I reached into my back pocket and pulled out the card. It was wrinkled and ripped in one corner. I tossed it onto her lap.

"What's this?" she said, unfolding it. "When did you make this?"

"Today. During art." I paused. "It's why I left school. I wanted to give it to you."

Her eyes softened. "Sweetheart, it's a lovely card. I appreciate the gesture. But this impulsive behavior of yours ..." She smoothed the construction paper between her palms, trying to get it to lay flat. "You can't just do what you want, when you want."

"I know."

"Well." She held up the card in front of us. "It *is* beautiful." I studied her profile as she gazed upon my card: her delicate nose, her creamy skin, her curly hair that looked good no matter how she wore it. "But you need to promise me, Iris, that you won't walk out of school again. It's dangerous."

No shit.

"Mom?" Daisy called from the doorway. "Can I have some ice cream?"

"In a minute," Mom called back and then to me: "Well? Do you promise?"

I nodded. She patted my hand, stood, and went inside. I stayed on the steps, kicking at the ground, squashing ants that got in my way, and throwing rocks up in the air. I was still there when Dad drove up, early no doubt because of Mom's birthday and their anniversary. He stepped out of the cab, whistling, and spotted me.

"Hey, Buttercup," he said. "Why the long face?"

"I'm in trouble." As I said the words, I realized that there'd been no discussion of consequences, of grounding. It was only a matter of time, I was sure, but it was still weird.

"Oh, yeah?" he sighed as he sat down next to me, a cup of Dunkin' Donuts coffee in his hand. "What'd you do?"

"I ditched school."

He raised an eyebrow. "Again?"

"Yep," I said, and I lowered my eyes, ashamed.

"I thought we talked about this last time. Why now?"

"Because she wanted to give me a birthday card," Mom's voice said from the screen door.

Dad turned to look at her and then back to me. "Is that right, Iris?"

"Yes."

"I see." He sipped his coffee. "You know what this means?"

"No shooting lessons?" *Ever in my life, most likely.*

He nodded. "I say we'll need to postpone our plans. For a month, anyway. I told you I had a deal with your mother, right?"

"Yeah, you told me."

"And while it was nice of you to want to give your mom a birthday card—"

"I know, I know," I pouted. "I shouldn't be so 'pulsive."

"So what?"

"'Pulsive."

"You mean impulsive?"

"I guess."

"Do you know what that means?" he asked, trying not to laugh.

"It means I shouldn't do whatever I want, when I want."

Daisy and Rosie exploded through the door and ran past us, laughing, with Mom right behind.

His eyes followed them, and he nodded. "Yeah. That's about right."

#

What I remember: wrestling with the window at Aunt Kat's house the night I ratted out Mom about her relationship with Jamie. I knew I'd screwed up the minute I'd opened my mouth and spilled, the moment I saw Dad's pained face and the horror on my mother's. I loved Dad, love him still, but even then I knew what he could be like, especially if he had any booze in him.

"Help me lift this up," I'd said to Rosie, desperate to leave and go to them, to Mom and Dad and make sure everything was okay.

"Iris, quit it," Rosie said. We were crammed into Aunt Kat's guest bedroom, sleeping bags on the floor side by side. Rosie had been reading Daisy a story. "You're gonna get us in trouble."

I ignored her, determined and unable to shake the feeling that something bad was going to happen—to Mom, to Dad, maybe to both of them. I knew that whatever it was, it would be my fault. But I couldn't tell Rosie and Daisy that. I hadn't even told them about Jamie.

"I don't care. I'm going home," I said, trying the window again. It moved.

Rosie jumped up. "No, you're not."

She was skinny, fragile like a bird. Even though she was older than me, I was taller and tougher. She knew it. I knew it.

I pushed the window all the way up, did the same with the screen, and surveyed my surroundings, grateful we were at ground level. "Yeah, I am."

"It's freezing, and it's dark."

"I got a coat, and I don't care. I ain't a scaredy cat like some people," I added for effect.

"*Not*. You're *not* a scaredy cat."

"Exactly," I said while rolling my eyes, annoyed that Rosie couldn't stand anyone bastardizing the English language, even for effect. Mom was the same way. *Mom.* Shit, I had to get out of there.

"Fine," Rosie said. "Go. Get in trouble. I don't care."

"Rosie!" Daisy said. "You can't let her go."

But I was already halfway out the window. Once on the ground, I felt their eyes on me as I zipped up my coat, slid my hands into my mittens, and made sense of where I was. I'd walked between Aunt Kat's and my house thousands of times. It wasn't far. It would have probably been even faster if I cut through the woods, but though I never admitted it to anyone then, sometimes I got scared of the dark. So I hummed and walked and ran, hiding in shadows whenever I heard the crunch of tires on gravel. When I finally spied our house, the lights on in the window, Dad's pickup in the driveway, I was relieved, but also queasy. I hadn't sorted out what I was going to say. Should I say I'm sorry? Should I lie for Mom and say I made it up? I held my breath, turned the knob, and pushed open the door. I listened and heard nothing, at first. But then, there it was: a deep drawn out guttural wail.

I stood still for a moment, not sure if I should run toward the sound or away from it. A definite part of me wanted to run away, to run back to Aunt Kat's and pretend I was too scared to go much beyond her street, and to beg forgiveness. But there was the other part. The curious part. The part that knew the sound was human and that the human was in pain. My feet moved forward, one in front of the other, until I was standing on the threshold to my parents' bedroom.

What I remember: a kaleidoscope of silver, gray, and red, lots and lots of red— swirling, swirling, swirling, until there's nothing left to swirl.

#

I sit up in bed with a start and feel the sweat dripping down my face. The memory—what happened, what *really* happened—is there beyond my peripheral vision, just outside of my reach. I can feel it. I lie down again, close my eyes, and will myself to remember.

Mom kneels next to Dad in their bed. She's holding a gun to his head. He's not moving.

I scream and lunge. I somehow knock her to the floor, and we roll toward the door and into the hallway. There's a bang, a firecracker, so close, like it's going off right in my ear.

I'm on the floor. She's on the floor. Blood pours from the side of her face. I try to move, but can't. I'm heavy. My body is heavy. My hand is heavy. My hand. I look down. I'm holding a gun. Teardrops fall onto it.

"Iris."

My name. Someone is calling my name. It's her. She holds her hand to her cheek. There's blood. On her. On the wall behind her.

"It's okay. It's okay. Come here, baby."

But I can't. I can't move. I'm too heavy. I'm too confused. I'm too scared. She begins to crawl toward me.

"Iris, come here." Her voice is more insistent. "Give me the gun. Iris, please." She reaches out her arms. "Give me the gun. Before your father wakes up."

The room spins and my mind attempts logic. She's going to kill him. She's going to kill him. She's going to kill him.

Teeth, gritted. Veins, popping. Eyes, bulging. Head, pounding. Room, spinning. Gun, lifted. "No."

"Iris!"

"I won't let you hurt him."

"Iris. Listen to me."

Tongue, spits. "Whore."

Heart—hers—broken. Room, twists.

"Whore!"

Room, spins.

"Whore!"

Room, whirls.

"Whore!"

"Iris! Wake up."

Eyelids open. Rosie and Daisy stand over me. I battle my way to a sitting position, head throbbing, hands shaking. Daisy sits next to me and rests her head on my shoulder. I shake her off.

"What'd I say?" I ask. They don't answer. I look at Daisy and then Rosie, who's fingering the glass animal figurines on my dresser. "Tell me. Please."

"You said 'whore,'" Daisy answers. "You screamed it, actually. Four times."

"Do you remember something?" Rosie asks.

"Yes," I say, but I shake my head. "No. I don't know. None of it makes sense. They say she fell to her death, right? That she was pushed. There was no—"

"There was no *what*?" Rosie asks.

"No gun."

"That's what you remember?" Daisy whispers. "You think she was shot?"

I look down at my hands and wonder if what I'm feeling is the gun's grip or if I'm imagining it. "I don't know. It's just in the dream ..."

Rosie joins us on the bed. She takes my hands in hers and rubs her thumbs along my knuckles, trying to comfort me like the big sister she is. "Who shot her? In your dream, I mean. Was it Dad?"

"No," I say, while shaking my head. "It was me."

April 2014

Chapter 36

Wayne

I glance beyond the curve of her hip to her digital clock on the nightstand. It's 4:40, and I need to get going since the girls will expect me home in time for supper.

As if she can sense what I'm thinking, she stirs, turns, and faces me. It's a pretty face, a little Marilyn Monroe-esque with her platinum blonde curls, big red lips, and eyelashes long and thick with mascara. I've never seen her face naked, which is funny, I guess, considering our clothes never stay on long, considering I often find her in bed waiting for me on Friday afternoons. I've never slept over, have never gotten intimate with her in the way people do when they transition from lovers to long-term commitments and all that goes with it: no makeup, morning breath, body odor. I'm as much an escape for her as she is for me, and after four years of doing what we've been doing, I don't see it ever turning into anything more.

I met Honey Wallace at, of all places, the cemetery where my parents and Carl are buried, where Koty's parents are buried, and where we'll be burying Koty, too, in a fresh new plot all her own. It was the spring after Koty's disappearance, and I'd taken to walking the cemetery, the only place that I could be by myself without any eyes on me wondering, questioning, accusing. I'd started going to AA meetings once the roads cleared after the ice storm, and, as expected, that other road—the one to recovery—was littered with mental debris, bad memories, and desperate moments. The cemetery's silence helped quiet my mind and helped me, on more than one occasion, stop myself from going to the local watering hole.

I'd walk up and down in between tombstones and markers, reading the names, the years, and studying the headstones themselves, recognizing my grandfather's handiwork on many of the older ones. Grandpa did more than build the stone culverts in the area; he also made monuments for the dead, just as his father had done, and just as I wanted to do in addition to restoring old stone walls. He died before my apprenticeship had finished and before I could properly take over the business. Instead, my father sold it to a family named Hanson, a family that still operates the same monument showroom that Grandpa ran for almost fifty years in Granite Creek. Today, I take care of their plumbing, and sometimes they let me pretend I belong there.

Anyhow, one warm April day at the cemetery, a woman sat on one of the granite benches facing a headstone. Normally, I steered clear of people, but there was something about her, something so out of place. She was a larger woman dressed in pink from top to bottom, complete with a pink hat and high heels. I approached from the side, saw she was crying, and began to retreat, but she turned and faced me, her eyes sparkling from her tears. She was pretty, despite her girth, all made up movie-star like.

"You're a regular ol' taphophile," she said with a hint of southern drawl. *What the fuck did she just call me?* "Excuse me?"

"A taphophile. Lover of cemeteries and all things having to do with them like tombstones and their etchings." She smiled. "I've seen you here before."

"Well." I nodded. "Didn't mean to intrude."

"No intrusion," she said. She stood and walked to the headstone she'd been facing: *Sylvester P. Wallace. 1958–2008.* "I had a verse I wanted to add to this tombstone when Sylvester died, but I couldn't afford it." She ran her hand, complete with long pink fingernails, over the top.

"They could add it now, you know. Without removing it from the cemetery."

"Right," she said, but she was frowning. "Can't afford it still, I imagine."

I'm not sure what overcame me in that moment. Pity. Compassion. Lust. "I could get it done for you," I heard myself say. "I know the folks at Hanson's Monuments in town. They owe me a favor or two."

She turned away from the stone and faced me again. "Well, that's mighty kind of you, mister—"

"Wayne. Wayne Fowler."

"That's mighty kind of you, Mr. Wayne Fowler." She held out her hand, and I walked to her and shook it. "I'm Honey. Honey Wallace. This here is Sylvester, but I guess you already knew that." And she laughed.

That's how it began with Honey and me. Friendly at first, with me helping her out with the lettering on the stone, then fixing a leaky faucet in her house, and then, well, me fixing her in a stolen afternoon here, a stolen afternoon there, until we fell into the routine of Fridays. She's what most people would call a floozy, and I might even use the term if I didn't know her and didn't hear her occasionally pull words like "taphophile" from her ass, showing she's smarter, deeper, than most people probably give her credit for. What she offers in return for all my handiwork is a place for me to be me with no questions, accusations, or expectations. She listens, too. For someone who has always considered himself more of the strong silent type, I find myself opening up to her, this almost-fifty-year-old floozy who's never worked a day since I've known her, who gets by on God's good graces and the kindness of people like me, and listens more intently than any woman I've ever known.

#

She watches as I pull on my boxers, jeans, and sweatshirt and then rolls over, lifts the blinds, and sighs. "Still light out. Not bad for April 4."

Shit. The date hits me and I fall onto the bed.

She knows me well enough not to ask questions. Instead, she disentangles herself from the sheets (they're silk, I might add), straddles her big naked self behind me, wraps her legs around my middle, and squeezes.

"The date. Carl's birthday. He'd have been thirty-seven," I say, explanation enough, and she hugs me tighter, still silent.

#

I'm pensive on the ride home, Carl's soul, ghost, whatever you want to call it, so close that I can feel the hairs on the back of my neck stand up on end. I'm used to him haunting me—Koty, too—and I think back to the first time they met and the warning he gave her (of course she told me): "Don't let him end up back here. No matter what."

Yet here I am, on my way back to the house I grew up in, the house I now share with my three daughters, to the memories of Koty and Carl, to the promises made, to the promises broken, and to the "almost" promises. Like the one where Carl asked me to accept him when he told me he was gay, not even three weeks before he was killed, and all I could say was I needed time to think about it. "Promise me you will," he'd said. Time, of course, turned into forever, thanks to the bastard (or bastards) who killed him. I never told anyone, not even Koty or Hank, what Carl revealed to me, and I spent the rest of my life—up until Koty disappeared—acting like the homophobe I was expected to be, thanks to my family name. Today, though, I try to make up for it—all of it, like the broken promises—by staying sober, by letting Carl's cold case remain just that (thank you, third step), by trying to be open to other ideas and lifestyles, and by being there for Rosie and Daisy and Iris.

Especially for Iris.

Chapter 37

Iris

The year I was born, a band named the Goo Goo Dolls released a song called "Iris," and I guess it was a big deal back then and won Grammys or was nominated at least. Oh, and it was part of the soundtrack to *City of Angels*, a movie starring someone named Meg Ryan and Nicolas Cage, who plays an angel and falls in love with Meg Ryan's character and needs to decide if he's willing to give up angel-hood for this girl. Mom said she didn't name me after the song, but I guess after I was born, a lot of people asked her if there was a connection. I've heard the song, of course, but the lyrics are kind of cryptic. I mean, the word "iris" isn't even in the song. I'd read that someone in the band named it after a country singer. But I also read that the name is supposed to be a tribute to a Greek goddess named Iris who left her messages in rainbows. (I like that explanation way better than the country singer thing.) Anyhow, I'm not sure what the song means, but there's a line that's repeated a bunch of times about wanting people to know who we are, who we *really* are. I think it's supposed to be a reference to the angel dude from the movie, but I like how it can refer to any of us. Isn't that what we all want? To have people know who we are and like and love and accept us anyway, no matter what?

I think Rosie and Daisy know I'm gay. We don't talk about it, mainly because there's nothing to talk about, but I think someday, maybe I will. I don't think they'll care. It's Dad I worry about.

Ever since Mom's been gone, he's mellowed in some respects. (The fact he doesn't drink and goes to AA helps.) But that doesn't mean his values have changed. Despite the gaps in my memory on the night Mom disappeared, my memory tends to be long and detailed on other things. I remember his rants about "faggots" when gay marriage in New Hampshire was legalized. "Not right," he'd said. "It's not natural." I've overhead him and Uncle Hank jawing about some "homos" in town, and when a history teacher at school was caught carrying on with a nineteen-year-old former male student, even though everything was consensual and all, Dad was among the first to call for the teacher's resignation.

So what would he do if I ever went to him and said, "Dad, I'm gay"?

Thinking about it is enough to make my hands sweat, my mouth dry up, and my belly ache. I hate to be a disappointment to him, especially since he's worked so hard at protecting me (from what, I can't remember, but that's beside the point). I wish he knew how much I wanted to be normal for him: straight, girlie, ordinary. But maybe our family lost its chance at normal a long time ago.

#

We stand in the funeral home, and Daisy runs her hands along a gleaming slate blue casket, which, according to the brochure, is one example from the "wide selection" of caskets that "are kept on site at all times." This one is called "Heading Home."

"Blue was her favorite color," Daisy says. "I think she'd like this one." Rosie nods, and I don't say anything because this moment is too surreal for words. Dad and the funeral director talk in hushed voices in the other room. I tug at my scarf as the heat rises up my chest, my neck, and my cheeks. The room spins, and I stumble to the couch.

Rosie sits down next to me. "You okay?"

"Hot."

She nods. "Yeah. These places always are."

Dad and the funeral director—Thomas something-or-other—return. Thomas is dressed in an all-gray suit with one of those pocket watch chain thingies around his middle. His mouth turns down in a perpetual scowl, not that I blame him. I mean, who'd ever choose to do this for work? The sign out front said *Hubert & Sons Funeral Home*. A family business. Just like Dad's. Maybe Thomas didn't have a choice. I glance at Dad, curious now, because the thought had never occurred to me before: did he have a choice? Was plumbing what he dreamed about when he was a kid?

"So," Dad says. "Have we decided?" He'd told us we could choose whatever casket we wanted, as if it were as simple and as fun as choosing flavors of ice cream.

Daisy nods and points. "The blue one."

"A fine, fine choice," Thomas says, and I roll my eyes because of the insincerity in his voice. Like what would he have said if we'd chosen the one called "Praying Hearts" or "Golden Empire"? That those choices sucked? Rosie catches my eye and giggles, and, before I know it, we're both laughing, smack dab in the middle of a funeral parlor. Daisy laughs as well, mainly because we are.

"It's been a long day," Dad says to Thomas as they shake hands, even though it's not even lunchtime yet. "Thank you for your help."

"I understand, Mr. Fowler. I understand."

All I want to scream is, "Do you, Thomas? How many murdered women have you and your brothers and father buried in the last however many years you've been doing this?" But, of course, I don't.

#

We order flowers next, an easier task than the casket since there's no decision to make: we want each of our names represented in the arrangement (the florist called it a blanket) that sits on top of the casket. Dad requests a bouquet of sunflowers, and when he sees our questioning eyes—I can't remember Dad buying Mom sunflowers ever—he shrugs. "The summer we started dating, I'd sometimes leave a sunflower under the windshield of her car." Once again, I find myself looking at him differently, like I don't know him, just like he doesn't know me, and maybe, just maybe that's all he wants, too. For us to ask him how it was with her, with him, in the beginning before they had us, before he used to drink too much, and before she stopped caring about him in the way most women care for men.

We stop at Friendly's on the way home, as if this were some special weekend outing, a father with his three kids. We order burgers and fries. Daisy gets a Fribble, Rosie and Dad get regular shakes, and I get a lime rickey, but when everything arrives, we all push our food around.

"So, like, what'll happen at the service?" Daisy asks as she moves a fry around in a swirl of catsup. We've all been baptized, this much I know, mainly because I've seen the pictures in the photo albums. I have vague recollections of "going to church" for Christmas and Easter during my first few years of school.

Dad leans back in the booth and wipes his mouth with a paper napkin. "It's been awhile, I'll admit. There will be readings. The priest will say some words. There will be something called Communion. Some final prayers and blessings. Then we'll go to the cemetery."

Daisy continues her catsup design. "Will there be music?"

"Yep."

"What kind?"

He thinks her question over. "Appropriate."

"'Amazing Grace'?" Daisy asks.

"We can ask them to sing that, if you want. We're allowed to have input. Didn't know how much input we'd have to offer since, well, it's been awhile for all of us, I guess."

"What sort of things will the priest say?" I ask.

"Oh, I don't know. Appropriate things about her life. Who she was."

"But he didn't know her. Did he?" I say.

"He knew who she was, but no, he didn't know her personally. Not like we knew her." He pauses. "Why? Is there something you want me to ask him to talk about, Buttercup?"

I shrug because thinking about it makes my eyes all misty.

Rosie pipes up. "Maybe we should write down some memories about Mom and give them to the priest. You know, an inside view on how we saw her. What we remember."

Daisy nods, and Dad's eyes remain on me. "Iris?" he says. "How's that sound to you?"

"Sure," I say.

"You don't have to if you don't want—"

"I said, 'Sure.' Why do you always have to question me to death about every decision I ever make?" I cross my arms and glare at his wounded eyes.

Our waitress appears and starts clearing away dishes. "Anything else?" she says, an afterthought almost, and Dad shakes his head no. She plucks the check from her front pocket and tosses it onto the table. Dad examines it, pulls out his wallet from his back pocket, takes two twenties, and hands them and the check to Rosie.

"Why don't you and Daisy go on up and pay?" He places six one-dollar bills under his glass. "Tip's all set."

Rosie nods, and she and Daisy slide out of the booth.

"So," he says once they're gone, "want to tell me what that was all about?"

"What was what all about?"

"You jumping down my throat for asking a simple question. Kind of like what you're doing right now."

"I'm sick and tired of you always asking me things twice at least. You don't do that with Rosie and Daisy. But you always do it with me."

"That's not true. I—"

"Yes, it is, and you know it." I stop and take a deep breath. "What did I do, Dad?"

"What do you mean?"

"That night. What did I do?"

Before he can respond, Rosie and Daisy are standing by the booth. "All set," Rosie says, as she glances from me to Dad. She takes the keys off the table. "We can go wait in the car, if you want."

Dad nods, and Rosie and Daisy leave. I watch them through the large-glass window as they climb into Dad's suburban.

"So?" I say. "What is it? What did I do?"

He shakes his head.

"Your silence is an answer, you know," I say. "If I hadn't done something, you would have said, 'Don't be silly, Iris. What are you talking about? You didn't do anything.'"

He rolls his eyes. This conversation isn't new. We've had it before over the years, but it's different now because of my dreams and because of the pieces I'm remembering and because I'm older and wiser and can take apart any logical arguments he throws back.

"You're remembering things," he says, and it's a statement, not a question. I shrug, and he leans into the table. "Talk to me, Iris. What are you remembering?"

I lower my eyes and shake my head. "I don't know."

"Tell me. Whatever it is. Just tell me."

"I remember a gun. Your gun. Me holding it and pointing it at Mom. She was bleeding." I look up, and my mind debates whether to tell him everything, but my mouth moves before I can stop it. "I called her a whore."

He waits and finally nods. "That it?"

I search his face, expecting him to be more surprised by my dream than he is. Instead, I swear I see a glint of recognition, like he's been waiting for this missing piece to surface. "Isn't that enough?"

"You didn't shoot her, Buttercup."

"How do you know that?"

"Well, first, by what they say killed her. It wasn't a bullet."

"Right. She fell or was pushed or whatever," I say.

"And, second, where is this mystery weapon? You were ten, Iris. *Ten.* We hadn't even started our shooting lessons because you had gotten in trouble, remember?"

"You don't need lessons to shoot a gun. That's how accidents happen, right? A kid finds a gun and shoots his leg off?"

"But I didn't find you with a gun, Iris. That morning, when I woke up, you were in bed, sick. Remember?"

"I remember you sitting by my bed and giving me saltines and ginger ale. I remember the smell of bleach."

He nods. "You'd been sick. I had to clean up."

"I remember coming home the night before. I was scared I'd be in trouble, and I was upset about what I had said that afternoon, about telling on Mom about, well, you know."

"I know. I know."

"I remember walking into the house and hearing something. Something angry and sad."

He nods again. This part isn't new either.

"And then, that's all. It's blank after that. Well, until I started remembering the gun."

"I think the angry-sad thing you heard was your mother's voice, and it was directed at you. No doubt, she was probably upset with you—for good reason, I might add—for walking out of your Aunt Kat's in the middle of the night. Knowing her, she sent you to bed."

"Why don't I remember that then? Why do I remember a gun?"

"You were probably already coming down with something. A fever can do weird things to our heads, our memories. And then, well, the shock of Mom disappearing, the guilt you no doubt felt and still feel." He stops and shakes his head.

"What if I caused her to fall?" I say.

"What do you mean?"

"Couldn't I have shot her, and the bullet, I don't know, hit her, but didn't, you know, stay lodged inside or whatever. And what if we were somewhere high up when I did it, and the force of it—the bullet—what if that caused her to fall?"

"Iris. You're watching too much TV. It doesn't work that way."

"How do you know?" I ask. "How does it work?"

"Look. I don't know why you're remembering what you're remembering but if I had to guess, I'd say it has to do with guilt, and the guilt is manifesting into these memories. Right around the time Mom disappeared was when you were hounding us to learn to shoot, and it was during that time when you were getting into a lot of trouble." He pauses and shifts his position in the booth, and I follow his gaze to Rosie, who's sitting in the driver's seat with Daisy right next to her. He fixes his eyes back on me. "Your mind is probably feeling guilty and creating images that might seem related—like the gun—even though a gun had nothing to do with what happened to your mom." He stops and stares out the window again.

"I didn't hurt that cat, you know." I wait until he turns back to me. "Kenny Landau's cat? I didn't cut off its ear."

"I know, Buttercup."

"Mom thought I did. She didn't even ask me. She just assumed."

"Mom was going through a mixed-up time. Plus, like I said, you'd been getting into trouble."

"I keep thinking that if I hadn't gone over Kenny Landau's house that afternoon, none of this would have happened. I keep thinking it was the one thing, you know, that set everything in motion. No matter how you look at it, it was my fault." I fiddle with a straw wrapper on the table, tearing it to shreds. He covers my hand with his own. Even though I'm tall, I have freakishly small hands for my size, and his hands—which are manly and large to begin with—look enormous on top of mine.

"It wasn't your fault." He rubs his thumb along the inside of my wrist. "You had nothing to do with your mother's death. *Nothing.* Iris? Do you hear me?"

"Yeah, I hear you."

"You believe me, right?"

"I don't know, Dad."

"Try, okay? Try to believe, to let it go. You can't carry this around with you forever, kiddo. Especially when it wasn't your fault. None of it was your fault."

The urgency in his voice gets me. For a moment, I wonder if we're still talking about me or something else.

"Okay," I say.

"Okay, what?"

"Okay, I'll try to believe and let it go." I attempt a convincing smile. He raises an eyebrow.

"Hmm," he says. "Not sure that one smile is enough to make me believe you, but it's a start." He slides out of the booth, and I follow.

"Dad?"

"Yeah?"

"How come you never wanted me to talk to anybody? You know, like the police. Or a shrink, like Aunt Kat wanted."

"Because," he says as he holds the door open for me, "cops and shrinks are notorious for planting seeds in kids' heads. You didn't need that. Whatever you remembered, *if* you remembered, needed to happen naturally."

"But you just said that even I couldn't trust my mind. That it might be playing tricks on me and creating images that never happened."

He stops walking and looks at me. "Exactly. Those images shared with a shrink or the cops, even if they're not real, *especially* when they're not real, could be dangerous. Right?"

Something in his eyes indicates that he's waiting for a specific response: a big old "yes" from me. He waits, taking his coat off in the process, the weather downright balmy for early April.

"Right," I say. I don't have the heart to point out he's gone and planted a memory garden all his own.

Chapter 38

Daisy

I tell everyone that I'm going to drive with Aunty to the wake. No one says anything, and I'm sure they're not surprised, since I tend to spend more time at Aunty's house than I do at ours.

I think, at first, Dad worried that she'd become a replacement mother, and then I think he was happy she was there, since she taught me how to cook (something everyone's asked me to do more of since most of Rosie's cooking is, like, totally gross). She taught me how to sew, which is awesome, since everyone knows I want to be a fashion designer when I grow up. Last summer, we even took a pottery class together. I love Aunty, and, of course, I love the attention I get when it's the two of us, but part of me feels sorry for her, too, because she's all alone.

See, after Mom disappeared, Aunty became obsessed—and I mean *totally* obsessed—with finding her. She drove the cops mental with all her theories, leads, and private investigators (she went through two in a year and a half). She said Mom never would have left, but when the cops pointed out she'd done it once before, Aunty pointed out that *1)* Mom had taken us with her and *2)* she'd come back on her own. One of the detectives, the one Daddy doesn't like—Panzieri—believed her. Panzieri also believed Daddy had something to do with Mom's disappearance, and Aunty believed it as well, at least in the beginning.

I don't remember seeing her much during those early months. Right around the one-year anniversary of Mom's disappearance, Daddy said he'd had enough, and he and Aunty had a long talk and somehow he convinced her he wasn't involved. She'd let up after that, mostly, but in some ways—in important ways—it was too late: Uncle Dennis had already walked out on her, none of her girlfriends talked to her anymore, and the accounting business she ran out of her house had "gone down the shitter," as Daddy likes to say. She'd lost touch with her step-kids as well (our step-cousins?). Even Rosie and Iris had kinda turned against her in the beginning. Things have mellowed since then, but I don't think Rosie's ever forgiven Aunty for accusing Daddy. I'm not so sure about Iris. I think Iris worries everyone blames her and that if she hadn't taken off from Aunty's house, maybe Mom would still be alive. Who knows? She might be right. I don't blame Iris, though. She was a kid. Besides, whoever hurt Mom had no right to do that.

#

"Can you zip me up?" Aunty says as she comes out of her bedroom, her arms behind her and her fingers tugging at the zipper.

I get up from the dining room table where her laptop hums and dozens of folders lay scattered. It's tax season, her busiest time of year. By the looks of everything, this might be the busiest she's been with work since Mom disappeared.

She turns around, and I zip her up and attach the clasp at the top. It's a sleeveless black dress with a scoop neck. We made it together when she was teaching me how to sew. She faces me. "There. What do you think?"

I think she looks tired and too skinny. We all lost weight after it happened, but after a while, when it became clear Mom wasn't coming back, we'd all started eating normal again. All, except for Aunty. Right now, she looks totally "ana," her bones and veins practically bursting through the skin on her neck, her arms, her legs.

"You look good," I say.

She examines her reflection in a mirror hanging on the wall and wipes the corners of her mouth with her index finger and thumb. Aside from her tight curls, which are just like Rosie's and mine, we don't share any other traits that I can see. Aunty is tall. Not as tall as Iris, but a lot taller than Mom and Grandma were. She has boobs, too. Mom was flat-chested, and so are Rosie and Iris. I still hold out hope, even though I'm almost thirteen. (Okay, in seven months. Whatever. Everyone says I think much older than that anyway.)

"Well," she says while she deposits a tube of lipstick in her black clutch. "Ready?"

I nod, but as I do, tears squirt from my eyes. How can I possibly be ready for this, a wake for my murdered mother? Aunty wraps her arm around me. She smells like ivory soap and vanilla.

"Oh, honey. I know," she says, as if she'd read my mind. "Trust me, I know."

But having her know isn't enough.

#

We pull into the funeral home's parking lot the same time Daddy does. Rosie and Iris follow in the old pickup that Rosie uses and will eventually share when Iris gets her license later this year. It's light out, even though it's almost five, and normally I love this time of year when we change the clocks and the air smells different and the flowers start to bloom. I love color— Aunty says this'll be my trademark in fashion. Right now, though, I feel like I might hurl.

"Why didn't you guys come with Daddy?" I whisper to Rosie as we squeeze together through the door and the funeral home dude ushers us into a room.

"We thought we'd go out afterwards and talk about tomorrow and stuff."

"Who's we? And talk about what?"

"You, Iris, and me. Talk about the funeral and whether we want to say anything."

The idea of speaking in front of a crowd of people under the best of circumstances scares the bejeezus out of me. There's no way in hell I'm doing it at my mother's funeral. "Okay, I'll come, but I don't want to say anything."

Rosie ignores my response, and I see why. She's staring straight ahead at the blue casket we'd picked out over the weekend. Our flowers cover it: roses, irises, and daisies. A tall lime green vase of sunflowers sits on the floor next to it, along with baskets and other arrangements. I glance at Iris and Rosie, their faces pale, and I know they're thinking the same thing I am: our mother is in that box. Our dead mother. Our murdered mother. Her remains. Not even a complete body, like most people get to bury, but bones. Broken bones.

I'm going to be sick.

I teeter like I'm walking a tight rope. The new strappy heels I'd saved for with my allowance and somehow convinced Daddy to let me wear tonight are not helping.

"Whoa, there," the funeral home dude says as he catches my arm and places his hand on the small of my back, actually a little lower than he should. *Perv.* "You okay?"

Aunty swoops in, takes my arm, and leads me to some chairs. "Let's sit," she says and then to the room: "Can someone get her a glass of water?"

A paper cup appears in front of my face, handed off by I don't even know who, and I take a small sip and wait. Rosie, Iris, and Daddy hover nearby.

"You okay, DD?" Daddy asks, and I nod. "You sit," he says. "We can stand."

"No, I'm okay." I stand, wobble for a moment, and then straighten. "See?"

I take my position next to Iris, and Aunty stands next to me. I spot Uncle Hank and Aunt Veronica and my cousins Henry and Michael on the other side of the room. People begin filing in: neighbors, cops I recognize from six years ago, teachers from school, my friends and their parents. My feet hurt, and I keep shifting from foot to foot as I shake people's hands, thank them for coming, and give hugs. I'm a robot simply going through the motions, any feelings I had draining out of me along with my sweat. It has to be, like, a hundred degrees in here, and when I glance over at Rosie and Iris, I see they're sweating, too.

When the crowd thins out, I step out of line and ask the pervy funeral director dude for another cup of water. He leads me into another room with a water cooler. I down two cups, fill another, and wander back. That's when I see the easel and the poster board overflowing with pictures. I must have missed it on the way in, consumed with trying not to yak on the carpet. I know Rosie has a photo album under her bed filled with pictures from when she was a baby and little kid, and even Iris has a picture on her nightstand of her and Mom, but I don't have any pictures displayed in my room or even my laptop. I know we have a bunch of files saved on the house computer, the one Dad uses for his business and for bills and that we've had, like, forever, but I never think to look in there, and we don't have many pictures hanging around the house of her either; it's mostly pics of us girls. So seeing so many images of Mom all at once is kinda weird.

"She was beautiful, wasn't she?" Aunty stands next to me, and I nod. "See?" She points to a picture of a frizzy-haired girl—Rosie, I think— splashing in a plastic pool. "That's her when she was five. She would have been your age in this one," she says while tapping her index finger on a shot of a girl wearing full makeup, some sort of weird black leotard-like top, and tight black jeans.

"She was allowed to wear makeup at my age?" I ask, and all of a sudden, I'm pissed because I've had to beg to wear a little mascara and pink lip gloss.

Aunty laughs. "Oh, she tried." Aunty sighs and points again. "Here she is holding you, right after you were born."

I've never seen the picture before, and I study it: the look of sheer joy on Mom's face, the purple headband holding back her thick curly hair, the soft pink of the blanket wrapped around me, the lime and blue teddy bears on the teeny-tiny cap on my head. It's weird, totally freaky even, looking at a picture of her hours after I entered the world, both of us alive, and today, one of us isn't, and hasn't been for a long time. I tremble, despite the tropical temperature.

"You okay?" Aunty asks.

"No," I say, surprised at myself.

Aunty squeezes my hand. "You will be."

I squeeze back and wonder if she's right.

#

Rosie and I sit side by side, across from Iris, and wait for our order of mozzarella sticks and fries, even though I bet we won't eat any of it. I stir the straw in my Diet Coke and watch as Iris shreds the paper from her straw, something she always does whenever we go out to eat. Drives Daddy insane.

"So," Rosie says. "Dad said we can say something, if we want, but we don't have to. Whatever we're comfortable with."

"Is it normal," I say, "for kids to say something at their parent's funeral? I mean, kids like us?"

Rosie shrugs. "I don't know."

I sip my Coke. "Do you want to say anything?"

"I don't," Iris says, her voice soft.

"Me either," I say. "I almost hurled when we had to do an oral report in English first term."

"Yeah," Rosie says. "I'm not sure I could get through it. So, I guess we're decided."

"Wait," Iris says. "So does that mean no one is saying anything?"

"Daddy said the priest will," I say. "We can tell the priest things to talk about."

"When are we supposed to do that?" Iris says, and I shrug. The waitress arrives and places the appetizers and three plates in front of us. I take a mozzarella stick and dip it in marinara sauce.

Rosie opens the bottle of catsup, turns it upside down above her plate, and smacks the bottom. "We'll be meeting at the funeral home before we go to the church. We can do it there."

"So, like, what are you guys wearing?" I ask in between mouthfuls.

"You would worry about that, DD," Iris says, and not too nicely I might add.

"Sorry. Can't help it if I actually *care* about how I look. Unlike some people."

Iris ignores me and stuffs a fry in her mouth. "Your boyfriend going to be there?" she says to Rosie.

I tug on Rosie's blouse. "Hey! I didn't know you had a boyfriend."

Rosie blushes, wipes her mouth, and stares at Iris. "I don't."

"Whatever," Iris says.

Rosie throws her napkin on the table. "What's your problem?"

I continue yanking on her sleeve. "Who is it?" I ask.

"No one," Rosie says, shaking me off.

Iris smirks. "Jamie Briggs."

"What? But isn't that the guy who …" I stop myself. We all know who Jamie is, and what he was to our mother. Not to mention he's also Rosie's boss, which is, like, totally weird and not something we talk about at home since it upsets Daddy. He and Rosie had a fight a few years ago when Rosie first started working at the Center. Some people think Rosie's all quiet and stuff, but she didn't back down on that one. I think Daddy gave in out of shock more than anything else.

"Yeah," Iris says. "Same guy."

"Why are you doing this?" Rosie says. "Why tonight of all nights?"

Iris shrugs, lowers her eyes, and goes back to shredding the shreds.

I lean into Rosie. "You're dating Jamie Bri—"

"Shh," she hisses. "And no. I'm not."

Iris looks up. "But you like him."

"Whether I do or not doesn't matter because he doesn't like me. At least not in that way. Happy?"

Iris doesn't respond.

"Wait," I say. "You do like him? In *that* way?"

"Shut up," Rosie says.

"I'm just asking! You guys don't tell me anything."

Rosie bangs her cup. "There is nothing to tell. Okay?"

"Jeez. Okay, okay. I'm not the one who brought it up."

"Is he going to the funeral?" Iris asks.

"How am I supposed to know?" Rosie says, miffed. "I'm not his keeper. But I'd think not, since—"

"Since he was fucking our mother and if he hadn't been, maybe she'd still be alive?" Iris scowls and crosses her arms.

"So that's it?" Rosie leans back in the booth and shakes her head. "You need someone else to blame so you can stop feeling guilty?"

"You saying I have something I should feel guilty about?"

"Only *you* know the answer to that." Rosie smacks the side of her head. "Oh, wait. That's right. You can't remember."

"Guys," I say, because the waitress is walking toward our table. She frowns when she sees Iris's mess.

"You girls need anything else?"

"No, thanks," I say, and she places the check on the table. I look at my phone: 10:11. "It's getting late. We should probably go home."

Rosie pulls out a five from her wallet and counts some one-dollar bills before leaving them poking out beneath her plate. She nudges me to move out of the booth. I do, and Iris puts some more singles on the table.

I shrug into my coat. "But I haven't put any money in."

"Forget it," Rosie says, and I know she means more than the money. Iris is already out the door and marching toward the truck.

"What's up with Iris?" I whisper.

"It's everything, I guess. It's hard, you know?"

"Yeah," I say. "It is." But having Rosie and Iris know isn't enough either.

Chapter 39

Iris

Rosie and Daisy don't say anything to me on the ride home or when I bump into Rosie on my way to the bathroom to brush my teeth or when I go to the kitchen to fill the water dispenser for Moonbeam, my teddy bear hamster, and I find Daisy standing at the sink eating ice cream right out of the container. I don't say anything to them, either.

I feel like a jerk. I don't like fighting with my sisters. I don't like fighting with anybody, honest. It's just that sometimes I get so angry, I can't help it. Angry because she's dead. Angry because people blamed Dad and some still do. Angry that Rosie has a crush on the guy Mom was sleeping with. Angry that I saw them—Mom and Jamie—and can't seem to forget that. Angry for who I am, what I am. Angry, maybe, because I can't have a crush, not now, anyway. Maybe not ever.

#

It's early morning, and the house is still in darkness as I lace up my running shoes. It'll be another half hour at least before any hint of light outside, but I don't care. Everyone's given up on telling me when I should and shouldn't run, and Dad doesn't question me anymore when I run at odd hours, like four in the morning.

Today, it's not quite that early. The clock in the kitchen says 5:55, and I know the coffee maker is set to go off in five minutes, which is when Dad gets up. I stretch my quads, my calves, my hamstrings, but I often wonder if this is a formality because my muscles always feel ready to work out.

Running is my second favorite pastime next to spending time with my pets. I ask Dad every year if we can go down to Boston to watch the marathon runners, but we never do. Next year I'll be able to drive myself, maybe. The Kenyans are always so fast, but even they are slow in comparison to animals. Did you know cheetahs can run seventy miles per hour? Some people think they're the fastest animals on the planet, but that's actually wrong. They're the fastest mammals. Sailfish reach the same speed in water, making them the fastest fish. The fastest insect is something called the hawk moth, which can reach thirty-three miles per hour, and the fastest reptile—the spiny-tailed iguana—can reach twenty-four miles an hour. But all of these are beaten by birds in flight. The peregrine falcon can fly at ninety miles an hour and dive at two *hundred* miles an hour, and it is truly the fastest animal on the planet. At least, the fastest one researchers know about. I like to think that somewhere—a Brazilian rainforest or the Outback in Australia, maybe—there's a bird we've never seen before, and it flies and swoops faster than fast. I picture it being a shy bird, leery of everything and everyone—human and animal alike, even its own kind—and it only comes out when it absolutely needs to. I bet there's a bird like that. Probably more than one. While part of me gets excited at the thought of being part of a research team when I grow up that discovers new bird species, another part of me hopes they're never discovered. Ever. Because if no one knows about them, they can live in peace.

#

I run. I try not to think and instead focus on the rhythm of my breathing, on the sound of my sneakers as they smack against the road, on the way everything wooshes in my ears, but, inevitably, my mind shifts and thinks and thinks and thinks.

I run.

I'm not sure I'm going to be able to keep it together this morning. I'm not sure how or if it's even possible. How can I sit up front, all eyes on my back, when I know what they're thinking: *Why can't she remember? She knows something. Who's she protecting?*

I run.

Some people think the beauty of small-town living is that everyone knows everyone else. But that also means everyone knows everyone's business and secrets. What I couldn't remember that day has been remembered for me in a variety of different "theories." The uncreative theory: Mom had decided she didn't want her life here anymore and had simply walked away. She'd since been "spotted" in California, Florida, and—my personal favorite—Gary, Indiana. I was the last person to have seen her that fateful morning, and her saying good-bye to me somehow traumatized me into forgetting her farewell.

I run.

The conspiracy theory: Dad and Hank had stumbled on the identity of my Uncle Carl's killers and they'd done Mom in as a warning. I'd witnessed the slaying. Or the fall, I guess. Whatever.

I run.

The causal theory: Dad had killed her in a drunken rage when he discovered she was having an affair with the guy in town who'd lost his legs and arms in Iraq. I'd walked in when it was happening.

I run.

You'd think that if any of these theories were correct, they'd somehow have eventually triggered my memory of them. But they haven't. I know deep in my gut that they're all wrong. The fact we're burying my mother today and that she's been dead for as long as she'd been missing should poke holes into the first two theories. People don't always like the facts, though, especially when they're pointed out by a teenager.

I stop, pant, and bend over with my hands on my knees. As I straighten, I take in my surroundings. Where am I? I've run almost every road in Granite Creek, I think, and the ones surrounding it, but sometimes I get lost in my head, and my feet simply take me places. I mentally retrace the last street I remember being on, Dairy Farm Road (real inventive). It's long, and I think this one is off it. Still, nothing is familiar, not the bend where I've stopped, not the landscape, not the house I'm facing, which sits alone away from the road. To its left stands an old weathered barn and a fenced in area, a pasture of sorts maybe. Something moves in the pasture, and so do I. Closer.

Despite past events, I'm not a timid person, never have been and probably never will be. There's a difference, I think, between being timid and being quiet. With me, most people assume one and then the other. I don't bother to correct them.

I trudge up the driveway toward the barn, the sky getting lighter with each step, and my breathing returns to normal. In the fenced in area a woman walks a small-ish brown horse (maybe a pony?) back and forth, back and forth. She doesn't acknowledge me until I'm right at the fence, which I lean over while I watch. She doesn't stop. She's older—*old*, actually—with gray hair that's loose and curly and wild and reminds me of Daisy's when she teases it. Dad calls it "80s hair." She's skinny, though, with no butt to speak of, and wears blue jeans, work boots like Dad's, a flannel shirt with a turtleneck underneath, and heavy-looking gloves.

"Yeah?" she says, and she doesn't sound particularly concerned that I'm standing there watching her. The horse wears a bright red halter, and she leads him by a rope attached to it.

"You exercising him?" I ask, partly confused and partly embarrassed because I don't know enough about horses to know if it's a male or if this is how you exercise them. Birds are more my specialty since I can watch those for free in the woods. And, of course, cats and hamsters since I have one of each.

"Colic," she says.

"Huh?"

"She's got colic. Have a call into the vet, but doubt he'll get here for another hour anyway."

"Oh." I nod even though I have no idea what colic is. I've always thought it was something babies got.

"Who are you?" she says.

"Me?"

She keeps walking. "Yeah, you. Unless there's someone else hiding there in the shadows."

"No, it's just me. My name's Iris."

"Well, Iris. I'm Rebecca. How do you do? I'd shake your hand, but I can't stop walking ol' Chestnut here."

"How come?"

"You ever get a stitch in your side when you run?"

"How'd you know I run?"

"What, you think I start talking to random people who come up to me this early in the morning? I saw you come down the street and practically collapse in front of my house."

I laugh. "I wasn't going to collapse. I was catching my breath."

"And if you hadn't caught it, you would have collapsed, right? Anyhow, you didn't answer my question. When you get a stitch in your side, it's uncomfortable, right?"

"Yep."

"Now imagine you're a horse with a horse-sized abdomen and horse-sized intestines and you have that sort of stitching feeling. Now multiply the feeling by a hundred and it's running through your belly."

"Ouch."

"Exactly. That's colic. When it gets real bad, a horse will roll around and even refuse to get up. That's never a good sign. It's dangerous."

"Why?"

"Because when a horse rolls—and I mean thrashing—it can tangle its innards."

"For real?"

"You betchya. Twisted gut. That's why I gotta walk her. So she doesn't roll. Hoping I caught it early enough. Right, ol' girl?" Her voice softens a bit. "You got yourself some gas, Chestnut?"

"Gas? You mean like—"

"Yeah, like when you have to fart, but you have to hold it in and it hurts. Kinda like that. Right, Chestnut? You gotta let one rip?"

I laugh. The woman seriously must be on something. But she's funny. She glances at her watch and slows down right in front of me.

"Well, we'll let her rest a bit now. I like to walk her for twenty minutes, then let her rest a little, then walk her some more. As long as she stays standing." She juts her chin in my direction. "Go on. You can stroke her."

I reach out my hand, tentative at first, and Chestnut sniffs it. Her huge nostrils flare, and her breath is hot against my hand. I don't think I've ever been this close to a horse. I stroke her down the white part of her nose. "So how did you know something was wrong? Did you find her rolling on the ground?"

"Hell no," Rebecca says. Her eyes are pale blue and surrounded by endless wrinkles. "At that point, I doubt I'd have had any luck getting her on her feet. No, I just had a feeling something was off. Chestnut and me have been together for thirty years. That's longer than my two marriages combined." She throws her head back and belts out a laugh that turns into a phlegm-filled cough. "Anyhow, thankfully, I'm an early riser, up at four most mornings. I looked in on her and I could tell. I've seen enough colicky horses and ponies in my lifetime to spot it a mile away."

"Was she doing something specific? What were her symptoms?"

"Well, she didn't come greet me like she usually does. When the friendliest pony in the universe doesn't do that, you know something's up. She was also curling her lips and showing her teeth and putting her neck out straight. All signs." She pauses and watches me stroke her nose. "You like animals. You're good with 'em, too. I can tell."

"I don't know too much about horses. I have a cat. Well, it's my sister's cat, but—"

"But the cat likes you best," she finishes for me.

I nod. "I also have a teddy bear hamster. Oh, and a beta. You know, one of those fishes that flare up when they see their reflections in a mirror. So, you said Chestnut is a pony?"

"Yep. Her mother was a generic pony, her father was a registered Morgan stallion, but her size makes her a pony, not a horse. And yeah, I know there're miniature horses out there, but she's still a pony."

I nod and commit these details to memory. I'll research Morgan stallions online later.

"You in school?" she says.

"Yep."

"Where you go?"

"Granite Creek High."

She arches a barely-there eyebrow. "High school?"

"Yeah. I'm tall for my age."

"I'll say. What year?"

"Sophomore."

"Well, Ms. Iris, I'm no busybody, but shouldn't you be at school right now? Or at least getting ready for school instead of out here yapping my ear off?"

I'm yapping her *ear off?* "Oh, I'm not going to school today."

"How come?"

I stop stroking the pony. "I have a funeral to go to."

"I'm sorry to hear that."

"It's okay."

I kick at the ground and avoid her eyes because I can feel them boring into my skull. I wait for the inevitable question: *Who died?*

"So you got a job, Iris?" she asks instead, surprising me.

"Nope."

"You want one?"

"What do you mean?"

"I mean here." She points to the barn. "There's more where this girl came from. I got me two donkeys, three goats, a whole mess of chickens, one extra cocky rooster, and some rabbits. Not to mention a lazy-ass sheep dog who's asleep inside the house."

"Wow. It's like a farm."

"Yeah, and ever since Fred died nine months ago, it's been too much work for this old broad to handle on her own."

"Was Fred your husband?"

"Fred was my live-in for the last seventeen years. Good man. Lousy gambler, but good man." She laughs her ragged laugh. "Don't ever get married, Iris. Live in sin, but don't let him convince you to get hitched." And she laughs again.

"No chance of me marrying a 'him.' I guarantee that." *Oh my God. Did I just come out to an old woman walking a colicky horse on the morning of my mother's funeral?* The words tumbled out of my mouth, that's the honest truth. (Okay, maybe I wanted them to.) Either way, I immediately regret them hanging there between us and wonder if she'll understand their meaning.

She tilts her head and sizes me up. "Ah, hell, you'll probably be better off lovin' a woman instead of a man. Sometimes I wished I'd been wired that way." She takes the rope from the halter and wraps it around her gloved hand. "Anyhow. That mean you're in?"

"Yeah. I mean, I guess."

"We can figure out proper compensation. You got some grownup or something you need to ask permission?"

"My dad, probably."

She nods. "Well, then. You ask your daddy if you can help Rebecca Woodhull over on East Meadow Road four or five days a week. Three or four weekdays, but one weekend day is a must. More during the summer, if you want it. You like gardening?"

"I don't know. I've never done it."

"Well, I keep gardens in the summer. You can help me with that if you want." She stops and points to the pony's mouth, her lips curling. She does look like she's smiling. "I best get Chestnut walking some more."

"Right." I step back and watch Rebecca lead the pony.

"My condolences," she calls out.

"What?"

"The funeral you have to go to. My condolences."

"Oh. Thanks." For some insane reason, part of me wants to tell her the funeral is for my mother. But I don't. "So when do you want me to start?"

"Whenever you're ready. I'll be here. Next week. Week after."

"Okay."

"Okay, then. Bye, Ms. Iris."

#

I run.

Could it be okay? Loving a girl? Marrying a girl?

I run.

Did I just get a job working with animals?

I run.

Steam rises from the streets, and sunlight pours over the treetops. The air smells like wet leaves and moss, like grass when you walk through right after a rain shower.

I run.

Excitement bubbles up in my belly, a feeling I remember getting when I was younger before everything happened and everything changed, like the day I'd found a ten-pound snapping turtle on the road or the first time I saw an owl in our woods or that last summer we were all together, a hot August day in the middle of the week, and all of us—Mom, Dad, Rosie, Daisy— went to Salisbury Beach and hung out, happy.

I run, stretch my arms to the sky, let the feeling overtake me, and pray it will somehow last.

Chapter 40

Rosie

We stand side by side: me, Daisy, Iris. The crowd has thinned out, and cars pull away, their tires crunching on the gravel path that leads to this secluded spot deep inside the cemetery. It's a newer section, recently excavated to hold more bodies, and the nearest tombstone is a good twenty-five feet away. Her casket sits over the grave on a platform. It won't be lowered and officially buried until after we're gone.

"She's all alone," Daisy says. "I don't want her to be lonely."

I wrap my arm around her. She's almost as tall as I am in her high heels, which isn't saying much, considering Iris towers over us both. "Just her bones," I say. "Her spirit is everywhere."

Daisy peers up at me, her eyes red-rimmed and puffy. "Do you really believe that?"

"I don't know, but today I need to."

"I'm sorry," Iris whispers, and we both turn to her. Tears trickle down her face. Her hair is pulled back in a ponytail, and it glistens in the sun. It's warm for early April, summerlike almost, and drops of sweat bead at her hairline.

"You okay, Iris?" Daisy says.

"It's my fault," she says. "I killed her."

Daisy gapes, her face contorted in horror.

"No, Iris," I say. "You didn't. You were a kid. You didn't push mom from a building, balcony, whatever. And you didn't bury her body in some woods in Maine."

She turns to us. "But if I hadn't told on her. If I hadn't gotten in trouble that afternoon and told Dad I'd seen Mom with, you know. And if I hadn't come home that night and whatever. Chased her out or got mad at her or threatened her. Then she wouldn't have left, and this—" She pauses and points to the casket. "This wouldn't have happened." She stops and sniffles. "I'm sorry," she says again, and I realize now that she's directing it at us, not the grave, not Mom.

When I work at the Center with the kids and one child hits another or takes a toy or pulls another kid's hair, I always tell the offender the most important thing he or she can do is be genuinely sorry and ask for forgiveness. Then I tell the "victim" that the best thing he or she can do is offer the offender the *gift* of forgiveness. Never in the last five and a half years had it ever occurred to me that the one thing my sister needed was this gift I'd encouraged so many kids to offer so freely. Or that forgiving might be as important to me as it is to her.

"I forgive you," I say, and I mean it.

Daisy looks at me and then at Iris and nods. She takes Iris's hand in her own and squeezes it tight. "Me, too."

Iris shudders and lets out something in between a sob and a wail, and we both circle her and hug her, something she rarely allows since she's not a touchy-feely sort of person.

#

On our way back to the car (Dad had the good sense to say no to the limos offered by the funeral home, figuring we might want to linger at the end; he drove us and left me with his keys while he hitched a ride back to the church with Uncle Hank), I spot someone standing a few hundred feet away.

Daisy points. "Isn't that—"

"Yeah," I say. "It's him."

Iris follows our gaze. "We'll wait for you at the car."

I watch as they walk up the hill, arm in arm. Then, I face Jamie. He doesn't move, so I take a deep breath and go to him. He wears a navy blue suit, and if you didn't know it, you probably couldn't tell he has prosthetics for legs and arms. I look around, wondering if he's by himself or if someone brought him here, and I spy his van, alone, far down the path.

"Hey," I say.

"Hey."

We stand awkwardly for a few moments until I can't take the silence anymore. "Were you at the funeral?" Most of the service was a blur, but I'd steal looks over my shoulder every now and then to see if he was there, sitting in the back or in the balcony.

He shakes his head. "Didn't think it'd be appropriate."

"Oh. Right."

"I'm sorry, Rosie."

Unlike Iris, I know he's not asking forgiveness for anything specific, at least I don't think he is. He's merely offering his condolences. "Thanks," I say. "What do they call it? Closure."

"Won't be that until they find who did it."

"I guess." I glance back at the grave. Daisy's right. It does look lonely. "Well, you probably want to be alone."

"I would like to say good-bye to her."

"Right. Well, I'll—"

"But I could use some help, actually," he says. "Terrain here's a little more uneven than I expected." The tips of his ears turn red, something I've noticed happens when he's angry or has to ask for help, like it's a weakness or failure on his part.

"Oh, sure," I say. I extend my arm but realize I don't even know how to help him. "What can I do?"

"Stand on my right side, and hold onto me at the elbow. And then we'll take it slow."

I follow his directions, and we make our way together, arm in arm. He smells incredible, a combination of freshly showered and something else: aftershave, cologne, or maybe just him. I pretend we're going on a date or to my prom. I pretend he's my boyfriend. I pretend we're taking a romantic walk in the countryside and that my sisters aren't up on the hill gawking. I pretend we're not walking toward my mother's grave. I pretend and pretend and pretend, hoping that if I pretend hard enough, this fantasy of mine will pass through me to him and that everything will be different.

Chapter 41

Jamie

The air smells different in a cemetery. I don't know if it's the dug up earth or what, but it's not normal. Of course, what is normal? Normal for me ended on May 4, 2005, when my Humvee and the two riding behind mine were hit by an IED. Whether you consider me one of the lucky ones is purely subjective. I was one of three severely injured, while five of my brothers were killed. Out of the three of us who survived the initial blast, I'm the only one who lived beyond six months. And that's all you'll get out of me. I don't remember much about that day, and what I do, I'd rather forget.

\#

She leads me down the hill, which isn't as steep as I thought. I probably could have maneuvered it on my own, and now I regret asking her for help. We reach the grave, and she releases my arm and steps back.

"I can wait over here," Rosie says, her voice low. "If you want."

"No, that's okay. You're fine where you are." How many gravesides have I stood by? Even though I stopped counting long ago, I remember them all, starting with my father's. I stare at the casket, which is blue and gleams in the sunlight, and I think about death, the most routine thing in the world. It happens every second of every day of every year. Yet there's nothing routine about the process of dying, everyone's experience unique to them.

That first day Koty and I met, had either of us thought it would end like this, with her taken, brutalized, murdered? (I don't think Rosie knows the full story, and that's probably best. There's always stuff they don't tell the families.) When I enlisted, even though injury and death are reality in soldiers' lives, especially those serving in war zones, did I expect this would happen to me? No. We don't think about or expect those things, because if we did, we'd stop everything. We'd stop living. Why was I given a pass, a second chance, when my brothers weren't so "lucky"? Why was Koty killed? I spend my days focusing on the questions I can answer: how to form a wheelchair basketball team, how to manipulate a prosthetic leg so your stump doesn't ache, how to satisfy a woman with nothing more than your tongue. But it's moments like this one when all the unanswered questions come tumbling forth with no answers to catch them with. All I can do is wait it out, once again at the mercy of the universe or God or time.

#

"Okay," I say to Rosie. "I'm ready to go back." She appears puzzled at first, as if maybe she'd expected me to cry or take more than a couple of minutes standing in silence. Then, she nods, and her face dissolves into some semblance of understanding. Shit, she reminds me of her mother.

She takes my arm, and we walk up the hill and then down the path toward my van. We stop.

"Well," I say.

"Well," she says. "Thanks for coming. I appreciate it. I know she would have. That she does."

I nod. "I'm sorry." What I want to say: *I'm sorry if I had a hand in this. If my presence in your mother's life led her here.* But I don't.

"I know," she says, and I hold her gaze and see that she does. Her eyes are a shade lighter than her mom's dark brown. They're softer, too, but maybe Koty's eyes looked this way when she was seventeen and before life threw shit at them.

She reaches for me, and I allow her to hug me, even though I stand stiff, my back straight. It's not that I don't want to hug her; I can't. She lingers, and finally I pull away. "I should let you go," I say. "Your sisters are waiting."

She nods, and I ignore the tears about to spill from her eyes. "Bye," she says. "See you next week."

"Right," I say, and I watch her walk away.

May 2014

Chapter 42

Wayne

I stand in one of the interview rooms in the police department, wondering if this is the beginning or the end. Panzieri had called earlier in the day, asking me to come in.

"Should I bring a lawyer?" I had asked.

"That won't be necessary."

"And I should believe you why?"

"There's been a break in the case. The Feds believe they've determined who your wife's killer is. Thought it best to share the details in person."

I'd told him I could be there at two o'clock and hung up, while ten million different emotions washed over me: relief, curiosity, guilt.

#

Panzieri walks in, and even that—the man's self-important swagger—is enough to transport me back to the days and weeks following Koty's disappearance and my overwhelming desire to slug him on a daily basis. He'd been an overzealous detective hell bent on finding me guilty, despite the fact Koty had walked out before, despite the fact her affair became public, despite the fact I'd passed a polygraph.

"Thanks for coming in, Mr. Fowler," Panzieri says, a folder in one hand and his other extended in greeting, the same hand that pointed a finger in my face five and a half years ago. I ignore it, and he nods, barely, and pulls back. He motions to two chairs in front of a desk. "Have a seat."

"I'll stand, thanks. Tell me what you have to tell me."

"Right."

"You said you've found the person?"

"Yes, the Feds believe so." He flips open the folder. "Porter Clemson. White male. Age fifty-one. Had been serving a life sentence for the kidnapping, rape, and murder of twelve prostitutes from New Hampshire and Maine, killed between 1988 and 2009. Clemson was caught in 2009 and convicted in 2012." He looks up. "And murdered nine months ago."

"Murdered?"

"Yes. By a fellow inmate."

What the fuck? I let out a low whistle because I'm incredulous more than anything else, and I need to channel my energy somewhere. I need to be alert to play this hand, whatever it is: a bluff, a gift, a pardon.

"Clemson was a serial killer, Mr. Fowler. Dubbed the 'Jezebel Killer' by the Feds, and they think your wife was one of his last victims."

"I remember that case. Big news around here." I rub my jaw, deciding how to frame my question. "But there's something I don't understand. You say Clemson killed prostitutes?" Panzieri nods, and I choose my next words carefully. "My wife was a lot of things, but she was no prostitute."

"No, of course not."

"So what's the connection?"

"The Feds have their theories, and I'd be happy to connect you with someone in the Bureau if you have more questions, but the short of it goes like this: your wife and the other victims shared strikingly strong physical characteristics with Clemson's ex-wife, who apparently was a serial cheater."

"He kill her, too?"

"No. She filed for divorce, however, and took up with one of her lovers. This was back in 1988, which was when he started killing. Clemson had an interesting history before that, of course, as most serial killers do. His mother died when he was five, and his father was a drunk and beat him regularly. Clemson was incredibly bright—genius, actually—and did well in school. That is until he dropped out his junior year of high school. Had an 'inappropriate' relationship with one of his teachers. Some believed the teacher in question had been raped by Clemson, but she refused to press charges." He consults the folder again. "Anyhow, the genius part about him ensured he never had problem finding work. Clemson was in computer sales of some sort. Made a shitload of money. Worked from home but traveled a lot."

I wait, and so does he, his eyes on mine. I don't blink.

"You going to tell me the rest?" I say. "Or am I supposed to guess?"

"Clemson was in the area on December 10, 2008."

"The area?"

"He'd been in Connecticut on business on December 10. Started for home—he lived in Maine—but decided, apparently, to stop at a motel in Portsmouth for the night. Turns out it was the twenty-year anniversary of his wife filing for divorce. He'd been served papers on December 10, 1988, and the date held significance for him. Apparently, he left his hotel room abruptly before midnight. Turns out he had tried calling his ex-wife, but she had hung up on him. Clemson didn't check out or anything, and he had damaged the room. Put a hand through a wall. That's why the Feds were able to piece this together. We had a police report on file. We think he picked up Koty somewhere on his way back to Maine."

I can't fucking believe what I'm hearing, but I play along. "Picked up?"

"She didn't have her car when she left, right? We have to believe she was on foot. Perhaps hitchhiking. Shit luck. Wrong place. Wrong time. Wrong car for her to get into."

I rub my face again and try to process everything, including how the hell I'm supposed to respond. "I'm not a cop or a lawyer, but is that it? Doesn't seem like an ironclad case."

"How much do you want to hear?"

I study his poker face. The prick is having way too much fun with this. "All of it," I say. "I'll censor what I tell my girls."

He nods. "There's also the manner in which he killed his victims. He tortured them, Mr. Fowler. Kept them awhile in his house. Raped them. Beat them. What killed them, however, was this: he pushed them out a third-story window, thus the connection to Jezebel, a biblical character who was defenestrated."

"*Defenes*—what?"

"Defenestrated. Means throwing someone out of a window. 'Jezebel' means an immoral woman."

"I know what Jezebel means."

"Clemson had a huge house in Maine on secluded property. While it might have been possible to survive the fall with proper medical attention, the women had already been through so much, and, of course, he didn't get them help. Likely let them suffer before he disposed of the bodies. Your wife's injuries are consistent with a fall like that." He pauses. "Mr. Fowler, didn't you wonder why we didn't come around asking you all sorts of questions after your wife's body was discovered?"

"I wondered."

"Once the medical examiner determined the types of injuries, the way in which she died, where she was buried, the Feds immediately focused on Clemson. Also, there's the physical evidence that was discovered on the victims. The remnants of a silk nightgown were found with your wife's remains. The other victims were found with similar material. Lingerie. This part had never been revealed to the press; it didn't come out until Clemson's trial. So the Feds were able to rule out a copycat killer."

I ignore the images popping in my head and struggle for something to say. "Lingerie?" I manage. "Like that shit from Victoria's Secret?"

"More like that shit from Frederick's of Hollywood. The Feds believe he was trying to humiliate them, cheapen them even more, by burying them in outlandish stuff. We're not talking sexy stuff, but hardcore. He went after prostitutes because he equated their 'sin' with his wife's transgressions. He'd said all along, up until his death, that we hadn't found all his victims."

"But Koty wasn't a prostitute."

"No, but let's say she was hitchhiking." He shuffles through paper in the folder. "Cell phone records show Koty tried reaching Mr. Briggs that fateful night. She made one call to him at 10:06. Didn't last more than a couple of seconds."

Hearing Jamie Briggs's name makes me want to punch a wall, even to this day. "He said he didn't see her that night."

"So he said. But there was a window of opportunity, right? Mr. Briggs's mother was at the grocery store that night when Koty made her call. Maybe he *did* see her. Maybe she wanted 'in.' And maybe he said no."

I clench my jaw because I know the prick doesn't believe this. He's trying to get a rise out of me. *Bastard.* "Interesting theory."

"It might explain why Mrs. Briggs found Koty's cell phone in the driveway the next day. Perhaps spurned by her lover, and knowing the wrath she might face from her husband and even her children, Koty runs. She's somehow lost or dropped her phone. She has no money. So she hitchhikes."

"Enter Porter Clemson."

"That's right. He sees her and picks her up because she fits his type."

"Except for the prostitute part," I remind him.

"True. But if your wife, if Koty, opened up at all about *why* she was hitching, well that could have set him off." He pauses, regards me, and continues. "Think about it. What if she told him about her own difficulties in her marriage and her transgression with Mr. Briggs? It might have been enough to push him over the edge. An edge that, by all accounts, he was dancing precariously close to anyway. The location fits as well: Koty's remains were found in a wooded area off the Maine Turnpike, as were six of his victims, the other six being found along wooded areas off I-95 in New Hampshire."

I allow my eyes a quick intake of the room and wonder if I'm on camera, if this is a trap, if the state police are going to burst in at any moment, or even the Feds. But Panzieri says nothing more.

"What about, you know, DNA?"

"Clemson was meticulous. He didn't leave behind any of his DNA. It's one of the reasons why it took so long to catch him. The Feds believe he took as much time preparing the bodies for disposal as he did with killing them."

I shake my head. "You keep saying the Feds believe."

"Excuse me?"

"You keeping saying, 'the Feds believe this,' and 'the Feds believe that.' What do you believe?"

"I believe I owe you an apology." He closes the folder, crosses his arms, stares me square in the eyes, and I know he doesn't believe a single word of what he's told me. "Don't I?"

"You do or you don't, I don't give a shit. Nothing you say or I say is going to bring her back."

"True. But I would think you'd want closure."

What the fuck does he know about what I want? I want him to shut the fuck up. I want to get the fuck out of here. "What makes you think I don't?" I wait for him to say something, but he doesn't, so I continue. "Ever since this happened, my number one priority has been my daughters."

"Of course. No one would argue with that."

"So unless closure is going to bring their mother back, then it doesn't amount to a whole helluva lot, does it?"

He strokes his chin, a thoughtful expression spreading across his face. "Interesting."

"What's that?"

"How much your philosophy has changed since your brother was murdered. You wanted nothing but blood back then, as I recall."

Hearing Carl referenced, even after all this time, still throws me off, despite all the goddamn AA meetings I attend and conversations with well-meaning members about forgiveness and moving forward. "As any twenty-something kid probably would."

"Ah, yes. Today, you're older. Wiser." He pauses. "Smarter."

"So," I say. "We done here?" I hold his gaze, determined that he sees my eyes and that I don't flinch, not even for a millisecond.

"Looks that way, Mr. Fowler." He smiles. "Looks that way."

#

Outside, I walk to my truck, get inside, turn the key, and pull away from the curb. I feel eyes watching me, but I don't look around. Is it possible it's over? That I can live without fear for Iris? Will this put the images that Iris is remembering to rest, once and for all? Can she finally live in peace? Can I?

December 11, 2008, is a day I'd like to forget, but I know no amount of time will allow me to and that no amount of forgiveness exists to absolve me from what I did to Koty on her last night on earth. My one hope, growing brighter now, is that the actions I've taken since then have saved a life: our daughter's. Koty would have wanted that, I have no doubt.

I grip the steering wheel.

The engine hums.

My mind wanders back, and I'm there again on that day, that morning, in that surreal moment when everything changes.

It's not until I'm on my way back from the john that my eyes begin to focus, and my peripheral vision returns. There's a lump at the far end of the hall, and, at first, I think it's her, Koty.

"Christ almighty, get up from the goddamn floor."

She doesn't move, and I wonder if she's dead. My mind rewinds as best it can to the night before, spitting images out of order.

"Fuck me." I stumble toward her body, fall on my knees, and that's when I see that it's not Koty. It's Iris, curled tight like a snail, her hand wrapped around the butt of a gun.

"Iris!" Her eyes are open, staring blankly ahead. She blinks once, but that's all. "Iris!" I wave my hand in front of her eyes, but there's no connection, no acknowledgement. "Iris, can you hear me? Are you hurt? Say something!" She doesn't.

What the fuck happened? I twist on my haunches, fall over as I do, right myself, and survey my surroundings. That's when I see the blood on the wall and the floor, with a trail leading down the hall. *Fuck!*

I turn back to Iris, lifting her head, her arms, her legs, searching for evidence, for a source of the blood. I sniff her hand and the barrel of the gun. It's been fired. I'm not imagining this. I look at the blood again. Someone's been shot. But who? And that's when it hits me. *Koty's* been shot. And Iris— oh my God, Iris!—shot her.

I stand and stagger down the hallway, following the blood until I get to the front door, which I throw open. My feet are bare. I jump down the steps. "Koty?" I yelp. "Koty?"

Nothing.

I mount the steps and race down the hallway back to Iris.

"Iris," I hiss as I slide on the hardwood floor to where she's balled up, fetal-like. "Iris, can you talk? Are you hurt?" I reach for her and stroke her shoulder. She doesn't flinch. She doesn't do anything.

The gun.

My senses are waking up. I need to get the gun out of her hand. I cover my right hand over hers, so small, and can barely believe this is happening. I pry. I try to pry.

"Iris. You need to let go, okay? C'mon, sweetheart. Please. You know you're not supposed to touch Daddy's gun."

She must be able to hear me, because with those words, her fingers loosen, and I'm able to pull the gun from her grip. My head pounds, my eyes bulge, and my tongue cottons. *What the fuck happened, what the fuck happened?* My brain's covered in tar. Logic tries to move through the sludge to get to my memory. *Last night. Last night. What the fuck happened last night?* I lean against the wall, writhing in pain that's beyond physical.

I have to find Koty. I return the gun to my bureau and haul ass through the house: the bathroom, the kids' rooms, the kitchen, even closets, just in case she's still here. She's not, and the blood trail out the door shows me where I need to search next. But first, I need to help Iris. I go down the hall, get on my knees once more, crawl to Iris, and stroke her cheek. "Iris, I need you to listen to me carefully, okay? I need you to get up. I need you to get up and go to your room and stay there until I get back, okay?"

She blinks, says nothing.

"Dammit, Iris!" I slam my fist on the floor, and, for the first time, I notice I'm crying, snot dripping down my nose. "Listen. I think Mommy's hurt. I need to go find Mommy. But I need you to stay here."

She doesn't move. I rub my face and pull myself up.

"Okay, okay. Here's what we're going to do. I'm going to pick you up. I'm going to pick you up and put you in your bed. Because you're sick, Iris, okay? You're sick, too sick to move. I understand that. So I'm going to put you in your bed, and I'm going to go out, and you're going to stay in bed, you hear? Don't get up for the door, the phone, nothing, okay? And when I come back, I'm going to …" I stop, cough, struggle. "I'm going to give you saltines and ginger ale and chicken soup. Whatever you want."

She's a contorted ball of dead weight. I can't recall someone so little being so goddamn heavy. I carry her to her room, place her on her unmade bed, pull the covers tight over her body, still formed into a doughnut.

"There. Isn't that better?" I ask, except this time I don't expect a response.

#

I throw on my boots, my parka, my gloves, my hat, and check the door to make sure it's unlocked in case Koty comes back. I glance at the junk table by the door where she usually charges her cell phone, but the charger is empty. *My cell.* I run into the bedroom, grab it from the bureau, and note the time: 6:51 a.m.

I walk out the front door. Her van sits in the driveway. The sky bulges with snow. It's cold, fucking cold, even for here, even for now. I don't need to think where she'd go. I know her, despite what she thinks. I know about her long walks in these woods, her escape from me, our girls, our life, how she knows this land as well as I do, how these woods separate us from the good side of town, how they separate me from him, the crippled kid fucking my wife.

I have no idea if she's leaving me and going to him for good, and, in this moment, I don't care. All I can think about is Iris, about the gun, about the blood, about all the trouble Iris's been in, been causing, and I won't let anything happen to her, won't let them take her away, regardless of what she's done to her mother. I know despite all our disagreements, about the fact we don't see eye to eye on anything anymore, that Koty would agree with me on that.

I follow what appears to be blood, kicking at it with my boots, as it leads me around back, toward the woods. It's not as much as I'd expect from a gunshot wound. You wouldn't notice it, if you weren't looking for it, or at least looking for something. Perhaps she's not as hurt as I originally thought. Grazed, startled, in shock, no doubt, but not severely injured. Maybe a flesh wound, enough to scare her, enough to hurt, enough to disorient her, make her walk out in the early morning hours.

"Fuck!" I yell as I break a tree branch for the hell of it.

Normally, I'd relish a morning like this: cold, calm, peaceful even. The calm before the storm. Just me, the woods, the elements. Instead, I feel nothing but urgency, and dread. I quicken my pace, hoping the route I'm taking, the most direct route I can think of, is the same one Koty took. The woman was never good with directions.

I walk.

Maybe she's already made it to his house. Maybe she's even in a hospital. But no, I reason, I'd have heard by now. I dig into my pocket, make sure I still have my cell, that it's on, and it is. 6:56. No messages, no missed calls. The booze seeps out of my pores, and with each step, my reasoning returns. This isn't making sense. When the fuck did Iris come home? Sometime this morning? Sometime last night? Either way, Koty'd have ended up somewhere by now, right? I stop, rotate three hundred sixty degrees, consider my surroundings, take my phone out again, dial our home number—hoping perhaps a message awaits or maybe even Koty herself answers—and continue walking, my impatience mounting with each unanswered ring. Finally, voice mail kicks in. I hit the right combination of keys, and a familiar voice chirps: "You have no new messages."

Damn.

Had she returned home, she'd have picked up the phone, right? If only because of Iris. Unless she took Iris to the hospital.

I dial her cell. I don't expect an answer, even if she does have it, since she'll see it's me. I wait for the beep: "It's me. I'm in the woods looking for you. If you get this, call me. It's okay, just call. I'm not mad. I need to know you're okay. Iris needs you. Please. Call me."

I walk.

What if she doesn't listen to her voice mail, especially if she sees it's my number?

I walk and walk and walk.

I decide to text her: *Where r u? need 2 know ur ok. something wrong w/iris.* I send the message. 7:03 a.m.

I walk.

I run.

I scream, only once, "Koty, please!"

Time collapses.

A hawk screeches overhead. Branches and dead leaves crack beneath my weight. The earth thumps. A white birch stands out, stark against the grays, browns, and pine greens. A squirrel dashes up the side of a tree, scolding me the whole time.

I wish I had my rifle.

I make out the old culvert ahead, the sorry excuse for a "creek" running through the enormously high-ceilinged tunnel, and the steep embankment that leads to the road some twenty feet above, the same road where the kid lives. Anger tears at my insides. It would be just like her to put me in a situation where I needed to go to that house, that fucking house where I installed a goddamn fucking "roll in shower" so this kid could wash his stinking ass in comfort.

I pull out my cell, a picture of my girls on the front. Rosie uploaded it as a screen saver because I couldn't figure out how. I run my thumb over Iris, over all of them, and note the text displayed at the bottom: Thurs. Dec. 11. 7:13 am.

Fuck, fuck, fuck.

The cell vibrates in my hand. It's Kat. *Shit.*

"Hello?"

"Wayne, it's Kat." Panic drips from her voice. "I tried the house, but no one picked up. And Koty's cell goes to voice mail. Is Iris with you? I went to wake the kids, and she's not here. Rosie says she snuck out last night and was heading to your place."

"Yes. She's home." I keep walking, my eyes surveying the landscape, looking for signs. I head toward the culvert.

"Oh, thank God," she breathes. "Is she okay?"

"Might be coming down with something. Told her she should stay in bed and not pick up the phone." My mouth forms words, my brain is on autopilot, and I tense at the inevitable question I know is coming next.

"Oh. Where are you? Where's Koty?"

Somehow, I know any answer I give to this question could have long-term ramifications. Deep in my gut, my core, perhaps in that place where Koty insists the "old Wayne" is, I know.

"What?" I say. Loud. The tunnel's yawning mouth is directly ahead of me.

"Where's Ko—"

"What? Kat, you're breaking up," I interrupt, even though I can hear her perfectly. "Call me back." I hang up.

It's 7:14.

I turn off my phone, run my hands through my hair, and that's when I see her laying there where the creek should be running under the road above.

"Koty!" I scream, but nothing comes out of my mouth. I run, I fall, I pick myself up and run to her, kneel next to her, and turn her over. She's cold and stiff, and her face is a sickening, putrid shade of purple, like she'd been beaten. Her eyes stare at me, but they don't see. Her left leg, also purple, points in an unnatural direction, as if the bone is broken. She's wearing a nightgown, one I gave her years ago, with black lace and red trim, except it's covered now in blood and dirt. *What the fuck?* Leaves and branches tangle in her hair as if she'd been rolling around in a leaf pile, jumping in like she always does with the kids every fall.

God, no.

I grope her neck, searching for a pulse, even though I already know. She's gone.

Please, oh please, oh please, oh please.

I cradle her and cry, rocking back and forth, my mind spinning. *What the fuck happened?* I examine the piece of flesh pulling away from her cheek. I remember the blood back home. Iris holding the gun. But this doesn't look like a gunshot wound, more like she was grazed. So what the fuck happened? I attempt to piece it together. Somehow Iris got hold of my gun and shot it. A bullet grazed Koty's cheek, but there was still a lot of blood. She panicked and took off. Maybe she was afraid of what would happen to Iris. Maybe she was going to him. Maybe she didn't have a plan; she just ran. And then? I look around. Why here? Did she fall? Go into shock? What? I adjust her body in my arms, and as I do, the nightgown rides up, revealing the fact she's not wearing underwear. *Jesus.* And then I remember last night, and what I did.

My stomach turns and I wretch, but nothing comes up.

I remember something else, from yesterday afternoon: Iris saying she wished her mother was dead. Iris suffering because of what she saw her mother and that kid doing, Iris suffering and caught in the middle, like Carl always was. Iris suffering for being Iris. And then, I remember this morning, not even forty-five minutes ago: Iris holding the gun.

No way in hell I'll let anything happen to her. Not that anyone would believe it anyway, that she shot her mother by accident. Not after everything this piss-poor town believes about me, about my family, about the person Iris Fowler is becoming. Of course, there'd be the people who think I did it. And what if I had, partly? What about what happened last night? Aren't there tests they do that tell them when the sex is rough, if it isn't entirely consensual?

I wretch again and my brain hammers against my skull and I feel as if my eyeballs are going to jump out of their sockets.

What if I confess? My brain tries to manage the logic, the consequences. Despite the boozy fog, the shock of holding my dead wife in my arms, and the frigid air, I know it won't work. I'd lie for Iris if I knew that's all it would take, except that's just it. My lie would take me away from them. They'd lose a mother *and* a father all at once. I can't let that happen. I won't let that happen.

I stare down into Koty's face, and my tears follow. I know despite everything that's happened between us, she would agree. So I do the only thing that's left for me to do. I place her back on the ground, stand, pull out my cell phone, and pray.

#

I shake now, unaware of how long I've been driving or of where I am, the memories of that morning still so vivid, so real. I want a drink. I need a drink. But even more than that I have an overwhelming desire to see her.

I drive.

Is it really over? How could this possibly be happening, that there's a criminal, this Porter Clemson, accused of murdering Koty when I know better? When I know the truth? Or *do* I know the truth? They say Koty fell, that she was pushed. That that's how she died. I've tried resolving this information with what I remembered from that morning: the broken body, the blood, the dirt. Had she clawed her way to the road only to somehow trip and fall over the short stone wall above the culvert? Perhaps. Her remains wouldn't have had any evidence of the bullet graze to her cheek or bruises to her inner thighs (and elsewhere in that area), her flesh gone and decomposed after all this time. Any DNA found, if it were mine, well, that could be explained away, right? I was her husband. All that would be left would be bones. Broken bones, telling another story. The real story? A story Iris could accept and believe?

The girls and I had been doing so good lately at living our lives. I wouldn't say things were normal. You can't ever go back to normal after something like this. But after five years, shit. We'd learned how to live with it. How to manage. How to get up and go about our business and come home and have dinner and go to bed and do it all over again.

And then.

Koty's remains found. Finding her was supposed to bring closure to my girls and to me, being able to bury her properly and all, but it also changed the normalcy, the life management, I'd worked so hard at creating. Completely turned it on its head.

And now, this. This reprieve. This mulligan. This, *this*.

I find myself in front of my destination, even though I have no memory of how I got here. I glance in the rearview mirror, wondering if I'll spot a suspicious car tailing me, if everything Panzieri had said was a load of bull and I'm under some sort of surveillance. If I am, I wonder if this will seem normal, or odd. If it will make me look innocent, or guilty.

I open the door and step out into the bright sunlight. I kick at the dirt, rocky but level now with grass sprouting in patches. Most of the flowers scattered about are dead, even though the interment was only a few weeks ago. There's one bouquet, however, fresher than the rest: a couple of red roses, purple irises, white daisies. I bend and pick it up and spot a card tucked inside, the words "I miss you" written in neat cursive, in Rosie's handwriting.

"Hey," I say to her gravestone and immediately feel like an idiot. It's an ornate stone, with flowers chiseled in ribbons around the top and angels flanking both sides. Too gaudy for my taste as it would have been hers, I imagine, but the girls had insisted.

The girls. Our girls. My girls.

I hadn't wanted Rosie, I'm ashamed to admit. Hadn't wanted any of them, actually, not at first. Now, I can't imagine my life without them, even though I realize—and probably a helluva lot sooner than I care to think—they'll one day be gone.

What I said to Panzieri was the truth: everything I've done for the last five and a half years has been for them. For Rosie. For Daisy. For Iris. And maybe even for me.

In a way, I guess, it feels done now.

I'd made a promise to Koty in those moments after I found her, in that space between my phone call to Hank and my waiting for him to arrive to take her away. Hank never told me where he'd buried her or how, and I'd never asked; I simply thanked him after he came to get me on the eve of the ice storm and we pretended to search for Koty.

Koty.

The promise I made was this: that I'd protect Iris, no matter what. I'd protect her like I couldn't—didn't—protect Carl, like I couldn't—didn't—protect Koty. Today, that promise has been fulfilled. No one will have to suffer now, not Iris, not me, not even the person accused but innocent, at least of this crime.

If I were a man of faith, if I believed that there was something more after we took our last breath in this world, I might say that Koty had a hand in this, at least in how it's turning out, at the chance at peace our family might have.

Yes. I might just believe that.

Chapter 43

Mrs. Briggs

Through the open window, the wind blows one of those breezes that carries with it summer's promise, and it flutters the term papers I've been grading. Then, just as fast, the breeze dies down, and everything is still. In the distance, a car stereo (do they even call them that anymore?) blasts and tires squeal. I had thought the change in scenery, the move from my classroom desk to this one in the teachers' lounge would be exactly what I'd need to get through these papers. Perhaps I was simply looking for company, a grading companion, someone with whom to commiserate, to countdown "only five more to go." But at four o'clock on the Friday of Memorial Day Weekend, no one is left, and I am alone.

Sighing, I toss my red pen high in the air, and it lands with a light thump on the weekly newspaper that the town still somehow manages to put out, although my colleagues and I have bets as to how much longer it will last.

I lean across the table, stretching my torso and arms until my fingers graze the paper (I'll never understand the allure of those electronic reading devices), and pull it toward me.

Immediately, I wish I hadn't. On the front page is a picture of her, of Koty Fowler, the woman gone missing five and a half years ago, her remains recently found, and her killer identified but also deceased. The headline reads "Gone, But Not Forgotten." A picture of her three daughters appears near the bottom of the article, each girl's name carefully labeled: Daisy, Iris, Rosie. The latter is someone I've come to know quite well, since she's my advisee, and—dare I say it?—someone whom I've grown rather fond of, despite myself. Despite, well, everything.

I push the paper aside and shake my head, trying to ignore the images that have been haunting me ever since the news broke a few weeks ago about Koty's case, how it was solved, and who was involved. These images involve the moments nobody knows about. Nobody but me, and her.

It was an accident, I remind myself. Then it wasn't, anger getting the better of me. But I was going to make it right again, except when I came back for her, she was gone. *Gone.* That must be when this serial killer—this Porter Clemson—found her. And finished her.

All this time, I've lived with debilitating guilt, thinking I'd delivered the final blow, that I played a part—a big part—in the death of a mother, of a wife, of a woman, in my only son's heartbreak.

For five and a half years, I've kicked myself, I've repented, I've given back, I've lost weight, I've taken up the drink, I've distanced myself from my son (Not completely; I am his mother, after all, and he needs me, loves me. He couldn't be all that he is without me, you know. Behind every successful man, remember.).

Now, it turns out, my role in it was minimal, a *cameo* at best. Perhaps, one could reason, that my role and the way I played it sent her on the path that ultimately led to her demise. I think, however, that's giving me too much credit. Fate, you see, no doubt, stepped in and performed.

I tell myself all this, but it doesn't stop the memories, the flashbacks, her voice pleading with me. Why was she on the side of the road, in a nightgown for God's sake, in the middle of the night? Up to no good, that's for sure, the little tramp.

I'm sorry. I don't mean to speak ill of the dead, but that's what she was: a tramp. Luring my son into a trap, a trap that would have done nothing but snapped shut around his heart, breaking him down further.

She had no right. *No right.*

I don't care what was going on in her life, what her husband did to her, what she felt. My son had almost been taken away from me once. I'd be damned if I'd see him taken from me again. Because that's what she wanted. It's what she said.

I wouldn't have even been out that night, if not for her. After our run-in that fateful afternoon, it became clear to me that Jamie and Koty's "relationship" had to end, for myriad reasons. She was trouble: a cheater, white trash, pregnant in high school. Oh, I remember. I was appalled that the school allowed her to stay and complete her education, showing off her pregnant belly as if it were something to be proud of, a sign she'd been chosen, a sign of her fertility. One of the greatest ironies of life is the ease in which some females get pregnant. So often, it's the ones who don't want it and who don't know the first thing about nurturing or responsibility. Then there are those of us who could be poster children for domesticity, who were born to mother, yet who cannot get pregnant—or who *can,* like I could, but who could not carry a child to term. Six miscarriages. *Six.* That's how many I had before I turned thirty. A decade of heartache, of tears, of physical and mental pain beyond compare. Then came my reward from God for my patience and suffering: Jamie.

Let me set the record straight: I did not coddle him. Yes, he was an only child. Yes, I had longed for him. But, you see, I'm an educator. I teach classes on early childhood development. I raised a healthy, well-balanced son.

He was not supposed to go off to war, you see. He was supposed to go off to college, get married, and raise a family of his own. Had I been able to take his commitment back, I would have. I tried, showing up at the recruitment office, but they said he was an adult, that he had made his decision, that he had signed, that it was an honor to serve our country.

I had a bad feeling from the very beginning. "Ma," he'd say. "You worry too much. You worked too hard to get me. You don't think God is going to take me away now, do you?"

Turned out, he was right. God did not take him away, not all of him. In essence, God gave me exactly what I prayed for: my son back, out of the army, with no chance of ever returning. A part of me wonders if I somehow played a role in that as well.

I worked too hard bringing him into this world, and I worked too hard in those weeks and months after he was injured in keeping him in this world, in my world, that I would be damned if some woman with loose morals took him away from me.

After she left my house that fateful afternoon, after it was clear that she was more confused than I had originally thought, I went in to see Jamie, to share the details of my day, to hear about his. When I knocked on his door, received no response, and entered anyway, I found him as he had been only a few months before: sitting in his wheelchair, staring out the window, at what, I don't even know, since darkness had already fallen.

He didn't respond to my questions or acknowledge my presence, and anger tore at the edges of my soul. What had the little tramp done now? How was it possible that she could take him away from me when she wasn't even present?

I left him alone and convinced myself that he needed a little time, an hour perhaps, maybe two. Two hours later, however, he was still in the same position.

"What would you like for dinner, sweetheart?" I said. He didn't respond. I walked to him, crouched next to him, put my arm around his shoulders. "You need to eat."

"Not hungry."

"Jamie—"

"What part of that don't you understand? I'm not hungry."

I stood, left, went to the kitchen, and began cooking anyway. An hour later, I returned with a bowl of soup, which he promptly rejected. An hour after that, I brought him tea and a platter of fruit and cheese. He ignored me. An hour later, ice cream. Still nothing.

It was almost ten o'clock, and I was beyond frantic. I was determined—*determined*—to get him to eat something because that one gesture would indicate I'd won him back, that we'd be okay, that he wasn't giving up completely. I realize now it sounds crazy, but in that moment, perhaps I was.

I entered his room, dragged the rocking chair to where he still sat in his wheelchair by the window.

"Is there anything you'd like to talk about?" I asked.

He didn't respond.

"I'm here, you know. I'm happy to listen to whatever is on your mind."

Still, nothing.

"Did something happen between you and Ko—"

"Do you remember," he interrupted, "after Dad died, and you couldn't get me to eat? You remember what finally worked?"

"Of course." I smiled. "Breakfast for dinner. Eggs, bacon, and—"

"Your secret French toast recipe."

"Shall I?" I asked as I lifted myself from the chair and walked to the door.

"Sure," he said.

I ignored the dejected I'm-just-doing-this-to-please you tone in his voice. Instead, I practically skipped to the kitchen, giddy as a schoolgirl who'd gotten her crush to agree to have lunch with her. I hummed as I pulled out the ingredients: first the milk, eggs, butter (it was important that they reach room temperature), the flour, baking soda, salt, cinnamon, nutmeg, and—where was my ground ginger? The secret was the ginger.

I rummaged through my cupboards and spun the lazy susan, all of my spices carefully labeled and in alphabetical order. Nothing. I pawed through my pantry where I had backups of every ingredient imaginable. Then I remembered Thanksgiving, the ginger I'd used up in a new pumpkin pie recipe, how I kept meaning to add it to my shopping list, but hadn't.

The ginger *made* the French toast. It wasn't the same without the ginger, and I needed this dish to be perfect. I glanced at the clock. 10:03. There was a 24/7 Stop & Shop not even ten minutes away. What about Jamie? He'd be okay, I reasoned as I buttoned my coat. I poked my head into his room.

"I'll be right back."

"Where you going?"

"To the store."

"Forget about—"

"Nonsense. I'll be back, lickety split."

I didn't wait for a reply, simply walked out, got into my car, and drove, a little faster than I normally would down my street, in the dark, but it was late and no one was around.

It happened so fast. As I approached the old stone culvert, there was nothing there. But then, there was movement. An animal, I thought at first, but no—it was larger, and standing up. I swerved, or at least I tried, that's the honest truth, but it couldn't be avoided. I hit it.

"Jesus, Mary, and Joseph!" I jumped out of the car, ran to the passenger's side, and there a person lay. Female? Yes, on her back, her head resting at the base of the short stone wall that lined both sides of the road, a poor-excuse of a guardrail if you ask me.

"Hold on! Don't move." She didn't. She wasn't. For a moment, I stood paralyzed, thinking I'd killed her or severely injured her. I remembered the first aid kit in my trunk. "Always be prepared," I'd tell my students. I ran back to the driver's side, popped the trunk, and remembered the little flashlight on my keychain, too. I turned off the ignition, tore the keys out, ran to the trunk, grabbed the kit, and by the time I got back to her, she was moaning.

I struggled to my knees, arthritis be damned, and bent my body over hers. "Are you hurt?" I pointed the flashlight into her bloodied face. *Sweet Jesus. Koty!* The front of her was soaked in blood as well, but my word! What was she wearing? Some gauzy see-through nightgown? I pointed the flashlight lower, toward her naked legs on up to her thighs and to her naked everything. Her mission was obvious: the tramp was on her way to see my son.

She mumbled something, but I couldn't make it out. Her head moved from side to side, but her eyes were open, trying to focus. I put my face right in front of hers and watched as her eyes recognized mine. She gripped my arm. "Please," she said, her voice hoarse, barely audible. "Take me to him."

"You need to go to the hospital."

"No! Jamie. I need Jamie. We need to get away."

"*What?*"

"Please."

"No."

She moaned. "Please."

I ignored her pleas, and began to pull away, but I'd underestimated her grip. As I attempted to get up, she pulled me down toward her, and my head clashed against the side of the stone wall. "Jesus, Mary, and Joseph!" I winced.

"Help me." She struggled to sit up.

"I'm going to help you. Let me go."

She didn't. If anything, she held on harder. "I tried calling him, but he didn't answer." She hoisted herself onto her knees and attempted to stand, wobbling the whole time.

I stood as well and reached for her elbow. "Shh. Be still."

"He loves me. That's what he said today."

"Be quiet!"

"I know we can make it together." She wrapped her hands around my wrists, vice-like. "Help us."

I tried wriggling free from her grip, but she held on, the whole time teetering on her legs. "Let go."

"Please. If you love him, you'll help us."

"Enough! He doesn't love you. He doesn't know what he's talking about."

She shuddered. "You bitch."

I'm the bitch? "Koty—"

"Why won't you help us?"

"Because *you* need help. Meaning a doctor. I can take care of my son."

"He doesn't *want* you." She gripped my arm tighter. "He wants me. *Me*, do you hear? And I want him."

"Shut up!" I yelled, shaking her off, pushing the little vixen away from me, and just like that, she went over the stone wall. *Dear Lord!* I peered over, pointing my flashlight. The drop had to be at least twenty feet to the dried up creek and rocks below. She lay motionless, face down, and I knew she was dead, or close to it. "Stupid, stupid girl," I cried. *No! What have I done?* It was her own fault, my brain reasoned. She shouldn't have been sneaking out to see my son in the middle of the night. She was married. A mother to three little girls. My son deserved more than what she had to offer. So much more.

He'd never forgive me, of this I was certain. He'd be miserable. He'd shun me. I wasn't going to lose him to her. Not in life. Not in death. I'd nearly lost him once already.

Let me say this: nothing can prepare you for the phone call that tells you your son is one step away from death. Nothing. Logically, I always knew it was possible. I was a war wife, after all. But emotionally? It's easy to understand how horrifying and terrible the calls are that tell you your child is dead. Those limbo notifications, however, when you plead with the person on the other end to tell you what's going to happen to your child and the voice responds with "Ma'am, we don't know"? In one moment, you feel an enormous amount of hope because he is, in fact, still alive. Then the reality of the situation sets in. The tubes, machines, and bags that cover your boy, snaking in and out of blankets and sheets. The body parts, removed. The hope, dwindling. The wait, excruciating. The fact that if he dies, a piece of you dies, too. And then, all of sudden, hope flickers once more. His eyes open and speak, *I'll fight for you, Mom. I'll fight. Don't give up on me.*

These were the thoughts—compressed and disjointed but there nonetheless—that filled the space between the moment I knew Koty was dead and the moment I stood, brushed myself off, walked to the front of my car, and pointed the flashlight around. A cell phone—hers, I assumed—lay on the ground. I picked it up, put it in my coat pocket, and shone the light on the front of my car. A broken passenger headlight. A dent on the side. Some scratches on the hood. The windshield was intact. I hadn't been going that fast. I hadn't hit her hard. If she hadn't been out in the middle of the godforsaken night, this never would have happened. It was an accident. *An accident.*

I pointed the flashlight over my coat, looking for signs of her, and noticed specks of blood, possibly dirt. I took the coat off and got back in my car. Turned the key in the ignition. Gripped the steering wheel. Stepped on the gas. I drove to the store, parked, and glanced at myself in the rearview mirror, fingering where my head had hit the stone wall, a bump forming. I'd been wearing a heavy wool sweater and turtleneck because the heater in my classroom had been on the fritz. I decided I looked warm enough and that it wouldn't cause too much alarm to see a woman dash into the store without a winter jacket. Heck, I wasn't running around half-naked in a nightgown.

I got out, walked into the store, got my ground ginger, smiled at the daydreaming cashier, a teenage girl I'd vaguely recognized from the hallways at school and who asked if I wanted a plastic bag. "No, thank you,"

I'd said cheerfully while depositing the small box in my purse. "Thinking of the environment." I walked out of the store, got in my car, and turned on the radio. My favorite oldies station had been playing Christmas music non-stop since the day after Thanksgiving. I drove and hummed along with the remaining notes of "The Most Wonderful Time of the Year." I drove and belted out the words to "I Saw Mommy Kissing Santa Claus" along with the Ronettes. I drove down my street, over the culvert, into my driveway. I got out of the car and walked inside without ever looking back.

I made French toast, bacon, scrambled eggs. Jamie and I ate together and caught the end of the eleven o'clock news: sports and weather. A storm was headed our way. Jamie didn't have much to say, but he was grateful, I could tell, for the food, for the fact I'd gone out to fetch the secret ingredient, for having me there to help him ready for bed, get tucked in, wait by his side until he fell asleep.

I fell asleep in his rocking chair, waking with a start at three in the morning. My bones creaked as I lifted myself from the chair and hobbled down the hall to my bedroom. We were definitely in for some weather, if my joint and bone pain were any indication. I fell onto my bed, still dressed in my clothes, but my eyes refused to shut this time.

Had she screamed when she'd fallen over? The scene replayed in my mind, and I decided that she had, once. It was an accident, I kept telling myself. An accident. But I left her. How could I have left her? She was a mother. She had children.

I shuddered.

Should I go back? Now? But she was dead. Going back now would suggest something more nefarious on my part. Intention, even.

I tossed and turned, and my stomach moved in the opposite direction. Bile filled my throat. I leaned over the side of my bed and heaved, the contents of my stomach splattered on the hardwood floor and the oval throw rug. I attempted to get out of bed, but the room spun and my head ached. I needed to make it right. In the morning. I'd make things right in the morning. I'd say I hit something last night on my way to get the ginger, that I thought it was an animal, nothing more. I'd say I stopped at the culvert this morning, because that's where it had happened, and that I'd looked over the side and saw her there. I'd call 911 from that spot. Yes, this was what I would do.

And Jamie?

I'd plead for his forgiveness. I'd tell him it was an accident, a horrible, horrible accident. He'd understand. Maybe not at first, but he, of all people, understood the law of Wrong Place, Wrong Time. He'd forgive me. I was his mother, after all. I was all he had now.

My stomach settled, and I must have drifted off, because when I awoke, light filled my bedroom. Too much light for my normal wake-up time of five a.m. I rolled over and glanced at the clock: 7:38. I sat up fast, groggy, my mouth dry, and put one foot onto the floor and then the other. Something wet soaked my socks. I looked down, saw my vomit, and remembered.

The next ten minutes blurred. I wiped up the floor. I checked on Jamie, who was still sleeping. I called the school and told them I'd overslept and that I'd be there in time for second period. I changed clothes.

"Hey, Mom?" Jamie called out. I walked down the hall and opened his door.

"Morning, sunshine," I said with as much cheerfulness as I could muster.

He glanced at the clock, his face confused.

"I'm running late," I said. "Shall we?" I gestured to his prosthetic arms and legs, even though I'd seen him do it by himself before. But that can take time—a lot of time—and I figured he needed to use the bathroom.

He nodded, and we got his legs on and his arms. He walked to the bathroom, and I hung outside the door, checking and rechecking my watch. 8:02. Already halfway through first period, Child Growth and Development.

The toilet flushed. Jamie walked out.

"All good?" I said.

"Yeah." He studied my face. "You okay?"

"Stomach's a bit off," I said as I walked down the hall to the closet and donned my winter coat. "Breakfast at eleven at night. That's probably the culprit." I turned around. He stood in his doorway. "You all set?"

"Sure."

I nodded, picked up my purse and briefcase, and walked out. In the light of day, the damage to the car seemed worse. Much worse. I paused in front of the broken headlight and then placed my bags on the passenger seat. I walked around the front of the car, my eyes scanning the scratches in the hood, slid into the driver's seat, took a deep breath, and turned the key in the ignition.

I drove carefully, slowly, not like the Department Head of Family and Consumer Sciences, late for homeroom and first period. As I approached the culvert, I held my breath. My hands shook. I pulled over, stepped out of the car, walked to the edge, and peered over. I didn't see anything but rocks below. I crouched and splayed my hands flat on top of the stone wall and leaned over, way over, trying to see into the tunnel's vast mouth, but couldn't. I considered my clothes: slacks, which I seldom wore, another sweater, and boots, since the forecast had said the weather we were in for might start before school let out. I'd forgone fashion years ago in deference to my bad knees. I couldn't afford to fall, but I couldn't afford not to find this woman either.

"Jesus, Mary, and Joseph," I muttered under my breath and scrambled, if you could even call it that, down the embankment, which was much steeper than it looked, to the earth below. "Koty," I whispered. I studied the rocks, searching for evidence, but I had never been much for hiking or hunting or wildlife study, despite having lived in New Hampshire my whole life. I didn't know what I was looking at or looking for.

I pulled out my keys and switched on the flashlight, which had gotten more use in the last twelve hours than the last twelve months combined, and pointed it into the shadows of the arched tunnel with its high ceilings. "Koty? Are you in there?" I took one step forward and then another and pointed the light to the ground, looking for what? Footprints? Blood? I stepped forward again, and, this time, I tumbled and lurched, catching myself at the last minute. Debris—branches, beer bottles, an old tire, I think—littered the interior. If she had gone in this direction, I reasoned, she wouldn't have gotten far, not even to the other side, a few feet away, the light shining through, but I crossed to the other side anyway, hopeful, scared, and then, ambivalent, when once again there was no sign of her. I retraced my steps to where I started, grateful to be in open air and out from under the cold granite stone covered in moss and lichen and Lord knows what else.

My mind raced. Had she somehow survived that fall? She was young, sprightly even. It was possible, wasn't it? Had she wandered back through the woods? For all I knew she was at her house right now, clean and resting and taken care of. But no. I had seen her lying there, crooked and broken. Or had I? Was it possible I imagined the whole scene last night? What about the damage to my car? Maybe it *had* been an animal. Maybe in my fatigue, my anxiety—

"Mrs. Briggs? That you down there?"

I stood back and craned my neck. Wearing his hunter's cap with earflaps, Richard Bates stood on top of the stone wall and gazed down at me. A former student of mine. A classmate of Jamie's in high school. Owner of the general store in town.

"Yes, Richard. It's me." I dug my hands into my coat pocket, thinking it would make the whole scene appear casual. My left hand touched something. A cell phone. *Koty's cell phone.*

"You okay?"

"Fine," I said as I started my way up and realized it had been much easier going down, which wasn't saying much. I held onto limbs and branches that seemed sturdy enough to support my weight and pulled and climbed and pulled. Richard ran down, offered his hand—which I gladly took—and led me to the road.

"Ah, yes." I gulped air. "Thank you very much."

"I thought I recognized your car. Saw the damage to the front and was concerned."

"Right. I hit something last night. Happened so fast. I'm not sure what it was. Maybe a raccoon or possum. Stopped to see what I could see this morning."

He glanced at the front end of my car. "Mighty tall possum or raccoon, given the damage."

I followed his gaze. "Indeed. Perhaps I don't want to acknowledge what it was." He looked at me, confused, and I continued. "A deer. I know they're pests, but I've never been comfortable with hunting Bambi. Left that to my husband and son." He considered the damage again, tilting his head right and left. "Speaking of which," I added before he could question me further, "I'm sure Jamie would love to see you."

He stuffed his hands in his pocket, and a sheepish expression flooded his face. "Yeah. How's he been?"

"Doing well, thank you. You should stop by for a visit sometime."

He nodded and kicked the dirt with his boot. "Yes, ma'am. Perhaps after the holidays. Busy time, you know."

I said nothing and waited until he had no choice but to look me in the eyes. I stared at him until he squirmed the same way he did when he was sixteen and had to sit through my Reproductive Health class.

"Well, I should get going," he said. "Just wanted to make sure you were all right." He walked to his pickup and climbed inside.

"I'll tell Jamie to expect you." I waved, and he nodded and drove away. All I could do was hope that what he'd remember about this moment was the guilt he felt for not checking in on his old crippled friend from high school. I watched until his truck disappeared from view. Sighing, I got back in my car. What else could I do? Wait! *The cell phone. What should I do with the cell phone?* I pulled it out of my pocket and inspected it. A little envelope icon fluttered across the screen. Four missed calls. One text message. I turned it over in my hands. My fingerprints were on it. There was no good reason for me to have it unless I said I found it in my house. No, *outside* the house. As if she'd dropped it.

I turned the key in the ignition and hoped beyond hope that she was somehow still alive or I'd imagined the whole scenario to begin with. I drove to school, got through the day, left the minute I could, and prayed I'd see Koty's car when I pulled into the driveway. It wasn't there. When I knocked on Jamie's door, his face filled with so much hope and then disappointment when he saw it was only me.

"Koty already leave?" I asked.

"She never showed."

"I found this outside on my way in." I displayed the cell phone in my hand. "I think it's hers. She must have dropped it, maybe on her way out yesterday. Perhaps I should call her and let her know?" I held my breath, unsure of the answer I wanted from him. Sadness filled his face, and he shook his head.

"I said something to her yesterday that I shouldn't have." He sighed. "Upset her, I think. Scared her."

"What was it?"

He shook his head, unwilling or unable to answer.

"Well," I said. "Would you prefer I don't call her, then? Let her come around on her own?"

He nodded.

"Okay." I placed the phone on his bureau and pointed to the window. "We're in for some nasty weather. I best go take care of a few things."

The weather came, as predicted, fast and furious. After supper, one of Koty's girls called. Turned out it was Rosie, a girl I didn't know then, but one I'd get to know quite well a couple of years later, thanks to her interest in childhood education, her desire to be a teacher, her love for my son (yes, I see it; I'm sure I'm not the only one). I heard and felt the panic in Rosie's voice, but I remained calm, at least until I'd hung up the phone. Only then had I realized I'd forgotten to tell her about her mother's cell phone. Where had Koty gone? I'd hit her. She'd fallen. Where was she? Had an animal run off with her? I hadn't seen any signs and there would have been. Right? I shook my head, refusing to let the images take hold. If she'd been missing since last night, people would be out searching for her, wouldn't they? Her husband? The police?

I didn't even realize I was still holding the cordless phone until Jamie hobbled in. "Who was that?" he asked. "What's going on?"

I had a choice: lie or tell the truth. I told him the truth. Well, not all of it. I told him that one of Koty's daughters had called looking for her and that I told her she had never shown up today. His eyes darkened, and I wondered if this was how his face appeared when he lost someone in his unit or when he woke up, groggy from surgery, to discover his limbs gone. I reached for him, but he shrank away and retreated to his room.

The storm picked up, an ice storm like we hadn't seen in these parts in decades. Wind battered windows. Branches hit and bounced off the roof. We lost power shortly before midnight. It would be eleven days before it would come on again, although Richard Bates, out of guilt perhaps, checked in on us on the third day and brought a generator—his recently deceased father in law's—and helped me get it started.

"You hear about the Fowler woman?" Richard had asked once he, Jamie, and I were in the kitchen and I was able to start a pot of coffee. Of course, we hadn't. Without power, we had no access to news, and little contact with people since our road was littered with trees, branches, and downed wires.

"No," I said, while glancing at Jamie. "We haven't. What happened?"

"Gone missing," he said. "Or run off. Some cops come by the store this morning, asking if I'd seen or heard anything."

"That explains why we haven't heard from her about her cell phone," Jamie said, mostly to himself. "I figured it was because of the storm." Then, to Richard: "They check with her no-good husband?"

Richard shook his head. "Don't know. She's run off before, though. Seven years ago. I remember hearing about it. It was right after my granddad died and my dad took over the store. It was right before 9/11."

I'd forgotten about that, but he was right: she had run off once before, or so the rumors in town suggested as much.

"Yes," I said as I poured coffee into a mug and handed it to Richard. "I remember that now. She was pregnant, wasn't she? With the third one? Simply walked out one day with the other two. Was gone for a few days or something like that."

Richard sipped and nodded. "I heard she'd hitchhiked and shacked up with some guy in a motel down in Hampton Beach. The cops found her and the girls, her credit cards missing and drug paraphernalia strewn about."

I'd heard this as well but figured it was false, one of those erroneous reports that gets started by wagging tongues and spins off into a life of its own. I hadn't been a high school teacher for forty years and not learned a thing or two about gossip. In that moment, however, I didn't correct Richard. I sipped my coffee and watched Jamie's expression out of the corner of my eye.

"That's a damn lie," Jamie said.

Richard shrugged. "Just repeating what I heard."

"Yeah, well," Jamie had replied. "Maybe you should make sure what you're repeating is facts."

#

Facts. I stare at a student's paper in front of me, which discusses, incorrectly I might add, age-appropriate language skills for the average three-year-old. Despite the fact we discuss this in class, that I provide additional handouts, that there are chapters in their text devoted to language development, there's always at least one student, sadly often more than one, who warps the facts, mixes them up, or disregards them completely.

Facts. The fact is a woman is dead. The fact is the police have concluded how she died. The fact is I am no closer now than I was on that morning five and a half years ago to knowing what role, if any, I played in her death. A part of me—the tired part, a part that grows deeper and longer and wider with each passing year—thinks it's time I let it go, that these recent developments show, definitively, that my role, if any, had little bearing on her demise. Another part of me, however—the part that's a mother, that was once a wife, that is still very much a woman, despite the fact I'm fast approaching my seventh decade on this earth—can't let go of the possibility that had I not hit her and left her, that perhaps she wouldn't have ended up dead. The fact it was ultimately at someone else's hands is irrelevant. Lives have been forever changed as a result, including my own.

The door to the teachers' lounge opens, and a lanky, jeans-clad janitor backs in while pulling a trash can on wheels. He tugs on his ears buds until they pop out and nods at me. "Sorry, Mrs. Briggs. Thought everyone had left for the weekend."

"Yes." I smile, stand, and slide the papers into my leather laptop briefcase. "Everyone has."

He nods again and grins, and as I slip past him, I detect cigarettes and sweat. The hallway is empty, a long row of gray and blue lockers on either side. It strikes me how some things never change: high school hallways. Lockers. A rite of passage we all must survive to get to the other side of life.

I walk through one set of double doors, down a stairway, and through another set to the empty parking lot. My eyes seek out the passenger side headlight of my car, the side panel, and the hood that had been repaired, re-painted, and buffed long ago, no questions asked, thanks to the infamous ice storm of 2008.

Facts. The fact is no matter how hard we try, we don't have the power to empty our heads of bad memories. Only the memories themselves can decide when enough is enough.

I open the door, slide on the seat, buckle myself in, start the car, turn up the radio, and pray, as I always do, that maybe today they'll leave me be.

Chapter 44

Iris

There are horses on the beach.

Daisy sees them first and points them out: three of them, with a young girl on each, a man and woman leading the way.

It's my sixteenth birthday, Memorial Day Weekend, and we're together at Salisbury Beach just like we were when I turned ten. A trip to Markey's Lobster Pool for fish and chips is in our future, followed by go-carts and Skee-Ball and ice cream at Hodgies.

Daisy races ahead, twirling her arms like a windmill. Rosie and Dad walk together, arm in arm. And me, I'm in between, feeling more alive today than I have in almost six years, maybe ever. I've been officially "out" for nine whole days to the people who matter most: Rosie. Daisy. Dad. The sky didn't fall. The earth didn't quake. They said it was okay. They said they still loved me, that they would always love me, no matter what.

Best of all, the images from that night so long ago have stopped haunting me, having faded away to almost nothing. When Dad told us the FBI had figured out who killed Mom, I realized what he'd been saying for the last five and a half years was true: whatever role I played was minor, at best. I probably arrived home that night, fought with Mom, was sent to bed, and woke up sick, Mom already gone. The fact I couldn't remember this for so long—and still can't, not completely, anyway—is because my brain wants me to focus on the good memories I have and not the ones from that last day.

It makes sense, I think.

A seagull squawks now overhead and the waves crash, the tide coming in. I drag my toes in the sand, making squiggly lines, and take a deep whiff of ocean air, a scent that—if you must know—originates from gases released from decaying organic matter. Not a pleasant thought, but a realistic one, because death, after all, is a part of life. Like forgiveness. And letting go. And moving forward.

#

Acknowledgements:

I'm eternally grateful to the following:

The Nobscot Niblets, my writing group: Dawn Swann, Colleen Cox, Steve Tannuzzo, Paul Ashton, Susan Weiner, Deb Mackey, Shelly Giordano, and Laura Matthews, who also served as my copy editor extraordinaire. You all rock my writing world!

Family and friends: Rita Bradley, Ron Bradley, Kevin Bradley, Don Kelley, Christine Junge, Beth Inman, Robin Chapman, Moneen Daley Harte (who provided her musical expertise on all things country).

Leah Hager Cohen, my faculty mentor at Lesley University, who encouraged and guided me with the short story, "Support Our Troops," on which the novel is based.

Stacy Rudnick Pollack, a friend and reader of "Support Our Troops." Stacy reminded me what I had always known to be true: the short story wasn't enough for these characters … I needed to go longer with a novel.

FictionWeekly.com, an online literary journal that published an early version of the short story in June 2009 and made me believe in it all over again.

The online video presentations by Lee Laster and John Ritenour on eHow.com; I spent a whole weekend watching these videos and learning about the parts of a gun, how to load a gun, and how to fire a gun, among other gun-related things.

Three experts: first, David Studley, who works in the Crime Scene Services unit for the Framingham Police Department in Framingham, Mass.; second, my wonderful proofreader, Diana Cox, who caught all my "oops" moments; and, third, "Emma," my quad amputee expert and (by way of Emma) her husband, who is an amputee. Thanks to all of you for your expertise and insight and for providing the story with the polish and authenticity it deserves.

Like what you've read?

Lend it out and/or tell others, especially book clubs. Consider leaving a review at Amazon, B&N, Goodreads, or wherever you bought the book. Thank you for reading my work!

Are you on Facebook?

Become a fan of my Facebook page and join our fun discussions about all things related to reading: http://www.facebook.com/RobynBradleyWriter.

Other titles by Robyn Bradley

Forgotten April - A Novel (available in paperback and as an eBook)

A Touch of Charlotte - A Short Story

Orange Pineapple - A Short Story

Support Our Troops - A Short Story

Crush - A Short Story

The Object - Flash Fiction

All are available as eBooks through Amazon, Barnes & Noble.com, the iBookStore, and Lulu (for all other eReaders).

About Robyn Bradley:

Robyn Bradley has an MFA in Creative Writing from Lesley University. Her work has appeared in FictionWeekly.com, *Metal Scratches*, *Writer's Digest*, and *The MetroWest Daily News*. When she's not writing or sleeping, Robyn enjoys watching *Law & Order* marathons, drinking margaritas, and determining how many degrees really separate her from George Clooney. Visit www.robynbradley.com for more info. Robyn loves hearing from readers. Email her: robyn@robynbradley.com.

30672070R00202

Made in the USA
Middletown, DE
02 April 2016